A Sunless Sea

ANNE PERRY

A SUNLESS SEA

A William Monk Novel

BALLANTINE BOOKS • NEW YORK

Published in the United States by Ballantine Books, an imprint of The Random House Publishing Group, a division of Random House, Inc., New York.

BALLANTINE and colophon are registered trademarks of Random House, Inc.

Library of Congress Cataloging-in-Publication Data

Perry, Anne.
A sunless sea : a William Monk novel / Anne Perry. — 1st ed.
p. cm.
ISBN 978-0-345-51064-8 (hardcover : alk. paper)
eBook ISBN 978-0-345-53593-1
1. Monk, William (Fictitious character)—Fiction. 2. Private investigators—England—London—Fiction.
3. Murder—Investigation—Fiction. 4. London (England)—History–1800–1950—Fiction. I. Title.
PR6066.E693S87 2012
823'.914—dc23
2012022484

Printed in the United States of America

First Edition

2 4 6 8 9 7 5 3 1

Book design by Karin Batten

To Frances and Henry

A SUNLESS SEA

CHAPTER

1

THE SUN WAS RISING slowly, splashing red light across the river. The
drops thrown from Monk's oars glowed momentarily in the air, like
wine, or blood. On the other seat, a yard or so in front of him, Orme
leaned forward and threw his weight against the drag of the current.
They worked in perfect rhythm, used to each other now; it was the last
week of November 1864, nearly two years since Monk had taken command of the Thames River Police at the Wapping Station.

That was a small victory for him. Orme had been part of the River
Police all his adult life. For Monk it was a big adjustment after working
first for the Metropolitan Police, and then for himself.

The peace of his satisfaction was shattered by a scream, which was
piercing even above the creak of the oarlocks and the sound of the
wash from a passing string of barges breaking on the shore. Monk and
Orme both turned toward the north bank and Limehouse Pier, which
was no more than twenty yards away.

The scream came again, shrill with terror, and suddenly a figure
appeared, black against the shadowy outline of the sheds and warehouses on the embankment. It was someone in a long coat, waving
their arms and stumbling around; it was impossible to tell whether it
was a man or a woman.

With a glance over his shoulder at Monk, Orme dug his oars in again and swung the boat round toward the shore.

The low clouds were parting and the light became stronger; the figure materialized into a woman in a long skirt, standing on the pier, waving her arms and crying out to them, her words so jumbled in terror they were unintelligible.

The boat bumped at the steps and Orme tied it up.

Monk grasped the closest wooden beam and clambered out, going up the steps as fast as he could. When he got to the top he saw that the woman was now sobbing and putting her hands to her face as if to block out all possible vision.

Monk looked around. He could see no one else, nothing to cause such hysterical fear. Nor could he immediately see any evidence of a threat to the woman. The pier was empty except for her and Monk, and then Orme, coming up the steps.

Monk took her arm gently. "What is it?" he asked, his voice firm. "What's wrong?"

She pulled away from him and swung round, jabbing her finger toward a heap of rubbish, which was slowly becoming more visible in the spreading morning light.

Monk walked over to it, his stomach clenching when he realized that what he had taken for torn canvas was actually the sodden skirt of a woman, her body so mutilated it was not instantly recognizable as human. There was no need to wonder if she was dead. She was twisted over, half on her back, her blue, sightless eyes turned up to the sky. Her hair was matted, and blood-soaked at the back. But it was the rest of her body that made his gorge rise and choked the breath in his throat. Her belly was ripped open, and her entrails were torn out and laid like pale, skinless snakes across her loins.

Monk heard Orme's step behind him.

"Dear God!" Orme breathed out the words, not as a blasphemy but a cry for help, for what he saw not to be real.

Monk swallowed hard and grasped Orme's shoulder for a moment. Then, stumbling a little on the rough boards of the pier, he went back to the woman, who was now standing trembling uncontrollably.

"Do you know who she is?" he said softly.

The woman shook her head, trying to push him away, but there was no strength in her. "No! God 'elp me, I dunno 'er. I come lookin' fer me man. Bastard's bin out all night! An' I find 'er." She crossed herself as if to ward off the horror. "I were terrified it were 'im, till I saw 'er, poor cow."

"You found her just now, when you screamed?" Monk asked.

"Yeah. Ye're River Police, eh?"

"Yes. What's your name?"

She hesitated only a moment. With that thing lying on the boards, almost close enough to touch, perhaps the presence of the police was not such a bad thing as usual.

"Ruby Jones."

"Where do you live, Mrs. Jones?" Monk asked. "And the truth, please. You don't want us coming looking for you, spreading your name up and down the riverside."

She looked at his eyes and decided he meant it. "Northey Street, be'ind the work'ouse," she answered.

"Look at her again, please," he said more gently. "Look at her face. It's not too bad. Keep your eyes off the rest. Think if you've seen her before."

"I don't! I don' know 'er!" she repeated. "I'm not lookin' at that thing again. I'm gonna see it the rest o' me life!"

He did not argue with her.

"Did you just come down here, or were you waiting here for a while, maybe calling out for your man?"

"I were lookin' fer 'im when I saw that. 'Ow long d'yer think I'm gonna stand 'ere, wi' that beside me, eh?"

"Not very long," he agreed. "Will you be all right to find your way home, Mrs. Jones?"

"Yeah." She jerked her arm sharply out of his grip. "Yeah." She took a deep breath, then looked toward the body, the horror in her face replaced by pity for a moment. "Poor cow," she repeated under her breath.

Monk let her go and turned to Orme. Together they went back to the corpse. Monk touched her face gently. The flesh was cold. He put a hand down to one of her shoulders, a little under the edge of her dress, feeling for any warmth at all. There was nothing. She had probably been dead all night.

Orme helped him turn her fully onto her back, completely exposing her ripped-open belly with its pale entrails bulging out, slimy with blood.

Orme let out a gasp of horror and for a moment he swayed, even though he was used to corpses. He was familiar with the destruction that time and predators could cause to a body, but this was a barbarity inflicted by man, and it clearly shook him to a point where he could not hide his shock. He coughed, and seemed to choke on his own breath. "We'd better call the police surgeon, and the local station," he said hoarsely.

Monk nodded, swallowing hard. For a moment he had felt paralyzed with horror and pity. The river he was so used to seemed suddenly cold and strange. Familiar shapes of wharves and wooden piles jutting out of the water closed in on them, seeming threatening as the sharp dawn light distorted their proportions.

Orme's face was grim. "Found her on the pier, means she's our case, sir," he said miserably. "But of course land police may know who she is, poor creature. Could be this is domestic. Or, if she's a local prostitute, then perhaps we've got a lunatic on our hands."

"Either way we have a lunatic on our hands. Even if it was domestic, no sane man could do this to his wife," Monk said incredulously.

"Who knows? Sometimes I think hate's worse than madness." Orme shook his head. "The local station's up the street that way." He indicated with his arm. "If you like, I'll stay here with her while you go get them, sir."

It was the sensible thing to do, since Monk was by far the senior of the two. Still, he was grateful, and said so. He had no wish to remain standing on the pier with the chill of the wind seeping into his bones, keeping watch over that dreadful corpse.

"Thank you. I'll be as quick as I can." He turned and walked rapidly across the pier itself, onto the bank and up toward the street. The sky was pale, the early sun silhouetting the wharves and warehouses. He passed half a dozen stevedores on their way to work. A lamplighter, little more than a gray shadow himself, reached his pole up and snuffed out the last lamp on the street.

An hour later, Monk and Orme were standing in the local police station, still shivering. There was a chill inside that even hot tea with whisky could not shift. Overstone, the police surgeon, came in, closing the door behind him. He was in his sixties, his gray hair thinning but his face keen. He looked from the local sergeant to Orme, then to Monk. He shook his head.

"It's a bad one," he said very quietly. "Most of the mutilation was almost certainly inflicted after death, perhaps all of it. Hard to be absolutely sure. If she wasn't dead already, that would have killed her. But there was still quite a lot of bleeding. She's been ripped open practically from navel to groin."

Monk looked at the man's strained face and saw the pity in his eyes. "If she was dead when that happened, what killed her?" he asked.

"The blow to the back of the head," Overstone replied. "Single one. Hard enough to break her skull. Piece of lead pipe, I'd say, or something like that."

He was standing by a wooden desk piled with papers of varying sizes, handwritten by many different people. There were neat bookshelves all around, the contents not stuffed back in place untidily like Monk's own. There were no pictures tacked up on the wall.

"Nothing else you can tell us?" Monk asked without much hope.

Overstone's mouth turned down at the corners. "Pretty vicious. Lot of weight behind the blow, but it could have been anybody between five and six foot tall."

"Left hand? Right hand?" Monk persisted.

"Probably right-handed, but could be either. Not much help," Overstone said apologetically. "Most people are right-handed."

"And the . . . mutilation?"

"Long blade: four or five inches, I'd say. The cuts are deep, edges pretty sharp. Butcher's knife, sailor's knife—or sailmaker's, for that matter. For God's sake, man, half the chandlers, lightermen, or boatbuilders on the river have something that could have cut the poor woman open.

Even a razor! Could be a barber, for that matter. Or any man who shaves himself." He seemed annoyed, as if his inability to narrow his answer stung him like some kind of guilt.

"Or any housewife with a kitchen," the sergeant added.

Monk glanced at him.

"Sorry, sir." The man lowered his eyes.

"No need," Monk replied. "You're right. Could be anyone at all." He turned to Overstone again. "What about the woman herself? What can you tell me?"

Overstone shrugged in a gesture of futility. "Mid-forties. Quite healthy, as far as I can tell at a quick examination," he replied. "About five foot four. Fairish hair, bit of gray at the sides. Blue eyes, pleasant face but no remarkable features. Good teeth; I suppose that's unusual. Very white. Slight crossover at the front. I imagine when she smiled that might have been attractive." He looked down at the worn, wooden floor. "Sometimes I hate this bloody job!"

Then instantly he lifted his head and the moment's weakness was past. "Might be able to say more tomorrow. One thing I can tell you now, with mutilation like this, feelings are going to run very high. As soon as word gets out there'll be fear, anger, then maybe panic. I don't envy you."

Monk turned to the sergeant. "You'd best keep it as quiet as you can," he ordered. "Don't give any details. The family doesn't need to know them, anyway. If she had one. Don't suppose anyone's been reported missing?"

"No, sir," the sergeant replied unhappily. "And we'll try." But his words lacked conviction.

MONK AND ORME BEGAN near Limehouse Pier and worked along the stretch of Narrow Street, north and south, asking everyone they passed, or in the shops now open, if they had seen anyone going toward the pier the previous evening. Did they know anyone who would return home that way after work, or prostitutes who might seek customers in the area?

The description of the woman was too general for the police to try to identify her: average height, fair brown hair, blue eyes. And it was too early for anyone to be considered missing.

They were told of several prostitutes, even one or two people who liked to walk that route, as Narrow Street offered a pleasant view of the river in places. They gathered a dozen names.

They moved inland up the alleys to Northey Street, Orme in one direction, Monk the other, asking the same questions. It was cold, but the wind had dropped and there was no rain. The low winter sun held no heat.

Monk was walking along the footpath in Ropemakers Fields when a small woman in gray came out of a door carrying a bundle of laundry balanced on her hip. Monk stopped almost in front of her.

"Excuse me, do you live here?" he asked.

She looked him up and down suspiciously. He was dressed in his usual dark, plain clothes, like those a waterman might wear, but the cut was far better, as if a tailor had made them rather than a chandler. His speech was precise, his voice gentle, and he stood with both grace and confidence.

"Yeah . . . ," she said guardedly. " 'Oo are yer as wants ter know?"

"Commander Monk of the River Police," he replied. "I'm looking for anyone who might have heard a fight last night, a woman screaming, perhaps a man shouting at her."

She sighed and rolled her eyes wearily. "If I ever 'ave a night when I don't 'ear nobody fighting I'll tell yer. In fact, I'll tell the bleedin' newspapers. Now, if yer don't mind, I got work ter do." She pushed her hair out of her eyes and with an irritable gesture began to move past him.

Monk stepped sideways to block her way. "This wasn't an ordinary fight. The woman was killed. Probably an hour or two after dark, on Limehouse Pier."

"Wot kind of woman?" she asked him, her face suddenly frightened, mouth drawn tight with a new anxiety.

"About forty or so," he replied. He saw her face relax. He guessed she had daughters who passed that way, possibly even stood around gossiping or flirting. "She was an inch or two taller than you, fair hair with a little gray in it. Quite pretty, in a quiet way." He remembered the teeth. "Probably a nice smile."

"Dunno," the woman with the laundry answered. "Don't sound like no one as I ever seen. Yer sure she were forty, like?"

"Yes. And she was wearing ordinary clothes, not like a woman looking for business," he added. "And there was no paint on her face that we could see." He felt callous speaking of her like that. He had robbed her of character, of humor or dreams, likes and dislikes; probably because he wanted to rob her also of her terror. Please God, she did not know what had happened to her afterward. He hoped she had not even seen the blade.

"Then 'er 'usband done 'er in," the woman replied, pulling an expression of weary grief. "But I dunno 'oo she is. Could be anyone." She pushed a few trailing hairs back off her face again and adjusted the weight of the laundry bag on her hip.

Monk thanked her and moved on. He stopped other people, both men and women, asking the same questions and getting more or less the same answers. No one recognized the woman from Monk's description of her. No one admitted to being anywhere near Limehouse Pier after dark, which at this time of the year was about five o'clock in the afternoon. The evening had been overcast and damp. Little work was possible after that. No one had heard shouting or anything that sounded like a fight. They were all keen to go home and eat, find a little warmth and possibly a pint or two of ale.

Monk met up with Orme at noon. They had a cup of hot tea and a ham sandwich at the corner stand, finding a little shelter in a doorway as they spoke, coat collars turned up.

"Nobody's seen or heard anything," Orme said unhappily. "Not that I expected them to. Word's out already that it's pretty bad. All suddenly blind and deaf." He took another bite of his ham sandwich.

"Not surprising," Monk answered, sipping his tea. It was hot and a bit too strong, but he was used to it. It was nothing like the fresh, fragrant tea at home. This was probably made hours ago, and added to with boiling water every time it got low. "Ruby Jones probably told her friends, and they told theirs. It'll be all over Limehouse by this afternoon."

"They should be frightened enough to want this butcher caught," Orme said between his teeth.

"They're shutting their eyes and pretending it's all miles away," Monk replied. "Can't blame them. I would if I could. That's how half the bad things happen. We don't want to know, don't want to be involved. If the victim did something wrong, something stupid, and brought it on themselves, if we stay out of it then it won't happen to us."

"But it isn't miles away," Orme said softly. He was leaning a little against a stanchion, gazing far away into the distance. Monk had no idea what he saw in it. There were startling moments when he felt he knew Orme intimately because of the bitter and terrible experiences they had shared, things that were understood but could never be put into words. But there were far more days like this when they worked together with mutual respect, something bordering on a kind of friendship, but the difference between them was never forgotten, at least not by Orme. "It's right here. Unless she came here by boat. Either way, she was killed there on the pier, and then cut open like that." His mouth tightened. His face was very pale under his windburn. "Or I suppose they could've killed her somewhere else, and then cut her here?" he suggested, his voice grating in his throat.

"She wouldn't have bled like that if she'd been dead awhile," Monk replied. "Overstone said that from the way the blood was, and the bruising, he reckoned she was just recently dead."

Orme swore under his breath, then apologized.

Monk waved his hand, dismissing it.

They both stood on the cold stones of the street, saying nothing for several moments. Other people were coming for the tea, their footsteps loud on the cobbles. Somewhere a dog was barking.

"Do you think they could've cut her up like that in the dark?" Orme finally broke the silence. "Not seeing what they were doing?"

Monk looked at him. "There were no streetlamps where we found her. Either they did it in the dark, or while there was still some daylight left."

"Why there, anyway?" Orme asked. He tightened his hunched shoulders as if his jacket were not enough to keep him warm. "It's not a place a prostitute would take a man. The riding lights of a barge would illuminate you long enough to be seen."

"Maybe they *were* seen," Monk thought aloud. "From the distance, a man struggling with a woman could look like an embrace. Lighter-men would just laugh at his boldness doing it out in the open, a kind of bravado. They would think he was taking his pleasure, not killing her."

"Not much point looking for anyone who saw," Orme said unhap-pily. "They could be anywhere by now, from Henley to Gravesend."

"Wouldn't help us much anyway," Monk replied. "They'd have no way of knowing if it was her they saw, or any other couple." The thought depressed him. A woman could be murdered and gutted like a fish, out in the open, in full view of the ships going past, on the most populous river in the world, and no one notice or understand what was happen-ing.

He straightened up, eating the last of his sandwich. He had to choke it down. There was nothing wrong with it, but his mouth was dry. The bread tasted like sawdust.

"We'd best see if we can find out who she was," he said. "Not that it will necessarily help us much. She was probably just in the wrong place at the wrong time."

"There'll still be people to tell," Orme responded. "Friends, even a husband."

Monk did not answer. He knew it. It was the worst part of the be-ginning in any murder case: telling those who had cared about the victim. In the end, the worst was finding the person who had done it, and those who cared about them.

Together they walked back up Narrow Street to the corner of Rope-makers Fields and then along it slowly. On the north side there were alleys every few dozen yards. Some led up to Triangle Place, and then on to the workhouse.

They asked there, giving as good a description of the dead woman as they could, but no one was missing. In any case, the dead woman's hands had not looked like those of a woman used to physical labor: red from long hours wet or submerged in caustic soap, scrubbing floors or laundering, or calloused from the constant prick of the needle while sewing canvas.

Was she a prostitute, well past her prime, perhaps desperate for a few shillings and easily persuaded to go anywhere, even the open space of a pier as darkness fell? With the money at least she could eat, or buy a few pieces of coal to keep herself warm.

In spite of himself Monk imagined it: the offer, the need on both their parts, the brief struggle, which she easily mistook for fumbling, clumsy desire, perhaps a man angry with himself for needing such a release, angry with her because she had the power to give it to him, and was demanding money. Then the crushing blow and the consuming darkness.

Why had he then mutilated her? Had he known her, and this was some uncontrollable personal hatred? Or was he a madman, and any victim would have done just as well? If that were so, then this would be only the beginning.

They walked the length of Narrow Street again, and Ropemakers Fields, and up and down the alleys, but no one had seen anything that helped, no man and woman together going toward the pier at dusk or shortly before, or if they had, they had barely noticed, or preferred not to remember. No amount of questioning elicited anything helpful.

They needed to find out who she was, who she had been before this.

"We'll get a drawing of her," Monk said as they walked back toward the local police station and the sky darkened into late afternoon. "There's a constable there who's good with a pencil to catch a likeness. We'll get him to make at least a couple of pictures. Try again in the morning."

MONK WAS TIRED ENOUGH to sleep well that night. He told Hester nothing about the woman on the pier, not wanting to shatter the brief peace of the evening. If she knew there was any worry, she was too wise or too gentle to say so.

He woke early the next morning and went out before breakfast to get at least a couple of the daily newspapers from the stand on the corner of Paradise Place and Church Street. By the time he had walked the hundred yards or so back home, he knew the worst. WOMAN HORRIBLY MURDERED ON LIMEHOUSE PIER, read one headline. WOMAN GUTTED AND LEFT TO DIE LIKE AN ANIMAL, said another.

He had them folded, headlines concealed under his arm, when he reached his own kitchen door. He smelled bacon and toast, and heard the kettle whistling on the hob.

Hester was standing with the toasting fork in her hand, taking the fresh piece off and putting it into the rack with the others, so it would stay crisp. She closed the oven door and smiled at him. She was dressed in her favorite deep blue. For a moment, looking at her, Monk could put off a little longer the thoughts of violence and loss, the chill on the constantly moving water and the smell of death.

Perhaps he should have told her last night about the woman, but he had been tired and cold, and aching to put the horror of it out of his mind. He had needed to get warm and dry, to lie close to her and hear her talk about something else—anything at all that had to do with sanity and the small, healing details of life.

She was looking at him now and reading in his face that something was badly wrong. She knew him far too well for him to dissemble—not that he ever had. She had been an army nurse in the Crimean War, a dozen years ago, before they had met. There were few horrors or griefs he could tell her that she did not already know at least as well as he.

"What is it?" she asked quietly, perhaps hoping that he could tell her before twelve-year-old Scuff came down for his breakfast, eager for the new day, and everything he could eat. About a year ago they and Scuff had mutually adopted each other, Hester and Monk because Scuff was homeless, living precariously on the river, mostly by his wits. It was not that he was an orphan, but that his mother had too many younger children to have time for him, or maybe his mother's new husband did not want him. Scuff had adopted Monk because he thought Monk lacked adequate knowledge of dockside life to do his job and needed someone like Scuff to look after him. Hester he had grown close to more reluctantly, in small steps, both of them being careful, afraid of hurt. The whole arrangement had begun tentatively on all sides, but over the year it had become comfortable.

"What is it?" Hester repeated more urgently.

"We found the body of a woman on Limehouse Pier at dawn yester-day," Monk replied, putting his folded papers on his chair and then sitting on them. "Badly mutilated. Hoped we'd keep the worst of it out of the papers, but we haven't. They're making a meal of it."

Her face tightened a little with only a tiny movement of muscles. "Who is she? Do you know?"

"Not yet. From what I could tell, she looked ordinary enough, poor but respectable. Middle forties, at a guess." An image of the woman's body came back to his mind. Suddenly he felt tired and chilled again, as if the lights had gone out, although the kitchen was bright and warm and full of clean, homey smells.

"The surgeon said the mutilation was done after she was dead," he went on. "The papers didn't say that."

Hester looked at him thoughtfully for a moment, as if she was going to ask him something. Then she changed her mind and served his breakfast of bacon, eggs, and toast, carrying the hot plate with a tea towel and setting it down in front of him. The butter and marmalade were already on the table. She made the tea and brought it over, steam coming gently from the spout of the pot.

Scuff arrived at the door, boots in his hands. He put them down in the hall and came in, looking first at Monk, then at Hester. In spite of almost a year here he was still thin, small for his age, his shoulders narrow. But now his hair was thick and shiny, and there were no blemishes on his fair skin.

"Are you hungry?" Hester inquired, as if it were a question.

He grinned and sat down in what he now regarded as his chair.

"Yeah. Please."

She smiled and served him the same as she had Monk. He would eat it all, then look hopefully around for more. It was a comfortable pattern, repeated every morning.

"Wo's wrong?" Scuff regarded Monk with a frown. "Can I 'elp?"

"Not yet, thank you," Monk assured him, looking up and meeting his eyes so Scuff would know he was serious. "Nasty case, but not mine, at least not yet." He knew that since it was in the newspapers, Scuff would unquestionably hear about it, but for now they could still have a few hours' peace. Since living here in Paradise Place, Scuff's ability to read had increased dramatically. He was not fluent—there were some longer or more complex words he still had difficulty with—but the plain language of a newspaper was well within his ability.

Scuff accepted his breakfast from Hester, but it did not distract his attention from Monk. "Why's it not yours?" he asked. "You're 'ead o' the River Police. 'Oo's would it be, then?"

"Depends on who she was," Monk replied. "We found her body on the pier, but she might have lived inland, so this case would belong to the local Limehouse police." Even as he said it he made up his mind. Lately the papers had been rife with criticism of the police for the violence and prostitution going on in the area close to the river. There had been several knife fights, one of which had degenerated into a full-scale street battle leaving half a dozen people wounded and two dead.

The newspapers had said the police were incompetent to handle it and had lost control. Uglier suggestions still were that they had deliberately allowed it to happen, in order to infiltrate it and get rid of a few troublemakers they could not handle legally, because the whole waterfront was slipping out of their control.

The only thing that might stop further destructive speculation after this crime was a quick solution.

"No, it don't belong ter them," Scuff argued. "They need yer ter 'elp 'em. If they killed 'er by the river, yer gotta do it."

Monk smiled, in spite of himself. "I'll offer to," he conceded. "It's not something I really want."

"Why?" Scuff asked, his face puzzled, fair eyebrows drawn into a frown. "Don't you care 'oo did it?"

"Yes, of course I do," Monk corrected himself quickly. "It's just that we don't know who she was yet, so we don't know where she lived. If it's inland, the regular police would know the people better."

"They in't better'n you," Scuff said with absolute certainty. "Yer gotta do it." He was watching Monk's face closely, trying to read what he felt, so he could figure out how to help. "It were a daft thing ter do," he went on. "If yer don't want something found, you 'ide it. Yer don't leave it out in the open so's any ferry or lighterman can see it. That's daft!"

Monk did not try to explain homicidal lunacy to Scuff over breakfast, or what kind of rage gets hold of a man that causes him to rip a woman's body open, even after she's dead.

Scuff rolled his eyes, then set the matter aside and started to eat his breakfast with intense pleasure. It would be years before he lost his excitement at a whole plate of eggs and bacon that was solely for him.

"Can you give it to Orme, or one of the other men?" Hester asked when Scuff had finished and left the kitchen.

"No," Monk said with a brief smile at her. "If she was on or near the river, it's ours. And it's going to be very bad. The newspapers are already calling for questions to be asked in Parliament about the vice in the port areas: Limehouse, Shadwell, Bermondsey, Deptford—in fact both sides of the river all the way down to Greenwich." He hesitated a moment. "Perhaps we can solve it soon."

She smiled at him without answer. There was a world of things between them that did not require words.

MONK WENT DOWN TO the water's edge to take a ferry across the river to the Wapping Station. It was a gray morning with a hard wind making the water choppy. He pulled his coat collar up around his ears as he climbed into the boat and they moved out into the open stretch of the river where the slight lee of the buildings no longer protected them.

They were in between the long strings of barges going up and down the waterway, laden with cargo. Close to the docks ships were moored, waiting to unload. The quays were busy, men beginning the hard labor of lifting, wheeling, guiding cranes and winches, always watching the wind and the tide. Even out on the water, in spite of the slap of the current against the sides of the ferry and the creaking of the oarlocks as the oars swept back and forth, he could hear the cry of gulls and the shouts of men onshore.

At the far side he paid the ferryman and thanked him. He was familiar with the ferrymen; he saw the same few almost every day and knew them by name. Then he went up the steep stone steps to the dockside and across the open space in the sharper wind to the Wapping Police Station.

Inside was warm and there was tea brewing. He had a cup while he checked the news of the night and gave the few instructions that were necessary. Then he took a hansom to Limehouse Police Station and looked at the drawings the young constable had made of the dead woman. They were good. He had a talent. He had given her features life, parting the lips a little to show the slightly crossed front tooth, making her an individual.

The constable saw Monk looking at it, and perhaps misunderstood the sudden moment of pain in his face.

"Isn't it any good?" he said anxiously.

"It's too good," Monk replied honestly. "It's like seeing her alive. It makes her death more real." He looked up at the man and saw the slight flush on his face. "You did very well. Thank you."

"Sir."

Orme came in a few moments afterward and Monk gave him one of the two drawings. They agreed where each of them would go: Orme to the north, Monk south, to the Isle of Dogs.

The wind funneled down the narrow streets, carrying the smell of the river and the dank odor of rubbish and wet stones, overrunning drains. Monk questioned everyone he passed. Though the news clearly had reached them, many affected to be too busy to answer him and he had to insist. Then they were angry, wishing to do anything to stop the horror and the fear from touching their own lives.

He was still down near the docks when he stepped in at a small tobacconist who also sold a few groceries and the local newspaper.

"I dunno anything about it," the man denied vigorously as soon as Monk told him who he was. He refused to look at the picture, brushing it away with his hand.

"It's not when she was dead!" Monk said testily. "That's what she looked like before. She could be a local married woman."

"Fine, 'ere," the old man held out his hand to take the picture again. Monk gave it to him and he studied it more carefully, before passing it back. "She could, an' all," he agreed. "But I still don' know 'er. Sorry. She din' work around 'ere, married or not."

Monk thanked him and left.

For the rest of the morning he walked miles through the gray streets, narrow and busy, all within the sight and sounds of the river. He spoke to several prostitutes but they all denied knowing the woman in the drawing. He had not expected them to admit it. They would want to avoid all contact with the police, whatever the reason, but he had hoped to see a flicker of recognition in someone's face. All he saw, though, was resentment—and always fear.

He was inclined to believe that the dead woman was not one of their number; she was too different from them. She was at least fifteen years older than they were, perhaps more, and there was a gentleness in her face. It looked more aged by illness than coarsened by drink or life on the streets. He thought her more likely to be a married woman ill-used.

He had asked the police surgeon if she had had children, but Overstone had told him that the mutilations had been so violent he could not tell.

It was Orme who stumbled on the answer, farther inland. At a small general store just over Britannia Bridge he had found a shopkeeper who stared hard at his version of the drawing, then blinked and looked up, sad and puzzled.

"Said she looked like Zenia Gadney, from up Copenhagen Place," Orme told Monk when they met up at one o'clock for a quick lunch at a public house.

"Was he certain?" Monk asked. Learning her name and where she lived made her death sharper, more real somehow.

"Seemed it," Orme answered ruefully, meeting Monk's eyes, understanding the same dread. "It's a good picture."

An hour later he and Monk were knocking on the doors at Copenhagen Place, which was just over a quarter of a mile from the river.

A tired woman with two children clinging to her skirts looked at the picture Monk held out for her. She pushed the stray hair out of her eyes.

"Yeah. That's Mrs. Gadney from over the way. But yer shouldn't be after 'er, poor thing. She in't doin' anyone no 'arm. Maybe she do oblige the odd gentleman now an' again, or maybe not. But if she do, wot's that hurtin'? In't yer got nothin' better ter do? Why don't you go an' catch that bleedin' madman wot cut up the poor creature you found on the pier, eh?" She looked at Monk with contempt in her pale, tired face.

"Are you sure that's Mrs. Gadney?" Monk said quietly.

She looked at him again, then saw something in his eyes, and her hand flew to her mouth. "Gawd!" she said in no more than a sigh. Her other hand instinctively reached for the younger of the children and gripped his hand. "That . . . that wa'n't 'er, was it?"

"I think it may be," Monk answered. "I'm sorry."

The woman seized the boy and picked him up, holding him close to her. He was perhaps two. Sensing her fear, he began to cry.

"What number did she live at?" Monk persisted.

"Number fourteen," the woman replied, nodding her head in the direction of the house opposite and to the left.

"Has she family?"

"Not as I ever saw. She were very quiet. Didn't bother no one."

"Who else might know more about her?"

"I dunno. Mebbe Mrs. 'Iggins up at number twenty. I seen 'em talking once or twice."

"Do you know if she worked anywhere?"

"In't none o' my business. I can't 'elp yer." She held the child tighter and moved to close the door.

"Thank you." Monk stepped back and he and Orme turned away. There was nothing further to ask her.

"Sir Oliver?" the judge said inquiringly.

Oliver Rathbone rose to his feet and stepped to the center of the courtroom floor. It was almost like an arena; he was surrounded by the gallery behind him, the jury on his left in their two rows of high seats, and the judge in front in the great carved chair, mounted as if it were a throne. The witness stand was almost above him, up the steps in its own little tower.

He had stood here in major trials for most of his adult life, as one of England's most brilliant lawyers. Usually he felt intensely about a case, whether he was acting for the defense or the prosecution. Often the battle was for a man's life. Today he was committed to the defense because it was his job—but he was still uncertain in his own mind if the accused was guilty or not. That gave him a rare feeling of emptiness. He could put no passion into this work, no fierce care for the sake of justice. He would be no more than competent, and that was far from enough to satisfy his nature.

But very little had been going well lately. The things that mattered seemed to have slipped beyond his control ever since the Ballinger case, and all the miserable decisions that had led to the final split between his wife, Margaret, and himself.

He concentrated on the witness, making himself recall the details of his testimony and one by one attack each point that was vulnerable, forcing the man to contradict himself so the jury would think him devious and unreliable.

He succeeded. This was the last witness of the day and the court was adjourned. Rathbone rode home in a hansom cab and arrived comparatively early. It was one of those calm, still evenings of deepening winter when the storms are all yet to come. It was not cold enough for frost. As he stepped out of the cab and paid the driver, there was no bite in the air. The last of the neighbor's chrysanthemums were still heavy with bloom, and their earthy smell was sweet as he passed them.

A year ago he would have been happy to be home with this extra time to spend. But that was before the whole business of the barges on the river with their obscene pleasures, their abuse of children, and their final descent into murder.

He and Margaret had been happy before all that— in fact increasingly so with each passing week. There had been tenderness, an understanding between them that filled all kinds of longings he had hardly acknowledged he felt earlier in his life.

Now, as he went in through the front door and the butler took his hat and coat, he felt the heavy silence in the house.

"Good evening, Sir Oliver." The man was polite as always.

"Good evening, Ardmore," Rathbone replied automatically. The butler, and the cook and housekeeper, Mrs. Wilton, might be the only people whose voices he would hear until he left his house again tomorrow morning. The soundlessness would grow thick and oppressive, almost like another presence in the home.

It was absurd. He was becoming maudlin. Silence had never bothered him when he was single, which had been a long enough time. In fact, back then he had found it rather pleasant after the constant noise of his chambers, or the courtroom. An occasional dinner with his friends, especially Monk and Hester, had been all the companionship he wished for—apart, of course, from visiting his father out at Primrose Hill. But just at the moment Henry Rathbone was traveling in Europe— Germany, to be precise—and he would be there until well into the new year.

Oliver would have liked to see him this evening. His father was still his dearest friend, as he had always been. But one did not visit friends with one's own emptiness; right now, there was no interesting problem to challenge Henry with, not even any specific loss or difficulty for which to seek his comfort. Just a sense of having failed. And yet, Oliver did not know what he would have or could have done differently.

He sat in the beautiful dining room that Margaret had designed. As he ate his dinner he went over it all yet again in his mind.

If he had fought harder to prove Ballinger's innocence, even if he had been able to think of some trick, honest or dishonest, surely it would have made no difference to the eventual verdict? All it would've done was tarnish his sense of honor.

But Margaret had never seen it that way. She believed that Rathbone had put his ambition before loyalty to his family. Ballinger was Margaret's father, and regardless of the evidence, she would not believe his guilt.

Was it better or worse that he had been murdered in prison before he could be hanged?

She had blamed Rathbone for that, too, believing that some sort of appeal could have been made, and Ballinger would have lived.

That was not true, though. There had been no grounds for appeal, and Rathbone, at least, knew that Ballinger had been guilty. In the end, privately between the two of them, Ballinger had admitted it. Rathbone could remember the arrogance in Ballinger's face as he had told the full story. In his own mind, Ballinger felt his actions were justified.

Rathbone ate mechanically, pushing the roast beef and vegetables around the porcelain plate and tasting little. It was an insult to Mrs. Wilton, but she would never know. He would thank her exactly as if he had thoroughly enjoyed it. The staff were all trying so hard to please him. It was touching and a little embarrassing. They saw him more clearly than he would have wished. It was said that no man was a hero to his valet; that acute perception seemed to extend to the butler and the housekeeper as well. It might even extend to the maids and the footman for all he knew.

Now that Margaret was gone, he had too large a staff, but he could not bring himself to let any of them go—not yet, anyway. Was that for their benefit? Or was it a refusal on his part to accept the situation as final?

His mind returned to Ballinger, and that last interview they had had together. Had Ballinger been justified, a little, in the very beginning? Clearly he believed so. The descent had come after that.

Or had the first step been wrong, and the rest always bound to follow?

Rathbone finished dessert: a delicate baked custard with a crisp, sweet crust. Mrs. Wilton was trying very hard. He must remember to compliment her for it.

He set his napkin beside his plate and rose to his feet. Without doing it consciously, he had made up his mind to go to see Margaret one more time. Perhaps it was the unfinished feeling that carved such a hollow inside him and made it impossible to close the acrimoniousness and begin to heal, whatever that might mean. He had not yet done everything he could to resolve the bitterness between them.

She was mistaken. He had not set his ambition before family. Ambition had not been on his mind at all. He had never flinched, even for an instant, from representing Ballinger. Moreover, he had believed, at least in the very beginning, that he could and should win the case. Margaret's accusation was unfair. He still stung from the injustice of it. Perhaps now, with a little time passed, she would know that.

He told Ardmore he would be out for an hour or two. After collecting his hat and coat, he went into the lamplit streets to look for a hansom.

He arrived at the new, far smaller house that Mrs. Ballinger had taken after her husband's death. It was the fifth place down on a very ordinary terrace, a dramatic fall from the wealth and fashion of the house in which they had lived before, the one in which Margaret had grown up.

As Rathbone stood on the pavement and looked at it, he felt a stab of pity, almost of shame, for the beautiful home he had moved into when he first married Margaret. She had done the interior, choosing the colors and fabrics, which were subtle and beautiful. They were more daring than he would have picked, but once they were in place he liked them. They made his previous conservative taste seem bland. She had placed the pictures, the vases, the best of the ornaments. Some of them were wedding gifts.

She had enjoyed being Lady Rathbone. He knew with sadness, and a bitter humor, that she had now stopped using the title, although she could hardly call herself Mrs. Rathbone. There was no such person. Neither of them had mentioned the subject of divorce, although the question of it hung between them, waiting for the inevitable decision. When would that be?

Perhaps he should not have come. She might raise it now, and he was not ready. He did not know what he wanted to say. Neither of them had sinned in the way usually accepted as making a marriage intolerable. Sometimes one or the other party invented an affair and admitted to it, but Margaret would never do that, and Rathbone realized as he stood on the front doorstep, that neither would he. Neither had wronged the other, in that sense. They were simply morally incompatible, and perhaps that was worse. It was not a matter of forgiving. The division was not in what either had done, but in what they were.

A parlor maid opened the door and her face registered her dismay when she recognized him.

"Good evening," Rathbone said, unable to remember her name, if he had ever known it. "Is Mrs. Ballinger at home?"

"If you'll come in, Sir Oliver, I'll ask if she's able to see you." She stood back to allow him into the narrow hall, so different from the handsome, spacious one in the old house. It was darker, somehow shabbier, in spite of the homely touches and the clean smell of polish.

There was no place for him to wait except there. The house had no morning room or study, just a simple parlor, dining room, and kitchens, probably just one to cook in, and a scullery for washing dishes. There was hardly need for more than a cook/housekeeper, one maid and a manservant of some sort, and perhaps one lady's maid for both Margaret and her mother. Rathbone wondered wryly how much of this was paid for by his very generous allowance. Wherever she chose to live, she was still his wife.

The maid appeared again, her face careful to show no expression.

"Mrs. Ballinger will see you, Sir Oliver, if you will come this way, please." She led him not to the parlor but to an unexpected small room next to the baize door into the kitchen. Possibly it was the housekeeper's room.

Mrs. Ballinger was standing inside. She wore black. Incredibly, it was only weeks since Ballinger had died—it felt like months had passed. Rathbone felt a wave of pity as he looked at her. She seemed smaller, as if everything in her life had shrunk. Her hair had faded and looked thinner; her shoulders sagged so that her gown hung awkwardly, even though it was an excellent one, kept from happier times. She did not fill it out as she used to. Her face was pale but there was a flicker of hope in her eyes.

Rathbone found himself floundering for words. He knew she wanted a reconciliation between himself and Margaret, hoped that their happiness could be rebuilt, even if her own could not. Margaret's anger and misery must weigh even more heavily on her than any other. Rathbone was certain of that as he looked at her face now. He had never really liked her. She had seemed to him self-absorbed, unimaginative, in many ways superficial in her judgments. Now he was overwhelmed with compassion for her, and he knew he could do nothing to help, except perhaps keep his temper, try harder to reach some accommodation with Margaret.

Had Margaret ever thought what her bitterness was costing her mother? Or was she too filled with her own pain to consider anyone else's? Rathbone realized with a cutting self-awareness that the very anger he wanted to control for Mrs. Ballinger's sake had welled up inside again, scalding him.

They were standing, facing each other in silence. It was up to him to speak first, to explain why he had come, uninvited and at this hour of the evening. Without planning to be, he was uncharacteristically gentle.

"I wanted to see how you were," he began, as if that were the kind of emotion he often felt. "There might be something I could do that I haven't thought of. If you would permit me?"

She was silent for several moments, weighing his intention behind the words.

"For Margaret's sake?" she asked finally. "You must still hate Mr. Ballinger and me because of him. I had no idea . . ." It sounded like an excuse, and she stopped as soon as she realized it.

"I never imagined that you knew," he said quickly, and honestly. "The shock of finding out such a thing, and beginning to understand what it meant is enough to paralyze almost anyone. And you had no alternative except loyalty. By the time you knew of it there was nothing to be done to save anyone."

She looked puzzled for a moment, as if trying to distinguish between his judgment of her, and his judgment of Margaret.

"You were his wife," he said, in self-defense as well as by way of explanation.

"Have you come to see Margaret?" Hope refused to die in her.

"If I may?" That was a polite fiction. Mrs. Ballinger had never refused him access to Margaret; it was Margaret herself who would not speak to him.

She hesitated. He knew she was considering not whether to take the message, but how; what manner would offer any chance of success.

"I will go to ask her," she said at last. "Please wait here. I . . ." She swallowed with difficulty. "I would rather not have a scene that would embarrass any of us."

"Of course," he agreed.

It was nearly a quarter of an hour before she returned, which showed a measure of the difficulty she had had in persuading Margaret. As Rathbone thanked her and followed her back across the hall, he found himself increasingly angry with Margaret, not on his own behalf but on her mother's. He could not even imagine the blow Mrs. Ballinger had taken from her husband's guilt, and then his murder cutting off all hope of a reprieve. Not that there had been any. He would have died with the hangman's noose around his throat. Her entire world had collapsed hideously. She had no one but her children on whom to lean. The failure of Margaret's marriage and her refusal to accept her father's guilt must keep all the wounds open and bleeding.

Margaret was standing in the middle of the overcrowded parlor, waiting for him. She was very plainly dressed. Like her mother, she was still in black, although hers was relieved by jet jewelry and a brooch set with seed pearls, a tiny glimmer of white against the darkness. As always, she stood with grace, her head high, but she was thinner than the last time he had seen her, and very pale, almost colorless.

She did not speak.

To ask how she was would be absurdly formal, setting a tone that would be hard to break. Her health had always been excellent and it was hardly the issue between them; any distress she felt now was emotional.

He felt awkward and knew that in his immaculately tailored clothes he must look out of place in this room with its drab walls, and too many family pictures on every surface. What could he say that was honest? Why had he come?

"I wanted to talk to you . . . ," he began. "To see if we could understand each other a little better, perhaps move toward some kind of reconciliation . . ." He stopped. Her face gave nothing away, and he felt both foolish and vulnerable.

Her fair eyebrows rose. "Are you saying what you think you ought to, Oliver?" she asked quietly, no lift in her voice. "Paving the way to justify yourself because you want to set me aside with a clear conscience? After all, you need to be able to tell your colleagues that you tried. It would reflect poorly on you if you didn't. Everyone would understand that an eminent lawyer like you would not wish to be married to the daughter of a criminal, but you should at least not make that offensively clear."

"Is that how you think of yourself: the daughter of a criminal?" he said with far more edge to his voice than he had meant to.

"We were talking about you," she responded. "You are here; I did not come to you."

That also hurt, although he should not have expected her to come to him. Right or wrong, it was always the man who pursued—except perhaps with Hester. If she had quarreled with someone she cared for, whether she had been right or wrong, she would have sought them out. He knew that from the past. Was he unfairly comparing Margaret with her? Hester had faults as well, but big, brave ones, never a pettiness of mind. He was the one who had not been daring enough for her. He should not be petty now.

He took a deep breath. "I came hoping that if we spoke, we might heal at least some of the breach between us," he said as gently as he could. "I have no idea what the future will bring, and I was certainly not trying to make excuses for it. I don't need to explain myself to anyone else—"

"Which is as well, because you can't!" She cut across him. "Not to me, or to my family."

He kept his temper with difficulty. "I was not thinking of you as someone else." They were both still standing, as if physical ease were impossible. He thought of asking if he could sit down, or even simply doing it, but he decided not to. She might take it as an implication that he thought he belonged here, and that he saw it as a right, not a privilege.

"How were you thinking of me, then?" she asked.

"As my wife, and—at one time at least—also as my friend," he said.

Without warning the tears filled her eyes.

For an instant he thought that there was hope. He started to take a step toward her.

"You threw that away," she said quickly, raising her head a fraction, as if to ward him off.

"I did what I had to do!" he protested. "Everything the law allowed me, to defend him. He was guilty, Margaret!"

"How often do you repeat that to yourself, Oliver?" she said bitterly. "Have you convinced yourself yet?"

"He admitted it to me," he said wearily. They had been over all of this before. He had lived out the whole wretched tragedy for her—Ballinger's desperate fight for life, then finally his admission of guilt. He had given her few details, to spare her distress, and her knowledge of details that were ugly and cruel, things she need never know.

"And that's enough for you?" She flung the words at him like an accusation. "What about the reasons, Oliver? Or didn't you want to know them? Can't you for once be honest and stop hiding behind the law? Or is it all you know, all you understand? 'The book says this! The book says that!'"

"That's not fair, Margaret," he protested. "I can't work outside the law—"

"You mean you can't think outside it," she corrected him, her eyes burning with contempt. "You are a liar, perhaps first to yourself; you can consider actual morality when you want to. You can for Hester. You'll bend all your own precious rules when she asks you to."

"Is that what this is?" he said with painful understanding. "Jealousy of Hester, because you think I would have done differently for her? Can't you understand that she would never have asked me to?"

Margaret gave a harsh, bitter laugh. The sound of it lacerated the last of his emotions. "You're a coward, Oliver! Is that why you care for her so much? Because she'll fight the battles for you, and never expect anything of you but to follow? What about Monk? Would you fight for him?"

He did not know how to answer her. Could any of what she said be true?

"Did you ask my father why he did all those things you accused him of?" she went on, perhaps sensing her victory. "Or did you not want to know? It might disturb your comfortable world of right and wrong where everything is decided for you by generations of lawyers from the past. No need to think! No need to make any difficult decisions, or stand alone. Certainly no need to take any dangerous action yourself, question any of your own comfortable certainties, or risk anything."

At last he was angry enough to reply. "I'll risk my own safety, Margaret, but not anyone else's."

Her eyes widened in amazement. "That man, Mickey Parfitt, he was filth!" she said with scorching contempt. "Worse than vermin. You know what he did."

"And the girl?" he said quietly.

"What girl?" She looked blank.

"The girl he killed as well?"

"The prostitute!"

"Yes, the *prostitute*," he replied coldly. "Was she vermin, too?"

"She would have had him hanged!" she exclaimed.

"So that justified him killing her? That's your courage, your brave morality? Personally deciding who lives and who dies, rather than leaving it to the law?"

"He had reasons, terrible choices to make." Now the tears ran freely down her cheeks. "He was my father! I loved him." She said it as if that explained it all. He began to realize at last that for her, it did.

"So I should forgive him, no matter what he did?" he asked.

"Yes! Is that so difficult?" It was a challenge, demanded in fury and despair.

"Then what a pity you did not love me also." He said the words so softly, they were little more than a whisper.

She gasped. Her eyes went wide. "That's not fair!"

"It's perfectly fair," he replied. "And since I cannot place your family before what is right, then perhaps I did not love you, either. That seems to be your conclusion, and by your way of measuring love, you are right. I am sorry. I truly believed otherwise." He stood still for a moment, but she did not say anything. He turned to leave. He had reached the door when finally she spoke.

"Oliver . . ."

He stopped, then looked back at her. "Yes?"

She made a helpless little gesture with her hands. "I thought I had something to say, but I don't." It was an admission of failure, a closing of the door.

The pain overwhelmed him, not for something lost so much as for the fading of a dream that had once seemed completely real. He walked out of the room.

The parlor maid was waiting in the hall, as if she had known he would not be staying. She handed him his coat, and then his hat. Mrs. Ballinger was not in sight, and it seemed faintly ridiculous to go looking for her to tell her he was leaving. It would only embarrass them both. There was nothing to say. Better simply to go.

He thanked the parlor maid and went out into the darkness. The air was cold now, but he barely noticed. He walked briskly until he came to the nearest cross street where he could find a hansom to take him home.

RATHBONE WALKED INTO HIS own wide, gracious hall to be told by Ardmore that there was someone waiting for him in his withdrawing room.

"Who is it?" he asked with some irritation. Whatever it was, he was in no mood to deal with it tonight. Even if some client had been arrested and was in jail, there was nothing he could do about it at this hour.

"Mr. Brundish, sir," Ardmore replied. "He says he has something of great importance to give you, and he is unable to return in the morning because of other commitments. I explained to him that you were out, and that I did not know at what time you might return, but he was adamant, sir."

"Yes, you did the right thing," Rathbone said wearily. "I suppose I had better go and take delivery of whatever it is. What is it, do you know? A letter of some sort, I suppose."

"No, Sir Oliver, it is quite a large parcel, and from the way he carried it, it seems to be of considerable weight."

Rathbone was surprised.

"A parcel?"

"Yes, sir. Would you like me to bring whisky, sir? Or brandy? I offered him both earlier, but he only accepted coffee."

"No, thank you. It will only incline him to stay." He was aware it sounded ungracious, but all he wanted was to accept the package and see the man leave. And very possibly, Brundish was as keen to get to home as Rathbone was to be left in peace.

He walked into the withdrawing room and Brundish rose from the chair he had been sitting in. He was a stocky man dressed in a striped suit. He looked tired and a little anxious.

"Sorry to call at this time of the night," he apologized before Rathbone had a chance to speak at all. "Can't come tomorrow, and I needed to . . . deal with this." His glance slid to the box on the floor beside his chair. It was approximately a foot in height and breadth, fifteen inches long. It appeared to be some kind of case.

"Deal with it?" Rathbone asked, puzzled. "What is it?"

"Your legacy," Brundish replied. "From the late Arthur Ballinger. I've been holding it in trust for him. At least, I held the key and the instructions. I only retrieved this today."

Rathbone froze. Memory came flooding back. Ballinger's message to him: that he had bequeathed him the blackmail photographs in a final irony as bitter as gall. Rathbone had assumed it was a dying joke, a threat empty of meaning.

He looked now at the case sitting on the beautiful carpet (another choice of Margaret's), and wondered if that was really what was in the box: pictures of men, important men, powerful men with money and position, indulging in the terrible vice that Ballinger had photographed and with which he had then blackmailed them. At least his blackmailing had usually been for good; Rathbone thought of the judge who had been disinclined to close down a factory polluting the land and causing terrible disease. The threat to make public his taste for the violent sexual abuse of small boys had changed his mind.

Each member of that hideous club had had to pose in a picture so lewd, so compromising, that the publication of it would ruin him. After this initiation, exercise of the vice was relatively free—until Ballinger needed their help in some favor or other.

Only after some years had it degenerated into payment with money rather than action. And then—when possession of the riverboat on which it had all taken place had satisfied Ballinger's own power for gain—finally to murder.

Rathbone did not know beyond doubt of Ballinger's guilt in, or even his knowledge of, the murders of the boys grown too old to please the tastes of such patrons, or too unwilling to be coerced anymore. He preferred to think that of those additional crimes, perhaps Ballinger was innocent.

None of this Margaret believed, and she had never seen or even imagined the pictures. Rathbone would fight with everything he had in order that she never did. Such things seared themselves into the mind and could not be erased. Rathbone himself still woke in the night soaked with sweat when he dreamed of them, of going into the boats themselves and feeling the pain and the fear drown him, like filthy water closing over his head.

"Thank you," he said, his voice hoarse. "I suppose you have to leave them here?"

"Yes," Brundish replied, his brows lifted slightly in surprise. "I assume from that remark that you do not wish for . . . whatever it is?" He pulled a small sheet of paper from his inside pocket. "However, I need you to sign this to confirm that I have delivered it to you."

"Of course you do." Wordlessly Rathbone took the paper over to the writing table in the corner, picked up a pen, dipped it in the ink-well, and signed. He blotted the signature lightly and handed the paper back.

After Brundish had gone, Rathbone sent Ardmore to fetch brandy, then he dismissed him for the night and sat in the armchair thinking.

Should he destroy them, now, without even opening them? He looked down at the box and realized it was metal, and locked. The key was tied to it on a ribbon, presumably by Brundish. He would have to open it and take them out before he could destroy them. Inside that box they were invulnerable, probably even to fire.

What else would destroy pictures? Acid? But why bother? Fire was easy enough. There was a fire in the grate now. All he needed to do was pile more coal on it, get it really hot, and he had the perfect method. By morning there would be nothing left.

He bent down and took the key, put it in the lock, and turned it. It moved easily, as if it were well cared for and often used.

The contents were not only paper as he had expected, but photographic plates, with paper prints beside, presumably duplicates used to prove their existence. He should have foreseen that. These were the originals from which Ballinger had printed the copies he had used to blackmail people. He had nearly said "the victims" in his own mind, but these men were not the victims. The true victims were the children, the mudlarks, orphans, street urchins taken and kept prisoner on the boats.

He looked at the pictures one by one. They were horrific, but obscenely fascinating. He barely looked at the children—he could not bear it—but the faces of the men held him totally, however much against his will. They were men whose features he knew, men of power in government, in law, in the Church, in life. That the sickness ran through them with such power that they would stoop to this shook him till his stomach clenched and his hand holding the plates trembled.

If they had paid prostitutes, or even done such things with adult men, or other men's wives, it would have been a private matter that he could perhaps shut out of his mind. But this was entirely different. This was the rape and torture of children, and—even to the most tolerant— it was a bestial crime. To the society in which they moved, which respected them and over which they had power, it was a sin beyond forgiveness.

The plates were glass. They would not burn. The fire in the hearth, however hot, would not be enough.

Acid? A hammer and blows violent enough to smash them to rubble? But should he? If he destroyed this evidence, then he was complicit in the crimes they had committed.

Should he take them to the police?

But some of those men *were* police. Some were judges, some advocates in the courts. He would overturn half of society. And if word of his possession got out, perhaps he would not even survive. Men had killed for infinitely less.

He was too tired to make any irrevocable decisions tonight.

He closed the box and locked it again. He must find a safe place to keep it until he could decide. It must be somewhere that no one else could find it, or ever think to look.

Where had Ballinger kept it? A bank vault or something of that nature?

He would deal with it tomorrow. Tonight he was too weighed down with grief.

CHAPTER

3

It was a bright, cold morning as Monk turned onto Copenhagen Place to continue knocking on the doors of Zenia Gadney's neighbors to see what he could learn about her. Orme was working the area closer to the river, searching for anyone who had seen her there, not only on the night of her death, but possibly at any other time. Why had she been on Limehouse Pier on a winter evening? It must have been cold, open to the wind off the water. Was she there as a prostitute, earning a quick shilling or two with someone who turned out to be a madman? The thought of it knotted Monk's stomach with revulsion, as well as anger for the desperation of both the man and the woman.

A group of men passed him, trudging along the road toward the docks. A vegetable cart passed the other way, piled with carrots and greens of one sort and another, and a few ripe apples.

Monk knocked on the door of number twelve, next to Zenia Gadney's house, and no one answered. He tried the next over and was sent briskly on his way by a woman in a long apron, already soiled and wet at the edges from the scrubbing of a floor. Now she was about to get busy with the front step, and told him smartly to take his great feet off it and let her get on with her job. No, she had never heard of Zenia Gadney and did not want to.

He retraced his steps and tried number sixteen, on the other side of where Zenia had lived, and found an old woman sitting in a room crowded with ornaments and mementos. She had been looking out the window at the street, and he had noticed her curious glance. Her name was Betsy Scalford; she seemed lonely, happy to have a much younger man wanting to talk to her, and—even better—to listen when she reminisced about the past.

She offered him a cup of tea, which he accepted because it gave him the excuse to stay at least half an hour. The longer they spent together, the more at ease she would feel.

"Thank you," he said appreciatively as she set the tray down and poured the steaming tea for him.

"Welcome, I'm sure," she answered, nodding vigorously. She was a gaunt woman, her bony shoulders making her look taller than she was. "In't seen you before." She looked him up and down, her eyes examining his face, the clean white collar of his shirt, the cut of his suit.

He had always spent too much on his clothes. When he had first woken from the accident a decade ago, robbed of all his memory, he had had to learn everything about himself from the start, including his character in the eyes of others. He had been appalled at the evidence of his vanity presented by his tailor's bills. At that time, necessity had made him trim them drastically. Now that he was head of the Thames River Police in Wapping, he indulged himself again. He smiled as he saw in the old woman's eyes approval of his well-polished boots.

"I haven't been here before," he said in answer to her question. "I'm River Police, not regular."

"River don't flood this far," she said with amusement in her eyes.

"Sometimes its events do," he countered. "And the currents of disaster it carries. You look to me like a very observant woman. I need information."

"An' you think I got nothing to do but sit here an' look out me window?" she retorted. She sat down opposite him. "You're right. Used not to be that way, mind. Time was I did all kinds o' business. Not now. Ask away, young man. But I'll be careful wot I tell you, all the same. Don't want a name fer tittle-tattle."

"Do you know the woman who lives next door at number fourteen?"

"I know where number fourteen is," she said a trifle sharply. "I 'aven't lost me wits yet. That'd be Mrs. Gadney. Nice enough woman. Widow, I think. What about 'er?"

Monk considered telling her immediately and decided against it. It might shock her too much to get any further help from her.

"Do you know her?" he began. "Can you tell me what she is like?"

"Why don't you go an' ask 'er yerself?" she asked. There was no criticism in her voice, just incomprehension and a sharpening curiosity.

He was prepared for that. "We can't find her. She seems to be missing."

"Missing?" Her white eyebrows rose. "She in't been anywhere else since she come 'ere, fifteen year ago. Where would she go? She in't got no one."

Monk felt the tension mounting. "How does she live, Mrs. Scalford? What does she do? Does she work at a shop, or a factory?"

"No. I know that 'cos she's at 'ome most days. I dunno wot she does, but she don't beg, an' she don't ask no favors." She said that with a slight lift of her chin, as if she identified with the pride of it. "An' far as I know, she don't owe no one," she added, nodding her head.

Monk looked at the old lady more carefully, meeting the washed-out blue eyes without flinching. Could this old woman possibly be ignorant of the fact if Zenia Gadney had been a prostitute? It was far more likely she was protecting the reputation of a neighbor, possibly a younger woman who reminded her in some way of herself, thirty years ago.

"To be admired," he said gravely. "Do you know of any family she has?" He intentionally spoke of her still as if she were alive.

Mrs. Scalford considered that for several moments, sipping her tea.

"She did 'ave a man," she said finally. "Come reg'lar, until a couple o' months ago. Dunno if 'e were a brother, or mebbe 'er dead 'usband's brother, or wot. Could be 'e looked after 'er."

"But he stopped coming about two months ago?" Monk pressed. In spite of himself, he sat forward a little.

"In't that wot I jus' said?"

"Do you know why?"

"I told yer, young man. I don't know 'er ter 'ave 'er explain all 'er business to me. I jus' see people come an' go along the street. I spoke to 'er 'alf a dozen times, mebbe. Good morning, an' nice day, that kind o' thing. I see 'er go past 'ere an' I know 'ow she's feeling 'cos yer can see that much in a person's face."

"And how was she feeling, Mrs. Scalford?"

"Most times she were neither good nor bad," she replied with a sigh. "Like most folks, I s'pose. Some days she 'ad a really pretty smile. I reckon as she were 'andsome when she were younger. Got a bit tired-looking now. S'pose we all do." Without thinking she put her hand up and smoothed her own white hair.

"And the last two months?" he asked.

"Yer mean since 'e stopped coming? Sad. Terrible sad, she were, poor thing. I seen 'er walking along 'ere with 'er 'ead 'angin', an' draggin' 'er feet like she lost all 'er spirit."

"Could he have been someone close to her? A brother, maybe?" he asked.

She looked at him through narrowed eyes. "Why d'yer want to know all this, then? Yer 'unting for summink? Wot's she got ter do with the River Police?"

"She's missing, Mrs. Scalford," Monk said grimly. "And we've found the body of a woman we think may be her."

She went pale and her shoulders stiffened as if she hardly dared breathe.

"I'm sorry," he apologized. He meant it. "We could be wrong." He pulled the constable's drawing out of his inside pocket, unfolded it, and passed it to her.

She took it and held it in gnarled hands, which trembled a little.

"That's 'er," she said huskily. "Poor little beggar! What she ever do ter deserve bein' cut up?" Her voice dropped even lower. "That's 'oo yer talking about, in't it? 'Er wot was cut open an' left on the pier?"

"Yes, I'm afraid so."

She looked up at him. "Yer goin' ter get 'oo did it and 'ang 'im, ain't yer?" It was a demand as much as a question. She was shaking now, her cup clattering in its saucer.

"If you help," he answered, taking the cup from her and putting it down. "Tell me more about this man who visited her, and stopped coming two months ago. Can you describe him for me? And don't tell me you don't remember him. Of course you do. I'd lay odds you could describe me, if someone else came and asked you."

She smiled as if in some bleak way it amused her. "Course I could. Ain't many around 'ere as looks like you." There was approval in her voice and he saw a glimpse of the young woman she must have been half a century ago.

"So tell me," he prompted.

She gave a deep, weary sigh. "I s'pose I better 'ad. I dunno, mind, but I reckon as she were one o' them tarts that 'as just one customer, like, an' either 'e got tired of 'er, or 'e died." She nodded toward the window. "I saw 'er goin' up and down 'ere a few times since, an' I thought, yer poor cow, yer ain't going ter find much lookin' like that. Only them as is desperate. An' a man only gets ter pick up 'er age o' tart if 'e in't got the money fer a younger one." She shook her head slowly, the sadness so deep in her, Monk had no doubt now that she saw herself as she could have been.

"Can you describe him?" he asked again.

She returned her attention to the present and looked him up and down, thinking. "Almost your height, I should think, but bonier. Kind o' more awkward. Gray 'air, goin' thin across the top. Clean shaven. Well dressed, like a gentleman, but ordinary. I lay odds 'e didn't pay 'is tailor like you pay yours."

"Thank you," Monk said drily. "Anything else? A coat? An umbrella, perhaps?"

"No. Coat in the winter, not in October, when he last come. Never saw 'im with a brolly. Saw 'im close, too, once. Nice face 'e 'ad. Sort of . . . gentle. He looked kind of sad, an' 'e smiled at 'er."

"He went to her house?"

"Course 'e did. What d'yer expect? They was going to do whatever they did in the street?"

"Might have gone to some other place," Monk pointed out.

"No, 'e went inter 'er 'ouse."

"For how long?"

"'Alf hour, mebbe more."

"But you saw him?"

"Course I saw him. Couldn't tell yer if I 'adn't, could I? You suddenly gone soft, or summink? You find 'im! She don't deserve to be cut up like that." She swallowed with difficulty, struggling to overcome her anger.

"What I mean, Mrs. Scalford, is did he come when it was clear daylight, when you could see clearly who came and went to the house?"

"In't nothin' wrong wi' me eyes." She thought for a moment. "Afternoon, it were, usually. Funny, come to think of it. Why wouldn't 'e come when it were dark?"

"I don't know," Monk replied. "But I shall find out."

There was little more to be learned from the old woman. He thanked her, left, and went on along the street.

Almost opposite number fourteen he spoke to Mr. Clawson, who kept a general hardware store.

"Not that I know of," Clawson said indignantly when Monk asked him if he had seen Zenia Gadney with anyone other than the one man he already knew had visited her. "We may be a bit shabby around 'ere, but we're perfectly respectable," he added, sniffing hard and wiping his hands on the sides of his apron.

Monk wondered if it was worthwhile trying to persuade Mr. Clawson that he had not meant to imply otherwise, but decided it was not worth the effort. Everyone around seemed concerned with keeping up appearances.

"So if she were on the streets, then she went somewhere else to do it?" Monk asked a trifle abruptly.

"I dunno wot she did!" Clawson was angry now. "I took it as she were a widow. Always looked a bit . . . sort o' . . . sad. Put a good face on it, poor soul, but I think things were 'ard for 'er."

"Did she ever come in here, Mr. Clawson?" Monk looked up and down the shelves of sewing articles, kitchenware, patent cleaning liquids, and boxes of nails, screws, and tin tacks. There were also neat wooden drawers for snuff and various potent remedies for one ache or another. He noticed one marked CLOVES for toothache, another with PEPPERMINT for indigestion. Several were unmarked except with letters representing longer words not spelled out, pills for liver or kidneys, creams for itching, ringworm, or burns. And of course there were the usual penny twists of opium, the cure for almost every pain from cramps to sleeplessness.

Clawson followed his glance. He looked less comfortable. "Now and then," he said. "For 'eadaches, and so on. She didn't always keep so well. People don't."

"Any illness in particular?"

"No."

Monk knew the man was lying; the question that mattered was why. There was nothing wrong with selling remedies. Most small local shops did.

"It would be better, Mr. Clawson, if you told me whatever you know about her, rather than oblige me to pull facts out of you one by one."

"You got some complaint about her?" Clawson asked. He was a small man, blinking up at Monk through black-rimmed spectacles, but just at that moment he looked angry and ready to defend a woman he knew against the intrusive questions of an outsider.

"None at all," Monk answered him soberly. "The opposite. We are afraid that someone has hurt her, so we need to know who it could be."

Clawson's face tightened. " 'Urt 'er? 'Ow'd they do that, then? She never done anything wrong. Why'd you want to go looking into that? 'Aven't you got any proper crimes to go after? She was just a poor woman past 'er youth, 'oo got by best as she could. She didn't bother no one. She didn't go around the streets dressed cheap an' she didn't bother no man wot was mindin' 'is business. Let 'er be."

"Do you know where she is now, Mr. Clawson?" Monk asked gravely.

"No I don't. Nor I wouldn't tell yer if I did." Clawson was defiant. "She in't 'urting no one."

Monk persisted. "Do I understand correctly, she used to have one friend who came to see her regularly, until about two months ago, and after that she fell on hard times and had to go out and find the odd bit of business, just to pay her way—but she was discreet about it?"

"Yes. What of it?" Clawson demanded. "There's 'undreds o' women like 'er, do the odd favor, to make ends meet. Fancy bastard like you comes round 'ere, wi' yer swank clothes and shiny boots, askin' questions. I don't know where she is, an' that's all I'm saying."

"Did you learn about the body that was found on the pier, the day before yesterday?"

Clawson's response was instant. "She wouldn't know anything about that, an' neither do I."

"I imagine you don't," Monk agreed, sorry for what he was about to say to this little man who was so quick to defend a woman he barely knew. "But if Mrs. Gadney is not at home, and we don't find her alive and well, then we will know that the body was hers."

Clawson went white and grabbed the counter to steady himself. He stared at Monk, unable to find words.

"I'm sorry," Monk said sincerely. "Now perhaps you understand my need to know more about her. I have to find out who did that to her, and to be frank, Mr. Clawson, I very much want to. The more I hear of her, the more I want to find him."

Clawson closed his eyes, his fingers still white-knuckled. "She were a quiet little woman 'oo came in 'ere an' bought a penny twist of opium for 'er 'eadaches, an' ter pass the time o' day, because she were lonely," he said. "When 'er one . . . customer . . . stopped coming by, she were all on 'er own. If she went out there to make a few shillings for 'erself, or even for a bit o' comfort, it don't mean she should get cut up an' murdered! You find that animal wot did it an' cut 'im up the same! There's a few folk around 'ere as'll be glad ter 'elp yer." He opened his eyes and glared at Monk.

"I'll find him," Monk promised rashly.

Clawson nodded slowly, happy to believe. "Good." He nodded again. "Good."

Monk left him and finished inquiring along the rest of the road, and in one or two local shops in the nearby streets. But by the end of the day he was tired and hungry, and he had learned nothing more that was of any value.

As he stood on Limehouse Pier waiting for the ferry, he went over what he knew in his mind. Was that what had got her killed? Inexperience and desperation caused by the sudden death of her solitary supporter? Had he died, or merely abandoned her? Or had some domestic crisis meant he could no longer indulge himself in keeping a mistress? It seemed tragically likely.

Who was he? No one had given a description of him that would identify him out of thousands of outwardly respectable, middle-aged men in London, or even beyond it. Perhaps he saw her so infrequently because he lived some distance away and came to London on business? Then he could be as far as Manchester, Liverpool, or Birmingham. It would be almost impossible to find him.

"We'd better find this man who knew her," Orme said the next morning as they stood by the riverside on the dock at Wapping New Stairs. The tide was high and the river was running fast, just after the turn. The wind was rising again and there was a keen edge to it. There usually was when it came from the east, and the open water.

Monk pulled his coat collar a little higher. "I'll do what I can to find him. He could have come from anywhere."

"Hansom cab," Orme suggested. "Sounds from what you say as if he wasn't local. He wouldn't come by omnibus. Want me to help? I got nothing to follow up or down Narrow Street. All blind, or she never went there, except with a woman friend once or twice. Mostly she were just alone."

"No. You'll do better with the locals around Limehouse Pier up to Kidney Stairs," Monk replied. "Somebody saw her, and they must have seen him, too. They'd notice anyone not local. We just need to waken their memories."

"They're terrified," Orme replied grimly. "Papers aren't helping. They've got everyone in such a sweat they're looking for a monster, something raving and slavering like an animal with a kill."

"Only on the inside," Monk said, shaking his head. "On the outside he probably looks like anyone else. How long does it take people to learn that? Poor woman probably thought he was perfectly ordinary, maybe just awkward."

"What a trade," Orme stared across the water. "God know how many of them get beaten or killed."

"Not as many as die of disease," Monk said grimly, thinking of all those whom Hester had helped in her clinic on Portpool Lane.

"I'll start looking," Orme promised, fastening his coat. Giving a little salute, he turned and walked along the dockside, hunched against the wind, then down the steps to the boat.

IN THE END IT took Monk only two days to trace the man who had visited Zenia Gadney every month. He began with asking all the local hansom cab drivers, but they were unable or unwilling to help. They did not look closely at faces, and early October was a long time ago. It seemed that the man Monk was looking for had picked cabs at random, sometimes on Commercial Road East, at other times on the West India Dock Road, or even walking east to Burdett Road. It was painstaking and time-consuming to find out even this much, but finally he narrowed down his search to half a dozen people and eliminated them one by one.

In the end he was left with Joel Lambourn of Lower Park Street in Greenwich.

Rather than approach him at home, Monk decided to ask a little about him at the local police station, and thus face the man armed with at least a degree of knowledge.

The desk sergeant looked up at Monk as he came in. His round face was politely blank. "Morning, sir. Can I help you?"

"Good morning, Sergeant," Monk replied, introducing himself. "I am making inquiries about an event that may involve a Mr. Joel Lambourn, who lives in your area." He saw the man's face crease in sudden, sharp sadness.

"I'm not sure as I can 'elp you, sir," the sergeant said coldly. "Don't really know nothing about it, sir. Sorry to be a bit formal, like, but may I see summink as proves to me 'oo you are? Can't go talking about people without knowing." He did not bother to hide his hostility.

Puzzled, Monk produced his warrant card as proof of who he was.

"Thank you, sir." The chill remained. "What is it you think we may be able to 'elp you with, Mr. Monk?" Deliberately he omitted the courtesy of rank.

"Do you know Mr. Lambourn?"

"Dr. Lambourn, sir," the sergeant corrected him smartly. "Yes, I did know 'im to speak to."

"You did? You don't any longer?" Monk was puzzled.

"Seein' as 'e's dead, may God rest 'im, no I don't," the sergeant snapped.

"I'm sorry." Monk felt clumsy. He could not have known, but perhaps he should have guessed. "Would that have been about two months ago?"

The sergeant winced. "Are you tellin' me as you didn't know?" Clearly that was incredible to him.

"No, I didn't," Monk answered. "I'm inquiring into the murder of a woman whose body was found on Limehouse Pier, five days ago. It was likely that Dr. Lambourn knew her. I was hoping he might be able to tell us something more about her."

The sergeant looked startled. "That poor soul what was cut up by some bleedin' butcher? Beggin' your pardon, sir, but you got that wrong. Dr. Lambourn was a quiet, very respectable gentleman. Wouldn't 'urt anyone. An' 'e wouldn't know any woman in that way o' business."

Monk wished to point out that many people appeared different in public from the way they might be in private, in the darkness of a back-street far from where they lived. However, he could see in the man's face that he was not open to any such suggestion about Lambourn.

"What kind of a doctor was he?" he asked instead. "I mean, what sort of patients did he treat?"

"'E din't treat patients," the sergeant replied. "'E studied, learned things about sickness an' medicines an' such."

"Do you know what kind of illnesses?" Monk persisted. It might not matter at all, but so far Dr. Lambourn was the only person who seemed to have known Zenia Gadney as more than just a casual neighbor. So he would take any details he could get.

"No," the sergeant replied. "But he asked a lot of questions about medicines, especially opium and laudanum, and stuff like that. Why? What's that got to do with this poor creature you got in Limehouse?"

"I really don't know, except that she took opium sometimes, for headaches and things."

"So does 'alf England," the sergeant said derisively. "'Eadaches, stomachaches, can't sleep, baby's crying, cutting its teeth, old folks got rheumatics . . ."

"Yes, I suppose so," Monk conceded. "What was Dr. Lambourn studying that he asked about opium and the medicines containing it? What sort of questions did he ask, do you know?"

"No, I don't. He was always a very quiet gentleman, with a good word for everyone. Not meaning any disrespect, Mr. Monk, but you must 'ave been misinformed some'ow. Dr. Lambourn was as decent a man as you'll find anywhere."

Until he had further information on the subject, he would gain nothing by arguing. He thanked the sergeant and walked outside into the street. Lambourn may well have paid Zenia Gadney sufficient money to live on, but he could tell them nothing now, and he could not possibly be responsible for her death, since he himself had apparently died two months earlier. Still, Monk would like to know more about him, even if only for the light it would throw on Zenia Gadney's life.

"Sir!" the sergeant said abruptly from the doorway.

Monk turned back. "Yes?"

"Don't go botherin' Mrs. Lambourn, sir. It was all 'ard enough at the time. Leave the poor lady alone."

So there was a Mrs. Lambourn. Monk wanted to ask more about her, but something in the sergeant's expression troubled Monk, an anger that seemed out of place.

"What did Dr. Lambourn die of?" he asked instead.

The sergeant looked down at his hands. "'E took 'is own life, sir. Cut 'is wrists. Leave 'er alone . . . sir." It was a warning, as much as he dared make it.

4

Monk had no choice but to go and speak to Joel Lambourn's widow. If she knew nothing about her husband's relationship with Zenia Gadney, this would be a very hard time to learn about it. If she did know, perhaps that was part of the reason he had taken his life. Monk did not want to hurt the poor woman any further, but Zenia Gadney also deserved some justice. It was urgent that Monk catch the butcher who had killed her and see him hanged; the newspapers were spreading the panic with their wild articles. There were rumours of half-men, half-beast creatures prowling the dockside area. Monk had even seen some irresponsible fool suggesting that a monster had arisen from the river, come in on the tide from some deepwater lair.

Half an hour later he was at the Lambourns' front door in Lower Park Street, a few hundred yards from Greenwich Park, with its trees and walks, and of course the Royal Observatory, from which the world's time was taken. The street was an area of quiet, solid houses for people who lived hardworking and private lives. He hated doing this, but he knew there was no choice so he did not hesitate.

The door was opened by a parlor maid dressed in a plain, stiff blouse and skirt and a crisp white apron. She looked at him inquiringly. "Yes, sir?"

He introduced himself and asked if he might speak to Mrs. Lambourn. He apologized for intruding on her privacy, and quickly mentioned that it was a matter of importance, or he would not have come.

He was shown to a pale green morning room overlooking the street. The curtains were half drawn, leaving the chairs in shadow and one warm patch of sunlight on the patterned carpet. There was no fire lit, but it was likely that Mrs. Lambourn was not receiving many visitors at the moment.

Monk thanked the maid. When she had gone and the door was closed, he looked around the room. The walls were lined with bookcases, all of them full. He walked over to read the titles. They covered all sorts of subjects, not merely medical texts and histories, but general British history, Chinese history (which he had not expected to see), and some very recent texts on the modern history of the United States of America.

On the opposite wall he found philosophies, the complete works of Shakespeare, Milton's *Paradise Lost,* and Gibbon's *The History of the Decline and Fall of the Roman Empire.* There were even a number of novels.

He was still looking at them when Dinah Lambourn came in. The slight sound of her closing the door startled him and he turned to face her.

"I'm sorry," he apologized. "You have a most interesting selection of books!"

"My husband's," she said quietly.

Under normal circumstances she would have been a striking woman. She was tall, and had high cheekbones and a strong face, which now looked vulnerable, almost bruised with grief. She wore black unrelieved by any jewelry at all. Her rich, dark brown hair was the only color about her, apart from the dark blue hue of her eyes.

Her sadness was so palpable Monk felt a stab of guilt again for having come to her with such a wretched question to ask. What sort of a man had Joel Lambourn been that he could have left a woman like this and gone all the way across the river and west to the Limehouse area to find a drab woman like Zenia Gadney? Was he weak, and Dinah overpowered his dull personality? Did he fail to answer her needs, emotionally or physically, and he wanted some plain, ordinary woman who asked nothing of him? Or perhaps who dared not criticize?

Or did he have a darker side that he had not wanted Dinah to know of?

She was waiting for Monk to explain himself. How could he tell why he had come and cause her the least pain possible? And yet he must learn the truth.

"Did you know a woman named Zenia Gadney, who lived in Copenhagen Place, in Limehouse?" he asked quietly.

She blinked, as if the question puzzled her. She stood still for several moments, as though searching her memory. "No, the name is not familiar," she said at last. "But you said 'did I know.' Has something happened to her?"

"I'm afraid it has. This is unpleasant, Mrs. Lambourn. Perhaps you would prefer to sit down." He said it in a tone that made it more a request than merely a suggestion.

She complied, slowly, her face going even paler, her eyes fixed on his. "How does that concern me?" Her voice trembled.

"I regret to tell you that she is dead," he answered.

"I'm sorry." It was a quiet murmur, but conveyed a feeling that went far deeper than mere good manners would require.

"But you said you didn't know her," he responded, already a chill touching him.

"What has that to do with it?" She lifted her chin a little. "I am still sorry that she is dead. Why do you come here? Limehouse is miles away, and the other side of the river. I know nothing about it."

"I believe your husband knew her."

Her grief almost slipped out of control. "My husband is dead, Mr. Monk," she said huskily. "And I have never met Mrs. . . . . Gadney."

"I know your husband is dead, Mrs. Lambourn, and I am deeply sorry for that." He wanted to express condolences for what he was about to add to her grief, but it seemed shallow in the circumstances. "Those I spoke to said he was a remarkably fine man," he went on. "However, it seems that he knew Mrs. Gadney quite well, and over a long period of time."

She had to clear her throat before she could force herself to speak. Her slender white hands were locked around each other in her lap.

"What are you implying, Mr. Monk? When did this Mrs. Gadney die, and how? It must've been serious; if you came here despite the fact that you knew my husband has been dead for some little time?"

"It appears that your husband met with Mrs. Gadney in Limehouse at least once a month," he replied. He watched her face for shock, disgust, defensiveness, but he saw only grief that he was certain of. There were other emotions there as well, but he could not read them.

"When did she die, and of what cause?" she asked very quietly.

"Nearly a week ago. She was murdered."

Her eyes widened. "Murdered?" She could hardly say the word. Her tongue stumbled and there was horror in her eyes.

"Yes." He felt brutal. "You may have heard word of it, by the papers. There was a woman killed and her body mutilated, near Limehouse Pier."

"No. I had not heard." Dinah Lambourn was now so pale he was afraid she might faint.

"Would you like me to ring for your maid, Mrs. Lambourn?" he offered. "She could bring water, perhaps smelling salts. I am afraid I have brought very ugly news for you. I'm sorry."

"I shall . . . be all right." She forced herself to sit more upright, but it was clearly an effort. Her voice wavered. "Please say whatever it is you have to say."

"You did not know her?" Monk asked again.

She evaded the answer. "Do you know who did this thing?" she asked instead.

"No, not yet."

Her eyes widened slightly. "But you think I can help you?"

"Possibly. So far Dr. Lambourn seems to have been her only friend. And judging by the patterns of her expenditure in the local shops, she seems to have had money each time after he visited her. Quite often she paid her bills then." He left the implication in the air.

"I see." Mrs. Lambourn folded her hands in her lap and stared down at them. She had long fingers with elegant nails. Her skin was unblemished.

"Tell me something about Dr. Lambourn," he requested. He wanted to keep her talking to make some judgment about what kind of woman she was. He still was not sure whether he believed that she had not known Zenia Gadney. And was she still so numb with grief that she had no curiosity about the other woman who had held so much of her husband's loyalty and attention—not to mention his money?

She spoke quietly, as if remembering for herself rather than informing Monk. He had the sudden, complete conviction that she did not expect to be believed. She never once looked up at him in any attempt to persuade.

"He was a gentle man," she began, struggling to find the words at once large enough and precise enough to convey what she saw in her own mind. "He never lost his temper with me, or with our daughters, even when they were young, and noisy." She smiled briefly, but it vanished as she controlled her emotions with an obvious effort. "He was patient with people who were genuinely not very clever. And compared with him, that was very many. But he couldn't abide liars. He was quite stern with the girls if they lied to him." She shook her head slightly. "It only happened about twice. They loved him very much."

Outside in the street a carriage passed, the sound of it barely penetrating the quiet room.

Monk allowed a few moments before prompting her to continue.

"I'm sorry," she apologized again. "I still keep expecting to hear his step. That's ridiculous, isn't it? I know he's dead. Every inch of my body knows it, every thought in my mind is filled with it. And yet when I go to sleep I forget, and in the morning I wake up, and for a second it is as if he hasn't gone. Then I remember again."

Monk tried to imagine what his own house would be like if Hester never returned. It was unbearable, and he forced the idea out of his mind. His job was to learn who had killed Zenia Gadney. There was nothing he could do to change the fact of the suicide of Joel Lambourn. How did anyone deal with such a painful tragedy, find the answers that allowed them to continue on? Daily life must seem absurd and completely meaningless after such a thing. He supposed having children both hurt and helped. You would force yourself to keep going, for their sakes, even if the sight of them was a reminder of what you had lost.

But what about at night when you lay alone in the bed you had shared, and the house was silent? What could you think of then that allowed you live with pain?

"Mrs. Lambourn, please go on."

She sighed. "Joel was very clever; in fact, he was brilliant. He worked for the government on various kinds of medical research."

"What was his latest work?" Monk was not really interested; he just wanted to keep her talking.

"Opium," she replied without hesitation. "He was passionately angry about the harm it is doing, when it isn't labeled properly. And he said that happens almost all of the time. He had an enormous amount of facts and figures on the number dead because of it. He used to sit in his study and go over and over them, weighing every story against the evidence, checking to make sure he was always correct and exact."

"To what purpose?" In spite of himself Monk was now curious.

For the first time she looked up at him. "Thousands of people die of opium poisoning, Mr. Monk, among them many children. Do you know what a 'penny twist' is?"

"Of course I do. A small dose of opium powder you can buy at a corner shop or apothecary." He thought back to Mr. Clawson and his general hardware shop with all its remedies, and his fierce defense of Zenia Gadney.

"How much is in a dose?" Dinah Lambourn asked.

"I've no idea," Monk admitted.

"Neither has the man who sells it, or the woman who buys it to give to her child, or to take herself for her headache, or a stomachache, or because she can't sleep." She gave a little gesture of helplessness with her beautiful hands. "Neither have I, for that matter. That is what Joel was concerned about. He knew of thousands of cases over the whole country where this lack of knowledge led to death. Especially children. That was only part of his work, but that was what he did."

Monk was still trying to imagine the man who had gone to Limehouse to visit Zenia Gadney, who paid her every month. So far, the picture was so incomplete and contradictory as to be almost meaningless. And *why* had he taken his own life? So far that made no sense, either.

"Was he a successful man, financially?" he asked, feeling as if he were poking at an open wound.

"Of course," she said, as if the question were a little foolish. "He was brilliant."

"Scientific brilliance is not always financially rewarded," he pointed out. Was it possible she had no idea of his business affairs? Could he have gambled and lost badly? Or was it possible someone had black-mailed him over his visits to Limehouse, and when he could no longer pay, he had committed suicide rather than face the shame, and the ruin of his family? Other men, outwardly just as respectable, had done so.

"Look around you, Mr. Monk," Mrs. Lambourn said simply. "Do we appear to be in difficult times as far as money is concerned? I assure you, I am not ignorant of my situation. Joel's man of affairs has advised me very thoroughly in exactly what we have, and how to both use it and conserve the principal, so that we shall not fall into difficulty. We are more than comfortably provided for."

That at least would be easy enough to check, and he would have someone do so.

"I'm glad," he said sincerely. "Mrs. Gadney was not so fortunate. She lived very much from one month to the next."

"I'm sorry for her, but that is not my concern," Dinah replied. "In-deed, since the poor woman is dead, you say, it is not anyone's now."

He could not let it go. "Are you sure you did not know that your husband visited her every month?" he repeated. "It seems an extraordi-nary breach of trust, especially for a man who hated liars."

The color washed up her face and she drew in her breath sharply. She opened her mouth to respond, and then closed it when she quite clearly realized she did not know what to say.

Monk leaned forward a little and his voice was gentle. "I think it is time for the truth, Mrs. Lambourn. I promise you I'll find out either way, but it would be easier if you would just tell me. I give you my word that if your husband's relationship with Zenia Gadney has no connection with her murder, I will not make it public. So now I'll ask you again: Did you know about his visits to Zenia Gadney?"

"Yes," she said in a whisper.

"When did you learn?"

"Years ago. I don't remember how long."

He did not know whether to believe her or not. Certainly there was no shock or surprise in her now; but then if she had discovered it only two months ago, grief at Lambourn's suicide would have outweighed any other emotion in her. If she had known for years, how had she lived with it so happily, according to her? Perhaps a woman's acceptance of such an arrangement was something a man would never understand. He could not imagine how he would ever endure it if Hester were to betray him in that way. The idea was one he could not even look at.

Dinah was regarding him with the outward calm of one who has already faced the worst she can think of and has no energy left to fear anything more.

There had been a passionate hatred in whoever had ripped open Zenia Gadney and left her on the pier like so much rubbish.

"Was Zenia Gadney the only woman your husband visited and paid, Mrs. Lambourn?" he asked. "Or were there others?"

She froze, as if he had slapped her. "She was the only one," she replied with such certainty that he found it hard to disbelieve her. "I don't know if she . . . dealt with others. But you say she didn't."

"Not while Dr. Lambourn was alive," he agreed. "And after that there appeared to be no one regular."

She looked down at her hands again.

"Why did Dr. Lambourn take his own life?" Monk asked, feeling like a torturer.

She sat still for so long that he was about to repeat the words when finally she looked up. "He didn't, Mr. Monk. He was murdered." She took a long, deep breath. "I told you he was engaged in a work of great importance. If he had succeeded it would have saved thousands of lives, but it would also have cost certain businesses a good portion of their profit. Joel could not be bought. He would not bend the facts to suit them, nor hide the truth. The only way they could silence him was to mock his work, deny its validity. Then, when he still would not be silent, they made it look as if he had realized he was wrong and, in despair and shame, killed himself." She stared at him intently, her eyes brilliant, her face tense and passionately alive with the power of her feelings.

He did not believe her, and yet it was impossible not to accept that she believed it herself.

He cleared his throat, trying to steady his voice and keep his incredulity out of it. "What happened to his report?"

"They destroyed it, of course. They couldn't afford for it to remain."

Some vague mention of such a report stirred in his mind. It had been discredited, put down to one man's mistaken crusade, a man whose grasp on reality had finally snapped. The whole situation had been regarded as a tragedy.

"I knew you wouldn't believe me," Dinah said quietly. "But it is the truth. Joel would never have killed himself, and certainly not over poor Zenia Gadney. Perhaps they killed her, too."

"Who are 'they'?"

"Someone with a deep interest in the import and sale of opium," she answered.

"And why would they have killed Mrs. Gadney?" It made no sense. Surely even through her grief she could see that?

Her face looked bruised, desperately vulnerable. "Perhaps to make sure of his disgrace, so no one can resurrect his work," she answered.

"Did she have something to do with his work?"

She gave a helpless little gesture. "I don't see how she could."

Monk tried to imagine Joel Lambourn, disgraced in his profession because his colleagues thought his work worthless, coming home to a wife who believed in him so totally she had not even considered the possibility of his failure being real. Perhaps the one person who did not demand perfection from him was Zenia Gadney. Maybe that was what he saw in her: no standards to meet, nothing to live up to, simply accepted for who he was, both the strength and the weakness.

Maybe the pressure of it all had finally become unbearable, and he had taken the only escape he knew of.

It was possible, maybe even probable, that the murder of Zenia Gadney had nothing to do with Joel Lambourn, or even with opium. She was merely like hundreds of thousands of others who took the drug to relieve their pain. And perhaps Lambourn was wrong, and it did no true harm, apart from the occasional accidental overdose. But that wasn't a crime; after all, one could overdose on almost anything, including alcohol, which was sold and consumed just as freely.

Monk asked about any other family, just to finalize his inquiries, and she gave him the address of Lambourn's sister, Amity Herne.

He apologized again for disturbing her, and went out into the sun and the hard, cold wind. A sadness weighed heavily on him, as if he carried the fading light of the year within.

Monk was fortunate to find Lambourn's sister at home when he called in the early evening. The house was in highly fashionable Gordon Square. He had passed several carriages on his way here, some with crests on the doors, and liveried footmen, and all with perfectly matched horses.

The parlor maid asked him in and left him in an impressively furnished morning room while she went to see if Mrs. Herne would receive him.

Monk looked around the room. It was highly conventional. There was nothing individual here, nothing that would particularly please or offend. It was not only boring; it was, in an oblique way, deceitful. All traces of personality were concealed. Amity Herne's husband must be totally unlike her brother. Some of the books were similar, for example the Shakespeare and the Gibbon. But it was the way they were all matching and totally level with each other, as if they had never been moved, which irritated Monk.

He had some time to wait, but looking around he saw nothing that engaged his interest or gave him any insight into the passion or the beliefs of the man who lived here, except that he exercised a certain caution in all he showed.

Amity Herne came in and closed the door behind her. She was a handsome woman, in a brittle, elegant way. Her fair hair was thick and perfectly dressed, her skin without a blemish. She was almost as tall as her sister-in-law, but far thinner. In her dark, elegantly cut gown, her shoulders looked a trifle bony.

"How can I help you, Mr. Monk?" she asked, without inviting him to sit down. "I am afraid I am due to attend an exhibition of Chinese silks with the lord chancellor's wife this evening. You will appreciate that I cannot be late."

"Of course not," Monk agreed. "I will come immediately to the point. Forgive my bluntness. I am inquiring into the death of a woman named Zenia Gadney."

Amity Herne frowned. "I don't recall anyone by that name. I am sorry to hear that she died, but I cannot help you. I don't know what led you to imagine I could."

"Perhaps not," he conceded, without answering her oblique question. "But your late brother knew Mrs. Gadney quite well . . ." He stopped as he saw her face tighten. It might have been out of grief, but it looked to him more like irritation.

"My brother did not move in the same social circles as my husband and I," she said very quietly. It was plain she considered he was intruding, and—in view of her brother's apparent suicide—perhaps she was right. "He was . . . eccentric . . . in some of his opinions," she went on. "He became more so as he grew older. I'm sorry your time has been wasted."

Monk did not move. "His widow says that Dr. Lambourn knew Mrs. Gadney quite well, and our evidence from local people where she lived bears that out."

"That may be true," she agreed, also not moving from her position a yard or two inside the door. "As I tried to explain to you, my brother was a little eccentric. When he was convinced of an idea, nothing would change his mind, certainly not common sense, or evidence."

He caught the bitter tone in her voice. This was a different side to Joel Lambourn. It gave him no pleasure to hear it, but Monk could not let it go if there was even a possibility that it could somehow help lead to Zenia Gadney's murderer. He forced himself to picture her corpse lying half doubled over, looking smaller in death than she would have been alive. He pictured the waxy white face and the gutted body, the blood and the pale, bulging entrails.

"Mrs. Gadney was murdered," he said quietly, deliberately choosing the cruelest words. "Her stomach was slit open and her intestines pulled out. She was dumped on Limehouse Pier, like a sack of rubbish that had broken open. Dr. Lambourn knew her well enough to visit her every month," he went on more gently. "His widow says she was aware of that; indeed, that she had been for years. So far Dr. Lambourn is the only person with whom Mrs. Gadney appears to have had a relationship with, of any kind. Others knew her only well enough to exchange a word in the street."

A succession of emotions crossed Amity's face so swiftly, Monk could not identify them, except as forms of anger. If grief or pity were there, or fear, he did not see them long enough to know. But then, why should she display her vulnerability in front of him when he had been so brutal? Anger was most people's defense for that which hurt intolerably.

"You had better sit down, Mr. . . . Mr. Monk," she said icily. "I shall be as clear as I can, and as brief. There is obviously a great deal that you do not know, and I suppose in the wretched woman's memory, you need to. God knows, that sort of death should not happen to anyone."

She moved across to one of the large armchairs and sat down carefully. "My sister-in-law, Dinah, is a highly emotional woman and a complete idealist. If you have met her, as you say you have, then you are probably already aware of that. Her view of Joel was unrealistic, to put it at its kindest." She shook her head a little. "She was devoted to him and of course to their two daughters, Adah and Marianne. She cannot yet face the truth about him. I dare say she never will. I know it will certainly not help to try to force her. We all need something in which to believe, and she believes in Joel and his memory. It would be not only cruel, but also completely pointless, to say this to her now. I know, because I am guilty of having tried myself."

Monk could imagine it: Amity and Dinah with wildly opposing views of the same man, whom presumably they had both loved, but in such different ways. Did Dinah believe in him so consumingly, not because of who he had been, but because of who she had needed him to be, to fill her hunger and her dreams?

Amity was impatient. "Joel was a charming man," she went on, looking at Monk earnestly. "He was my elder brother, by seven years, and I always looked up to him. But clever as he was, he was also a man lost in his own ideas, a little . . ." A flicker of a smile touched her mouth and then vanished. "Otherworldly," she finished. "He would become obsessed with a cause, and then refuse to see the evidence against it. Perhaps that is good for a man of faith. It is not good for a scientist. He should have been a painter, or a dramatist, or something where realities and facts are not as important."

Monk did not interrupt her.

She sighed. "He used to be far more in touch with things, when he was younger. I suppose it's only in the last five or six years that he'd really lost his way."

Monk stared at her. Was she the wise one, the brave one, willing to look at the truth, rather than Dinah, who saw only what she wished to? There was a chill about Amity, but might it be only the armor she wrapped around herself as a shield from the pain of the situation, the fact that there was nothing she could do to help him now that he was gone, and maybe there never had been?

Amity lowered her gaze. "Most of his life he was very good at his job," she went on. "He was meticulous. He had a rare kind of integrity. Dinah will have told you that, and she was right. But he became fixed on this idea about opium and he got some of his original facts wrong, and from then on it all went bad. He just piled one error on top of another until there was no way out for him."

Her face was bleak, her concentration total, as if she were forcing herself to override all her inner misery and pain to a place where she could hide it, and continue only with the truth that had to be told. That way she could make Monk understand, and then he would leave. She could pick up the remnants of her life again and pretend normality, allow time to heal at least the surface of the wound.

Still, somehow, Monk did not like her.

"Errors?" he asked.

"His last report was a total failure, and the government rejected it," she answered. "They had no choice. He was just completely mistaken. He took it very hard. He couldn't believe he was wrong, in spite of the evidence against him. That was why he killed himself. He couldn't face his colleagues knowing. Poor Joel . . ."

"And Mrs. Gadney?" Monk asked more gently.

Amity shrugged. "I really don't know for certain, but it isn't hard to guess. Dinah is a beautiful woman, but demanding in . . . in her requirements." She said the word delicately, implying a deeper, more personal meaning. "She left him no room to fail. Perhaps he wished for someone who could be a friend, simply listen to him, and share his interests without the incessant need."

Monk thought about what it would be like to feel an unendurable loneliness, an emotional exhaustion, as the threat of being a disappointment, of having deceived others and let them down, became bigger, more suffocating with every slip, every error retrieved, and each new lie.

An ordinary, pleasant-faced prostitute, just as lonely, just as familiar with the taste of failure, would seem like a godsend. It would at last be someone to laugh and cry with, for once without judgment, without expectation of anything except fair payment.

Would Dinah have even begun to understand that? Probably not. And could she have required other things from him as well, of a physical nature, that he was too tired, anxious, or otherwise unable to provide? Love was a good deal more than a supply of constant praise and belief. Sometimes it was the ease of no expectations, of allowing a person to fail and still loving them the same way.

He thought back to the times he had failed. He had allowed his resentment of Runcorn, his old superior, to distract his attention from the truth more than once. And there had been other slips. Perhaps the worst was the arrogance that had ultimately led to Jericho Phillips being acquitted the previous year. But Hester had not blamed him or reminded him of it since.

When he had been most afraid of his own past, the ghosts that his amnesia had concealed but that had haunted him so badly in the early years, she had not called him a coward for fearing them. She had granted the possibility of his guilt in the murder of Joscelyn Gray, but not of surrender without a fight to the very last stand. Certainly it was the kind of love everyone needed in their darkest moments.

Had Dinah been unable to support Joel Lambourn when the possibility of failure loomed? Was that the reason he had given up?

Monk rose to his feet and thanked Amity Herne, even though what she had told him was so far from what he had wanted to hear.

As HE RETURNED HOME Monk thought about what Amity had said. Her view of Lambourn was so different from Dinah's that he needed some other opinion to balance them in his mind.

Dinah loved Lambourn profoundly, with a wife's love, perhaps distorted by a passion she still clearly felt. She was ravaged by the grief of his death and refused to believe it could have been self-inflicted. That was not difficult to understand, particularly since there seemed to have been no anger or despair leading up to his suicide; rather a determination to continue fighting for a cause he believed in deeply.

Or was that just what Dinah wished to believe—even needed to—in order to keep her own faith in all she cared about, and her ability to continue living and looking after her daughters? That would not be hard to understand.

Amity Herne had said that Lambourn was older than her. Seven years was a big gap between children. They would have led rather separate lives. He would've been caught up in his education and then his professional life. According to Amity, at that time they had lived sufficiently far apart geographically to have no more communication than letters, and therefore had not developed a friendship even then. Only recently had she learned much of his nature as a man.

Or was that also an emotionally tainted judgment rather than an impartial observation? Did she need to excuse herself from all blame in his suicide by painting him as a fatally flawed man whom she could never have believed in and was never close to?

Who else could Monk ask? Amity's husband, Barclay Herne, would be too tied by family bonds to answer freely, even if his opinion were more measured. Who had been in charge of the organization that requested Lambourn's report? They would have at least a professional opinion as to Lambourn's judgment, if not his personal life. Monk resolved to speak to them.

It did not take more than a few inquiries to learn that the government minister concerned was Sinden Bawtry, a gifted and charismatic man fast rising in political circles. He had a vast personal fortune and donated generously to many causes, especially cultural and artistic ones. His collection of fine paintings, and occasional donations of one or the other of them to museums, earned him much admiration.

But gaining half an hour of his time was less easy. It was late afternoon when Monk was shown into his office. He had had to stretch the truth a little as to the likelihood of Bawtry's information being able to help solve the murder of the woman on Limehouse Pier. He kicked his heels for three-quarters of an hour in the outer waiting room, growing ever more impatient.

He was expecting Bawtry to be a middle-aged man of austere disposition. But when he was finally summoned into Bawtry's office, he was met instead by a man whose vitality seemed to fill the room as he came forward and grasped Monk's hand.

"Sorry to keep you waiting," he said warmly. "Some people have no idea how to put things briefly. They think the more words they use the more important you will think their business." He smiled. "What can I do for you, Mr. Monk? Your message said it is to do with the late Dr. Joel Lambourn, and a possible connection with this appalling murder on Limehouse Pier. You have me puzzled as to what that connection could possibly be."

"There may not be any." Monk decided instantly not to try any deceit with this man, however slight. His handsome head and ready charm did not mask his intelligence or his consciousness of power. "But it appears that Dr. Lambourn knew the murder victim quite well," he went on. "I have received differing opinions of Dr. Lambourn from those close to him. I need an informed but more impartial view to balance them, particularly regarding the value of his work, and thus possibly his state of mind in the last year or so of his life."

"The opium report," Bawtry said with a slight nod of understanding. "I didn't know Lambourn personally. But I believe he was an unusually likable man, and affection can distort judgment, no matter how much you intend to be fair."

"Exactly," Monk agreed. He found himself relaxing a little. It was so much easier to deal with intellect unclouded by emotion.

Bawtry gave a tiny shrug, in a sort of wordless apology.

"A brilliant man, if a little unworldly," he continued frankly. "Something of a crusader, and in this case, he allowed his intense pity for the victims of ignorance and desperation to color his overall view of the problem." He lowered his voice a little. "To be honest, we do need some better control of what is put into medicines that anyone can buy, and certainly more information as to how much opium is in the medicines given to infants."

He looked bleak. "But that is one of the main reasons we couldn't accept Lambourn's report. Some of his examples were extreme, and based more on anecdote than medical histories. It would have done more harm to the cause than good, because it could so easily have been discredited."

He met Monk's eyes with a steady gaze. "I'm sure you have the same problem preparing a criminal case for the courts. You must offer only the evidence that will stand up to cross-examination, the physical evidence you can produce, the witnesses whom people will believe. Anyone that the defense can destroy may lose you the jury." He smiled, the question in his gesture. "He was a liability to us. I wish it had been different. He was a decent man."

Then all the light vanished from his face. "I was stunned by his suicide. I had no idea he was so close to despair, but I have to believe there was something else far different from the failure of the report behind that. Perhaps something to do with this miserable business in Limehouse with the woman? I hope that isn't the case—it would be so sordid. But I don't know. My assessment of him is professional, not personal."

"Do you know what happened to the report?" Monk asked. "I would like to see a copy of it."

Bawtry looked surprised. "Do you think it can possibly have some bearing on the death of this woman? I find it hard to believe her connection with Lambourn is anything but coincidental."

"Probably not," Monk agreed. "But it would be remiss of me not to follow every lead. Perhaps she knew something? He may have spoken with her, even confided something to her concerning it."

Bawtry frowned. "Like what? Do you mean the name of someone concerned with opium and patent medicines?"

"It's possible."

"I'll find out if there is a copy still extant. If there is, I'll see that you are given access to it."

"Thank you." There was nothing more that Monk could ask, and he had exhausted nearly all the time Bawtry could give him. He was not sure if it was what he had wanted to hear or hoped to discover, but he could not argue with it. It was careful, compassionate, and infinitely reasonable.

"Thank you, sir," he said quietly.

Bawtry's smile returned. "I hope it is of some use to you."

6

In the morning Monk went to the office of the coroner who had dealt with Lambourn's suicide. The findings of the inquest were public record and he had no difficulty in obtaining the papers.

"Very sad," the clerk said to him solemnly. He was a young man who took his position gravely. His already receding hair was slicked back over his head and his dark suit was immaculate. "Anyone choosing to end their own life has to make one stop and think."

Monk nodded, unable to find any reply worth making. He turned to the medical section of the report. Apparently Lambourn had taken a fairly large dose of opium, then slit his wrists and bled to death. The police surgeon had testified to it succinctly and no one had questioned either his accuracy or his skill. Indeed, there was no reason to.

The coroner had had no hesitation in passing a verdict of suicide, adding the usual compassion of presuming that the balance of the dead man's mind had been affected, and therefore he was to be pitied rather than condemned. It was a pious form of words so customary as to be almost without meaning.

The commiserations were polite but formal. Lambourn had been a man much respected by his colleagues and no one wished to speculate aloud as to what might have been the reasons behind his death. Dinah

Lambourn had not been called upon to say anything. The only witness of any personal nature had been his brother-in-law, Barclay Herne, who said that Lambourn had been depressed about the findings of his latest inquiry, and that the government's inability to accept his recommendations had troubled him rather more than was to be expected. Herne added that he regretted the fact deeply.

The coroner offered no further comment. The matter was closed.

"Thank you," Monk said to the clerk, giving him back the papers. "There must be a police report. Where is that?"

The clerk looked blank. "Not really a police matter, sir. No one at fault. Stands to reason."

"Who found the body?" Monk asked. He expected the man to say it was Dinah, and he tried to picture her horror—the initial disbelief.

"A man out walking his dog," the clerk said. "Might not have been seen for ages, except for the dog smelling it. They do . . . smell death, I mean." He shook his head, shivering a little.

"Where was he found?" Monk asked, somewhat surprised. He had assumed Lambourn would either have been at home or at work.

"Greenwich Park," the young man replied. "One Tree Hill. There's more than one tree on it, actually. He was in a bit of a dip, up near the top. Sitting there, with his back leaned against the trunk."

Monk was silent for a moment. What had happened to this man that he had abandoned his wife and daughters and gone by himself into the park, in the cold and the dark, then taken opium, waited for it to take effect, then cut his wrists so he bled to death where he would lie until some stranger found him? Forcing someone he knew, who cared, to be called in to identify what remained of him, and carry the news to his family. By all the accounts Monk had heard so far, Lambourn had been a gentle and considerate man. What had made him do something so unbearably selfish?

"The coroner's report doesn't mention his health," he said to the clerk. "Could he have had some terminal illness?"

The clerk looked taken aback. "No idea, sir. The cause of death was perfectly obvious."

"The immediate cause, yes, but not the reason," Monk pointed out.

The clerk raised his eyebrows. "Perhaps that isn't our concern, sir. Poor man obviously had something happen in his life so bad that he felt he couldn't live with it. Nothing we can do to help, except afford him a little privacy. It can't matter now, anyway." The implied criticism was clear in his tone as well as his choice of words.

Monk felt a flicker of anger. "It matters because Dr. Lambourn seems to have been the only person well acquainted with the victim of a very violent and obscene murder in Limehouse," he replied a little abruptly. "I need to know if he was aware of anything that led up to it, or if someone at least believed that he did."

He saw the clerk's look of alarm with momentary guilt. He had no evidence that understanding Joel Lambourn's death would help him know who had murdered Zenia Gadney, or why. It bothered him because there were so many aspects of their relationship that did not make sense—but perhaps it was part of a greater whole he wasn't seeing yet. And so far he had nothing else to follow, unless Orme found something, or a witness came forward.

The clerk was shaking his head as if to get rid of the idea that was forcing itself upon him. "Dr. Lambourn was a scientist, sir, a very respectable man. Worked for the government trying to get information for them. Nothing personal, not that sort of thing. It was about medicines, not about people. He wouldn't have cared in the slightest about murders, or the sort of people who get involved in such affairs. You said the crime was 'obscene.' That wouldn't be Dr. Lambourn, sir."

"How long had he been dead before he was found?" Monk asked.

The clerk looked at the papers again, then up at Monk. "Doesn't say, sir. I imagine it didn't affect the verdict, and they wanted to be as discreet as possible. Details distress the family. Doesn't help any."

"Who was the police surgeon?"

"Ah . . . Dr. Wembley, sir."

"Where do I find him?"

"Don't know, sir. You'll have to ask at the police station." The clerk's disapproval was now undisguised. He clearly considered Monk to be reopening a case that was decidedly closed, and believed that decency required it to remain so.

Monk noted the facts he needed, thanked the man, and left.

AT THE POLICE STATION they gave him Wembley's address, but it took him another hour to find the man's surgery and then gain the opportunity to speak to him alone. Then Monk was introduced to a man well into his sixties, handsome, with thick gray hair and mustache.

"Thank you." Monk accepted the seat Wembley offered him, relaxing back into the chair and crossing his legs.

"What can I do for the River Police?" Wembley asked curiously. "Don't you have your own medical people?"

"There is a case of yours that may have relevance to one of ours," Monk answered. "I dare say you've heard of the woman who was murdered and mutilated on Limehouse Pier?"

"Good God, yes! The newspapers are full of it. Giving you chaps a hard time." There was commiseration in both his face and his voice.

Monk decided to be frank about it. He judged Wembley would be offended by anything less.

"The only person we can find who knew the woman is unfortunately himself dead," he began. "It seems he supported her financially. He was her only known client, and saw her regularly once a month."

"She was a prostitute," Wembley concluded. "One client only? That's unusual. But if he's dead already then he can't have killed her. Isn't it reasonable to assume she picked up someone else, and was unfortunate enough to run into a lunatic?"

"Yes, that's a fair deduction," Monk agreed. "My men are following that line of inquiry, from the little there is to go on. So far it's a solitary case. No reports of anyone unusually violent or disturbed in the area. No other women attacked lately. No previous crimes similar enough to this one to assume it's the same perpetrator."

Wembley bit his lip. "Have to start somewhere, I suppose, but it does sound pretty violent for a first crime."

"Exactly," Monk agreed. "The alternative is that it was someone she knew, and the hatred was personal."

"Who the devil did the poor woman know to hate her enough to rip her entrails out?" Wembley's face creased with revulsion. "And why in such an open place as the pier? Wouldn't he risk being seen by any passing ferry, or lighterman?"

"Yes," Monk agreed. "Which all makes him sound more and more like a complete lunatic, someone possessed by a sudden, insane rage. Except he had the knife with him, or possibly an open razor. According to the surgeon, it was quite long, and very sharp indeed. If anyone saw them—which so far no one will admit to—then they took them for acquaintances, or if it was in the act, for a prostitute and client on the pier."

"A bit unusual, isn't it?" Wembley asked. "Why not an alley? There must be plenty more private places around there."

"Perhaps she thought she was safe with him in such a visible place," Monk replied.

Wembley pursed his lips. "Or he had some power over her. He could force her to go with him. God, what a mess!"

"Indeed." Monk smiled bleakly. "And it becomes more complicated. The man who supported her was Dr. Joel Lambourn, who apparently took his own life in Greenwich Park, just over two months ago."

Wembley took a deep breath, and let out a sigh. "A connection with him? That is a surprise. I suppose you're certain?"

"Yes, there seems to be no doubt. Both his widow and his sister, Mrs. Herne, say that they were aware of the relationship. They may not have known the woman's name, but they knew she existed."

Wembley shook his head. "I . . . I really am amazed. He is the last man I would have expected to do such a thing." He looked profoundly unhappy. "But then he is the last man I would have expected to commit suicide. So I have to grant that my judgment is pretty poor. You say Mrs. Lambourn knew about it?"

"She says so."

"But you doubt it?" Wembley pressed.

Monk gave a faint smile. "I find my judgment floundering also. I've missed something crucial, I fear, because the situation, this relationship, his death—none of it seems to fit with what I hear of the man. Did you know Lambourn personally?"

"Yes, but not well."

"But well enough to be surprised that he killed himself?"

There was no hesitation in Wembley's voice. "Yes."

"But you have no doubt that he did?" Monk persisted.

"Doubt?" Wembley was startled, then his eyes narrowed. "Are you suggesting that he didn't?"

"Mrs. Lambourn is convinced he was murdered," Monk replied. "But that may be because she cannot bear to accept that he wanted to die. I don't think I could bear to believe that my wife would kill herself, and that I hadn't even been aware that she was desperate, let alone suicidal. Could you?"

"No," Wembley said immediately. "What did his sister say? Or is she in the same category?"

"Not at all." Monk recalled Amity Herne's utterly different face, voice, and even more her attitude and mind-set. It was distasteful to repeat her words. "She seemed to find no difficulty in believing he killed himself," he replied. "She said he was a professional failure and something of a personal one as well. He could never live up to the perception of him that his wife held, and the strain of trying to do so, the pretense, finally overwhelmed him."

"I have no idea about his personal life," Wembley said with heat, as if he were offended by Amity's words. "But professionally he was outstanding. He had one of the finest minds in his field. It's true he held himself to a high standard. But I don't believe he ever fell short of it, and he was certainly robust enough to deal with a degree of failure. Good heavens, man, there's no doctor on earth who doesn't deal with failure every week!"

He jerked his hands apart in a gesture of frustration. "People die; people fail to throw off a disabling disease. You do your best. You might solve every case, I suppose, but you certainly don't prevent every crime!" It was something of an accusation. Monk's implied criticism of Lambourn had obviously angered Wembley.

Monk found himself perversely pleased. "So you cannot believe that he killed himself over a sense of professional failure?"

Wembley's face was tight and angry. "No, I cannot."

"Then over what?"

"I don't know!" He glared at Monk. "I am forced to go along with the evidence. He was found alone, in the early morning, in an out-of-the-way part of Greenwich Park. He had taken opium, enough to make him drowsy and lessen any physical pain and fear. He had slit his wrists and bled to death."

Monk leaned forward a little. "How do you know he took the opium himself, and cut his own wrists?"

Wembley's eyes widened and he leaned forward a little. "Are you suggesting that someone else did it, and left him there to die? Why, for God's sake? And why wouldn't he have fought back? He wasn't a small or weak man, and there was no evidence he was bound or restrained. The opium in his body was considerable, but it would not render him insensible immediately. He must have acquiesced in what was going on."

Monk's mind raced. "But his wrists were cut. Could the injuries have hidden signs of having been bound?"

Wembley shook his head slowly. "They were cut on the inside, to get the artery. If they had been bound, the marks would be on the outside."

Monk was not ready to give up. "Any other bruises?" he asked.

"None that I could see. Certainly nothing on his ankles."

"His face?"

"Of course not. I could hardly have missed that!"

"What sort of hair did he have?"

"Gray, thinning on top a little. Why?" But Wembley had hesitated.

"And at the back?" Monk asked.

"Thick still. Are you thinking there may have been a bruise hidden by his hair?"

"Could there?"

Wembley took a long, slow breath and let it out in a sigh. "I didn't think to look. It's possible. But there was no blood. I would have seen that."

"How did he take the opium?"

"I've no idea. What difference does it make?"

"Powder in a twist?" Monk asked. "And water to drink it down? Or a solution of some sort? Something like laudanum or some other patent medicine?"

"Why does it matter now?" Wembley spoke more slowly, his curiosity awakened.

"You can't carry opium loose," Monk pointed out. "And you can't take powder without something to wash it down with. Laudanum would've been carried in a bottle."

Wembley pursed his lips. "I saw no bottle, packet, or anything else. The police must have taken it away. I suppose I should have asked. It didn't seem important. It looked obvious what had happened. I admit, I was shaken." His tone was apologetic. "I admired his work, and insofar as I knew him, I liked him."

They sat in silence for a few moments. The sound of footsteps echoed outside in the passage, and then faded away.

Monk did not prompt Wembley to go on. He felt touched by the same sense of regret, even though he had never known Dr. Lambourn.

"He had a very nice sense of humor," Wembley went on quietly. "He had a keen amusement at the absurd, with a kind of affection, as if oddities pleased him." He stared into the distance, into the past, it seemed to Monk. "If there was something wrong, something strange about his death," he went on after a moment, "I'd be happy if you found it. It is one of those cases about which I would much rather be mistaken."

Monk RETURNED TO THE local police station in Greenwich but was not surprised when a young sergeant told him that the case was closed, and that such tragedies were best left alone.

"Dr. Lambourn was a very well thought of gentleman, sir," he said with a tight smile. "It shakes the whole neighborhood when something like that happens. Not really River Police business."

Monk struggled to think of a reason why he could ask if anyone had moved a bottle of water or alcohol, or something that could have contained a solution of opium, but the sergeant was right. It was not River Police business.

"I would like to speak with the policeman first on the scene," he said instead. "It may have a connection with a case that is our business. A murder," he added, in case the young man was inclined to take it lightly.

The constable's smooth face yielded nothing. He met Monk's eyes blandly.

"Sorry, sir, but that'd probably be Constable Watkins, and he's out Deptford way right now." He smiled very slightly. Monk did not know if it was meant to be charm, or insolence. He thought the latter.

"Not be back here until tomorrow," the young man continued.

"Couldn't tell you anything anyway. Poor gentleman'd been dead for hours, so the doctor told us. Is there anything else I can do for you, sir?"

Monk hid his irritation with difficulty.

"Who was in charge of the case?"

"Some senior man the government brought in, Dr. Lambourn being an important person," the young man replied. "Kept it . . . discreet." He loaded the last word with importance.

"And you don't know the name of this man?"

"That's right, sir, I don't." Again he smiled and met Monk's eyes boldly.

Monk thanked him and left, feeling thwarted, but also that he was wasting his time. Perhaps Lambourn had taken his opium in alcohol, possibly a lot of it, and it was a small kindness to conceal the fact. Grudgingly he acknowledged that those who found him might well have hidden it, for compassion's sake. He might have done the same himself.

He spoke to Orme the next morning at the River Police headquarters in Wapping. They were standing on the dockside in front of the station, staring across the river, watching the lighters as they made their way upstream in long strings, ten to fifteen of them carrying cargo to the Pool of London ready to be loaded and sent to every port in the world.

"Been through all the records I can find," Orme said unhappily. "Asked everyone. No crime similar enough to this to make it worth comparing, thank the Lord. Can't find anyone who's even been attacked in the last couple of years, except for the ordinary beatings or stranglings. No one sliced open and torn to pieces." His mouth pulled thin in distaste. "There's no trace of him doing this before, either side of the river." He shook his head. "I think this is a one-off, sir. And I don't know if it had anything to do with Dr. Lambourn or not. But I can't find anyone else she knew, except the odd local people to talk to. Shopkeepers, a laundress, old man a couple of streets away, but he's eighty if he's a day, and can hardly walk, let alone get himself to the pier."

"And Lambourn was two months dead by that time," Monk added. "Then we're left with someone connected to Lambourn. What could someone think he said or confessed to Zenia Gadney that was worth killing her for—and killing her like that?"

"To make us think it was a lunatic, and to do with Limehouse and her profession, not with Lambourn," Orme answered.

Monk did not argue. "And what made Lambourn kill himself when he did? Why not sooner, or later?" he asked, as much to himself as to Orme. "What changed so terribly?"

Orme said nothing. He knew he was not expected to reply.

THAT WAS ALSO WHAT Monk asked Lambourn's assistant a couple of hours later. He was a young doctor named Daventry, somewhat unhappy at now working for Lambourn's replacement, who was a stiff, busy man who had no time to speak with Monk himself, and was only too happy to find an excuse to send him to someone else.

Monk did not phrase his question quite so boldly. He was standing in a brightly lit laboratory full of jars and bottles, vials, burners, basins, and retorts. All kinds of glass and metal equipment stood around on surfaces. One complete wall was obscured by stacks of files.

"You worked closely with Dr. Lambourn before his death?" Monk began.

"Yes," Daventry answered, pushing his wild, dark hair out of his eyes and looking at Monk aggressively. "What are you after now? Why can't you leave him alone? He was a good doctor, better than that—" He stopped abruptly. "Don't waste my time. What is it you want?"

Monk was pleased he found someone loyal to Lambourn, even if it might make his own task more difficult.

"I'm River Police, not government," he said.

"What difference does that make?" Daventry challenged him. Then he peered forward to look more closely at Monk. "Sorry," he apologized. "I'm just tired of hearing Dr. Lambourn run down by a lot of people who didn't know him and didn't believe his findings."

Monk changed his approach instantly. "You did believe in them?" he asked.

"I don't know for myself." Daventry was scrupulously honest. "Except bits here and there. I collected some of the figures for him. But he was meticulous, and he never included anything he couldn't verify. Even cut some of my findings because I didn't double-check it with at least two sources."

"About opium?"

"Among other things. He worked on all kinds of medicines. But, yes, that was the one he cared about most recently."

"Why?"

Daventry's eyebrows shot up. "Why?" he said incredulously.

"Yes. What was he researching, and for whom?"

"The public's use of opium, because it's killing too many people. For the government, who else?" Daventry looked at Monk as if he were a particularly stupid schoolchild. He saw the confusion in Monk's face. "The government is looking to pass a bill to regulate the use of opium in medicines," he explained a little wearily, as if he had already said it too many times, to too many people who were apparently incapable of understanding.

"To stop people buying it?" Now it was Monk who was incredulous. A small dose of opium, as in a "penny twist," was the only way to kill pain, other than to drink oneself insensible to it, and to everything else. "Why, for heaven's sake?" he asked. "Nobody'll pass an act like that, and it would be impossible to police. You'd have two-thirds of the population in jail."

Daventry looked at him with heavy exasperation. "No, sir, just to regulate it, so that if you go to buy something with opium in it—such as Battley's Sedative, which is much like laudanum, except it's with calcium hydrate and sherry, not distilled water and alcohol—you'll know for sure how much opium it contains. And that it's pure opium, not opium cut with something else."

"Opium cut with something else?" Monk was puzzled.

"Do you know what's in Dover's Powder, sir?" Daventry asked.

Monk had no idea. "Apart from opium? No," he admitted.

"Saltpeter, tartar, licorice, and ipecacuanha," Daventry told him. "What about chlorodyne?"

Monk did not bother to answer this time. He waited for Daventry to list that as well.

"Chloroform and morphine," Daventry said. "But that's not what matters the most. If your child is crying with toothache, or a bad stomach, which one are you going to give him: Godfrey's Cordial, Street's Infant Quietness, Winston's Soothing Syrup, or Atkinson's Infant Preservative? How much opium is in each of them, and what else is in them?" He shrugged. "You don't know, do you? Neither does your average harassed mother who's getting half the sleep she needs, and probably half the food, and maybe she can't read well or understand figures, either. What would you say to having them regulated so she doesn't have to worry about it?"

"Is that what they're proposing?" Now Monk's interest was sincere and sharp, almost as sharp as Daventry's own.

"Part of it, yes."

"And Lambourn was getting the facts for them?"

"Yes," Daventry agreed, warming to it as he realized Monk's understanding. "And on other things, but opium was the chief thing."

"Why would anyone be against it?" Monk was puzzled.

"Lot of money in opium," Daventry replied. "Start telling people what they can and can't sell, you'll get their backs up. Also it means the government knows about it all. Under the counter as well as over. People who sell opium—and you'd be surprised at who some of them are— are very happy to hear how many people's lives are made easier by it, but not how many children die of overdoses, or how many people get dependent and then can't do without it. They don't want to be blamed for those unfortunate side effects."

He waved his hands around to encompass everyone in general. "Nobody wants to remember the Opium Wars. You'd be surprised whose fortunes were built on the opium trade. Don't want to rake all that up. Make yourself a lot of enemies."

"Do you know this for yourself, or did Dr. Lambourn tell you?" Monk asked gently.

The blush burned hot up Daventry's young face. "Dr. Lambourn told me most of it," he replied, so quietly Monk barely heard him. "But I believe it. He never lied."

"So far as you know . . ." Monk smiled to rob the words of some of their sting.

Daventry's expression was bleak, but he did not argue.

"Why do you think he took his own life?" Monk asked.

Daventry's face filled with a deep distress. "I don't know. It doesn't make sense."

"Do you know Mrs. Lambourn?"

"I've met her. Why?"

"She thinks he was murdered."

Daventry's eyes were brilliant. He caught his breath in sharply. "To hide his research? That would make sense. I can believe it. Are you going to find out who did it?" That was a very definite challenge, with all the sting of contempt if the answer were no.

"I'm going to find out if it's so, first of all," Monk told him. "Where is this research now?"

"The government people took it," Daventry said simply.

"But you have copies, working notes, something?" Monk insisted.

"I haven't." Daventry shook his head. "There's nothing here. I know because I've looked. If he kept it at home, they'll have taken that, too. I told you, there's a lot of money at stake—and a lot of people's reputations as well."

Several answers rose to Monk's lips, but he did not make any of them. He could see in Daventry's eyes that he did not know where Lambourn's papers were, and he was even more distressed by it than Monk was.

"How did Dr. Lambourn take the government rejection of his research?" he asked instead. That was what he needed to know. Was that the reason Lambourn had taken his life? Was the disgrace deeper than Monk had at first assumed it to be? Was it not just this report, but his whole reputation in other fields that was ruined?

Daventry did not reply.

"Mr. Daventry? How did he take the rejection? How important was it to him?" Monk insisted.

Daventry's expression hardened. "If he really took his own life over it, then something happened between the last time I saw him and that night," he answered fiercely, his voice charged with emotion. "When he left here, he was determined to fight them all the way. He was certain his facts were right and that a pharmaceutical act is absolutely necessary. I don't know what happened. I can't think of anything anyone could say to him that would have made it different."

"Could he have found a mistake in his figures that altered their validity?" Monk suggested.

"I don't see how." Daventry shook his head. "But if he really had been wrong, he'd have admitted it. He wouldn't have gone out to One Tree Hill and killed himself! He just wasn't that sort of man."

"I'm afraid he wasn't nearly as good as he believed himself to be," one of Lambourn's more senior assistants said unhappily, half an hour later. Nailsworth was a good-looking young man, and very confident. He smiled at Monk with a down-curved twist to his lips as if in apology. He shrugged. "He formed a theory and then looked for evidence to prove it, ignoring anything that called it into question." He smiled again, too easily. "Really, he should have known better. He used to be excellent. Perhaps he had a health difficulty we weren't aware of?"

Monk looked at the man with dislike. "Yes," he agreed a trifle acidly. "It is totally unscientific, in fact not even strictly honest, to create your theory and then look only at the facts that fit it. Even worse to bend the facts to make them fit, and then claim to have been impartial."

Monk was being sarcastic and expected a quick defense, but he was disappointed.

Nailsworth nodded. "I see you understand. I suppose there's a certain logical pattern to solving crimes as well."

"Indeed." Monk was unexpectedly angry. "Perhaps you would guide me through the logical steps you followed before deciding that Dr. Lambourn's research was in error, and that he was unable to accept that fact."

"Well, it's tragically clear that he was unable to accept his own failure," Nailsworth said tartly. "Unfortunately one can hardly avoid that conclusion!"

Monk stopped him. "Undeniably he is dead. But please start at the beginning, not at the end." His smile was more a baring of the teeth. "As you would if you were creating a theory yourself. Facts first."

Nailsworth's eyes were hard and bright. "Dr. Lambourn collected a great number of facts and figures about the sale of opium in different parts of the country and wrote them up in a report," he said icily. "The government compared them with other information they had, from several other sources, and found that Lambourn was in error in too many instances, and that his conclusions were flawed. They rejected his report and he took it very hard. It questioned his standing as a scientist and as a doctor. For some reason this whole issue of opium was one he took far too personally. He staked his reputation in it, and lost. Ending in the one fact you don't dispute, he is now dead, having cut his own wrists."

His eyes never moved from Monk's face. "I'm sorry. He was a very agreeable man, and I think he had every intention of being honest, but he allowed his emotions to govern his thought." He sounded anything but sorry. There was condescension perhaps, but not grief. Monk wondered what Lambourn had done to sting Nailsworth's vanity so deeply.

"His recommendations were both restrictive and completely unnecessary," Nailsworth continued. "'Overblown' was the word they used about his results. He was humiliated, and he couldn't face it. Now if you have any compassion at all for his family, you'll leave the matter alone."

Monk watched and listened. Nailsworth was deeply angry, but the sharp edge in his voice betrayed something else. Something he dared not show? Some private concern over the opium issue? Jeopardy to his future career, should he speak out of turn?

As Monk thanked him and walked away, he thought it more likely to be the latter. Would Nailsworth have been in danger had he come forward as sympathetic to Dr. Lambourn?

Or, Monk wondered, was he now twisting the facts about Nailsworth to fit a theory of his own, already adopted, out of a wish for Dinah Lambourn to have some shred of comfort? Perhaps he was as guilty as any of them of selecting and interpreting the facts to fit the outcome he wanted.

7

Hester stood at the kitchen bench chopping onions to fry with the leftover potatoes from yesterday, and quite a large portion of cabbage. It would make bubble and squeak, one of Scuff's favorite meals, and—with sausages—one even Monk seemed never to grow tired of.

She had come home early enough to prepare a pudding as well, for the first time in several days. She ran a clinic for street women, in Portpool Lane, and she had been extremely busy. Lately there seemed to have been even more than usual to attend to.

The clinic was funded by charity, and Margaret Rathbone had been by far the best volunteer at raising money. But since the trial and death of her father, she had not been to the clinic at all. She regarded Hester as having betrayed her as much as Oliver had, and their friendship was broken—it seemed irredeemably.

Hester could not change her views. She had thought about it long and painfully, wanting to salvage a friendship that mattered to her. But what Arthur Ballinger had done was not possible for her to overlook just because he was Margaret's father. Especially the second murder he had committed, a young woman Hester had tried so hard to help. The grief of it still haunted her.

Finances for medicine, food, and fuel had all been more difficult to find since Margaret had withdrawn her help. Asking for money was not a gift Hester possessed. It required not only charm, but tact, and she had never mastered that art. She had no tolerance of hypocrisy or genteel excuses, and there always came the moment when she spoke too much of the truth. However, Claudine Burroughs had just the other day found the clinic a new patron, so the emergency had passed.

Scuff was upstairs struggling his way through a book, with a complex mixture of pride and frustration that Hester was sensitive enough to allow him privacy to deal with.

Maybe this evening Monk would be home in time to eat with them.

She had just finished chopping the onions when she heard his footsteps in the passage to the kitchen. There was heaviness in them, as if he was tired, and perhaps disappointed.

She put the knife down and washed her hands quickly to get rid of the onion smell. She was drying them on the towel hung over the rail of the oven door when he came in. He smiled when he saw her, but this could not disguise the weariness in his face. He walked over and kissed her gently.

"What is it?" she asked when he let her go. "What's happened?"

"Where's Scuff?" He evaded the question, glancing around.

"Upstairs reading," she replied. "He's not as good as he's pretending to be, but he's improving. Would you like a cup of tea before supper's ready?"

He nodded and sat down on the chair at the head of the table, leaning forward a little to ease his back, and resting his elbows on the scrubbed wood.

"Nothing on the case?" she asked as she pulled the kettle into the center of the stovetop and took out the tea caddy from the cupboard. There was no need to stoke the oven. It was already full and burning well, ready to cook in.

"I don't know," he replied. "The only person Zenia seems to have had any real connection with is a very respectable doctor who was preparing a report for the government on opium use and sales."

"Opium?" Hester stopped what she was doing and sat down at the table opposite him, her attention entirely caught. As a nurse, she knew a lot about the vast uses of opium. If one took it for a long time it could become addictive, only seriously so when taken as the Chinese did—not by eating it, but smoking it in clay pipes.

Briefly Monk explained Joel Lambourn's connection with the proposed pharmaceutical bill.

"What has that to do with Zenia Gadney's death?" she asked, not yet following his line of thought. "You don't suspect him, do you?"

He smiled bleakly. "He committed suicide a couple of months ago."

She was stunned. "That's terrible. Poor man. Why did he take his own life? And if he was dead when she was killed, why are you concerned with him at all? I don't understand."

"Neither do I," he admitted. "I'm not even sure if there is a connection, except that he knew her and seems to have provided for her financially."

Hester got up and made the tea and left it to sit for a moment or two to brew.

"Why did he kill himself?" she asked again. "You are sure it was suicide?"

"The official verdict is that he did it when the government rejected his report on the damage that unlabeled sales of opium can do. His reputation was destroyed and he couldn't face it."

"Was he so . . . fragile?" she said doubtfully. "If he really did kill himself, there must have been a better reason for it than that. Was he smoking opium himself? Or did Zenia Gadney end the affair, or threaten to make it public? Would she tell his wife—that he had very odd tastes, or something?" She leaned forward a little, frowning, the bubble and squeak temporarily forgotten. "William, I don't feel it makes sense, whether it has anything to do with Zenia Gadney's murder or not."

"I know."

"Did you see this report Joel Lambourn wrote?"

"No. All the copies have been destroyed," he replied. "And his wife, Dinah Lambourn, says she knew of his affair anyway."

Hester was puzzled. "Do you believe her?"

"I don't know."

"What is she like?" she asked curiously, trying to picture a woman who had lost so much and was trying desperately to hold on to some kind of meaning in her life.

"Very emotional," he said quietly. "But she has a kind of dignity you have to admire. She believed in him passionately, and still does. She thinks he was murdered."

Hester was startled, and yet perhaps it was the obvious straw to grasp for.

"Could he have been?" she asked doubtfully.

She saw the frown cross his face before he answered.

"I'm beginning to wonder about that myself," he said slowly. "He is said to have taken a fairly heavy dose of opium and then cut his wrists." He gestured slightly with one hand. "Up on One Tree Hill, in Greenwich Park."

"Said to have?"

Monk shook his head a little. "The evidence seems unclear. The doctor who examined him saw nothing containing opium, no powder wrappers, no bottle for a liquid or to drink water from. No knife or razor. And one of Lambourn's assistants said he wasn't distressed about his report being refused, that he intended to fight. But the other one says he was completely broken by it."

Hester stood up and fetched the teapot off the stove. She poured a cup for each of them. Its fragrant steam filled the air as she passed one cup across the table to him.

"His wife says he was strong, and his sister says he was weak," he said. "And even if he was murdered, I don't know what it can have had to do with Zenia Gadney's murder, except that his wife says there could be a connection."

"Why does she think that?" Again Hester was confused.

"I feel it's because she's desperate," he confessed. "I can't think of anything worse than for the person you love most in the world to take their own life, without warning you, and without explaining anything at all as to why, or giving you any chance to help or understand."

Hester felt an ache of pity for this woman she knew nothing else about. How could happiness be so impossibly fragile? One day you have a home, a place in society, and the only thing that really matters, a companion of heart and mind. Then the next day everything is gone, hideously and without reason. Everything you thought you knew swept away and what's left only looks like what you had, but it's empty.

"Hester . . . ?" His voice cut across her thoughts.

"Nor can I. Everything that matters—gone."

"Yes. Loving is always dangerous." He gave a bleak smile and touched her hand gently across the table. "As you have told me more than once, the only thing worse is not loving at all."

At that moment Scuff appeared at the door, looking pleased with himself and holding a book in his hand.

"I finished it," he announced triumphantly, meeting Hester's eyes for her approval. Then he looked over toward the stove. "Supper yet?"

"Not yet," she answered, keeping her face composed with difficulty. "You have chores to do. Then when you've finished it'll be sausages and bubble and squeak."

His grin was enormous. He glanced at Monk just to be sure for himself that he was all right, then he turned and left. They heard his feet clattering out into the scullery and the backyard to sweep and clean up.

"So much for safety of heart," Hester said, standing up again. "I'd better put the bubble and squeak on, and get on with the pudding, or it won't be cooked in time."

THE FOLLOWING MORNING, HESTER visited the office of a man she had known in her nursing days in the army, thirteen years earlier. She had seen him two or three times since then, and she hoped he would remember her.

Dr. Winfarthing was a large man in all respects. He was tall and rotund; his hair was thick, auburn touched now with gray, and flying all over the place. His features were generous and he regarded the world benignly through a pair of spectacles that always looked as if they were about to slide off his nose.

"Of course I remember you, girl," he said cheerfully. "Best nurse I know, and most trouble. Who have you upset now?"

She took no offense whatever. The remark was perfectly justified, and from him, almost a compliment. When she had returned from the Crimea she had had high and totally unrealistic hopes of reforming the nursing profession. She was impatient with delay, even more so with those who clung to the old because it was familiar, even if it was wrong. When she thought people's lives were at stake, she had not even tried to be tactful.

"No one just at the moment," she replied with a rueful smile.

Winfarthing waved expansively to offer her a seat in his spacious, chaotic office. As always it was crowded with books, many of them not even remotely connected with medicine. Indeed, some of them were of poetry, some fairy stories that had amused him or pleased his imagination over the years.

"Should I flatter myself that you have come simply to see how I am?" he asked with a crooked smile. "Ah, this will be good fun—let's see how will you answer now, without hurting my feelings, but still retaining a semblance of grace."

"Dr. Winfarthing!" she protested. "I—"

"Need help with something," he finished for her, still smiling. "Is it medical, or political?"

The question was so accurate, it reminded her just how well they had known each other, and how transparent she was to him.

"I'm not sure," she said candidly. "Did you know Dr. Joel Lambourn?"

The light vanished from Winfarthing's face and suddenly it was crumpled and sad, his years sitting heavily on him. "I did," he replied. "And I liked him. He was a remarkably decent man. You'd have liked him, too, even if he had exasperated you. Although, come to think of it, he probably wouldn't have. You really aren't any wiser than he was, poor soul."

Hester was taken aback. Winfarthing had always been able to do that to her. He was one of the kindest men she knew, yet his perception was scalpel-sharp, and if he liked you, he had no hesitation in speaking frankly. His trust in her was a compliment, as if they were equals, and pretense had no place in their communication.

"You knew him quite well," she concluded.

He smiled, knowing that she had evaded his comment on her, and done it with a degree of grace. "He was the sort of man that if he had any respect for you, he allowed you to know him honestly," he replied, blinking several times, oddly embarrassed by his emotion. "I am greatly flattered that he liked me. It was the best compliment he could have offered. Worth far more than telling me I was a great doctor—which I'm not. And don't argue with me, my dear. My medical knowledge is adequate. Perhaps a little outdated now. It is my understanding of people that you admire, and my ability to get the best out of them."

She met his eyes and nodded. He deserved the truth from her in that also. "Tell me more about Dr. Lambourn," she said.

He pushed his hand through his hair, leaving it wilder than before. "Why? What difference does it make to you now? He's gone."

"Did you know his wife as well?" Again she sidestepped the question.

"I met her," he said, studying Hester's face to find what she was really seeking. "Very fine woman, handsome. Again, why? I can keep asking as long as you can keep dodging me, and you know that."

"She doesn't believe he took his own life," she replied.

"Another one of your 'lost causes'?" He shrugged his massive shoulders. "I find it hard to believe, too, but they say the evidence is there. What else would it be? No one climbs a bare hill alone at night and cuts their wrists by accident, girl. You know that as well as I do."

She felt foolish, but she would not give up. If Winfarthing did not believe Dinah, then who would? "How important was the research Dr. Lambourn was doing into opium sales and use?" she asked. "Should there be a pharmaceutical bill to control opium?"

He frowned. "Is that what he was doing? For whom? He would be in favor of such a bill, of course."

"Are you?" she pressed.

"I'm insulted that you need to ask!" He said it sharply, but there was no anger in his face. "But it must be based on facts, not on religious or financial interests. Opium, in one form or another, is the only way most people have of dealing with pain. We all know that. God knows how many people get through the day on it—or the night." He said it with a heaviness of heart.

"As far as I know," she said, "what he wanted was for all remedies containing opium, which I know is hundreds—"

"At least! If not thousands," he interrupted.

"Should be regularized and labeled as to quantity and suitable dosage," she finished.

"Ah," he sighed. "Poor Lambourn. Heavy vested interests against him. Lot of money in the import of opium. Even some of the best family fortunes are built on it, you know?"

"Enough to try to crush Dr. Lambourn's report?"

Winfarthing's eyebrows shot up. "Is that what you think? Political pressure? You're wrong." He sat up straighter in his chair. "Joel Lambourn wouldn't have been persuaded by any man to cut his own wrists. He might have been a political innocent, but he was a first-class scientist, and far more important than that, he loved his family. He would never have left them that way."

He blinked again. "He had two daughters, you know, Marianne and Adah. Very proud of them." He looked at her almost angrily.

She looked down at the floor. "I'm sorry."

"Sorry for what? Reminding me of something I was trying to forget? I know it. Don't treat me like a fool." He sniffed. "Why did you come, anyway? Is this about Dinah Lambourn?"

"No." She looked up at him. "Actually it started about Zenia Gadney."

"Who the devil is Zenia Gadney?"

"The woman who was found murdered and mutilated on Limehouse Pier, over a week ago."

"What has that to do with Lambourn? Or opium?"

"Nothing to do with opium, so far as we know," Hester replied. "She bought the occasional penny twist, but so does half the population. Dr. Lambourn knew her quite well, well enough to go and see her once a month, and to support her financially."

"Stuff and nonsense!" Winfarthing said instantly. "Whoever said that is either malicious or a lunatic, or both."

"It was his sister, Amity Herne," she answered. "But only after a little pressing. His wife agreed that she too was aware of it, but not of where Mrs. Gadney lived."

"Mrs.? Was the woman married?" he said quickly. "Or is that a courtesy title?"

"Largely courtesy, I think, although people around her neighborhood thought she might be a widow."

"Supported by Joel Lambourn? A colleague's wife fallen on hard times?" Winfarthing still looked incredulous.

"Possibly," Hester replied with some doubt. "When Dr. Lambourn died, it looks as if she might have taken to the streets to survive."

"How old was she?"

"Middle forties, roughly."

"There's something wrong in this," Winfarthing said, shaking his head. "Somebody's lying. Has to be. Are you suggesting this poor woman was somehow connected with Lambourn's death?"

Hester evaded the question slightly, answering with one of her own.

"If he wouldn't kill himself because his report was rejected, and he doesn't appear to have had any fatal illness—or any illness at all, for that matter—then he killed himself for another reason," she said. "Could that have been an affair with a prostitute that was about to be exposed?"

Winfarthing's face filled with acute distaste. "I suppose we never know people as well as we think we do. As a doctor, I have certainly learned that. You wouldn't believe some of the things I've seen—and heard." He shrugged. "Or perhaps you would. But I still can't see Joel Lambourn conducting an affair with a middle-aged prostitute in Limehouse." His voice took on a more challenging tone, although it was the conclusion he fought, not Hester. "And if she were going to expose him, and he killed himself, that doesn't answer your question as to who killed her, does it? Why do you care, girl? Was she one of the women in this clinic of yours?"

She shook her head. "No. I never met her, or heard of her before this. Limehouse is a distance from Portpool Lane, you know. It's the manner of her death that is the worst. It's my husband's case."

"Of course." He grimaced, irritated with himself. "I should have worked that out. Well, I still find it hard to believe that Lambourn killed himself at all, over anything. I don't mind some of life's surprises, but I don't like this one."

"The alternative is that Dr. Lambourn was murdered as well, by someone who wanted his report suppressed," she said, watching his expression to judge what he thought of the idea.

He nodded very slowly. "Possible, I suppose. There are fortunes made and lost in opium. I . . ." He hesitated.

"What?" she said quickly.

He looked at her, his face creased with sadness. "I would hate to think there is corruption deep enough to have a man like Joel Lambourn murdered, and labeled as a failure and a suicide, in order to cover up the misuse of opium and prevent a regulating bill that is much needed, not only for opium but for the sale of all pharmaceuticals."

"Does that mean you won't consider the possibility?"

He jerked forward in his chair, glaring at her. "No, it does not! How dare you even ask?"

She smiled at him with rare charm. "To make you angry enough to help me," she answered. "But discreetly, of course. I . . . I don't want someone to find *you* on One Tree Hill with your wrists cut."

He sighed gustily. "You are a manipulating woman, Hester. Here am I thinking you were the only daughter of Eve who hadn't the art to twist a man around your fingers. I'm a wishful fool. But I'll help with this—for Joel Lambourn, not because you backed me into it!"

"Thank you," she said sincerely. "If you were looking for information to make the kind of report he did, what would you look for? Can you write it down for me, please?"

"No I cannot!" he said with sudden vehemence. "One Tree Hill is quite big enough for both of us. I'll do most of it. I've got excuses, reasons. You can try the ordinary apothecaries and common shops, midwives—peddlers in the street. Just see what you could buy. Ask, do you understand? Don't get it."

Hester nodded, and left him a quarter of an hour later with their plans made and agreed.

SHE BEGAN THAT DAY, walking the busy streets of the Rotherhithe area in the sharp winter sun. She was close to the river and she could smell the salt and fish odors on the wind, and hear the cry of the gulls. Occasionally as she turned north she saw the light on the water, glinting sharp between the rows of houses, or the dark lines of masts and spars against the sky.

She asked at small grocery shops, apothecaries, and tobacconists, and was surprised at the number of people who sold some preparation that contained an unspecified amount of opium. Of course she herself had used it at the clinic in Portpool Lane, but they had bought it in pure form and given it out very carefully measured, and as sparingly as possible. She would not have argued with anyone that it was not only the best remedy for pain, but in most cases the only one.

She began to ask the shopkeepers for advice as to how much to take, and how often. She inquired whether age or weight of the patient made any difference, and what other circumstances might alter its effect. Was there anything that would make it dangerous, such as taking other medicines at the same time, or having certain illnesses?

"Look, lady, either take it or don't," one busy man said to her exasperatedly, glancing at the queue of customers behind her. "Please yerself, just don't stand 'ere arguing wi' me. I in't got time. Now do yer want it or not?"

"No thank you," she replied, and went out of the cramped shop, past several strings of onions, dried herbs, and bins of flour, wheat, and oatmeal.

She did not need to spend a second day walking up and down the streets and calling at every likely shop. If it was so easy to buy opium in Rotherhithe, it would be the same anywhere else in London, and probably in every other city and town in England.

SHE DID NOT MENTION her activities to Monk when he came home late in the evening, having spent most of the day on the river dealing with thefts, and the murder of a sailor during a brawl. It was one of those senseless, drunken arguments that got out of hand. Abuse had been shouted, tempers high and out of control. The next moment a broken bottle had slashed a man's artery and he had bled to death before anyone could gather their wits and even think of helping him. The guilty man had run, and it had taken Monk and three of his officers most of the afternoon to catch him and arrest him without any further injury.

It had been late when he joined Orme, still searching for the "Limehouse Butcher," as the newspapers were calling him.

HESTER WENT IN TO the clinic in the morning, but only to ask the help of Squeaky Robinson, the reformed bookkeeper who had owned the buildings of the clinic when they had been one of the most profit-able brothels in the area. A clever trick of Oliver Rathbone's had manipulated Squeaky into saving himself from prison by giving the buildings to charity. Highly aggrieved, Squeaky had been suddenly made homeless, and with careful supervision and no trust at all, he had been permitted to remain in residence and manage the property in its new function.

Over the years since then he and Hester had come to respect each other, and now—at least in certain areas—Squeaky was both liked and trusted. This was a circumstance he enjoyed very much, to his own confusion. He would have denied it indignantly had anyone suggested such a thing.

Hester walked into the office where Squeaky had his files and led-gers. He was sitting at the desk looking almost like a clerk. Lack of anxiety and now regular nights had filled out some of the hollows in his face, but he was still long-nosed, slightly gap-toothed, and his hair was as straggly as always.

"Morning, Miss Hester," he said cheerfully. "Don't worry about money, we're not doing bad."

"Good morning, Squeaky." She sat down in the chair opposite him. "It isn't about money today. I need information about someone. Not here—in Limehouse. Who should I go and ask?"

"You shouldn't," he said instantly. "I know you. It's about that poor cow as was found on the pier, isn't it? Don't even go looking. A lunatic like that is trouble you don't need."

Hester had expected an argument and was prepared.

"She lived in the area," she told him conversationally, as if he had asked. "Someone must have known her apart from Dr. Lambourn. If she worked the streets at all, the other women would at least have known something about her. They won't tell the police, but they'll talk to each other."

"What is there to know?" Squeaky said reasonably. He looked her up and down and shook his head. "She was a tart, knocking on a bit and just about past it. Her steady bloke topped hisself, Gawd knows why, so she were broke, and she got careless. What else is there to know?"

"Maybe why he went to her in the first place?" she suggested.

"Now that's something you really don't want to know," he said sharply. "If he were bent enough that he had to go all the way from Greenwich over the river to Limehouse to get whatever it was he wanted, then it's something no lady needs to know about, nurse in the army or not." He frowned. "Which does make you wonder why she wasn't fly enough to deal with some bleeding lunatic what wants to cut her up, don't it? I mean you'd think she'd smell he was a bad 'un and leave him alone, not go clarting off onto the pier with him. She got real, real care-less. Damn stupid place to go fornicating, anyway! But that still don't matter to you."

"Or she was desperate," she said quietly. "Who do I ask, Squeaky?"

He sighed with exasperation. "I told yer! Leave it alone. Yer can't help her, poor cow. What's Mr. Monk going to do if you go and get yer-self cut up, eh? For that matter, what are we all going to do? Sometimes I think you haven't got the wits of a tuppenny rabbit!"

She smiled at him, ignoring the insult. "Then come with me, Squeaky."

He sighed heavily and put away everything on his desk with more care than necessary. Then he followed her out of the door into the hallway, and then the street.

He grumbled all the way to the omnibus, and when they got off on Commercial Road in Limehouse he stayed so close to her she all but tripped over him half a dozen times. But, walking along the narrow, dank, rain-chilled backstreets, she was very pleased to have his presence.

"Told yer," he said after the fifth person they had spoken to had, like all the others, denied ever having seen or heard of Zenia Gadney. "They're all too scared to say anything. Want to pretend they never heard of her."

"That's ridiculous," Hester retorted sharply. "They worked in the same streets. They have to have heard of her. And what do they think I want to know for, except to help catch the man?"

They continued for several more hours, but all they could learn of Zenia Gadney was what Monk already knew. She had been a quiet woman, well spoken. If you listened to her, she did not sound like the local prostitutes, or even like the shopkeepers, laundresses, and slightly more respectable housewives. No one they spoke to owned to particu-

larly liking or disliking her. Certainly none of the prostitutes considered her a threat.

"'Er?" one coarse-faced blond woman said indignantly. "Too old, fer
a start. I'm not sayin' as she were downright ugly or nothin'. In fact, not
bad, if yer took the time ter look, but dull. Dull as a bucket o' mud, if yer
know wot I mean?" She put her hands on her hips. "Got no fight in 'er,
an' no fun. A man wants yer ter more'n just stand there! If yer ain't got
looks, yer gotta 'ave something else, ain't yer?" She looked Hester up
and down, making her judgment. "Ye're too skinny by 'alf, but yer've got
fire. Yer might make enough ter get by."

"Thank you," Hester said drily. "If I need to fall back on it, it'd better be soon."

The woman's face split into a wide grin. "Ye're right about that,
love. Yer in't got too many years left ter 'ang around."

"Did she use opium much?" Hester asked suddenly.

The woman was startled. "'Ow the 'ell do I know? But if she did,
what of it? P'raps she'd got pains. 'Aven't we all? She don' sell it, if that's
wot yer mean. Quiet, she was. I 'eard someone say she read books. If yer
want the truth, I think she were all right once, an' she fell on 'ard times.
I'd say 'er 'usband died, or went ter jail. Left 'er 'igh an' dry. Got by the
best way she could, poor cow. Until some bleedin' madman got to 'er. If
the rozzers were any good at all, they'd 'ave 'anged the bastard by now."

Squeaky nodded as if he understood perfectly.

Hester glared at him, and he smiled back, showing crooked teeth,
several of them dark with decay.

"Well, even if you ain't got nothin' ter do," the woman went on, "I
'ave." And without adding anything more, she swirled her skirt and
walked away, swaying invitingly.

HESTER RETURNED TO SEE Dr. Winfarthing and found him sitting
hunched up in his office, his expression one of deep gloom. He barely
managed a smile as he hauled himself out of his chair to welcome her.

"What did you find?" she said without preamble.

"Barely scratched the surface," he answered. "But enough to know
there's a devil of a lot going on underneath. This is a rats' nest, girl.

Hundreds of rats in it, including some very big, fat ones with sharp teeth. Lot of money in opium. I asked enough to get some idea of how they bring the raw stuff into the country, which I suppose we all know, if we thought about it. They cut it with God knows what. But it goes back a lot further than that. Back to the Opium Wars in China, '39 to '42, then '56 to '60. There's a whole lot of that you don't want to know about. Lot of death, lot of cheating, lot of profit."

She sat down at last. "I know some people eat opium whom you wouldn't necessarily expect to. Artists and writers we admire."

He shook his head, his lips pursed. "It isn't the eating of it that's the big, ugly thing you're going to uncover, girl. It's the nice, respectable fortunes that were built on deceit, and the deaths of a lot of soldiers sent in to fight a filthy war, not for honor but for money. And God knows how many Chinese. Tens of thousands of them. Nobody's going to like you for showing them that. It's all right for foreign savages to behave like savages, but we don't want to hear that we did it—that Englishmen were without honor."

"Those of us with any knowledge of history already know it," Hester said very quietly. Even though she meant it, it was still painful to admit. Perhaps that, as much as the senseless death, was what infuriated her still about the Crimea.

He nodded. "Those of us who've seen it, and had to try to clear it up, not the rest. Did you ever meet anyone else who wanted to learn about it anymore, because as sure as hell's on fire, I didn't."

"Is that what was in Dr. Lambourn's report?" she asked.

"I don't know, but it's what would be in mine, if I made one. Some of the things we did out there would shame the devil." He glared at her, angry because he was afraid for her. "Leave it alone, Hester. You can't save Lambourn, God rest him. And it didn't have anything to do with this poor woman's death. She's just one more incidental victim."

"Thank you." She smiled at him bleakly.

"Don't thank me!" he roared. "Just tell me you'll leave it alone!"

"I never make promises I don't mean to keep," she answered. "Well, hardly ever. And not to people I like."

He groaned, but knew her too well to argue.

8

THE NEWSPAPERS WERE STILL writing black headlines about the murder of Zenia Gadney and the police failure to solve the crime. Monk walked briskly past one paperboy after another, ignoring them as much as it was possible. But he could not close his ears to the singsong voices calling out the headlines in an attempt to lure people into buying the whole paper.

"'Terrible murder in Limehouse still unsolved,'" one gap-toothed boy cried out, thrusting the paper at Monk. "'Police doing nothing!'"

Monk shook his head and walked on, increasing his pace. He and his men were doing everything he could think of. Orme was busy in the Limehouse area. Others were questioning lightermen and dockworkers, anyone regularly on the water, asking if they had noticed anything strange, or someone acting in an unusual manner. Nothing had been revealed so far. No one else in Copenhagen Place or its surrounding streets admitted knowing Zenia Gadney. To them she was an interloper, someone who disturbed the safe ordinariness of their lives and brought police questioning them. Worse than that, by being so viciously murdered, she had frightened away prospective customers. Who wanted to look for a prostitute with the police hanging around? If there were a madman on the loose, it was wiser to curb your appetites, or satisfy them elsewhere. It was only a ferry crossing to Deptford and Rother-hithe, or there was always the possibility of going west to Wapping, or east to the Isle of Dogs.

For the prostitutes there was nowhere else. Every street corner or stretch of pavement already belonged to someone. Interlopers were run off, as a strange dog is driven from the territory of another pack.

The only people everyone agreed to blame for the inconvenience were the police. It was their job to catch such lunatics and hang them. No one, decent or indecent, was safe until they did.

Monk had just that day received a summons from Barclay Herne, junior government minister and brother-in-law of the late Joel Lambourn. He wished to speak to Monk on the matter of Zenia Gadney's death, and requested that Monk be good enough to call upon him in his offices so that they might speak discreetly. Monk was curious to know what Barclay Herne might have to say. Surely it could only concern Joel Lambourn. What other connection could Herne possibly have with Zenia Gadney?

Monk caught a hansom. After half an hour's slow progress through the wet, busy streets of government buildings, he alighted outside Herne's offices in Northumberland Avenue. He was shown into a comfortably furnished waiting room, then spent fifteen minutes standing impatiently, wondering what Herne wanted.

When he eventually appeared, Monk was surprised. He had expected someone more impressive, less genial—at least superficially. Herne was barely average height, stocky in build, and with a face that was, at first glance, very ordinary. Only when he closed the door behind himself and stepped forward, hand held out, did that impression alter. His smile changed his whole aspect. His teeth were strong and very white, and there was a bright intelligence in his eyes.

He shook Monk's hand with a grasp so firm it bordered on being painful. It was a tangible intimation of the man's power.

"Thank you," he said with every aspect of sincerity. "I appreciate your time. A little early for whisky." He shrugged. "Tea?"

"No, thank you." Monk would have loved a hot drink after the long, cold ride, but he did not want to waste time with formalities. "What can I do for you, Mr. Herne?"

Herne gestured to Monk to sit down in front of a good, brisk fire, and immediately placed himself in the green leather armchair opposite.

"Rather a disturbing situation," he said ruefully. "It has come to my notice that you are looking into the death of my late brother-in-law, somewhat further than has already been done. Is that really necessary? My wife puts on a very brave attitude, but as you may imagine, it is most unpleasant for her. Are you married, Mr. Monk?"

"Yes." Monk pictured Amity Herne's cool, totally composed face, and agreed with her husband that if she was indeed distressed, she hid it remarkably well. But he chose his words carefully. "And if my wife were to sustain such a loss, I would be proud of her if she could keep so dignified a composure."

Herne nodded. "I am, I am indeed. But I still would greatly prefer it if we might offer whatever assistance we can now, and have the matter settled as soon as possible. Poor Joel was . . ." He gave the slightest shrug and lowered his voice a little before continuing. ". . . less settled in his mind than others seem to believe. One does not tell every Tom, Dick, and Harry of one's family difficulties. It is natural to try to protect . . . you understand?"

"Of course." Monk was curious to know what it really was that Herne wanted. He found it hard to believe that it was merely to avoid Monk distressing his wife with further questions. Monk hadn't even considered returning to speak to Amity; he doubted she would say anything different from her original statement: that Dinah was naïve as to Lambourn's weaknesses, and perhaps the pressure of her idealistic view of him had been difficult for him to uphold.

Herne seemed to be finding it hard to choose the right words himself. When he finally looked up at Monk he had an expression of candor.

"Some of our relationships were a little difficult," he confided. "When my wife and I were first married we lived in Scotland. To be honest we hardly ever saw Joel and Dinah. My wife was not close to Lambourn. There were several years between them so they grew up separately."

Monk waited.

Herne was tense. His hands were rigid so that his knuckles shone white. "It is only recently that I myself began to appreciate that Joel was a far more complicated person than he appeared to be to his friends and admirers. Oh, he was certainly charming, in a very quiet way. He had a phenomenal memory and could be most entertaining with bits and pieces of unusual information." He smiled uncomfortably, as if it were some kind of apology. "And of course jokes. Not the sort you laugh loudly at, more quiet jests in amusement at the absurdity of life." He stopped again. "He was very easy to like."

Monk drew in a breath to ask him what this had to do with either Joel's or Zenia's deaths, but then changed his mind. He might learn more if he allowed Herne simply to ramble a little longer.

Then suddenly Herne looked very directly at Monk. "But he was not the man poor Dinah chose to see him as." He lowered his voice. "He had a lonely, much darker side," he confided. "I knew he had this woman he kept in Limehouse. He visited her frequently. I don't know exactly when, or how often. I'm sure you will understand that I preferred not to. That was some ugly corner of his nature I would honestly have been happier not to know about." He made a slight gesture of distaste, perhaps for what he imagined of Lambourn, or possibly only for the fact that he had unintentionally learned more of another man's private life than he wished to.

"How did you find out, Mr. Herne?" Monk asked.

Herne looked rueful. "It was something Dinah said, actually. I only realized the implication afterward. It was really rather embarrassing." He shifted uncomfortably. "Joel always seemed so . . . unimaginative— rather staid, in fact. I couldn't even picture him with a middle-aged whore in the backstreets of a place like West India Dock Road." He frowned. "But since the poor man died before this unfortunate creature was killed, he couldn't possibly have been implicated in the horror. I can only presume she became desperate for money, and because he had looked after her for so long, she had lost her sense of self-preservation and become careless."

Monk was inclined to think the same thing, but he waited for Herne to complete what he wanted to say.

"My family . . ." Herne seemed to be finding it difficult to ask. "I would appreciate it very much if you did not publicly make any connection between Joel and this woman. It is hard enough for Dinah that she has to be aware of his . . . weakness, and, God help us, deal with his professional failure and his suicide. And of course for my wife; they were not close, but he was still her brother. Please . . . don't make his connection with this woman public. It can have no bearing on her murder."

Monk did not have to weigh it in his mind. "If it has nothing to do with convicting her killer, then we would have no reason to mention Dr. Lambourn," he answered.

Herne smiled and appeared at last to relax. "Thank you. I . . . we are greatly obliged to you. It's been hard for all of us, but most especially Dinah. She is a . . . a very emotional woman." He rose to his feet and held out his hand. "Thank you," he repeated.

It was only after Monk had left the office and was in a hansom on his way back to the River Police Station at Wapping, stuck in heavy traffic where the Strand becomes Fleet Street, that he realized exactly what Barclay Herne had told him. Dinah Lambourn had admitted that she was aware that her husband had an interest in another woman, but she had deliberately chosen to know no more of it than that. She had told him that she did not know where he went, or the woman's name.

Herne had told Monk that he had learned of the affair from Dinah, and then gone on to speak not just of Limehouse in general, but quite specifically of the West India Dock Road, which was a matter of yards from where Zenia Gadney had lived. Unintentionally, he had betrayed that Dinah knew exactly where Zenia Gadney lived, and thus he had exposed Dinah's lie.

The thought was repulsive. He tried to shut it out of his mind, but his imagination raced, painting picture after picture. Dinah had loved Lambourn almost obsessively. She had thought too well of him, set him on a pedestal that perhaps no man could remain on. Everyone has weaknesses, things over which they stumble. To ignore that, or deny it, places a burden too heavy to carry from day to day.

Love accepts the scars and the blemishes as well as the beautiful. Sooner or later the weight of impossible expectation produces evasions: perhaps only small ones to begin with, then larger ones, as the burden grows heavier

The hansom was barely moving in the traffic. It was raining harder now. Monk could see the drops bouncing up from the road, and the water swirling in the gutters. Women's skirts were sodden. Men jostled one another, umbrellas held high.

Had Dinah felt as if Joel had betrayed her? She had made an idol of him, only to discover he had feet of material even less pure than clay. Had the murder of Zenia Gadney been her revenge on a fallen god?

Or maybe that was complete nonsense? He hoped so. He wanted profoundly to be wrong. He had liked Dinah, even admired her. But it was inescapable that he must now find out.

He leaned forward and redirected the driver to take him to the Britannia Bridge, where Commercial Road East crossed the Limehouse Cut and became West India Dock Road. He must visit the shops again: the general hardware store, the grocer, the baker, and all the houses along Copenhagen Place.

By the time he got there the rain had stopped. There were a dozen or more children playing hopscotch on the pavement when he turned the corner from Salmon Lane into Copenhagen Place. A couple of washerwomen were standing with huge bundles of laundry on their hips, talking to each other. A dog was rooting hopefully in a pile of rubbish. Two young women haggled with a man beside a barrow of vegetables. A youth with a cap on sideways strolled along the edge of the pavement, whistling. It was a music hall song, cheerful and well in tune.

Monk hated what he was about to do, but if he did not test the idea, the possibility of it would haunt him. He began with the washerwomen. How would Dinah have dressed, if she had come here looking for Zenia Gadney? Not fashionably. She might even have borrowed a maid's shawl to conceal the cut and quality of her own clothes. Who would she have approached, and what questions would she have asked?

"Excuse me," Monk said to the washerwomen.

"Yer found 'oo done 'er in yet, then?" one of them said aggressively. She had fair hair, bright where the pale winter sun shone on it, and a heavy but still handsome face.

He was startled that they knew who he was. He wore no kind of uniform. But perhaps he should have expected it. He had learned that he was memorable. His lean face, the cut of his clothes, the upright stance, and the manner of his walk marked him as unusual.

"Not yet," he answered. "But we're closer to knowing who might have seen something." That was an evasion of the truth, but it did not trouble him at all. "Did either of you observe a woman around this area, looking for Mrs. Gadney, maybe asking questions? She would be tall, dark hair, maybe dressed quite ordinarily, but with the air of a lady."

They both looked at him narrowly, then at each other.

"Ye're soused as an' 'erring," the older of the two replied. "An' 'oo like that'd be lookin' fer the likes of 'er, then?"

"Someone whose husband she had been taking money from," Monk replied without hesitation.

"There y'are, Lil!" the fair-haired woman said jubilantly. "Told yer, din't I? She weren't up ter no good. I knew that, an' all!"

Monk felt his throat tighten. He would so much rather have been wrong.

"You saw her then?" he asked. "A woman looking for Mrs. Gadney? Are you certain?"

"Nah! But I 'eard about 'er from Madge up the street." The woman jerked her head to indicate the direction. "She were in ol' Jenkins's shop when it 'appened."

"When what happened?" Monk said quickly.

"When that woman were 'ere askin' questions about 'er that got 'erself killed, o' course. In't that wot ye're asking? Tight as a newt, she were, so they say. Poor cow." She looked at Monk narrowly. "Yer sayin' as it were 'er wot cut that other poor mare ter pieces an' left 'er on the pier? Listen, she might 'a bin off 'er 'ead, but one woman don't do that ter another, I'm tellin' yer."

" 'E din't say as she did it!" her friend responded. "Yer got bleedin' cloth ears, an' all? 'E said as she might know 'oo did."

"Thank you," Monk cut in, holding his hand up to stop her continuing. "I'll go and ask at the grocer's shop." He turned and walked briskly across the street and up Copenhagen Place. It was drier here than in the center of the city, but the wind off the river was cold. He pulled his coat a little closer around him.

He stopped at the grocer's and went in. There were three people ahead of him in the queue at the counter, a man and two women. He waited patiently, listening to their conversation, but learned little from it except that they were angry and frightened, because a crime had happened that they did not understand, and no one had solved it.

"She were 'armless," one of the women said with rising outrage. Her white hair was pulled back so tight into its pins that the strain of it all but obliterated the lines around her eyes. "Kept 'erself to 'erself all the years she were 'ere. Dunno wot the world's comin' ter when a poor creature like that gets cut open like a side o' meat."

"A pity they done away wi' drawin' an' quarterin', I say," the old man nodded sagely. "Course, they gotter get the bastard first."

"Yer'll be wanting oatmeal, sugar, and a couple o' eggs as usual, Mr. Waters?" Jenkins interrupted from behind the counter.

"Don't act like yer don't care!" Mr. Waters was offended. "She got all 'er groceries right 'ere in this store!"

"It must be very distressing for you all." Monk intruded into the conversation before it got any more heated.

All three of them swung around to stare at him. "An' 'oo are you, then?" Jenkins asked suspiciously.

"'E's the police," the other woman said with contempt. "You'd forget yer own name next, you would." She faced Monk. "Well, wot yer 'ere for this time, then? Ter tell us yer give up?"

Monk smiled at her. "If I had given up, I'd be ashamed to come and tell you so," he answered. Then before she could think of a suitable response to that, he went on. "The day Zenia Gadney was killed, or possibly the day before, was there a tall, dark woman in here asking about her?"

Both women shook their heads, but Jenkins looked at Monk with a frown. "So what about it? Sad ter see an 'andsome woman crazed like that."

"Oh, but it's all right if it's some ugly ol' bitch like us, eh?" the women said furiously. "Well, if that's wot yer think, don' expect me ter come back 'ere fer me tea an' 'taters." She slammed a shilling and two pennies down on the counter. She swung a large bag in one hand, knocking it against the door on her way out and swearing savagely.

"I'm sorry," Monk apologized to Jenkins. "I didn't mean to lose you your customers."

"Don't worry about it, sir," Jenkins replied, wiping his hands on his apron. "She's always losin' 'er 'ead about something or another. She'll be back. Can't walk farther than this an' carry 'er potaters anyway. Now, what can I do for you?"

"Tell me about this woman who was so upset in here, the day before Zenia Gadney was killed."

"You don't want ter take any notice of 'er, sir. She weren't from round 'ere. She were beside 'erself, poor thing. Raving an' mumbling, she were. Talking to 'erself somethin' rotten. Reckon she were lost."

"Can you tell me what she looked like, and as much as you can remember of what she said?"

"Didn't make no sense," Jenkins said dubiously.

"That doesn't matter. First, what did she look like, please?"

Jenkins concentrated, clearly seeing her again in his mind's eye. "Tall, fer a woman," he began. "Dark 'air, what I could see of it. Not black, like. She 'ad this old shawl 'alf over 'er 'ead. Proper 'andsome face. Told yer, she didn't come from 'ere, nor sound like she did neither. But the poor soul were 'alf out of 'er head. Too much o' that opium, I'd say. Now an' again it don't do no 'arm. Fact, it 'elps when mebbe nothing else does. But get too much of it an' it addles yer brain. It's smokin' the stuff that really does yer in. I reckon as mebbe that's what she'd bin doing. Lot of it, down by the docks, there is. It's mostly them Chinese. Got it something wicked out east, so they say."

Monk clenched his teeth and took a deep breath. "What was she mumbling about? Do you remember?"

Jenkins was oblivious to his impatience.

"Sort of," he said thoughtfully. "Couldn't make a lot of sense of it, but mostly about suicide an' whores an' things like that. But like I said, she were out of 'er 'ead. She weren't no whore. I'd lay money on that." He shook his head. "She was quality, even if she were 'alf daft. She went on about lyin', an' betrayal an' all sorts. I dare say if she were come to 'er senses, she'd be a different person. Yer shouldn't take 'er word for nothin', sir. An' I don't reckon as she knew Mrs. Gadney anyway. Yer couldn't think o' two women less like each other."

"Did she ask for Mrs. Gadney? Ask where she lived, or if you knew her?"

"Not as I recall. Just came in for penny twists, raved on about people killin' theirselves, and then went out again."

"Thank you. You've been most helpful." Monk bought a tin of treacle, in the hope that Hester might make a treacle sponge pudding for him and Scuff, and then went back out into the street again.

He asked the same questions in the other shops along Copenhagen Place. It was the tobacconist who finally told him that a tall woman with dark hair had been in looking for Zenia Gadney; apparently when she had been in his shop, she had been more or less composed, and he had told her that Mrs. Gadney lived farther along, toward the middle of the lane.

Monk spoke to others as well. Two more people had seen the woman, but they could add nothing further. Monk had all he needed to oblige him to go and face Dinah Lambourn.

HE WAS LOATH TO do so, so he delayed the task and went back to the station at Wapping and checked that everything was under control there. Then he put on his coat and went out onto the dockside. The quickest way to Greenwich would be along the north bank of the river, where he was, and then a boat from Horse Ferry across to Greenwich Pier. It would take some time. Hopefully, the chill late afternoon breeze in his face and the familiar sounds of the river would help him compose in his mind what he would say.

He stood on the dockside and looked across the busy water, which was getting a little choppy on the turning tide. The sky was darkening already, the light fading. In a little over a fortnight it would be the winter solstice, and, shortly after, Christmas. He could put it off; go home now, leave Dinah one more evening unchallenged, in her own home with her daughters. Poor girls, they had already lost so much. He wondered if they had anyone else—apart from Amity Herne. He could not imagine Amity giving them any warmth or comfort in the desperate time that might so easily be ahead.

That was an uncharitable thought! Amity might be quite a decent woman. People sometimes stretched to meet a challenge and were braver and kinder than even they themselves thought possible.

There was a ferry coming in toward the Wapping Steps. It would drop off its passengers, and he could take it home. He would be there in half an hour, in his own kitchen, and—far more than that—amid the emotional safety that his home offered to him. He and Hester could talk about what to get Scuff for Christmas: what he would want, and what might overwhelm or embarrass him. Monk had thought of getting him a pocket watch. Scuff had just learned to tell the time instead of guessing it. Hester wanted to get him books. Would both be too much? Would Scuff feel as if he had to get them each something?

He walked over to the top step, ready to go down to the boat.

Then he changed his mind and walked briskly across the dock and back toward the road. He would do it now, face it and get it over.

It seemed too short an hour before he was sitting in the withdrawing room and Dinah, grave and tense, was upright in the chair opposite him. Her face was almost bloodless, and her hands were knotted in her lap, clutching each other uneasily, knuckles white.

Monk began straightaway, because he knew there was no good way to ask her the questions he needed to ask anyway.

"Mrs. Lambourn, when I was here before, you told me that you knew your husband had an affair with another woman, but that you knew nothing about her, including where she lived. Did I understand you correctly?"

"Of course, I know now," she replied.

"But did you know before she was killed?" he persisted.

"No. Joel and I didn't discuss it."

"How did you know of her?"

Her eyes flashed up at him, and then down again at her hands. "One does know such things, Mr. Monk," she said quietly. "Small matters of behavior, distractions, explanations that you had not asked for, evasion of certain subjects. Finally I asked him outright. He admitted it but gave me no details. I didn't want details. Surely you can understand that?"

He nodded gravely. "But you didn't have any idea where she lived?"

She shook her head very slightly. "That was one of the things I didn't wish to know."

"Or her name?"

Her chin jerked up a little.

"Of course not. I preferred her to be . . . gray, without form." Her voice was tight. She was trembling very slightly.

Monk was certain she was lying. "On the day before she was killed, where were you, Mrs. Lambourn?"

Her eyes wandered. "Where was I?"

"Yes, please."

She was silent for several seconds, breathing in and out slowly as if composing herself for some major decision whose consequences terrified her. There was a nerve twitching in her temple, close to the line of her dark hair.

He waited.

"I . . . I went to a soirée with a friend. We spent most of the day together," she said at last.

"Your friend's name?"

"Helena Moulton. Mrs. Wallace Moulton, I suppose. She . . ." Again the deep breath. "She lives on the Glebe, in Blackheath. Number four. Why does this matter, Mr. Monk?" Her hands were clenched so tight her knuckles shone when the skin was stretched. If she was not careful, her nails would leave bruises in the flesh.

"Thank you."

"Why?" she said again. Her voice was so dry it rasped in her throat. "Joel couldn't have had anything to do with her death."

"Could she have had anything to do with his?" he asked.

"You mean . . . ?" Suddenly her eyes were wide, filled with anger, glaring at him. "You mean did she threaten to tell someone of their affair? Was she that kind of woman? Was she greedy, conniving, and destructive? Joel wasn't a very good judge of character. He often thought better of people than they deserved."

Monk recalled their earlier conversation vividly. "But you said that you believed he was murdered, because his report on the opium use was correct," he pointed out. "That would have had nothing to do with Zenia Gadney, right?"

She leaned forward and covered her face with her hands. She remained frozen for several moments. The seconds ticked by on the clock above the fireplace. Her shoulders did not shake, nor did she make any sound.

He waited, acutely unhappy. He would have to go to Blackheath and find Helena Moulton. He hoped intensely that she would agree that Dinah had spent the day with her—and that there would be others who would substantiate it. But he did not expect there to be.

At last Dinah straightened up. "I don't know, Mr. Monk. All that matters to me is that Joel is dead, and now this woman is dead also. You will have to find out how these things happened, and who is answerable." She looked exhausted, too tired to even be frightened anymore.

He rose to his feet. "Thank you. I'm sorry to have had to trouble you again."

Now she met his eyes fully, without flinching. "You have to do your job, Mr. Monk, whatever it entails. We must know the truth."

Monk walked some distance before he found a hansom and rode the rest of the way to the Glebe, on the edge between the town and the open country toward the Health itself. It was not a long road, and he soon found the home of Mr. and Mrs. Wallace Moulton.

He had to wait a half an hour before Mrs. Moulton returned from visiting a friend and he was able to speak with her.

"Mrs. Lambourn?" she said with some surprise. She was a pleasant-looking woman, carefully dressed. Her expression now showed complete puzzlement.

"Yes. Did you see her on the twenty-third of November?"

"For goodness' sake, why? I shall have to look at my diary. Did something important happen?"

"I'm not certain." He tried to keep the impatience out of his voice. "Your help would possibly answer that question for me."

She was very grave. "I'm not certain that I am willing to discuss my movements with you, Mr. Monk, or more particularly, Mrs. Lambourn's movements. She is a friend of mine, and she has been through a great deal of tragedy lately. If something unpleasant has happened, something even further than the terrible loss of her husband, I am not prepared to add to it."

"I will find out either way, Mrs. Moulton," he told her gravely. "It will take me a great deal longer than if you simply tell me, and of course it will involve questioning a number of other people. However, if that is what I am obliged to do, then I will. I find it distasteful as well. I have some regard, and a great deal of sympathy for Mrs. Lambourn, but circumstances leave me no choice. Will you tell me, or must I ask as many other people as it requires in order to find out?"

She was clearly distressed, and angry. Her eyes were sharp and bright, and the color a high pink in her cheeks. "Wherever Mrs. Lambourn said she was, then I have no doubt that it is the truth," she answered icily.

Monk's mind raced for a moment.

"She said you were at an art exhibition in Lewisham all afternoon, then had tea and discussed the work until early evening," he lied. He felt terrible doing it, but he didn't see another way to discern the truth.

"Then you know where she was," Helena Moulton said with a tight smile. "Why are you bothering to question me about it?"

"So she was telling the truth?" he said very quietly, feeling a coldness creep up inside himself.

"Of course." Helena was pale.

"Would you be prepared to testify to that in court, before a judge, if it should be necessary?" He felt brutal.

She gulped, and remained silent.

He rose to his feet. "Of course you won't, because you were not with Mrs. Lambourn."

"Yes, I was," she whispered, but she was trembling.

"She said you were at a soirée, not an art exhibition, and not in Lewisham." He shook his head. "You are a good friend, Mrs. Moulton, but this is beyond your ability to help."

"I . . . I . . ." She clearly did not know what to say, and she was now also afraid for herself, and embarrassed.

"May I assume that you have no idea where Mrs. Lambourn was on that day?" he said more gently.

"Yes . . ." The word was almost inaudible, but she gave a tiny nod of her head.

"Thank you. There is no need to rise. The maid will show me out."

She remained where she was, shivering and huddled into herself.

HE RETURNED TO LOWER Park Street. He now had no alternative but to arrest Dinah Lambourn. He could not imagine her attacking Zenia Gadney with such ferocity, to have hit her hard enough to kill her, and then disemboweled her there on the pier; but Dinah was quite a tall woman, and statuesquely built. She could have had a strength born of rage and despair. Zenia Gadney was several inches shorter and perhaps fifteen pounds lighter. It was possible.

The thought of it made him feel sick, and yet he could not deny the evidence. She had been seen in the area looking for Zenia, in a state of mounting anger. She had lied about where she had been. She, like anyone else, would have carving knives in her kitchen. Perhaps in irony she had even used one of Joel's old open razors.

Above and beyond all else, she had a passionate and compulsive nature. Zenia Gadney had robbed her of what she held dearest, the center of her life financially and socially, but—far beyond that— emotionally. Lambourn's love for her, and her belief in him, was the foundation of her own identity. Zenia Gadney had taken that from her. It appeared her need for revenge had obliterated everything else.

As he stood at the front door of the house in Lower Park Street, Monk tried to imagine what his own life would be if Hester had turned to someone else, made love with another man, lain in his arms and talked with him, laughed with him, shared her thoughts and her dreams and the intimateness of physical love. Would he want to kill that man? Even to eviscerate him?

He might.

The maid answered his knock and showed him to the withdrawing room. He stood, waiting for Dinah to come. He thought of her daughters, Marianne and Adah. Who would look after them now? What future would lie ahead for them, their father a suicide, their mother hanged for the terrible murder of his mistress?

He never got used to tragedies. The edges were never blunted. They cut to the bone always.

Dinah came into the room, walking very upright, her head high, and her face ashen white, as if she knew why he had returned.

"You weren't with Mrs. Moulton," Monk said quietly. "She was willing to lie for you. When I told her you had said you were together at the art exhibition in Lewisham, she agreed." He shook his head slightly. "You were seen in Limehouse, specifically in Copenhagen Place, where Zenia Gadney lived, asking about her, and in a state close to hysteria." He stopped because of the look of amazement in her face, almost stunned disbelief. For an instant he doubted his own knowledge. Could it be she was insane and had no idea what she had done?

"I didn't kill her," she said hoarsely. "I never even met her! If . . . if I can't prove that, will they hang me?"

Should he lie? He wanted to. But the truth would be hideously clear soon enough. "Probably," he replied. "Unless there is some extraordinary mitigating circumstance. I'm . . . sorry. I have no choice but to arrest you."

She gulped, choked for breath, then swayed as if she might faint.

"I know . . . ," she whispered.

"Have you resident staff to care for your daughters until someone else can be informed? Perhaps Mrs. Herne?"

She gave a bitter little laugh, which ended in a sob. It was a moment before she could compose herself sufficiently to speak again.

"I have resident staff. You won't need to call Mrs. Herne. I am ready to come with you. I would be obliged if we might go now. I do not like good-byes."

"Then please call whoever you wish to pack nightclothes and toiletries for you," he instructed. "It will be better than having me follow you upstairs."

She colored faintly, then almost immediately was as ashen as before.

The woman who came in answer to the summons was elderly, gray-haired, and plump. She looked at Monk with loathing but accepted Dinah's instructions to pack a small case for her, and to look after Adah and Marianne for as long as should prove necessary. The boot boy was sent to fetch a hansom cab and bring it to the front door.

Monk and Dinah rode down to Greenwich Pier for the ferry crossing in the dark. Then at the other side they took another hansom for the long chilly ride, cramped together as they jolted over the cobbles.

It was only then that she spoke.

"There is one way in which you can help me, Mr. Monk, and I think perhaps you will not refuse," she said quietly.

"If I can." He wished profoundly that he could, but he feared she was beyond anything he could do.

"I shall require the best possible lawyer to fight for me," she said with surprising calm. "I did not kill Zenia Gadney, or anyone else. If there is someone who can help me to prove that, I believe it would be Sir Oliver Rathbone. I have heard that you know him. Is that true?"

He was startled. "Yes. I've known him for years. Do you wish me to ask him to see you?"

"Yes, please. I will pay anything I have—everything—if he will defend me. Will you please tell him so?"

"Yes, of course I will." He had no idea whether Rathbone would take the case or not. It seemed hopeless. One thing he was certain of, money would not be the issue. "I will ask him this evening, if he is at home."

She sighed very softly. "Thank you." She seemed at last to relax a little against the back of the seat, exhausted of all strength, physical and emotional.

9

OLIVER RATHBONE ARRIVED HOME after an ambivalent conclusion to the trial he had been fighting. It was a partial victory. His client had been convicted of a lesser charge, thus carrying a considerably lighter sentence. It was what he believed was warranted. The man was guilty of more, even though there were mitigating circumstances. Rathbone might have achieved a better result for him, but it would not have been just.

He ate dinner alone, and without enjoyment. He had at last faced the fact that he did not want Margaret back, and that was a bitter knowledge. There was no ease between them, and now, not even any kindness. What he wished was that it could all have been different.

Had he been lacking in tenderness or understanding? He had not seen it that way. He had sincerely defended Arthur Ballinger to the utmost of his ability. The man had been found guilty because he was guilty. At the end Ballinger himself had admitted it.

That memory took his mind back to the photographs again. His stomach knotted and he felt as if a shadow had passed over him. Perhaps the evening was colder than he had thought. The fire burned in the grate but its warmth did not reach him.

He was sitting wondering if there was any purpose in asking one of the servants to fill the coal box so he could stoke the fire high, when a much larger thought occurred to him. Should he remain in this house at all? It was a home for two people at least. And he felt another strangely sharp stab inside him. Had he wanted children? Had he assumed that naturally, eventually, there would be?

Thank God there had not been any. That loss would have been far more difficult to bear. Or perhaps Margaret would have stayed, for the child, and they would have lived in icy civility with each other. What death of all happiness!

Or would Margaret have been different with a child? Would it at last have separated her from the previous generation and turned her fierce protectiveness toward her family of the present and future?

Rathbone was still contemplating this when Ardmore came in and told him that Monk was in the hall.

Rathbone was surprisingly pleased to hear that, in spite of the fact that it was after ten o'clock.

"Send him in, Ardmore. And fetch the port, will you? I don't think he'll want brandy. Maybe a little cheese?"

"Yes, Sir Oliver." Ardmore went out with a half-concealed smile.

Monk came in a moment later and closed the door. He looked tired and unusually grim. His hair was wet from the rain outside and, from the way he looked at the fire, he was cold.

Rathbone felt his momentary happiness evaporate. He indicated the chair on the other side of the fireplace and sat down himself.

"Something is wrong?" he asked.

Monk eased himself into a comfortable position. "I arrested a woman today. She asked me to help her get a good lawyer to represent her. Specifically, she asked me to get you."

Rathbone's interest was piqued. "If you arrested her then I assume you believe her guilty? Of what, exactly?"

Monk's face tightened. "Killing then eviscerating the woman whose corpse we found on Limehouse Pier a couple of weeks ago."

Rathbone froze. He stared at Monk to see if he could possibly be serious. Nothing in his face suggested levity of any sort. Rathbone sat up a little straighter, his hands laced in front of him. "I think you'd better tell me in rather more detail, and from the beginning, please."

Monk related the discovery of the body near the pier, describing it only briefly. Even though he had seen the headlines, Rathbone still found his stomach churning. He was glad when Ardmore brought in the port, and Monk too was happy to take a glass. The rich warmth of it was comforting, even if nothing could wipe the images of that morning out of his mind, the winter sunrise over the river and the hideous discovery of Zenia's body.

"You identified her?" he asked, watching Monk's face.

"A small-time prostitute in her forties, with one client," Monk replied. "It seems he kept her with sufficient generosity that she could survive on that money alone. She lived very quietly, very modestly, in Copenhagen Place, which is in Limehouse just beyond the Britannia Bridge."

"Sounds more like a mistress than a prostitute," Rathbone commented. "Is it the wife you've arrested?" It seemed like the obvious conclusion.

"Widow," Monk corrected him.

Rathbone was startled. "Did the dead woman kill the husband?"

"Why on earth would she do that? His death left her destitute," Monk pointed out.

"A quarrel?" Rathbone suggested. "Someone giving her a better offer, but he wouldn't let her go? Who knows? Did he die of natural causes?"

"No. Suicide—apparently."

Rathbone leaned forward a little farther, more interested now. "Apparently? You doubt it? His wife killed him, do you think?"

"No, she adored him, and now she is without means as well, except what he left. Not quite sure what that is yet, but probably not inconsiderable." He stopped. "Actually it's far more complicated than that. I have no idea what lay ahead for him. He had suffered a degree of professional disgrace. His prospects may not have been as good as before. On the other hand, he was determined to fight his way back, according to his wife."

Rathbone was intrigued. The story was full of passion, violence, and total inconsistency.

"Monk, there's something missing in this, something crucial that you are not telling me. Stop playacting and give me all of it," he demanded.

"The man was Dr. Joel Lambourn," Monk replied.

Rathbone was stunned. He knew the name. The man had been highly respected. More than once he had even been called as an expert witness in court regarding certain medical facts. Rathbone could picture him in his mind: grave, softly spoken, but with the kind of authority that would not be shaken by even the most stringent cross-examination.

"*The* Joel Lambourn?" he said with a sudden and deep sadness.

"I don't think there are two," Monk answered. "It is his wife, Dinah, who appears to have killed Zenia Gadney in revenge for her part in Lambourn's suicide. Dinah is convinced that the research that was touted as a failure was actually totally correct, and that Lambourn was innocent of professional error. She also—" He stopped abruptly, his face tight with anxiety. "It would be better if you went to see her yourself rather than my telling you secondhand what she said, and its inconsistencies."

Rathbone sat back in his chair, turning the matter over in his mind, very aware of Monk watching him, and the urgency of his emotions.

"Why are you so anxious about this, that you come to me at this time in the evening, rather than waiting to visit my chambers tomorrow?" he asked thoughtfully. "What is it that intrigues you so much? Is it pity for a widow who has been betrayed, bereaved, and now awaits trial and almost certainly the hangman? Is she handsome? Brave? And these are not idle questions, so give me the truth!"

"Yes, she's handsome," Monk said with a wry smile. "But I suppose the truth is that I'm not sure she's guilty. The evidence is strong against her, and so far we've found no one else at all to suspect, not even a suggestion. There's no other crime on the records like it, solved or unsolved. Limehouse is certainly a rough area, but Zenia Gadney had lived there for years without coming to any harm."

"Years?"

"Fifteen or sixteen at least."

"Supported by Joel Lambourn the entire time?" Rathbone said sharply. "That's a lot of money going from his household to her. Did the wife know about this? I mean, clearly you think she did at the end, but when did she discover it?" Perhaps the case was not as commonplace, or as sordid, as it first appeared?

"Her story's inconsistent," Monk answered. "At first she denied her husband's affair, then said she knew of it, but not the woman's name or where she lived."

Rathbone raised his eyebrows. "And she didn't want to find out? A remarkably incurious woman! Most women would want, at the very least, to see the competition."

"It is hardly competition in the ordinary sense," Monk told him. "Dinah Lambourn is, in her own way, beautiful. But what is far more attractive than that, she is unusual, full of character, emotion, and a remarkable dignity. Zenia Gadney was pleasant, but as ordinary as a boiled potato."

"Staple diet for most," Rathbone observed drily. "Does the wife have children?"

"Two daughters. At present still at home with the housekeeper."

Rathbone sighed. More victims of the tragedy. "I suppose I can go and speak to this woman, see what her account is. What does she say?"

Monk bit his lip. "I think I'll leave her to tell you that."

"So bad?" Rathbone asked.

"Worse." Monk drank the last of his port. "Worse as to what she thinks happened to Lambourn, and who killed Zenia Gadney and why. But at least listen to her, Oliver. Make your own judgments. Don't go on mine."

Rathbone stood up also. "I would welcome a challenge, as long as it's not absurd."

"It might be absurd," Monk answered him. "It certainly might be."

THE NEXT MORNING WAS cold. Winter was closing in.

Rathbone heard the prison door clang shut, steel on stone, and looked at the woman who stood alone in the cell in front of him. There was a table in the center of the floor with a chair on either side; apart from that, nothing at all.

"I am Oliver Rathbone," he said. "Mr. Monk said you would like to see me." He looked at her with curiosity. Monk had said she was handsome, but that hardly conveyed the degree of individuality in her face or her bearing. She was tall, within an inch or two of Rathbone's own height, and the way she carried herself, even here in this wretched place, gave her a dignity that was remarkable, as Monk had claimed. She was not truly beautiful in a classical sense—maybe there was too much character in her face, the mouth too generous—but there was charm, a power, even a rare kind of balance that was unusually pleasing.

"Dinah Lambourn," she replied. "Thank you for coming so soon. I am afraid I am in very deep trouble and I need someone to speak for me."

He gestured for her to be seated, and when she was, he sat in the hard-backed wooden chair opposite her.

"Monk told me some of what has happened," he began. "Before I look further into it myself, or hear what the police have to say, I would like you to tell me yourself. I have heard your husband's name, and know his reputation for professional skill. I even heard him testify once, and could not shake him." He smiled very slightly to assure her that the memory was a pleasant one. "You do not need to fill in that background for me. Begin with what you know of Zenia Gadney, and how you learned it, and perhaps also with the last few weeks of your husband's life, as you think it may be relevant."

She nodded slowly, as if absorbing the information and deciding how to tell her story. "It is very relevant," she said in a low voice. "In fact it is the heart of all this. The government is planning to pass an act to regulate the labeling and the sale of opium, which is presently available just about anywhere. You can buy it at dozens of small shops on any high street. It is in scores of patent medicines, in whatever amount the manufacturer cares to use. There is no label on it to tell the user the strength, what it is mixed with, or what would be an appropriate dose, or a dangerous one." She stopped, searching his face to make certain he was following her.

"Your husband's part in this?" he prompted.

"Gathering research to make sure the bill passes. There is very heavy opposition to it, backed by those who make a fortune from selling opium as it is presently permitted," she replied.

"I see. Please go on."

She drew in a deep breath. "Joel worked very hard indeed to gather facts and figures, to verify them by checking and rechecking, visiting individual people and hearing stories. The more he learned, the worse the picture seemed to be. He came home almost in tears sometimes, having heard stories of babies dying. He was not a sentimental man, but so many unnecessary deaths distressed him profoundly." Her face reflected her grief of the memory. "None of it was malice; it was all complete ignorance of what they were using. Just ordinary people: frightened, hurting, perhaps exhausted and at their wits' end, desperate for anything to ease the pain—their own, or that of someone they loved."

Rathbone began to see the outline of something far larger than he had imagined, and he suddenly felt absurdly privileged by his own physical well-being.

"Dr. Lambourn presented a report to the government?" he deduced. It was obvious, apart from what Monk had told him, but he must be careful not to leap to conclusions, or to put words in her mouth.

"Yes. And they rejected it." Clearly she still found it difficult to acknowledge. Monk had been right in his estimate of her loyalty to her husband.

"On what grounds?"

"They said incompetence, extreme bias toward his own opinions." Her voice caught and she had trouble repeating the words. "They refused to accept his facts. He said it was because his facts disagreed with their financial interests."

"The financial interests of those in the government?" he clarified. He could see that she believed absolutely what she was saying, but it did sound as if it could well have been bias.

She heard the inflection in his voice. Her lips tightened almost imperceptibly. "The interests of the government commission, of which Sinden Bawtry is the head and my brother-in-law, Barclay Herne, is a member." Now her bitterness was undisguised. "There is a strong faction in the government who believe that the bill would make opium inaccessible to much of the poorer part of the general public, and as such be highly discriminatory. And of course to measure and label accurately would cost a lot. It would reduce profit on each bottle or packet sold. Fortunes rest on that. All part of the legacy of the Opium Wars."

She leaned forward earnestly, her hands on the scarred table between them. "There is a great deal we don't speak of, Sir Oliver, painful things that many people are desperate to conceal. No one likes to have to admit that things their country has done are shameful. Joel was as patriotic as the next person but he did not deny the truth, however horrible it is."

Rathbone was growing impatient. "What has this to do with the murder of Zenia Gadney, Mrs. Lambourn?"

She flinched. "Joel was found dead two months . . . two months before Mrs. Gadney was killed." She swallowed as if there were something in her throat close to choking her. "He was sitting alone on One Tree Hill in Greenwich Park. He had taken quite a heavy dose of opium, and . . ." Again she found it difficult to force the words through her lips. "His wrists were cut so he had bled to death. They said it was suicide, because of his professional failure regarding the report, and the government's rejection of it. They were very damning of his ability."

Now she was speaking more rapidly, as if to say it all and get it finished. "They said he was overemotional and incompetent. That he confused personal tragedies with genuine assessment of facts. They . . . they made him sound silly . . . amateurish." She blinked away tears but they spilled over her cheeks. "It hurt him badly, but he was not suicidal! I know you will think I am saying that, believing it, because I loved him, but it is true. He had every intention of fighting them and proving that he was right. He cared about the issue so much he would never have given up.

"In the last few days before his death I found him working in his study at three and four in the morning, white-faced with exhaustion. I told him to come to bed, I begged him, but he said that after what he had heard, his nightmares were worse than any weariness he could feel. Sir Oliver, he would never have killed himself. He would see it as a betrayal of those he was entrusted to help."

Rathbone hated having to ask her, but he could not defend her without knowing the truth—and, whatever the past, whatever the truth of the opium issue, defending her was what he was entrusted with. It would be better to hurt her now than in court, where the damage would be public and almost certainly irrecoverable.

"If that is so, then I agree," he said gently. "The whole issue of the report's rejection was no reason for him to have taken his own life. Which forces me to ask: What was the reason? The prosecution is possibly going to agree with you that he was willing to fight the government, but that his affair with Zenia Gadney came to the surface in some way. Perhaps she threatened to expose him—"

"That's absurd," she said sharply. "She hadn't done so in fifteen years. Why on earth would she have suddenly chosen that time? If he were dead, she would have no income and be driven to seek money on the streets, which is both difficult for a woman her age, and—as has been made tragically clear—dangerous!"

"They will argue that she did not realize that," he said, watching her face.

Her response was instant. "She was an ordinary woman, not a fool! She lived in Limehouse. She knew people there, shopped there, walked the streets to get wherever she was going," she said derisively. "Do you think she had no idea how dangerous it was?"

"Then she did not realize that Dr. Lambourn might later take his own life rather than pay her more money," he responded.

Dinah looked at him with contempt. "She had known him for over fifteen years, and she did not know that?" Before he could point out the inconsistency of her argument she hurried on. "Of course she didn't know that—because it isn't true. Joel never would have killed himself over money, and I don't believe she was so greedy or so stupid as to have threatened him. She was in her mid-forties! Where on earth was she going to find another man to support her and ask nothing in return?"

"Nothing?" he questioned, a little surprised at the assertion. Did she really believe that? Could she possibly?

She flushed and lowered her eyes. "A visit once a month," she said quietly. "I know the prosecution may not believe that but even if they don't, the logic still holds. Whatever he asked, or she gave, it would still

be easier than walking the streets of Limehouse looking for casual customers."

Rathbone thought for several moments. "They might suggest it was
you who were blackmailing him to stop seeing Zenia?"

"Or I would do what?" she said with a rare spark of humor. "Hu-
miliate myself by making his affair public? Don't be ridiculous."

He smiled back, reluctantly. He admired her courage. "Then why
did he kill himself, Mrs. Lambourn?"

"He didn't." All the light vanished from her face again and grief
washed through it. "They killed him, because he was going to fight for
his report to be accepted by the people, if not by the government. They
made it look like suicide, to discredit him once and for all."

It sounded hysterical, a wild fiction to save herself from the shame
and the rejection of her husband's suicide, and yet he could not dismiss
the idea out of hand.

"You truly think it was murder?"

"How many people have already drowned in the dark sea of the
opium trade?" she asked. "Killed in the Opium Wars, murdered in its
aftermath of trade and piracy, dead of overdoses? How many fortunes
made or lost?"

"And who killed Zenia Gadney?" Rathbone asked, suddenly more
serious. "Was her death really only coincidence?"

"That seems so unlikely as to be impossible." She shook her head.
The fear in her was palpable. He looked at her with intense sorrow. He
knew exactly why Monk had asked him to see her and to take the case.

"I wanted to do all I could to clear Joel's name," she continued. "But
his papers are all gone. Someone took everything and destroyed it. I
was still trying to see if there were any other doctors who had the courage and resources to take up the issue."

"Even believing that he was murdered to silence him?"

"He was right," she said simply.

Rathbone returned to the earlier question. "Who killed Zenia?" he
said again.

"They did," she answered. "Whoever killed Joel."

"Why? What did she know? Did she have copies of his report?"

Copenhagen Place would not have been an unreasonable place to hide such a thing, if it existed.

"Maybe." She said it as if it had not occurred to her until then.

He could not let her get by with an answer the prosecution would tear to pieces. "Then why not simply burgle her house? That would draw much less attention. Or if she had hidden it and would not tell them where, why not beat her? And if they did have to kill her, why would they do it so grotesquely? This murder is so appalling that it has shaken all London into fear. It is in every newspaper and on everyone's lips. It makes no sense, in conjunction with your theory."

Dinah Lambourn put her hands up to her face in a gesture of weariness. "It makes excellent sense, Sir Oliver. As you have observed, all London is drawn into the horror of it. When the evidence ties it back to me, and to Joel, and if I cannot prove my innocence, then I will be hanged and Joel will be completely disgraced, once and for all. His report will be forgotten, and the bill will die quietly. What is Zenia's life, or mine, worth in comparison to the millions of pounds made from opium, and the continued burial of the secrets and sins of the Opium Wars?"

Rathbone did not know how much he believed her. The more he listened to her, the more credible the possibility seemed that, at the very least, Lambourn's report had been suppressed because it did not say what those who commissioned it had wished it to.

But could such a failure have led to first Lambourn's murder, and then Zenia's, in order to silence *Dinah*? Unquestionably the wealth at stake was enough to provoke murder. But could there really be such a hideous conspiracy at play?

Or was he being made a complete fool of because she was a beautiful woman, and her loyalty to her husband had caught him in the uniquely vulnerable place of his own wound? Was he losing his sense of perspective?

Was Dinah Lambourn risking her own life to save her husband's reputation? Or was she insanely jealous, had killed Zenia out of uncontrollable resentment, and was now lying desperately in order to try to save herself from the rope?

He honestly had no idea.

He wanted to believe her. Or, more truthfully, he wanted to believe that a woman would have that kind of loyalty to her husband. That even after his death, and his fifteen-year attachment to another woman, she would fight for him, for her memories of him, and all that they had shared.

Her own wounded feelings meant nothing. Not once had she spoken against him, or for that matter against Zenia Gadney.

She was obviously laboring in the grip of extreme emotion. She faced hanging if she was found guilty. After the manner of Zenia's death, and the public furor, there could be no question of mercy.

"I will take your case, Mrs. Lambourn. I cannot promise success; all I can commit to is that I will do everything I can to defend you," he said gravely.

She smiled at him and the tears of relief spilled down her cheeks.

Rathbone shook her hand and then turned for the door. What on earth had he done?

10

Oᴜᴛsɪᴅᴇ ᴛʜᴇ ᴘʀɪsᴏɴ, Rᴀᴛʜʙᴏɴᴇ stood on the icy pavement in the rising wind, astonished at his own rashness. He was stepping out into quicksand, and already it was too late to retreat. He had given his word.

Then perhaps rather than going to his chambers this early, to think on what he had committed to, he should continue on eastward and cross the river at Wapping, so he could go on to Paradise Place and tell Monk that he had taken the case. He would need more information from him than the minimum he had been given yesterday. Monk had talked Rathbone into this. Now Rathbone needed to talk him into helping untangle the almighty mess.

He walked briskly out to the main thoroughfare and took a hansom, directing the driver to go all the way to Wapping Stairs. He sat back as they weaved through the morning traffic and he thought about what he needed to know. How on earth could he raise reasonable doubt in any jury's minds without another suspect? In the sane light of a winter day, would he even have reasonable doubt himself?

Was Dinah Lambourn a woman who loved her husband in spite of all his weaknesses, the betrayal with another woman over fifteen long years, and finally his preposterous story about the government's refusal to acknowledge the truth about the use and abuse of opium? Surely if Lambourn's facts were even close to the truth, about opium or any other medicine, there would be no way for the government to ignore that truth indefinitely. All Lambourn's death would've achieved was a delay; an act would be passed eventually. Was that delay worth anyone's death, let alone an insane murder like that of poor Zenia Gadney?

Did Dinah simply refuse to believe in failure, her husband's or her own? The most likely answer of all was that she was touched by insanity herself, a victim of the facts she refused to acknowledge. Perhaps to survive she needed any answer at all that left her make-believe world unbroken.

He rode all the way to the ferry deep in other people's delusions, his own credulity swaying one way, then the other. He was glad to get out and pay the driver, then stand for a few minutes in the wind, listening to the sounds of the water until the ferry came.

He went down the stone steps, which were wet and a little slippery. He was very careful. The last thing he wanted was a drenching in the cold, dirty water. He climbed into the boat and sat down.

The river was running fast as the tide ebbed. Choppy little waves made it a rough passage, but he welcomed the sharper wind in his face and the smell of salt and mud, and the scream of the gulls above.

At the far side he enjoyed the walk up from Princes Stairs, across Rotherhithe Street and on up in a few hundred yards and several turnings to Paradise Place.

Hester welcomed him at the door. She looked well. He found himself smiling, although he had nothing to celebrate. He had nothing even to feel certain about, except their friendship.

"Oliver!" she said with pleasure. "Come in. How are you?" They were not empty words. Her eyes searched his face, probing for truth. Did she see the disillusion in him, the loneliness he would very much rather have kept hidden?

"I'm well, thank you," he replied, stepping inside. "But Monk has given me a near-impossible case. I will need his help. Please don't tell me he has gone already?"

"He's here," she assured him. "Would you like to sit in the parlor where you can be private? I'll bring you tea, if you wish, or even break-fast. It must be cold on the river."

"Don't you know about the case already?" he said with surprise.

She allowed a tiny smile to touch her lips. "He said he had been obliged to arrest Dinah Lambourn. Is that the case you have taken? So soon? How . . . rash of you." Now the smile was larger. Long ago, when she had first realized that he was in love with her, she had teased him about his caution, that he was too careful and well ordered to be happy with anyone as impulsive as she was. At the time he had thought she was right. Perhaps at that time it had been true. It was not true now.

"What man who was not rash would even contemplate it?" he said wryly.

"Then come into the kitchen," she invited him, leading the way down the hall.

Inside, the room was warm, a little untidy, very much the center of the house. Clean linen lay on one of the benches; the kettle was sim-mering gently just off the top of the stove. Dried herbs hung from hooks on the ceiling, as well as a couple of strings of onions. Blue-rimmed china lay waiting to be put away on the dresser.

Monk was sitting at the kitchen table and rose as soon as he saw Rathbone. He was eating a bowl of porridge and milk, which was pre-sumably why it had been Hester who had answered the door.

Rathbone suddenly realized he had not eaten this morning and was extremely hungry.

Hester saw him glance at Monk's plate. Without asking, she ladled him a bowl of porridge as well and set a place for him at the other side of the table. She did not ask if he wanted tea, but simply poured it.

"Well?" Monk demanded, his own food forgotten until he knew if Rathbone had accepted the case.

Rathbone gave a tight little laugh and met Monk's cool gray eyes. He sat down opposite him. "If I hadn't taken it I would have sent you a message at Wapping, and perhaps one here as well," he said ruefully. "But I'm going to need your help."

"I'm not sure what I can do." In spite of his words, Monk looked pleased.

"Well, to begin with . . ." Rathbone paused and took a tiny sip of his tea. It was a little too hot to drink, but the fragrance of it soothed him. Hester was right; it had been cold on the river. He had not appreciated it at the time; He had been too eager to get to Monk. "Is there anything you can swear to that can help? What else could there be about Zenia that would mark her out as a victim?"

Monk thought for several moments before he replied. "I suppose the fact that she had never had any other clients but Lambourn, as far as anyone knows, would leave her in a very awkward position, in trying to seek out new business," he said slowly.

"She was in her mid-forties, at least," Rathbone added, pouring milk on his porridge and taking the first spoonful.

Monk looked surprised. "How do you know?"

"Dinah said so."

Monk's eyebrows rose. "Really? Did Lambourn tell her that?"

Rathbone felt a needle prick of anxiety. "Wasn't she?"

"Yes, she was, but how did Dinah know? She claims never to have met her," Monk pointed out.

"Then I suppose Lambourn did tell her. Seems an odd thing for them to have discussed."

Hester was watching him. "You don't know whether to believe her or not, do you?"

"No, I don't," he agreed. "I have a very strong feeling she's lying about something, if not in fact then in omission. I just don't think I believe she killed and gutted that poor woman."

"Well, Lambourn didn't," Monk said. "By the time she was killed he was long dead, poor soul."

"If Lambourn couldn't have, and Dinah didn't, who did?" Rathbone asked. "Is it really just a ghastly coincidence that she ran into some murderous madman just at the time that Dinah came looking for her?"

"Did she admit to looking for her?" Monk asked.

"No. But you told me she'd been identified."

"Only roughly. A woman answering her description," Monk corrected him. "Tall, dark hair, well-spoken, but beside herself with rage or panic or opium—whatever it was, it made her behave hysterically."

"Opium makes people dazed, slow, and clumsy," Hester put in, "but not violent. They're more likely to fall asleep than attack you."

Rathbone was puzzled. "Dinah says someone in the government may have killed both Lambourn and Zenia Gadney," he said, "in order to discredit Lambourn's report, and then to have Dinah charged with murder and hanged, so the whole subject could never be raised again." He turned from Monk to Hester and back again. "Is that possible, in your opinion?"

"Yes," Hester said at the same instant as Monk said, "No."

"Perhaps possible," Monk corrected himself. "At least that someone *could* do it, but it wouldn't work, and anyone but a fool would know that. It would bury Lambourn's report, certainly, but not the Pharmacy Act in total. It would delay it, that's all."

"That's what I thought," Rathbone agreed. He bit his lip. "Which leaves me where I was before; Zenia may have been clumsy and vulnerable because she was out of practice at finding business, and also poor in judgment as to who was dangerous and who was as safe." He looked at Monk. "Is there any part of Dinah's story that can be proved?"

"Nothing I can think of that would make a difference to her case," Monk answered. "No one even imagined she had anything to do with her husband's death. At first she denied knowing about Zenia Gadney, and then she admitted that she did know of her, and that is what her sister-in-law, Amity Herne, says also. And from her slip to you regarding Zenia's age, she has to have known at least a few details. After all, even the newspapers didn't print such facts, because we didn't know for certain ourselves. Zenia certainly looked quite well for her age, to judge as far as you can by body and texture of skin, hair and so on. Her teeth were very good. One of the people I spoke to put her younger."

Rathbone remembered Dinah's face, and her words denying the possibility of Zenia having misjudged Joel Lambourn's nature. He frowned, setting down his spoon for a moment. "Dinah said that Joel and Zenia had known each other for fifteen years."

Monk looked up sharply. "How the devil did she know that?"

"I'm wondering myself." Rathbone was feeling more and more uncomfortable. He had never been confident in his judgment of women, and even less so since Margaret. Had he made a complete fool of himself in taking this case?

Hester touched him very lightly on the shoulder. "She's likely to lie, or at least evade, regarding her husband's affair with this woman," she observed. "She must feel like a complete fool. She'll try to find a way to explain it to herself, and not admit she was duped. I think anyone would, in her place."

"Do you believe her?" Rathbone asked, turning a little to look at her as she walked around behind him.

"I believe her regarding Lambourn's research," she replied, sitting down in the third chair at the table. "I spoke to an excellent doctor I know, and he agreed with it entirely. He said the number of deaths among children is appalling, and could very easily be mitigated with a degree of control and more information made available to the public."

"So Lambourn was essentially right in fact, even if his evidence was anecdotal?" Rathbone said.

"Yes. But I expect the anecdotes would only be added to give emotional power. He would have to have provided figures as well," she answered.

Rathbone turned to Monk again. "Exactly what concrete evidence is there on his suicide? Mrs. Lambourn is claiming that it was murder. Is that possible?"

Monk frowned. "I don't know. They say he was found on One Tree Hill in Greenwich Park with his wrists cut, and there was a considerable amount of opium in his body. I asked if there was a container of any sort found on his person, or near him, for liquid to swallow powder, or to dissolve it, or whatever form the opium was in. I got no answer, but I didn't speak to the person who found him. Frankly, I thought Mrs. Lambourn was simply refusing to believe it was suicide because it was too painful for her."

"That may be the case," Rathbone agreed. "But we need to know for certain."

Monk smiled. "We?"

Rathbone felt suddenly uncomfortably alone again. "You think she's guilty?"

"I don't know," Monk admitted. "I suppose I think she seems to be, and I wish very much that I were wrong. I accept 'we.'"

"Have you the authority to look into it?" That was Rathbone's real concern. He could attempt to do that legwork himself, in his standing as Dinah's lawyer, but he knew Monk's skills were far superior to his, both in seeking evidence and in knowing exactly what to look for and how to interpret it.

Monk debated within himself before replying. "I doubt it, but I can try. It's not my territory and, as far as I can see, it has no connection with the river. It's already been ruled a suicide, so it is not an unsolved crime. In fact it's hardly a crime at all, except in the eyes of the Church, and even that leaves some latitude, depending on the sanity of the person concerned."

"Opium?" Hester suggested.

They both looked at her.

"Well, a lot of opium comes in through the Port of London, a great deal of which ends up in Limehouse," she pointed out. "You could say that his report is of concern to you, particularly its reliability." She grimaced very slightly. "You could stretch the facts a little, and say that you heard he had information that would be of great use to you regarding smuggling?" She made it a question. "Couldn't you? It's probably true."

Monk smiled at Hester, amusement bright in his eyes. "I could," he agreed. "In fact I will. All in the interest of catching smugglers on the river, of course." He looked back at Rathbone again. "The evidence of suicide was noticeably missing when I asked before. And nobody seems to be able to account for his report. It's been condemned, but never shown."

"What about Lambourn and Zenia Gadney?" Rathbone continued, feeling that at last there was something he could work with. "Why did he go to her in the first place? It's all rather sordid, but her death itself is extremely violent. It suggests a hatred of an acutely personal nature, a sexual hatred. How hard have you looked for a lunatic who hates women in general, or prostitutes in particular?"

"Very hard," Monk replied. "And Orme is an extremely good man. There's been no crime at all that's comparable. The last prostitute murder we had was strangulation, and before that a beating that went too far. It was over money, and we got him. There was one knifing, but it was a single stab wound that was closer to the heart than the killer intended. It was her pimp and we got him, too."

Rathbone pursed his lips. "In your experience, have you ever seen a crime of this specific brutality toward a woman committed by another woman?"

"A few slashings by rival prostitutes," Monk answered. "They can be pretty vicious, but no, not one that cut open the stomach and hauled out the intestines and the womb. It's hard to imagine one woman doing that to another. That's partly why the outrage against Dinah is going to be so intense. Honestly, I have no idea how you're going to defend her. The public wants to see someone hanged. Have you looked at the newspapers?"

Rathbone winced. "Of course I have. You can hardly miss the headlines, even if you wish to. Doesn't that make it all the more important that we should be absolutely certain we have the right person?"

"Come on!" Monk said wearily. "You know as well as I do that most people don't think like that. They'd say of course they want the right person, but they already believe they have her, and to question that only makes them more defensive. For them to admit that she might not be the perpetrator means they have prosecuted an innocent victim, the police are incompetent, and worst of all, the guilty party is still out there and they are all still in danger. Nobody wants to hear all that."

Rathbone could not argue. He changed the subject. "I also need to know everything I can about Dinah Lambourn, so the prosecution doesn't spring any ugly surprises on me in court. If she is guilty, then it means she has a temper that's close to insanity. This can't be the first time she's shown at least signs of it. I'll find out what I can, but I need help."

Hester looked at him, puzzled and concerned. "And if she is guilty, Oliver, do you want to save her? That would mean she didn't just kill Zenia Gadney; she mutilated her in an obscene way. That's not excusable. There could be no provocation that would justify her actions."

"Hester—"

She overrode him. "And if she gets away with it, what will happen to the next person who crosses her? Added to that, if she is judged to be innocent, then the police will continue to look for someone else, someone who doesn't exist. The people of Limehouse will walk in fear, suspecting each other, because they think the murderer was never caught."

"You think she did it?" he asked bluntly.

"I have no idea," she answered. "But you need to decide now what you are going to do if you find she did."

He had not considered it. He had come to Paradise Place in the heat of emotion, ready for an almost impossible crusade. In part because it would absorb his mind and energy so he would, for a while, be oblivious to his own pain.

He turned to Monk. "Hester is right. I have to be sure. Will you help me?"

"You want me to help prove the innocence of the woman I've just arrested for one of the most brutal murders I've ever investigated?" Monk said softly.

"Are you certain she's guilty?" Rathbone asked.

"No. You know I'm not certain. But there's no other reasonable suspect."

"Then I just want you to help me find the truth, so we can be certain, one way or the other," Rathbone told him. He looked at Hester.

"William?" Hester in turn looked at Monk.

Monk shrugged, and conceded. "Yes, of course I will. I have to."

11

When Rathbone had left, Hester and Monk sat opposite each other across the table in the familiar, comfortable kitchen.

"What are you going to do to help him? What is there you can find?" Hester said it as an affirmation rather than a question.

"I don't know," Monk said. "I've already exhausted just about every inquiry I can. There's no other crime like it, no enmities that were more than a mere squabble in the grocery shop, or a difference of opinion on the weather. The poor woman didn't seem to have any relationships except with Lambourn. I can't even find what she did with her time, except the odd kindnesses for other people, small sewing jobs and the like. She read books, newspapers . . ."

"Could she have known something about someone, by accident?" Hester suggested. "Overheard something?"

"She could." He wanted to be able to agree, to offer some hope that was honest. "But there's nothing whatever to suggest it. She was almost an invisible woman. And even if she did know something, it could hardly account for the mutilation."

"No family?" she persisted, desperation creeping into her voice. There was a stray wisp of hair falling across her forehead, but she did not seem to be aware of it.

"No one knows of any," he replied. "We have looked."

"But you will keep on trying?" she urged.

"For Dinah Lambourn, or for Rathbone?" he asked with a slight smile.

She shrugged almost imperceptibly, her eyes suddenly soft. "Partly just for the truth, but mostly for Oliver," she admitted.

"Hester . . ." He reached over and smoothed the wisp of hair back. "I can't do very much. Lambourn's suicide really isn't part of my responsibility. I can ask a few questions, but I can't justify spending much time on it. They'll tell me Lambourn's report was destroyed, and I can't prove it wasn't. They might even say Lambourn destroyed it himself, because he knew it was flawed. They don't have to prove it's true."

"It's a long time since you had a holiday." She looked very directly at him. "You could take one now. I'll help. I've already asked Dr. Winfarthing to see what sort of information he can find, just to compare it with what Joel Lambourn said."

A chill of fear ran through him like a cold hand on his skin. "Hester, if anyone really did kill Lambourn for that report, then you could have put Winfarthing at risk, too!"

"I warned him," she said quickly, a very slight flush in her cheeks. "So you think there really is a danger, then?"

She had maneuvered him into admitting it not only to her, but possibly more important, to himself. Perhaps that was what she had intended.

"There might be," he conceded. "If what Dinah says about the report is correct, then there are very large amounts of money involved, and perhaps reputations as well. But that doesn't mean Lambourn was murdered, or that Dinah is innocent."

"I'll help you," she said again.

Monk was happy to yield to her, at least for now. There was something in Dinah's courage that moved him, in spite of the fact that logic told him she was guilty. Certainly he was unsatisfied with the idea that Lambourn's suicide was caused by his sense of despair over the rejection of his report. His career until then, and the way his colleagues had spoken of him, said that he was made of stronger material than that.

And he felt sufficiently conscious of his own happiness to want very much indeed to do anything he could to distract Rathbone from the bitterness of his current disillusions.

H E CHECKED IN AT the police station at Wapping first, and then went to the records department of the Metropolitan Police to learn who had been in charge of the investigation into the death of Joel Lambourn. He already knew that because of Lambourn's importance, the case had not been restricted to the local police in Greenwich.

He was startled to find that it had been Superintendent Runcorn, who at the beginning of his career had been Monk's friend and partner, later his rival, and later still his superior. It was a matter of opinion as to whether Runcorn had dismissed Monk from the force first, or Monk had given his resignation. Either way, it had been a heated and unpleasant exchange. They had parted anything but friends. Monk had spent the next few years as an agent of inquiry available for private hire. It had given him a great deal of freedom as to which cases to take and which to refuse, at least in theory. In practice it had been very hard work, and financially precarious.

During that time he and Runcorn had crossed paths on a few occasions. Surprisingly, they had each gained a better respect for the other. Later Monk had realized that his own manner had been unnecessarily aggressive, often intolerant. Being in command of men in the River Police had taught him how damaging to a force even one obstructive subordinate can be. It had profoundly changed his view of Runcorn.

When Monk had no longer been his junior in rank, but still constantly a step in front of him in reasoning, Runcorn had developed an appreciation of his skill, and a surprising respect for his courage and the handicap that his amnesia had once been.

Monk had never regained his memory of the majority of his life before the accident. There were occasional flashes, but no complete pictures. The separate pieces did not join up into a whole. Now it no longer haunted him. He did not fear strangers as he once had, always aware that they could know him, and he had no idea whether they were friends or enemies.

Facing Runcorn again was in some ways more awkward than dealing with someone who did not know him, but at least no explanations would be necessary. For all the enmity they had had over the years, they were past the times of misjudgment.

Monk went to the Blackheath Police Station, where Runcorn was superintendent, and gave his name and rank to the sergeant at the desk.

"The matter is very grave," he told the man. "It concerns a death in the recent past about which I have further information. Superintendent Runcorn should know immediately."

Monk was taken up to Runcorn's office within ten minutes. He went in and was not surprised to see how tidy it was. Runcorn had always been neat to the point of obsession, quite unlike Monk. Now there were even more books than before, but there were also very pleasant pictures on the walls, pastoral landscapes that gave an instant feeling of ease. That was new; quite out of character for the man he had known. There was a vase on a space on one of the shelves, a blue and white painted thing of great delicacy. It might not have been worth much in a monetary sense, but it was lovely, its shape the simplest of curves.

Runcorn himself stood up and came forward, offering his hand. He was a big man, tall and thickening in the middle as he grew older. He seemed grayer than Monk remembered him, but there was none of the inner anger that used to mar his expression. He was smiling. He took Monk's hand briefly.

"Sit down," he invited, indicating the chair opposite the desk. "Culpepper said something about information on a recent death?"

Monk had been preparing himself for a completely different reception—in a sense, almost a different man. He was caught off balance. But if he hesitated now it would put him at a disadvantage—something he could not afford with Runcorn—and it would also make him appear less than honest.

"I've been working on a particularly brutal murder, a woman whose body was found on Limehouse Pier nearly a fortnight ago," he began, accepting the proffered seat.

Runcorn's expression changed instantly into one of revulsion and something that looked like genuine distress.

Again Monk was surprised. He had rarely seen such sensitivity in

Runcorn in the past. Only once did he recall a sudden wave of pity, at a graveside. Perhaps that was the moment he had felt the first real warmth toward Runcorn, an appreciation for the man beneath the maneuvering and the aggression.

"Thought you'd arrested someone for that," Runcorn said quietly.

"I have. Newspapers haven't got hold of it yet, but it can't be long."

Runcorn was puzzled. "What has that to do with me?"

Monk took a deep breath. "Dinah Lambourn."

"What?" Runcorn shook his head in denial, as if he believed it could not be possible.

"Dinah Lambourn," Monk repeated.

"What about her?" Runcorn still did not understand.

"All the evidence says that it was she who murdered the woman by the river. Her name was Zenia Gadney."

Runcorn was stunned. "That's ridiculous. How would Dr. Lambourn's widow even know a middle-aged prostitute in Limehouse, still less care about her?" He was not angry, just incredulous.

Monk felt conscious of the absurdity as he answered. "Joel Lambourn was having an affair with Zenia Gadney, over the last fifteen years or so," he explained. "He visited her at least once a month and gave her money. He was her sole support."

"I don't believe it," Runcorn said simply. "But if he was, then when he died, she would be left with nothing. She probably went out on the streets again and ran into a bloody lunatic. Isn't that the obvious answer?"

"Yes," Monk agreed. "Except that we can't find any trace of a lunatic. A man who would kill like that doesn't commit just one crime with nothing before or after it. You know that as well as I do. He strikes with a few random acts of violence, which get worse as he gets away with it and his insanity increases."

"Someone just passing through?" Runcorn suggested. "A sailor. You can't find him because he doesn't belong there. His earlier crimes happened somewhere else."

"I wish that were the answer." Monk meant it. "This was terribly personal, Runcorn. I saw the body. A man insane enough to do that leaves traces. Other people up and down the river would have heard of him. Even a foreign sailor would have been seen by someone. Don't you think we've looked for that?"

"Dinah Lambourn would have been seen, too," Runcorn retorted instantly.

"She was . . . by several people. She made quite a scene trying to find Zenia Gadney. People in the shops at the time remember her; so does the shopkeeper."

Runcorn looked stunned. He shook his head. "You want me to testify to something about her? I can't. She seemed to me one of the sanest women I ever met: a woman who loved her husband very deeply indeed and was shattered by his death. She could hardly believe it." His own face was crumpled with grief. "I can't imagine how anyone deals with the fact that the person they love most in the world, and trust, has taken their own life, without even letting you know they were hurting, let alone wanted to die."

"Neither can I." Monk refused to think of Hester. "Imagine what it did to her to hear of his fifteen-year affair with a middle-aged prostitute in Limehouse."

"Did she know?"

"Yes. Her sister-in-law says she did, and Mrs. Lambourn herself admits it."

Runcorn sat motionless in his chair as if part of him were paralyzed.

"Does she admit to killing this . . . Gadney woman?"

"No. She says she didn't. She swore she was with a friend of hers at the time, a Mrs. Moulton, at a soirée . . ."

"There you are!" Runcorn was overcome with relief. Finally he relaxed, easing himself in the chair.

"And Mrs. Moulton says she was at an art exhibition, and under pressure, she admitted that Dinah Lambourn was not with her," Monk told him.

Runcorn stiffened again.

"What do you want from me? I can't testify against her. I know nothing about her but her dignity and her grief." Runcorn met his eyes with frankness, and quite open pity.

This was the most difficult part. Monk found himself uncharacteristically reluctant to offend Runcorn. It surprised him. In the past he had been happy enough actually to seek opportunities to quarrel.

"She begged me to ask Oliver Rathbone to defend her," he began a little awkwardly. "He agreed. Now he's asked me to help him. I don't know if he thinks she could be innocent. Nothing in the facts so far supports that. But the whole issue is full of ambiguities, and it matters far more than merely finding justice for Zenia Gadney."

"'Merely'?" Runcorn asked, his eyes wide.

Monk did not defend his choice of word. "It is a matter of justice for Dinah Lambourn also, and for Joel Lambourn, and it pertains to the whole question of the Pharmacy Act."

Runcorn frowned. "Joel Lambourn? I don't understand."

Monk plunged in. "Dinah says he did not take his own life. She says he was murdered because of the report he made on the sale of opium and the damage it does, particularly the deaths of so many babies and small children. She also claims that the same people who murdered him murdered Zenia Gadney, and framed her, in order to prevent her from raising questions about Lambourn's death, or raising too much interest in his report. The report itself seems to have vanished—all copies, and his notes."

Runcorn did not interrupt, just sat forward a little in his chair, tense and puzzled, his body slightly hunched.

"And, of course, if his affair with Zenia Gadney were to become public, which obviously it will," Monk went on, "then that provides an excellent motive for his suicide." He watched Runcorn's face and saw the revulsion, the anger, and then the pity. This was a Runcorn he did not know, a man of gentleness he had never seen before. Was it because Runcorn was utterly changed, or because something in Monk had changed, and he only now perceived what had always been there?

Runcorn thought for several moments before he answered. When he did, his words were carefully chosen, and his eyes did not leave Monk's face.

"I wasn't really happy about the verdict on Lambourn," he admitted. "I wanted to look into it more carefully, tie up all the ends." He shook his head very slightly. "Not that I could see any other answer. He was up there by himself, sitting on the ground half tumbled over, his back against that tree. His wrists were slashed and covered in blood. His clothes, too. I don't even know why I wanted to look any further, just that it's such a hell of a thing for a man with a family to do to himself." He stopped, as if he needed a space to weigh what he meant to say next.

Monk thought of Runcorn's solitary life and wondered if he had imagination of what it would be like to have a woman love him as Dinah Lambourn had loved her husband.

"The government was eager to close the whole thing as quickly as possible," Runcorn continued. "They said his work was sensitive just at that time, and that he had made some very serious errors of judgment. I don't know what errors precisely." He looked puzzled. "We know he was collecting facts about the import and sale of opium, where it is available, and the way it is labeled, that type of thing. So what error in judgment could he have made?"

"I don't know," Monk admitted. "Perhaps as to how much proof he needed before he accepted a story? Whether records of doctors were accurate or properly kept? Did they say?"

"No." Runcorn shook his head. "Just that for the sake of his reputation, and his family, it needed to be closed as quickly and with as little fuss as possible. I wasn't happy about the details, but I could understand their wishes, and the need for compassion. Are you saying there is a strong chance it is themselves they were protecting, not Dinah and her daughters?"

"I'm not sure." Monk was compelled to be honest. "And I need to be. Did you ever see this report of his?"

"No. They searched his house. I never did. The report would be government property anyway. They commissioned it and paid him for it. They said it was based on his emotional beliefs rather than scientific gathering of evidence, but that's all: no details." Runcorn sighed. "They suggested, without actually saying so, that it was evidence of the imbalance of his mind. They didn't seem surprised that he had taken his life."

"Did they mention his affair with Zenia Gadney?"

Runcorn shook his head. "No. They said he was eccentric in several ways. Perhaps that is what they were hinting at." He looked grieved. "What do you want to do?"

"Go over the evidence again," Monk answered. "See if there is any sense at all in Dinah Lambourn's story, anything that raises questions, or doesn't fit in with suicide, or the theory that he was losing his mind or was emotionally unbalanced."

"Are you sure he had an affair with this woman in Limehouse?" Runcorn's face still mirrored his disbelief. Surely Runcorn had been a policeman long enough to know that such an apparent aberration was in fact quite possible?

"Dinah denied knowing about it at first, but then she admitted it," Monk repeated.

"It doesn't sound right," Runcorn insisted, looking at the desk, then up at Monk again. "I'd welcome the chance to go over it all piece by piece, to see if there were mistakes, but we'll have to do it very quietly and unofficially, or we'll get the government stepping in and blocking us." There was no hesitation in his voice, no doubt.

Monk was not surprised, except at his courage. The Runcorn he had known in the past would never have defied authority, either openly or behind their backs. He held out his hand.

Runcorn took it. There was no need to give words to their agreement.

"I can get away at four o'clock," Runcorn said. "Come to my house at five." He wrote down an address in Blackheath on a small piece of paper. "I'll tell you everything I know, and we can plan where to begin."

MONK WAS EVEN MORE surprised when he arrived at the house at five minutes before five that afternoon. It was a respectable family home on a quiet street. The garden was well kept and from the outside it had an air of comfort, even permanence. He would never have associated it with Runcorn.

He was completely taken aback when the door was opened not by Runcorn, or a maid, but by Melisande Ewart, the beautiful widow he and Runcorn had questioned as a witness in a murder some time ago.

She had insisted on speaking to them when her overbearing brother had tried, unsuccessfully, to prevent her. Monk had realized at the time that Runcorn had admired her far more than he wished to, and that he would have been mortified with embarrassment had she guessed it. Indeed it was too sensitive even for Monk to have made any remark at the time. If the situation had been less delicate, Monk would have joked about it. Runcorn was the man least likely to fall in love, let alone with a woman of superior social rank and position, even though she had had no money and was dependent upon a brother she found oppressive.

Now she smiled at him with slight amusement and perhaps the faintest flush of color in her cheeks. "Good afternoon, Mr. Monk. How nice to see you again. Please do come in. Perhaps you would like a cup of tea while you discuss the case?"

He found his tongue and thanked her, accepting the offer of tea. A few moments later he was sitting with Runcorn in a small but charming parlor with all the signs of well-accustomed domestic peace. There were pictures on the walls; a vase of flowers on the sideboard, arranged with some artistry; and a sewing box stacked neatly in one corner. The books on the shelf were different sizes, chosen for content, not effect.

Monk found himself smiling. He could not remark on the difference he saw in Runcorn, the inner peace that had eluded the man all his life until now, and was suddenly so overwhelmingly present. Monk could not remember their early friendship, or how it had changed to become so bitter. That was part of his lost past. But he had found enough evidence of his own abrasiveness, the quickness of his tongue, the searing wit, the physical grace, the ease of manner Runcorn could never emulate. Runcorn was awkward, had always been in Monk's shadow and increasingly lacking in self-confidence with each social failure.

Yet now none of it mattered. Runcorn had taken the past off like an ill-fitting coat and let it drop. Monk was far happier for him than he would have imagined possible. He would probably never know how Runcorn had wooed and won Melisande, who was beautiful, more gracious and infinitely more polished than he. It did not matter.

Runcorn shifted a little self-consciously, as if guessing his thoughts.

"These are my notes from the case." He offered Monk a sheaf of neatly written papers.

"Thank you." Monk took them and read. Melisande brought the tea, with hot buttered toast and small cakes. She left again with only a word of consideration, no attempt to intrude. They both started to eat.

Runcorn waited patiently in silence until Monk had finished reading and looked up.

"You saw Lambourn where they found him?" he said to Runcorn.

"Yes," Runcorn agreed. "At least, that's what the police said."

Monk caught the hesitation. "You doubt it? Why?"

Runcorn spoke slowly, as if re-creating the scene in his mind. "He sat a little to one side, as if he had lost his balance. His back was against the trunk of the tree, his hands beside him, and his head lolling to one side."

"Isn't that what you'd expect?" Monk said with a whisper of doubt. "Why do you think they might have moved him?"

"I thought at first it was just that he didn't look comfortable." Runcorn was picking words with uncharacteristic care. "I haven't seen many suicides, but those who have done it relatively painlessly looked . . . comfortable. Why would you sit so awkwardly for such a thing?"

"Perhaps he fell awkwardly as he was dying?" Monk suggested. "As you said, as his strength ebbed away, he lost his balance."

"His wrists and forearms were covered with blood," Runcorn went on, his face puckered a little at the memory. "And there was some on the front of the thighs of his trousers, but more on the ground." He looked up at Monk, his eyes steady. "The ground was soaked with blood. But there was no knife. They said he must have thrown it somewhere, or even staggered and dropped it. But there was no trail of blood leading to where he lay. And why on earth would you throw a knife away after you've cut your wrists? Would you even have the strength to hold it, let alone hurl it far enough so no one would find it?"

Monk tried to imagine it, and could not.

"What time was it?" Monk asked.

"Early morning, about nine when I got there."

"Then whoever found him must have found him very early," Monk observed. "About seven or so. What were they doing in the park on One Tree Hill at seven on an October morning?"

"Out walking," Runcorn answered. "Exercise. Hadn't slept well and went out to clear his head before the day, so he told us."

"Could he have taken the knife?"

"Not unless he's a lunatic," Runcorn said drily. "Come on, Monk! What sane man steals the knife a suicide has just slashed his wrists with? He was a respectable middle-aged man. Worked for the government at something, I don't remember what, but he told us."

"For the government?" Monk said quickly.

Runcorn caught his meaning. "I looked for blood leading to the place. There wasn't any. And the knife wasn't ever found. I looked for it everywhere within a hundred yards of where he was. It's open ground. If it had been there we'd have seen it."

"An animal carried it away?" Monk suggested without conviction.

Runcorn curved his lips down. "Taking the knife but not disturbing the blood on the corpse? You're slipping, Monk!"

"So who took the knife, and why? What were they doing there? Was it at the time of this death, or afterward?" Monk gave words to what he knew they were both thinking. "That's where we begin. There's a lot to follow."

"I'll go back over the witnesses," Runcorn offered, his face bleak. "We'll have to be discreet, as if we're trying to close any door in the face of this new trial. The government men were . . ." He shrugged. "I assumed they were strong-arming me out of compassion for the Lambourns, but now it's beginning to look as if that was their guise for keeping me out."

Monk nodded. "I'm taking some time off. It's overdue. Give me the names and addresses of witnesses, and I'll say exactly that: I'm trying to make certain that Dinah Lambourn's defense doesn't open anything up." He was not certain if the excuse would be believed, or if he would be fobbed off with the same stories, but he could think of no better way to start their investigation.

He bade Runcorn farewell, and thanked Melisande. Then he went out into the darkness of the quiet street, prepared to walk until he could find a hansom to take him home, although in truth it was not so very far.

MONK BEGAN THE NEXT morning by telling Orme what he was about to do. Then he went back to Greenwich determined to speak directly to the people who had seen Lambourn's body. He had not previously been given the name of the man who had discovered Lambourn, but now he had it from Runcorn. This time he would also persist until he found Constable Watkins, the first policeman on the scene, wherever he was on duty, or off.

He would also go back to Dr. Wembley. He could say it was to protect his own case against any accusations Dinah might make. He half acknowledged to himself that he hoped to find that Lambourn had not committed suicide, either over his failure to produce a report that the government would be obliged to accept, or because his personal life had crumbled to pieces around him. But that acknowledgment annoyed him—he was made of better fiber than to be so sentimental.

He walked briskly in the pale sun, but it was nearly ten o'clock when he reached the quiet, well-ordered office of Mr. Edgar Petherton, just off Trafalgar Road. This was the man who had found Lambourn's body, and Monk introduced himself and explained to him immediately who he was.

Petherton was in his fifties, but already silver-haired. His eyes were unexpectedly dark, his features showing both humor and intelligence. He invited Monk to sit down in one of the two handsome, leather-upholstered chairs by the fire, while he took the other.

"What can I do for you, sir?" he asked. His voice was quiet and full of curiosity. "Are you sure it is me you wish to speak to, and not my brother? He works in the Naval College. His name is Eustace. We are occasionally confused."

"I might be in error," Monk admitted. "Was it you or your brother who was walking your dog very early in the morning about two and a half months ago, and found the body of Dr. Joel Lambourn?"

Petherton made no attempt to disguise his pain at the memory.

"No error, I'm afraid. It was I. I have already answered all the questions the police asked me at the time, and those of a gentleman from the government. Home Office, I believe."

"I'm sure." Monk now gave the explanation he had been planning. "I dare say you read of the very violent murder of the poor woman found on Limehouse Pier, at the beginning of this month?"

Petherton's shock was transparent. "What on earth has that to do with Lambourn's death? The poor man was gone long before then."

"Lambourn's widow has been arrested and charged with killing the woman," Monk replied. "We are trying to keep down the public hysteria, in order to have some semblance of a fair trial."

"Mrs. Lambourn?" Petherton shook his head in disbelief. "That's preposterous! Why, in God's name, would she do such a thing? You have to have made some hideous mistake."

"Possibly," Monk conceded, wondering if it really was possible, or if he was just mouthing conciliatory words. "Because of the nature of her likely defense, I am rechecking all the facts so they cannot be twisted to support a story that is not the truth."

"And if it is the truth?" Petherton challenged.

"Then she may well be innocent, and we shall have to look further to find whoever butchered this poor woman," Monk answered.

Petherton frowned. "Can you really believe any woman, never mind a civilized and dignified lady, could do such a thing to another of her own sex?" He looked at Monk as if he were some curiosity of nature, not quite human.

"I've been in the police for a long time," Monk told him. "I can believe a lot of things that I wouldn't have ten or fifteen years ago. Even so, I find it hard to believe it of Mrs. Lambourn. That is why I need to learn the details of the case for myself. Perhaps another explanation is possible."

"I can only say what I have already said." Petherton looked as if he wished very much that he could find the imagination or the courage to lie.

"Do you often walk your dog so early?" Monk asked him. "And is it usually to Greenwich Park that you go?"

"Quite often in the park," Petherton answered. "Far more often than not. But to answer your first question, no, not usually so early. I could not sleep and it was a fine morning. I went a good hour earlier than is my habit."

"And you usually go to One Tree Hill?"

"Not often. I wanted to think that day. A certain personal matter had been causing me concern. I wasn't really paying much attention to where I was. I only became aware of my surroundings when Paddy—my dog—started to bark, and I was afraid he was bothering someone. It was an unusual sort of sound, as if he were troubled by something. Which of course he was. I ran after him and found him bristling, hackles raised, staring at a man sitting with his legs out in front of him, his back against the tree. He had lolled a bit to one side, as if he were asleep. Except, of course, he was dead."

"Was that immediately clear?" Monk asked quickly.

"I . . ." Petherton hesitated, clearly thinking back with some distress. "I rather think I did know it right away. His face was very pale indeed, almost bloodless. He looked dreadful. And of course his wrists were scarlet with blood, and there was blood on the ground. I didn't touch him at first. I was rather . . . shaken. When I gathered my wits I bent down and touched his forearm, above the slashes—"

"His sleeve was rolled up?" Monk interrupted.

"Yes. Yes, his shirtsleeve was quite high."

"Jacket?"

"I . . . as I recall he had no jacket on. No, he definitely was in a shirt only. I touched his arm and the flesh was cold. His eyes were sunken. I could find no pulse at his neck. I didn't try his wrists—the blood." He took a deep breath. "And I didn't want to . . . to leave a mark where I . . . I admit, I didn't want to put my fingers in his blood. It seemed not only repellent, but intrusive. The poor man had already reached the lowest hell a living person can. His despair should be treated with . . . with some decency."

Monk nodded. "Certainly that was the right decision. And where was the knife?"

Petherton blinked. "I didn't see it."

"Wouldn't it have been close to his hand?" Monk continued almost casually.

"It wasn't." Petherton shook his head. "Perhaps he had moved, and it was half under him?"

"Hidden by his jacket?"

"I told you, he didn't have a jacket, just a shirt," Petherton repeated.

"Were you wearing a jacket?"

"Yes, of course I was. It was October and early in the morning. Barely light. It was cold." Petherton was now frowning and clearly troubled. "It doesn't make complete sense, does it? Would a man intent on committing suicide walk half a mile, or more, in the cold, before dawn? I never thought of that before." He chewed on his lip. "He must have been half out of his mind with despair over something . . . and yet he looked so peaceful, as if he had just sat down there against the tree and let it happen." He stopped there and looked at Monk.

"He had taken a lot of opium," Monk said, watching Petherton's face. "That was probably why he looked so calm. He was probably all but insensible from it."

"Then how did he climb that hill?" Petherton said immediately. "Or is that what you are saying—he took it once he got up there? Then he'd still want a jacket while he was walking. I wonder what happened to it."

"Did you see the footprints of anyone else there?" Monk asked.

Petherton looked surprised. "I didn't look. It was very early daylight. Only just enough to see by. You think someone was with him?"

"Well, as you point out, he surely would have worn a jacket, unless he went out early the previous evening, and didn't intend to go so far," Monk replied.

Petherton saw what he was leading to. "Or meant only to go for a short walk, and return home? As I remember, it was actually a very mild evening the previous day. It turned cold overnight. I was outside myself. Pottering in the garden until quite late."

Monk changed his direction of approach.

"Did you see anything that could have had opium in it, or water to take a powder with?"

"No. I didn't search his pockets!" Again the faint revulsion showed in his face.

"But could he have had a bottle or a vial in them?" Monk persisted.

"Not a bottle. A small vial in a trouser pocket, I suppose. What are you saying happened?"

"I don't know, Mr. Petherton. That is what I need to find out. But for your own sake as well as that of the investigation, please do not discuss this with anyone. God knows, we have had sufficient tragedy already." He said the words easily, but he felt a weight in his mind as he struggled to think of any answer but suicide, and failed to find one, in spite of the small anomalies they had just discussed. Was it even conceivable that Dinah had gone out after him, followed him up a path that perhaps he often took? Was it she who had found him and removed the knife and the vial to make the death seem more suspicious than it was?

Monk thanked Petherton again, and left him looking just as confused as he himself felt. He walked out into the fresh air and turned west toward the police station to look for Constable Watkins.

THAT PROVED TO BE far more difficult than he had expected. First he was mistakenly directed to Deptford, an awkward journey that took him over an hour, only to discover that Constable Watkins had already left and gone back to Greenwich.

In Greenwich, Watkins was involved in an investigation and Monk was told to wait. After an hour he asked again. With profuse apologies, the sergeant told him that Watkins had been called away and would not return until the following day. And no, he did not know where Watkins lived.

It was too late to find Dr. Wembley again, and until Monk had confirmed Petherton's story with Watkins, there was no purpose anyway. He had wasted a whole day, and he went home angry and more sure than ever that he was being intentionally misled, although whether to protect Lambourn or to hide some secret, he did not know.

He was at the police station in Greenwich the next morning by half-past seven, much to the dismay of the sergeant at the desk. He waited there until Constable Watkins came in. The sergeant attempted to block

Monk, but there was an old woman in a drab cotton dress and torn shawl who was distracting his attention, complaining about a stray dog.

"Constable Watkins?" Monk said loudly and clearly.

The young man turned around to face him. "Yes, sir. Morning, sir. Do I know you?" There was absolutely no guile in his wide blue eyes.

"No, Constable, you don't," Monk replied with a smile. "I'm Commander Monk of the Thames River Police at Wapping. I need to ask you very briefly about an incident that was reported to you, just to verify certain facts. Perhaps you'd like a cup of tea to start the day? And a sandwich?"

"Not necessary, sir, but . . . yes, thank you, sir," Watkins accepted, trying to hide his relish at the thought of a fresh sandwich, and not making much of a success of it.

The sergeant shifted his weight from one foot to the other, drawing in his breath sharply. Monk knew in that moment that he had had orders not to let this happen.

"Constable!" he said sharply. "Mr. Monk—Constable Watkins has duties, sir. He can't just . . ." He looked at Monk's face and his voice wavered.

"Have you received orders from your senior officers that you are not to permit Constable Watkins to cooperate with the River Police in *any* investigation, Sergeant?" Monk asked very clearly. "Or with one investigation in particular?" He said it with an edge to his voice that would have cut glass.

The sergeant stammered a denial, but it was obvious to Monk, at least, that that was exactly what he had been told to do.

Monk went with Watkins to the peddler at the next street corner from the station and bought hot tea and sandwiches from him. It was a cold morning, the light only just broadening. A stiff wind blew up from the river, cutting through the wool of coats and scarves.

Watkins was uncomfortable after the exchange between Monk and the sergeant, but he recognized that he had no choice but to cooperate. Monk knew he would have to do what he could to protect the man from the ire of his senior officers.

"Constable, you were first on the scene of Dr. Joel Lambourn's death, up on One Tree Hill, about two and a half months ago."

"Yes, sir."

"I spoke to Mr. Petherton, the man who had found Dr. Lambourn. He was most helpful. But you understand I also need a more trained eye to tell me if his observations were correct."

"Yes, sir." Constable Watkins sipped his tea but his eyes never left Monk's.

Monk repeated precisely what Petherton had told him, including the shirt, the rolled-up sleeves, the blood on Lambourn's wrists, and the ground, both in shape and degree.

"Was there anything else?" he asked. "Please think carefully, Constable. It would not do to have to add anything later. It would look gravely incompetent, at the very best. At the worst it would seem like deliberate dishonesty. We can't have that. A man's death is very serious, any man's. Dr. Lambourn's importance to the government makes his even more so. Have I just described it as you witnessed it? Bring it to your mind, your recollection as a police officer, and then answer me."

Watkins closed his eyes, was silent for several moments, then opened them and looked at Monk. "Yes, sir, that's perfectly correct."

"So Mr. Petherton is both accurate and honest?"

"Yes, sir."

"He didn't leave anything out? Nothing else to see at all? Footprints? Marks of a scuffle? Anything?"

"No, sir, nothing at all."

"Thank you, Constable. That's all. I must not hold you from your duties any longer. You may tell your sergeant I am obliged to him, and that all you did was confirm your own recollection, as you gave it before. You never added anything or changed anything. You can swear to that in court, if need be."

Watkins gave a sigh of relief and the color flooded up his face. "Thank you, sir."

MONK SAW DR. WEMBLEY again, but the doctor could not recall or add anything significant; he simply repeated the evidence he had given before.

Later that evening, in fine, cold rain, Monk went to Runcorn's house and told him the results of his day.

They were in the small, comfortable parlor with the fire burning well and fresh tea and slices of cold chicken pie on the table between them. This time Melisande was also there. She had initially come in simply to bring the food, but Runcorn had signaled her to stay. Considering the firmness with which he did so, Monk did not raise any objection. He did not want to distress her. He had little knowledge of her personality, except for the courage with which she had insisted on giving evidence during the case they were investigating when they had first met her. He glanced at her face once or twice, and saw only pity and intense concentration.

"That's the same as they told me," Runcorn said when Monk had finished his account. "I went back over the instructions I was given." He looked faintly embarrassed. "I thought at the time they were to protect Lambourn's reputation, and his widow's feelings. Now they look a good deal more as if they were to conceal the truth. And if someone went to that much trouble to conceal the truth, we have to wonder why."

"He walked up there in his shirtsleeves," Monk reasoned aloud. "Or else he had a jacket and someone removed it. But Petherton said that the evening before was mild. He was out in his own garden. The night turned cold and by morning it was definitely chill. It looks as if Lambourn might not have intended to go so far, and definitely not to stay there."

Runcorn nodded but did not interrupt.

"Petherton was certain there was no knife, and nothing with which to carry liquid—unless it was very small indeed, and in his trouser pocket. Watkins agreed, except he was also certain there was nothing in Lambourn's pocket. I don't think they are both lying. And you can't swallow those things dry."

"Someone else was there, then, and at best took away the knife and whatever Lambourn drank the opium with after Lambourn had committed suicide," Runcorn concluded. "Or at worst, Mrs. Lambourn was right, and he was murdered." He looked at Monk, his brow furrowed.

"And they expected to be able to conceal it," Monk thought aloud. "But they were careless. No knife. Nothing to take the opium with. No jacket to walk that distance on an October evening. Was that because they were caught by surprise and had to act quickly, without preparation? Or was it just arrogance?"

Melisande spoke for the first time. "It seems very stupid," she said slowly. "The knife should have been there beside him. He should've been wearing a jacket. Why didn't they leave those items there, even if it was murder?" She looked from one to the other of them. "Was there something in the knife or the vial that would have made it obvious who the killer was?"

No one needed to answer her. Runcorn looked at Monk intently. "Is it really possible someone killed him to silence him, and bury his report? But why?"

Monk answered, his voice a little hoarse. "Yes, I am beginning to think it is possible. And there has to be a reason, something deeper than just wanting to delay his report, and thus the bill."

They sat without speaking for several moments. The fire burned gently in the hearth, creating a warm light and a soft, whispering sound.

"What are you going to do?" Melisande said at last, looking at Runcorn. There was fear both in her voice and in her face.

Runcorn looked back at her. Monk had never before seen emotion so naked or so intensely readable in his face. It was as if he and Melisande were alone in the room. He cared intensely what she thought of him, yet he knew he must make the decision alone.

Monk barely drew breath, willing Runcorn to give the right answer.

Ash collapsed in the fireplace and the coals settled.

"If we do nothing, we become part of this . . . conspiracy, if there is one," Runcorn said at last. "I'm sorry, but we must learn the truth. If Lambourn was murdered then we must find out and prove who did it, and who concealed it, and why." He put out his hand gently and touched hers. "It may be very dangerous."

She smiled at him, her eyes bright with fear and pride. "I know."

Monk had no need to answer her question for himself. He had come to Runcorn in the first place because this was precisely what he feared. He admitted to himself now that if he had truly believed Dinah Lambourn was guilty, he would not have taken the case to Rathbone, let alone pursue the evidence himself.

Runcorn stood up and stoked the fire.

They talked a little more, making further plans to report to Rathbone. Then Monk said good night and went outside into the dark street. The rain had stopped, but it was colder. At this late hour, it might be difficult to get a cab. He would have a better chance if he went toward the lamplit streets in the center of the town, where there were clubs and theaters with other people looking for transport, perhaps even a place where cabbies ate, or waited for fares.

He was walking briskly along the footpath, seeing clearly enough in the light from a few lamps at front doors, when he was aware of someone behind him. His first thought was that it might be another person hoping to find a hansom. Their steps were quiet and they seemed to be moving very rapidly. He stepped aside to let them pass. It was at that instant that he felt the blow on his shoulder, so hard it numbed his whole left arm. Had it landed on his head it would have knocked him senseless.

His assailant regained his balance and swung again, but this time Monk lashed out with his foot hard and high. He caught the man in the groin and the attacker pitched forward. Monk raised his knee under the man's jaw as he collapsed, snapping his head back so hard Monk was afraid he might have broken his neck. The cudgel clattered away across the pavement and into the gutter.

Monk's own left arm was still paralyzed.

The man rolled over, gasping, struggling to get up onto his hands and knees.

Relieved that he was alive, Monk kicked him again, hard, in the lower chest where it would knock the wind out of him.

The man coughed and retched.

Monk straightened up. There was another figure on the far side of the street, not running toward him, as someone might do if he meant to help, but moving easily, carrying something in his right hand.

Monk swung round. There was a dense shadow ahead of him also, maybe the bulk of someone half concealed in a doorway. He turned on his heel, his left arm still leaden and throbbing with pain. He ran as fast as he could back the way he had come.

He was less than a mile from Runcorn's house. He did not know how many more attackers there might be. He was in an area he did not know, and it was close to midnight. His left arm was useless.

He did not go directly back to Runcorn's house. Whoever was after him would expect that. He kept to the broader streets, going as fast as he could, around the back, through other people's gardens, and eventually arrived at Runcorn's kitchen door, searching desperately for a sign someone was still up.

He saw nothing. He crouched in the back garden, trying to be invisible among rows of vegetables and a potting shed. He could not imagine Runcorn doing anything as domestic as gardening. He smiled to himself, in spite of the fact he was beginning to shiver. He could not stay out here. For one thing it was extremely cold and beginning to rain again, and he was hurt. More urgently, sooner or later they would think to look here for him. Very likely, it would be sooner!

He picked up a handful of small stones out of the earth and tossed them at one of the upstairs windows.

Silence.

He tried again, harder.

This time the window opened and Runcorn put his head out, just visible as a greater darkness against the night sky.

Monk stood up slowly. "They're after us," he said in the dark. "I was attacked."

The window closed and a moment later the back door opened and Runcorn came out, a jacket over his nightshirt. He said nothing but helped Monk in, locked the back door again, and shot the bolt home, then looked Monk up and down.

"Well, at least we know we're right," he said drily. "We've got a spare room. Are you bleeding?"

"No, just can't move my arm."

"I'll fetch you a clean nightshirt, and a stiff whisky."

Monk smiled. "Thank you."

Runcorn stood still for a moment. "Like the way it used to be, isn't it?" he said with a bleak satisfaction. "Only better."

12

OLIVER RATHBONE SAT IN his chamber in the Old Bailey trying to compose his mind to begin the defense of Dinah Lambourn, on the charge of murdering Zenia Gadney. It was the highest-profile case he had appeared in for some time. He had already received considerable criticism for taking it at all. Of course, the remarks had been oblique. Everyone knew that all accused persons had the right to be represented in court, whoever they were and whatever they were charged with, regardless of the certainty of their guilt. That was the law.

Personal revulsion was an entirely different matter. Acknowledging mentally that somebody should represent her was quite different from actually doing it yourself.

"Not a wise move, Rathbone," one of his friends had said, shaking his head and pursing his mouth. "Should have let some hungry young beggar take it, one who has nothing to lose."

Rathbone had been stung. "Is that who you'd want defending your wife?" he had demanded.

"My wife wouldn't hack a prostitute to death and dump her in the river!" the man had replied with heat.

"Maybe Dinah Lambourn didn't, either," Rathbone had responded, wishing he had not been foolish enough to allow himself to be drawn into this discussion.

Perhaps the man had been right. As he sat in the big, comfortable chair and looked at the papers spread out on his desk, he wondered if he had been rash. Had he accepted this as a sort of suicide of his own, a self-inflicted punishment for failing Margaret?

The newspapers were running banner headlines about the trial. Some journalists had described Dinah as a woman consumed with hatred toward her own sex. They suggested she was insanely jealous, given to delusions, and had driven Lambourn to suicide with her possessiveness.

Another paper's editorial pointed out that if the jury sanctioned a woman committing a hideous and depraved murder because her husband had resorted to a prostitute, there was no end to the slaughter that that might lead to.

And of course Rathbone had heard some women siding with Dinah, saying that men who consorted with prostitutes defiled the marriage bed, not only by the betrayal of their vows, but more immediately and physically by the possibility of returning to a loyal wife and bringing to her the diseases of the whorehouse, and thus of course to their children. And what about the money such men lavished on their own appetites, even while in the act of denying their wives household necessities?

To some men whom Rathbone had overheard at his club, Dinah was the ultimate victim. To others she was the symbol of a hysterical woman seeking to limit all a man's freedoms and to pursue his every move.

One writer had presented her as the heroine for all betrayed wives, for all women used, mocked, and then cast aside. The heat of emotion carried away reason like jetsam on a flood tide.

Rathbone had prepared everything he could for this defense, but he knew he had far too little. Neither Monk nor Orme had been able to find a witness who had seen Zenia with a man near the time of her death. The one person she had been seen with, briefly on the road by the river, was unquestionably a woman. He had no wish to draw attention to that.

All he really had to defend Dinah with was her past loyalties to both Lambourn and Zenia, and her character. He would rather not put her on the witness stand to testify. She was too vulnerable to ridicule because of her belief in a conspiracy for which there was no proof. But in the end he might have to.

Monk and Hester were still searching for solid evidence, as was Runcorn, when he had the chance. The trouble was, everything they had found so far could just as easily be interpreted as evidence of her guilt as her innocence.

The attack on Monk had been brutal, and well organized, but there was nothing to tie it to the murder of Zenia Gadney. There had been no second attack, so far.

Rathbone was glad when the clerk came to interrupt his growing sense of panic and call him to the courtroom. The trial was about to begin.

All the usual preliminaries were gone through. It was a ritual to which Rathbone hardly needed to pay attention. He looked up at the dock, where Dinah sat between two wardens, high above the floor of the court. On the left-hand wall, under the window, were jury benches, and ahead was the great chair in which the judge sat, resplendent in his scarlet robes and full-bottomed wig.

Rathbone studied them one by one while the voices droned on. Dinah Lambourn looked beautiful in her fear. Her eyes were wide, her skin desperately pale. Her thick, dark hair was pulled back a little severely to reveal the bones of her cheeks and brow, the perfect balance of her features, her generous, vulnerable mouth. He wondered if that would tell against her, or for her. Would the jury admire her dignity, or misunderstand it for arrogance? There was no way of knowing.

The judge was Grover Pendock, a man Rathbone had known for years, but never well. His wife was an invalid and he preferred to remain away from the social events to which she could not come. Was that in deference to her, or an admirable excuse to avoid a duty in which he had no pleasure? He had two sons. The elder, Hadley Pendock, was a sportsman of some distinction, and the judge was extremely proud of him. The younger one was more studious, it was said, and had yet to make his mark.

Rathbone looked up at Grover Pendock now and saw the general gravity of his rather large face, with its powerful jaw and thin mouth. This was a very public trial. He must know all eyes would be on his conduct of it, expecting—indeed, requiring—a swift and completely decisive conclusion. The sooner it was ended, the sooner the hysteria would die down and the newspapers turn their attention to something else. There must be no doubt as to justice being done, with no unseemly behavior, and above all, absolutely no chance for an appeal.

The counsel for the prosecution looked grim and full of confidence, as if already spoiling for a fight. Sorley Coniston was in his late forties, taller than Rathbone and heavier, smooth-faced. When he smiled there was a slight gap between his front teeth, which was not unattractive. He was almost handsome. Only a certain arrogance in his manner spoiled the grace with which he rose to call his first witness.

As expected, it was Sergeant Orme of the Thames River Police. Rathbone had known it would be, but it still puzzled him that Coniston had chosen Orme rather than Monk.

Then, as he saw Orme's solid, calm face when he climbed the steps to the witness box and looked down at the floor of the court, he understood the choice. Monk was lean and elegant. He couldn't help it. The air of command was in him: in the angle of his head, the bones of his face, his remarkable eyes. Orme was ordinary. No one would think him devious or overly clever. He would be believed. Anyone attacking his honesty would do more harm to themselves than to him.

Coniston walked out into the center of the floor and looked up at Orme, who was already sworn in and had given his name and his rank.

"Sergeant Orme," Coniston began courteously, as if they were equals. "Will you please tell the court of your experience on the morning of the twenty-fourth of November, as you approached Limehouse Pier? Describe the scene for those of us who have not been there."

Orme had been prepared for this, but he was uncomfortable nonetheless. It was obvious in his face, and the way he leaned forward a little, both hands gripping the rail. Rathbone knew it was the request for a description of something he was not used to putting into words for others, that made him behave so. To the jury it would look like distress at what he had seen. Coniston was already preparing them for the horror. Rathbone was impressed. He could easily have taken less trouble and assumed the mood would follow naturally.

"Mr. Monk and I were coming back from looking into a robbery farther up the river," Orme began.

"Just two of you?" Coniston asked. "Were you rowing?"

"Both of us," Orme answered. "One behind the other, sir, an oar each."

"I see. Thank you. What time of day was it? What was the light?" Coniston asked.

"Early sunrise, sir. Lot of color in the sky, and across the water, too." Orme was clearly unhappy.

"Were you close in to shore, or out in the current?" Coniston continued.

"Close in to shore, sir. Out in the stream an' you'd be in the way of shipping, ferries an' the like."

"In the shadow of the docks and warehouses? Paint the picture for us, Sergeant Orme, if you please."

Orme shifted his weight to the other foot. "About twenty yards out, sir. Buildings sort of . . . looming up, but we were not in their shadow. Water was smoother closer to shore. Out of the wind."

"I see. You describe it well," Coniston said graciously. "So you and Commander Monk were rowing back to Wapping after being called out before dawn. It was cool. The breeze made the river choppy except close to shore, almost in the shadow of the docks and the warehouses, rising sun spilling red light on the smooth, dark water around you?"

Orme's face tightened as if the attention to beauty in the circumstances were distasteful to him. "Something like that, sir."

"Did anything occur that caused you to stop?"

There was absolute silence in the courtroom, apart from the slight rustle of a skirt as someone shifted position.

"Yes, sir. We heard a woman crying out, on Limehouse Pier. She was screaming, and waving her arms. We couldn't see why until we got right up to the pier and climbed the steps to the top. There was the body of a woman lying crumpled up on her side. Her . . . the body'd been ripped open and there was blood soaking her clothes . . ." He could not finish, not only because of his own emotion, but also because of the rising sound of gasps and groans from the body of the courtroom. In the gallery a woman was already crying, and there was a murmur of voices trying to offer comfort and telling others to be quiet.

"Order! Please, ladies and gentlemen," Pendock said from the bench. "Let us continue. Allow Sergeant Orme to be heard."

"Thank you, my lord," Coniston said soberly, then turned again to Orme. "I assume you and Commander Monk examined this poor woman's remains?"

"Yes, sir. There was nothing we could do for her. She was past all human help," Orme said hoarsely. "We asked the witness's name and address, and all she could tell us, which wasn't anything. She had just come there looking for her husband. Then I stayed with the body, and Mr. Monk went for the local police."

"The local police?" Coniston said with raised eyebrows. "But since she was found on the pier, was she not within your jurisdiction?"

"Yes, sir. But the first thing we wanted to know was who she was," Orme pointed out reasonably.

Coniston smiled and relaxed his tense position a fraction. "Of course. We will come to that. She was not known to you?"

"No, sir."

"And could you describe the body for us, Sergeant?" This time he made no apology.

Rathbone would like to have objected, but there were no grounds. The crime was appalling. Coniston was entitled to horrify the jury until they were sick and weeping. Had Rathbone been prosecuting he would have done the same.

Orme swallowed hard. Even from where he was sitting, Rathbone could see the muscles of his neck and jaws tighten. The effort it cost him to maintain his control would be just as visible to the jurors.

"Yes, sir," Orme said quietly. He gripped the rail in front of him and breathed in and out several times before beginning. "She wasn't a young woman, maybe forty, but not gone to fat. Her skin was very white, what we could see of it. Her clothes had been torn, or cut, and her . . . her bosom laid bare. Someone had slit her open right from . . ." He moved a rather jerky hand to the middle of his own chest and then slowly down below the rail to where his groin would be. He swallowed again.

"And her entrails were pulled out, sir, an' left lying all over her. It . . . it wasn't easy to see if everything was there, sir, an' I wouldn't know anyway."

Coniston looked pale himself. "Was that the full extent of her injuries, Sergeant?"

"No, sir. There was blood matted in her hair, as if she'd been hit pretty hard."

Coniston stood with his head bowed. "Thank you, Sergeant. Would you please remain on the stand in case my learned friend for the defense has any questions for you?" He looked across at Rathbone with a courteous smile. There was nothing for Rathbone to question, and they both knew it.

Rathbone stood up and addressed the judge. "Thank you, my lord. But I think Sergeant Orme has already told us all that he is able to."

Orme left the stand, and his place was taken by Overstone, the police surgeon who had examined the corpse. He held himself with military precision and looked straight at Coniston, his face bleak, his thinning hair smooth to his head. He looked tired, as if he had done this too many times, and it was getting harder rather than easier for him. It flickered through Rathbone's mind that it was requiring all the man's strength of will to speak with a steady, unemotional voice.

"You examined the body of this unfortunate woman that the police found on Limehouse Pier, Dr. Overstone?" Coniston began.

"I did," Overstone answered.

"Describe it for me, if you please. I mean what manner of person had she been in life?"

"About five foot, three inches tall," Overstone replied. "Of average build, thickening a little around the waist. She appeared to be well nourished. I would estimate her age to be middle or late forties. Her hair was light brown, her eyes blue. As much as one could tell, she must have been very pleasant-looking in life. She had good teeth, fine-boned hands."

"Any sign of illness?" Coniston inquired, as if it were a reasonable question.

Overstone's face tightened. "The woman was hacked to bits!" he said between his teeth. "How in God's name would I know?"

Coniston flushed slightly, even though he had incited the answer. In that instant Rathbone knew he had done it intentionally. The emotion in the room was taut as a violin string. Rathbone felt his own muscles lock and his neck ache with the effort of trying to breathe deeply and relax. Some of the jurors were looking at him, wondering what on earth he would do to defend anyone accused of such a crime. Possibly they wondered why he was here at all.

Coniston's penitence was brief. He addressed Overstone again.

"But you could ascertain the cause of her death, couldn't you, sir?" he said respectfully.

"Yes. A violent blow to the head," Overstone answered. "It crushed her skull. She would have died instantly. The mutilation was done after her death, thank heaven. She can have known nothing about it." There was a very slight defensiveness in Overstone's face.

"Thank you, Doctor," he said calmly. He walked back toward his seat, then at the last moment turned around again and looked up. "Oh . . . one more thing. Would it have required great strength to have struck the blow that killed her?"

"No, not if it were wielded with a swing."

"Did you ever find what it was that was used?"

"They brought the body to me, man!" Overstone said irritably. "They didn't take me onto the pier to look at it."

Coniston's face remained impassive. "Just so. Have you any idea what the weapon was? What do you think most likely, if you please?"

"A heavy piece of metal: a length of piping, something of that order," Overstone answered him. "I doubt a wooden bar would have had the weight, unless it was hardwood, even ebony."

"And the mutilations? Would they have needed particular strength or skill?"

"Just a sharp blade. There was nothing skilled about it." Overstone said the words with loathing.

"Would a woman have the strength to have done it?" Coniston finally asked what everyone in the room was thinking.

"Yes." Overstone did not add anything.

Coniston thanked him and turned to Rathbone. "Your witness, Sir Oliver."

Rathbone tried desperately to think of anything to say that would make the slightest difference. Dinah must be wondering why on earth she had hired him. Her life was in his hands.

"Was there anything about the injuries, anything at all, to indicate what manner of person had inflicted them?" he asked, looking up at Overstone.

"No, sir," Overstone replied.

"Nothing to suggest their height?" Rathbone elaborated. "Strength? Whether they were left- or right-handed, for example. Male or female? Young or old?"

"I said nothing at all, sir," Overstone repeated. "Except perhaps, considering the power of the blow, it might have been two-handed." He lifted both his own arms above his head, hands clenched together, and brought them down and sideways, as if holding a two-handed sword. "But that hardly helps. All it does is make height irrelevant."

"So it could have been anyone, except perhaps a child?"

"Just so."

Rathbone nodded. There was nothing more he could ask. Overstone was dismissed.

Next Coniston called Monk to the stand.

Monk was immaculately dressed, as always, elegant even to his polished boots. But he climbed the stairs to the witness bar as if he were stiff, and stood with one shoulder a little higher than the other.

To begin with, the court seemed less tense, not knowing what to expect from him. They thought the worst horror was past. Nevertheless the jurors watched him gravely, faces pale, several of them fidgeting with discomfort. They knew the people in the gallery were looking at them, trying to guess what they thought. Rathbone did not see a single one of them look toward Dinah Lambourn sitting high up in the dock, with burly woman jailers on either side of her.

Coniston seemed aware this time that he was dealing with a potentially hostile witness, in spite of the fact that it was Monk who had arrested Dinah. Rathbone's long friendship with Monk must be widely known. Coniston was far too clever not to have made certain he was aware of such things and the effect it might have on his case.

"Mr. Monk," he began softly. The gallery was silent, to be sure they missed nothing. "You were with Sergeant Orme when you first discovered the body of this poor woman, that dawn at Limehouse Pier. You and he heard the screams of the woman who found her. Orme remained with her to guard the body, and you went to call the local police, in case they could identify her, and appropriate authorities to take care of the corpse?"

"Yes," Monk agreed, his face carefully expressionless.

"Did the local police know who she was?" Coniston asked casually, as if he did not know the answer.

"No," Monk replied.

Coniston looked a little startled. He stood motionless, stopped in mid-stride. "They had never had occasion to arrest her, or at least caution her regarding her activities as a prostitute?"

"That is what they said," Monk agreed again.

"If she was indeed a prostitute, do you not find that remarkable?" Coniston asked with a lift of surprise in his voice.

Monk's face was expressionless. "People often don't recognize someone when they have died violently, especially if there is a lot of blood involved. People can look smaller than you remember them when they were alive. And if they are not dressed as you know them, or in a place where you expect to see them, you do not always realize who they are."

Coniston looked as if that was not the answer he had wanted. He moved on. "Did you then make inquiries to find out who she was?"

"Of course."

"Where did you inquire?" Coniston spread his hands, encompassing an infinity of possibilities.

"We spoke to local residents, shopkeepers, other women who lived in the area and with whom she might have been acquainted," Monk answered, still hardly any emotion in his voice.

"When you say 'women,' do you mean prostitutes?" Coniston pressed.

Monk's face was bland. Probably only Rathbone could see the tiny muscle ticking in his cheek.

"I mean laundresses, factory workers, peddlers, anyone who might have known her," he said.

"Were you successful?" Coniston inquired courteously.

"Yes," Monk told him. "She was identified as Zenia Gadney, a middle-aged woman who lived quietly, by herself, at Fourteen Copenhagen Place, just beyond Limehouse Cut. She was known to several other people in the street."

"How did she support herself?" Coniston was still calm and polite, but the tension in him was not missed by the jury. Watching them, Rathbone could feel it himself.

"She didn't," Monk answered. "There was a man who called on her once a month, and gave her sufficient funds for her needs, which appeared to be modest. We found no evidence of her having earned any money other than that, except for the very occasional small sewing job, which might have been as much for goodwill and companionship as for money." Monk's face was somber, his voice quiet, as if he too mourned not only her terrible death, but the seeming futility of her life.

Knowing him as he did, Rathbone had no difficulty reading the emotions in his face and his choice of words. He wondered if Coniston read it also. Would he judge him with any accuracy?

Coniston hesitated a moment, then went on. "I assume that, as a matter of course, you attempted to identify this man, and the kind of relationship he had with her?"

"Of course," Monk answered. "He was Dr. Joel Lambourn, of Lower Park Street, Greenwich."

"I see," Coniston said quickly. "That would be the late husband of the accused, Mrs. Dinah Lambourn?"

Monk's face was a blank slate. "Yes."

"Did you go to see Mrs. Lambourn? Ask her about her husband's connection with Mrs. Gadney?" Coniston said innocently. "It must have been unpleasant for you to have to inform her of her husband's connection with the dead woman." There was a touch of pity in his voice now.

"Yes, of course I did," Monk answered him. His own expression was ironed clear of compassion as much as he could, and yet it still shone through.

The jury watched intently. Even Pendock in the judge's seat leaned forward a little. There was a sigh of breath in the gallery, as if the tension had become too great.

"And her reaction?" Coniston prompted a little sharply, as if he was annoyed at having to ask.

"At first she said she did not know Mrs. Gadney," Monk replied. "Then she admitted that she was aware that her husband had supported her until his death two months earlier."

"She knew!" Coniston said loudly and clearly, even half turning toward the gallery so no one in the whole courtroom could have missed it. He swung back toward Monk. "Mrs. Lambourn knew that her husband had been visiting and paying Zenia Gadney for years?"

"She said so," Monk agreed.

Rathbone made a small note on his paper in front of him.

"But first she denied it?" Coniston pressed. "Was she embarrassed? Angry? Humiliated? Afraid, even?"

Rathbone considered objecting on the grounds that such a judgment was not in Monk's expertise, then changed his mind. It would be futile, merely drawing attention to his own desperation.

The shadow of a smile crossed Monk's face, and then disappeared. "I don't know. She was in the grip of some powerful emotion, but I have no way of knowing what it was. It could easily have been shock and horror at the manner of Zenia Gadney's death."

"Or remorse?" Coniston added.

Rathbone started to rise to his feet.

Pendock saw him. "Mr. Coniston, you are speculating inappropriately. Please restrict yourself to questions the witness can answer."

"I apologize, my lord," Coniston said contritely. He looked up at Monk again. "But it would be accurate to say that Mrs. Lambourn was in a state of extreme emotion, Mr. Monk?"

"Yes."

"Considering what you had learned of Dr. Lambourn's connection with the victim, and that Mrs. Lambourn at some point or other had become aware of it, did you take steps to find out if Mrs. Lambourn had ever visited Zenia Gadney herself?"

"Yes." Monk's face was tight with unhappiness, but he did not evade the answer. "Several witnesses saw someone answering her description in Copenhagen Place the day before Zenia Gadney's corpse was found on the pier. They say she was making inquiries to find Mrs. Gadney, specifically in the shops."

Coniston nodded slowly. "She was searching to find the victim. Did anyone mention her state of mind? Please be exact, Mr. Monk."

"She was in great distress," Monk replied. "Two or three people described her as behaving wildly. That was why they remembered her."

"Did you ask Mrs. Lambourn about this?"

"Of course."

"And her answer?"

"At first she told me that she had been at a soirée with a friend. I visited the friend, who told me otherwise."

"Is it possible that this friend was mistaken—or worse, that she lied?" Coniston pressed.

"No," Monk said flatly. "I merely asked her where she had been at that day and time, and she told me. She was in company with many other people, and we have since verified her whereabouts. There was no such soirée as Mrs. Lambourn said she attended."

"So she lied?" Coniston said, again loudly and clearly.

"Yes."

Coniston smiled very slightly.

"To sum up, Commander Monk, your evidence is that the accused, Mrs. Dinah Lambourn, knew that her husband had visited the victim for many years, and paid her money on a regular basis. On the day before the murder she went to the street on which the victim lived, searching for her, asking people where she could find her. Several people told you that she was in a state of great distress, almost hysterical. When you asked her about this, she lied to you and said she was somewhere else, which you have proved to be untrue. Is that correct?"

"Yes," Monk said miserably.

"At that point, did you arrest her and charge her with the murder of Zenia Gadney?"

"Yes. She said she had not killed her, and insisted that she had not been to Copenhagen Place," Monk replied.

"Thank you, Commander Monk," Coniston said with visible satisfaction. He turned to Rathbone. "Your witness, Sir Oliver."

Rathbone walked out slowly into the center of the open space and looked up at Monk. He was aware that every person in the courtroom was watching him, waiting to see what he could possibly do. He had a sudden vision in his mind of a Christian entering an arena full of lions. He was hoping for a miracle, and not at all sure that he believed in them.

"Mr. Monk, you said that Mrs. Lambourn admitted to knowing that her husband had been visiting Mrs. Gadney for many years. By the way, was she married, or are we using the title as a courtesy?"

"Neighbors said that she claimed to have been married," Monk answered. "But we found no trace of anyone called Gadney, nor any record of him."

"And Dr. Lambourn had been supporting her financially all the time she had been there?" Rathbone continued.

"Approximately fifteen years," Monk agreed.

"I see." Rathbone frowned. "And you say that apparently Mrs. Lambourn knew of this all that time, or at least most of it? Are you certain?"

"Yes."

"Because she admitted it? And of course you believed her?" Rathbone allowed a small lift of incredulity into his voice.

Monk looked at him with a flash of humor, there an instant and then gone again. "Because another witness also told me," he corrected him.

"Ah. So you have no doubt that she did indeed know of Mrs. Gadney for some considerable time, probably years?"

"That's right."

"And Dr. Lambourn had been dead how long when Mrs. Gadney was murdered?"

"Nearly two months."

Rathbone could see in Monk's face that he knew exactly what the next question was going to be. Their eyes met. "And what reason did you find that caused Mrs. Lambourn, two months into her widowhood, suddenly to go to Copenhagen Place searching for Zenia Gadney, hysterical with emotion, allowing even shopkeepers and their customers to see her in such a state? What did she want with Zenia Gadney then, and so urgently, after years of knowing all about her? There was no more money going to her, was there?"

Several jurors leaned forward as if to be certain of catching every word of the answer. One frowned and shook his head.

There was a rustle of movement in the gallery and a sharp hiss of indrawn breath.

Pendock was staring at Rathbone, his face furrowed with apprehension.

Monk did not seem perturbed. Rathbone wondered for a moment if perhaps he had walked into a trap. He calmed himself by remembering that while it was Monk who had arrested Dinah, it was also Monk who had sought out Rathbone to defend her, and worked in his own time to find new evidence about the case.

"She claimed that she did not go to Copenhagen Place," Monk said slowly and distinctly. "She believes that her husband, Dr. Joel Lambourn, was murdered because of his work to prove that opium is sold in this country—"

Coniston shot to his feet. "My lord!" he said loudly. "This is absolutely irrelevant and misleading. Opium is a common medicine prescribed by doctors and available in every apothecary in England, and thousands of ordinary shops. If Mrs. Lambourn took it, for pain or any other reason, it does not excuse what she did. Millions of people take opium. It relieves distress and sleeplessness; it does not drive to insanity or give any excuse for murder."

"Taken too heavily, too often, it can cause addiction, especially if smoked," Rathbone said tartly. "And taken in overdose, it kills."

Coniston turned to him. "Zenia Gadney was not addicted and she did not die of an overdose of opium, Sir Oliver! She was beaten over the head with an iron pipe and then obscenely mutilated. Her intestines were torn out and—"

"Order," Pendock barked furiously. "We are aware of how she died, Mr. Coniston! Sir Oliver! Are you suggesting that Mrs. Lambourn took opium, and that it in any way excuses this terrible crime?"

"No, my lord, I—"

"Good," Pendock snapped. "Then please proceed with your questions to Mr. Monk, if you have any more. Otherwise we are adjourned for luncheon."

"Only a few more, my lord." Without waiting for Pendock to grant him permission, Rathbone turned to Monk again. "You believe that her sudden decision to look for Zenia Gadney had something to do with her husband's death?" he demanded.

"Not his death so much as the ruin of his reputation," Monk replied. "And she did not believe he had taken his own life."

Again Coniston rose to his feet. "My lord, the tragic suicide of Joel Lambourn—"

Pendock raised his hand. "I am quite aware of it, Mr. Coniston." He turned sharply to Rathbone. "Sir Oliver, Dr. Lambourn had already been dead for two months by the time Mrs. Lambourn began to look for Zenia Gadney. If she believed Mrs. Gadney in some way responsible for Dr. Lambourn's suicide, then you must show some evidence to that effect. Have you any?"

"No, my lord."

"Then please move on." It was an order.

Rathbone drew in his breath to find some other question. He hated to retreat now; it looked as if in some way he were surrendering. And that was also how it felt. He had nothing else to ask Monk. Clearly, whatever he said that raised the issue of Joel Lambourn's death, or any area of his work related to the report on opium, was going to be disallowed, unless he could make it so clearly relevant that to refuse it would be grounds for appeal.

"Nothing further, thank you, my lord," he said with as good grace as he could manage, and retired to his seat.

AFTER THE LUNCHEON ADJOURNMENT, Coniston called evidence regarding the death of Joel Lambourn and its effect on his widow. Rathbone's interest sharpened. Perhaps he would have an opportunity to open up the subject in such a way that Lambourn's suicide could be questioned after all. Monk had certainly given him sufficient evidence to debate, if he could get a toe in the door. It would need only the smallest error of judgment on Coniston's part, one slip by his witnesses, and the subject could be raised.

Rathbone glanced behind him and noted how many journalists were sitting attentively, pencils in hand. They would not miss the slightest inflection, even if the jury did.

Then, as Rathbone was turning back to face the judge and the witness box, his eye caught sight of a face he knew. He had even met him half a dozen times at one function or another. It was Sinden Bawtry, an ambitious man in the government with a reputation for philanthropy. His fortune was built on the manufacture of patent medicines, particularly one known as Doctor's Home Remedy for Pain.

Rathbone avoided catching his eye, without being certain as to why. He did not want Bawtry to know that he had seen him, at least not yet, although he was a handsome man, and would not go unnoticed by the press. By tomorrow every newspaper reader would know he had been here.

Now Rathbone's attention was needle sharp. Bawtry's interest in Lambourn's connection to the case was obvious. Was he here privately, or as a representative of the government's interest?

Rathbone watched carefully as a policeman he did not know climbed the steps to the witness box. Monk had told him that Runcorn had been in charge of the investigation into Lambourn's death. So who was this man, Appleford, and why had Coniston chosen him?

"Commissioner Appleford," Coniston began smoothly, "I believe the tragic death of Joel Lambourn was referred from regular police inquiry, up to your command. Is that correct?"

"Yes, it is." Appleford was of average height, slim although running very slightly to fat around the waist. His light brown hair was thinning drastically, but he was smart and appeared very confident, as if he were here only to be helpful and clear up difficulties lesser men might find beyond them.

"Why was it not left to the superintendent of the nearest police station? That would be Mr. Runcorn, at Blackheath, would it not?" Coniston said with every appearance of being casual.

"Mr. Runcorn did deal with the first evidence," Appleford replied with a slight smile. "When it was realized that the dead man was Joel Lambourn, a fine man, an excellent scientist, who had had some recent . . ." He hesitated, as if looking for a suitably delicate word. "Emotional distress," he continued. "Her Majesty's Government wished to be discreet about as much of his personal affairs as was possible, without any perversion of the law. There was no way to avoid admitting that his death was suicide, but the more immediate facts were not made public. There was no purpose to be served, and his family could be protected. It seemed a merciful thing to do for a man who had served his country so well."

"Indeed." Coniston bowed his head, then looked up again. "Was anything pertinent concealed from the law? I mean was there any possible question whatever that his death might not have been self-inflicted?"

"None at all," Appleford replied. "He took opium, quite a heavy dose, presumably to deaden the pain, and then slit his wrists."

"Thank you, Commissioner." Coniston turned to Rathbone. "Sir Oliver?"

Rathbone knew even before he began that he would achieve nothing with Appleford. But he refused to be cowed into not trying.

"Is it particularly painful, slitting one's wrists?" he asked. "I mean sufficiently so that one requires opium to bear it?"

"I have no idea!" Appleford said with a touch of sarcasm.

"I apologize," Rathbone said, with an equally cutting edge to his voice. "I thought you had been called upon as an expert, more so than Superintendent Runcorn. Is that not the case?"

"I was called in to take on the responsibility of keeping the matter discreet," Appleford snapped. "That was not within Runcorn's power."

"Apparently not," Rathbone agreed. "Yet every man and his dog seems to know that Joel Lambourn was profoundly discredited and, in despair because of it, he committed suicide in Greenwich Park. It did happen in Greenwich Park, didn't it? Or is that where the discretion comes in?"

Coniston stood up, exasperation clear in his face and his manner. "My lord, Sir Oliver is simply trying to embarrass the witness because he has no useful questions to ask him. May we not, in decency, leave Dr. Lambourn's final tragedy in the little privacy it has left? It has no bearing on Zenia Gadney's murder."

Rathbone swung around. "Has it not? Then it appears you have been given a great deal of information about it that I have not. Your whole prosecution rests on the fact that you believe Mrs. Lambourn killed Zenia Gadney over something to do with Dr. Lambourn." His voice dripped sarcasm. "Are you suggesting some other connection between the two women, one of whom is a highly respected doctor's widow in Greenwich, the other a middle-aged prostitute across the river in Limehouse?"

"Of course he is the connection!" Coniston said with some heat. "But his life, not his death."

"Are they totally separate matters?" Rathbone asked incredulously.

There were several rustles of movement in the gallery as people craned forward, afraid of missing something.

In the jury box the members looked from side to side, and then up at the judge.

"Yes," Coniston said boldly. "Insofar as the professional despair that caused his suicide was completely separate from the domestic jealousy that caused his wife to murder Mrs. Gadney." He too looked up to the judge. "My lord, the defense is seeking to muddy the case by raising issues that considerably precede Mrs. Gadney's murder and have nothing to do with it. Mrs. Lambourn had no involvement in her husband's work for the government; therefore it cannot have had anything to do with the murder of Zenia Gadney."

Rathbone rose to protest. The conclusion was totally unwarranted. "My lord—"

"Your point is very well taken, Mr. Coniston," Pendock cut across him. "Sir Oliver, if you have no relevant questions to ask Commissioner Appleford, the court excuses him, and we will proceed to the next witness. If you please, Mr. Coniston?"

Rathbone sat down feeling as if he had been crushed by a weight he should have seen falling on him, and yet he had not. He had no idea where he could turn next. The ruling was unfair, and yet if he protested again he would earn Pendock's fury without being able to prove anything in Dinah's favor, because frankly, he did not have anything.

He felt suddenly very close to despair.

As the trial of Dinah Lambourn was beginning, Hester set out on her own investigation. The whole issue of the sale of opium was one that drew her in with increasing urgency with every new piece of information she found. Because most of her nursing experience had been with soldiers suffering from appalling injuries, or from the fevers and dysentery of war, she was familiar only with the advantages of opium as a means to reduce pain.

Her later work in the clinic on Portpool Lane had been with prostitutes. Some were as young as twelve or thirteen; but she hadn't known of the devastation inflicted on smaller children from remedies containing opium before Dr. Winfarthing had told her.

However, as far as Dinah Lambourn was concerned, there was no time now to justify Lambourn's report to the government. Before anything else, they must find out who killed Zenia Gadney. To do that, they needed to learn more about Gadney than the bare facts of her life in Copenhagen Place.

Most of the street women who came to the clinic in Portpool Lane were from within a mile or two of the clinic itself, but some with more chronic diseases had come now and again from farther away. There was usually not much Hester could do for them, but anything to ease their distress even a little was a help. Now she set out to find one woman in particular with whom she had sat up many nights, nursing her through pneumonia and back into sufficient health for her to return to the streets, until next time. That would probably be this winter when hunger, exposure, and exhaustion might well kill her.

Gladys Middleton was nearly forty, and had been bought and sold since she was twelve, but she was still surprisingly handsome. Her hair was thick and unmarked by gray. Her skin was fading, but there were no visible blemishes, at least in candlelight. The last illness had reduced her weight, but at this point, the loss was flattering. She still had generous curves, and walked with surprising grace.

It took Hester most of the day to find where Gladys now lived. Even after she had discovered the right lodging house, she had to wait, standing as discreetly as possible in a doorway, until Gladys returned from the public house on the corner.

Hester followed her at almost fifty yards' distance until Gladys went through the door, and then she went in after her. She made a couple of mistakes, having to apologize before she knocked at the right room.

Gladys opened it cautiously. It was early to expect custom. There was still daylight outside, and a prospective client might far too easily meet someone he knew on the street. His presence here might be difficult to explain.

"Hello, Gladys," Hester said with a quick smile. There was no point in pretending she had come other than for a favor. Gladys knew the way of survival and would not appreciate being patronized by lies.

Hester held up a bottle of the tonic cordial she knew was Gladys's favorite.

Gladys regarded it with pleasure, then suspicion. "I ain't sayin' as I'm not grateful, nor pleased ter see yer, but wot d'yer want?" she said skeptically.

"Not to stand at the door, for a start," Hester replied, still smiling.

Gladys backed in reluctantly.

Hester followed her. The room was cleaner than she had expected. There were no signs of trade here, only a faint odor of sweat, and recently eaten food.

"Thank you." Hester sat down on the edge of one of the chairs. She kept the bottle of cordial in her hand. It should be understood that this was a bargain, not a gift.

Gladys sat down opposite her, also on the edge of her chair, uneasily.

"Wot d'yer want, then?" she repeated.

"Information."

"I dunno nothin'." The response was instinctive and immediate.

"Rubbish," Hester said briskly. "Women who know nothing don't survive very long. Don't lie to me, and I won't lie to you."

Gladys shrugged, admitting at least a degree of defeat. "Wot are yer askin'?"

"Did you know Zenia Gadney?" Hester replied.

The color drained out of Gladys's face, leaving her ashen. "Gawd! I don't know nothin' about that, I swear!"

"I'm sure you don't know anything about the murder," Hester agreed, telling something close to the truth. "I want to know what she was like."

"Wot d'yer mean, wot she were like?" Gladys blinked in confusion.

Was she playing for time, or did she really not understand? Hester put her hand lightly on the cordial bottle. "This stuff is quite good for your health," she remarked.

"Well, it in't goin' ter cure a slit throat!" Gladys said huskily. "Or yer guts torn out an' tied around yer waist, is it!"

"Why should anyone do that to you?" Hester raised her eyebrows. "Anyway, her throat wasn't slit. She was hit on the back of her head. She wouldn't have known anything that happened after that, poor soul. You didn't have an affair with Dr. Lambourn, did you?"

Gladys was startled. "Course I din't! 'E weren't like that. All 'e wanted were ter know 'ow easy it were ter buy opium, an' if I knew wot was in the stuff I got ter 'elp me sleep, or when I got a bellyache."

"And did you?" Hester tried to keep some of the eagerness out of her voice. She could not afford to have Gladys sense how much she needed the information. "Did you know what was in it, and how much to take? Or how long before you could take more?"

"I know it works, I don't need ter know nothin' else, do I!" Gladys retorted.

"Is that what he asked you?"

"'E weren't askin' me, 'e were askin' them wot 'as kids. I were just there."

"Did you know Zenia Gadney?" Hester went back to her first question.

"Yeah. Why?"

"What was she like?"

"Yer said that already. Wot kind o' thing d'yer want ter know?" Gladys shook her head. "She were older'n me, quiet, not much ter look at, but clean. It's all on wot yer like, in't it? Some folk like 'em ordinary, but willin' ter do anything, if yer get me meanin'? Like their wives, but easier."

"Yes, I understand you. Is that what Zenia was like? Actually, she's not much like Mrs. Lambourn at all."

"Wot's Mrs. Lambourn like, then?" Gladys was curious.

Hester remembered what Monk had said, and the effect she appeared to have had on him. "Handsome, very striking indeed," she replied. "Tall and dark, with very fine eyes."

Gladys shook her head, completely bewildered. "Well, Zenia weren't nothin' like that. She were as dull as a mouse, all browny-gray and quiet. In fact, she were a real bore, but nice, like, if yer know wot I mean? Din't talk down at nobody. Din't lose 'er temper nor tell lies about yer. Nor she din't steal nothin'."

Hester was puzzled as well. "How did you come to know her?"

Gladys rolled her eyes at Hester's stupidity. "'Eard about 'er 'cos she got wot we all want, din't she? One real nice gent wot only needed ter see 'er once a month, treated 'er like she were a lady, an' paid all 'er bills. If that 'appened ter me, I'd reckon as I'd died an' gone ter 'eaven. 'Ow'd she do it, that's wot I'd like ter know. It weren't 'cos she knew 'ow ter make a man laugh, or feel as if 'e were the most interestin' man as she ever met, or the 'andsomest, neither."

"Did Dr. Lambourn love her, do you think?" Hester asked. "Was she especially gentle, or kind?"

Gladys shrugged. "'Ow'd I know? I reckon as she must 'ave been willin' ter do some real strange things fer 'im. All I can think. An' 'e looked as decent as yer like, jus' straightforward. Goes ter show, yer never know wot's be'ind them ordinary faces."

It was a possibility Hester had already thought of, distasteful as it was. She had never even met Dinah Lambourn. Why did it trouble her so much that she might have deeply loved a man with deviant tastes? Perhaps it was her own imagination of how she would feel were she to discover such a thing of Monk.

If it were so, would she want to kill the woman who had catered to him, as Dinah was accused of having killed Zenia? Possibly. Not as violently, as brutally, but kill her? It was strange and disturbing that murder was something that she could even imagine.

Now the whole situation looked different—sad, ugly, and unimaginably painful.

"Do you think Zenia loved him?" she asked Gladys. Was that a question that even made sense to the woman? Gladys lived, worked, and thought only to survive. Love was a luxury she would probably never be able to afford. Perhaps she had not even allowed herself to dream of it. In a hundred different disguises, that was probably true of millions of women of all ranks, from servant to aristocrat. Children would have much to do with it; neither Hester nor Gladys would have children, but Hester had love. She was perfectly sure of that.

But then many women believed they had love. Maybe even Dinah Lambourn.

She looked at Gladys again. She was sitting with her brow furrowed, a look of deep concentration on her face.

Hester waited.

Gladys looked up at last. "Mebbe. Don't really matter," she said slowly. "It were terrible wot 'appened to 'er. I don't care wot she done, that weren't right."

Hester was not sure what to say. "Did she do something so bad?" she asked. She was afraid she would drive Gladys back into silence, but she was increasingly conscious that the other woman knew more than she had said.

"That's it," Gladys bit her lip. "She were kind o' secretive, sometimes a bit la-di-da, like she were better'n the rest of us, but she were kind, in 'er own way. She acted like she'd come down in the world, but I thought that mebbe she 'ad. Something she said once. Tillie Biggs were drunk 'alf out of 'er mind. Lyin' in the gutter like it were the only place left for 'er. Couldn't fall out of it, likely. An' Zenia were the only one wot 'ad time ter pick 'er up. Rest of us said the stupid cow brought it on 'erself, but Zenia wouldn't 'ave it. Said we all brought things on ourselves, don't mean we didn't need 'elpin'."

"What did she do?" Hester felt a tightening in her throat, the beginning of an emotion she could not control.

Gladys made a small, sad gesture. " 'Eaved 'er up an' dragged 'er into an alley doorway where it were dry, an' nobody'd fall over 'er. Propped 'er up there, an' left 'er. In't nothin' else yer can do. She knew that." She stopped, struggling with whether to say more.

Hester did not know whether to encourage her or not. She drew in her breath to speak, then changed her mind.

"Reckon as maybe she'd fallen in a few gullies 'erself," Gladys said quietly. "She told me once that she'd bin married. Mebbe 'e left 'er 'cos o' the drink. Or she left 'im. Dunno." She shook her head. "But she weren't one o' us, like from round 'ere."

"Where did she come from, do you know?" Hester asked gently. Gladys's answers had made Zenia far too real: a woman with dreams and sudden kindnesses, capable of feeling grief and pain.

"She never said. She were an odd one. Liked flowers. I mean she knew 'ow ter grow 'em, wot kind o' soil they liked, that sort o' thing, 'cos she used ter talk about it sometimes. Wot month they was out, an' the like. Don' get no flowers round 'ere. She used ter stand on the pier sometimes an' look over the water, like mebbe she were from south o' the river." She shrugged. "Could a' bin just ter be by 'erself, like; think a bit. Dream as yer could get on one o' them boats an' go somewhere. I think that, sometimes."

Again Hester waited before she broke the moment.

Gladys looked up at her and smiled a little self-consciously. "Daft, eh?"

"No," Hester replied. "We all need to dream of things, now and then. Who else knew her? What was Dr. Lambourn like? Did she ever talk about him?"

"No. But then I reckoned as she knew 'e were worth keepin' for 'erself, like. Couldn't share nothin'. Weren't enough to go round."

"Jealous?" Hester said quickly.

"Course we was, but Gawd, we wouldn't do that ter nobody! Wot the bleedin' 'ell d'yer think we are?" Gladys was indignant, even hurt.

"I didn't think so," Hester retracted. She really did not know what to ask next. Since finding Gladys and talking to her, she began to believe that perhaps Dinah had lost her sanity, temporarily, and maybe it was she, after all, who had ripped Zenia apart. Could an otherwise normal woman feel so betrayed that she would indulge the darkest, bloodiest side of her nature? Had the wounds been so deep—failure, self-disgust, hatred—that they drove her beyond sanity?

It no longer seemed unimaginable.

She changed the subject. "The shopkeeper said Mrs. Lambourn came to Limehouse looking for opium. Dr. Lambourn did, too, didn't he? Asking questions, I mean."

"I 'eard. 'E never asked me, but 'ow would I know anything?"

"Did you meet him?"

"Yeah, couple o' times. I told yer, 'e were askin' all sorts o' things o' people."

"About opium?"

"Yeah. 'E wanted ter find Agony."

Hester was taken aback. "What?"

"Agony Nisbet. Least I reckon 'er name is really Agatha, or summink like that, but everyone calls 'er Agony, 'cos she 'elps folks wot got real terrible pain."

"With opium?" Hester said quickly.

"O' course. You know anything else wot'll 'elp when pain is that bad?"

"No," Hester admitted, "I don't. Did he find her?"

"Dunno. S'pose, 'cos 'e didn't come back lookin'."

"What was he like?" She asked more from curiosity than because she thought it would help. And she was not sure what she was trying to gain anymore; she had begun with the idea of finding some explanation for Zenia Gadney's murder that would prove Dinah innocent. Now her own emotions were disturbed to the depth where she could imagine getting lost in a madness of grief, where acts of violence might be quite possible, and she was no longer certain there *was* another explanation to find.

Could she take that back to Monk, and to Rathbone? Would that be surrender, or just realism?

Gladys gave the characteristic lift of one shoulder again. "Not like I'd 'ave thought," she said with surprise still lingering in her face. "'E were soft-spoken, real gentle. 'E treated me like I were . . . someone instead of no one. I guess yer can't always tell about folks, can yer?"

Hester remained a little longer, but Gladys did not know anything more except the places where Hester might begin to look for "Agony" Nisbet. So she thanked her and left.

She spoke to several other people in Copenhagen Place, including the shopkeeper that Monk had visited, and heard his account of Dinah's visit, which added nothing new to what they already knew.

Then she went out into the cold, gusty thoroughfare. As the eaves dripped on her and people jostled her on the wet footpath, she tried to put herself in Dinah's shoes. Apparently Dinah had known for years that her husband had visited Zenia Gadney, and paid her. What had happened that had changed her from a compliant wife, tolerating the fact, even agreeing to it, into a woman who had lost all hold on humanity?

If Hester had discovered something like that about Monk, it would have defiled her love for him. But would it have destroyed her own values of compassion and honor?

She might have been hurt beyond bearing. She might have wept herself exhausted, unable to eat or sleep, but if her despair had been complete she would have taken her own life, not someone else's.

Wouldn't she?

Was it conceivable that it was Dinah who had actually killed Joel Lambourn? Had either Monk or Rathbone even thought of that, and weighed it without the tangle of emotion her pain caused in them?

But Lambourn's death had looked like suicide. It was even gentle, with the opium to dull the pain. There was no hatred there, not even any anger. But it robbed Dinah of the respectability, the social status, and most of the income to which she was accustomed. What about Adah and Marianne? Had she even thought of them? Did a woman

ever really forget her children? What had Lambourn left? Enough for
them to live on, for Dinah to raise and successfully marry the two young
girls?

Was it even physically possible that Dinah had done it alone? Had
she lured him up to One Tree Hill in the middle of the night? Persuaded
him to take the opium, then sit there while she cut his wrists, calmly
picked up the bottle and the knife, and walked back home again to her
children? Why take away the bottle and knife? That made no sense. If
he had really committed suicide, they would have been there. And the
fact that they were from her home wouldn't need concealing, because it
was his home, too!

If she were capable of such cold-blooded planning, why the insane
rage in mutilating Zenia Gadney? And what could have provoked her,
after years of knowing about the whole arrangement? Why suddenly
commit two murders, two months apart?

It made no sense. There had to be another answer.

HESTER SPENT THE REST of the day speaking to people in the area
and learning a little more about Zenia Gadney, but nothing that altered
the picture Gladys had given her of a quiet, rather sad woman. Apparently she had destroyed her youth with drink, but she also appeared to
have beaten whatever demons had driven her then. For the last fifteen
years she had lived in Copenhagen Place. She had done the odd job of
sewing or mending for people, but more as a friend than for money. It
was a way of associating with others, and having the occasional conversation. She appeared to be supported by Dr. Lambourn sufficiently that
if she was careful, no other income had been necessary.

Several people said they saw her out walking quite often, in all
weathers but the very worst. Most often it was along Narrow Street,
beside the river. Sometimes she would stand with the wind in her face,
looking south, watching the barges come and go. If you spoke to her she
would answer, and she was always agreeable, but she seldom sought conversation herself.

No one spoke ill of her.

Hester went to stand in Narrow Street herself, the wind stinging her face, gray water glinting in the light. Hester had a strong sense of Zenia's loneliness, perhaps of the regret that must have crowded her mind so many times. What had started her drinking in the first place? Some domestic tragedy? Perhaps the death of a child? A marriage that was desperately unhappy? Probably no one would ever know.

There seemed to be nothing in Zenia's life that led to her terrible death, unless it was her association with Joel Lambourn. If it was not that, then she was no more than a chance victim, sacrificed to opportunity and insane rage.

Hester had begun with pity for Dinah, a woman robbed not only of the husband she loved, but, in a sense, of all that she had believed of the happiness in her life. The sweetness of her memories were now tainted forever. Soon she would lose her own life in the awful ritual punishment of hanging.

Now as Hester stood watching the gray water of the river swirl past her, her pity was for Zenia Gadney. The woman's life had held so little comfort, and in the last decade and a half, almost no warmth of laughter, sharing, even touching another human being, apart from Joel Lambourn once a month, for money. Hester refused to try to picture that in her mind. What could he have wanted that was so strange or so obscene that his wife would not grant it to him, and he paid a sad prostitute in Limehouse instead?

She was glad that she did not need to know.

The water was loud on the shingle as the wash of a boat reached the shore on the low tide. A string of barges passed in midstream, laden with coal, timber, and bales stacked high. The men guiding them balanced with a rough, powerful grace, wielding their long poles. The wind was rising and smelled of salt and rain. Gulls screamed overhead, a long, mournful cry.

Hester felt she had exhausted the subject of Zenia Gadney. She wondered if there was any point in trying to find out more of Dr. Lambourn's search for information about opium. Probably not. The light was fading and it was getting colder as the tide turned. It was time to go home where it was warm, not just away from the wind off the water, but away from the impressions of death, from rage and despair, and the hunger that in the end had destroyed everything that was precious for these people.

She would make Scuff something he really liked for supper, and listen to him laugh about something trivial, say good night to him when he was scrubbed and clean, smelling of soap and ready for bed.

Later she would lie with Monk, and thank God for all the things that were good in her world.

It took Hester all the next day, and half the day after to find Agatha Nisbet. She had walked along the narrow path westward, past Greenland Dock and inland to Norway Yard. She asked again in Rotherhithe Street, and it was only a few dozen yards farther to a large, unused warehouse where there was a makeshift clinic for injured dockworkers and sailors.

She went in, walking boldly; head up as if she had the right to be there. One or two people looked at her curiously, first a young woman with a mop and bucket busy scrubbing floors, then a man with blood on his clothes, who appeared to be some kind of orderly. She smiled at him, and he relaxed and did not challenge her.

She passed two or three middle-aged women. They looked tired and harassed, their clothes crumpled as if they had been in them all night as well as all day. They brought back sharp memories of her own hospital days: cleaning, rolling bandages, changing beds, and helping sick and injured people eat, above all taking orders. She remembered the weariness, and the comradeship, the grief shared and the victories.

There were straw palliasses on the floor, all of them occupied by men, pale-faced and dirty, arms, legs, or bodies bandaged. The fortunate ones seemed to be asleep. If Agatha Nisbet had given them opium and bound up their injuries, Hester for one would have no criticism of her. Those who found fault should try a week or two of lying on this floor with bruised and broken bodies, with no ease during the long, bitter hours of the night in the cold and the darkness when even to draw breath was all but unbearable.

She had reached the end of the huge room and was about to knock on one of the doors of the cubicles at the end when it burst open. She found herself looking up at a woman who was well over six foot tall and with the broad, heavy shoulders of a navvy. Her hair was frizzy and of a fading auburn color. Her features were powerful, and had probably even been handsome thirty years ago in her youth. By now time and hard living had coarsened them, and sun and wind had roughened her skin. Fierce blue eyes regarded Hester with contempt.

"What do you want here, lady?" she asked in a soft, slightly sibilant voice. It was a little high, and did not sound as if it could possibly have come from her enormous body. There was contempt in her use of the word lady.

Hester bit back the tart response she would like to have made.

"Miss Nisbet?" she asked politely.

"What of it? 'Oo are you?"

"Hester Monk. I run a clinic for street women on the other side of the river. Portpool Lane," Hester answered loudly, and without backing away.

"Do you now?" Agatha Nisbet's eyes looked her up and down coolly. "Wot d'yer want with me, then?"

Hester decided to plunge in. Niceties were going to get her nowhere. "A better source of opium than I have at the moment," she answered.

"Yer mean cheaper?" Agatha said with a curl of her lip.

"I mean more reliable," Hester corrected her. "Cheaper would be good, but I believe that as a rule you get what you pay for." She gave a slight shrug. "Unless you're very new to it, and then you get less. There are plenty of dealers who would happily shortchange the sick." She looked Agatha up and down equally frankly. "I should imagine they don't do it to you a second time."

Agatha smiled, showing large, strong, unusually white teeth. "Any sense an' they don't do it the first time neither. Word gets round."

"So what you have is as reliable as it can be?" Hester reaffirmed.

"Yeah. But it'll cost yer some."

"Did Dr. Lambourn come here?" she asked quickly.

Agatha's eyes widened. "He's dead."

Hester smiled as artlessly as she could manage. "And now maybe there won't be a bill through Parliament to regulate the sale of opium because of it, at least not for a number of years."

Agatha's eyes narrowed.

Hester felt a sudden chill of fear, and realized that perhaps she had made a mistake, even put her own life in danger. She must not let this big woman see her unease. "Which will give me a little more latitude," she said aloud. She was certain that her voice was husky.

Agatha stood motionless, one hand on her hip. Hester could not help noticing the size of her fist, the shining, bony knuckles.

"An' what is it you mean by that, exactly?" Agatha asked. Her voice was so soft, had Hester not been able to see her, she might have thought she was listening to a child.

Her mouth was dry and she could not swallow. Her throat tightened. She gulped air. "That I can't do my job if I can't get supplies," she answered. "The men in government don't think of that, do they? Rich men can buy opium to give them nice dreams, but people in the streets and in the docks, people who are beaten or broken, get what they can, where they can. Do I have to explain that to you?" She allowed the final question to be tinged with a note of disgust.

Agatha's large body relaxed and she allowed the ghost of a smile into her face. "Want a cup o' tea?" she asked, stepping back a bit so Hester could come into the room. "I got the best. Get it from China special."

Hester blinked. "Doesn't all tea come from China?" She followed Agatha into the room, which was surprisingly tidy, even clean. There was a slight smell of smoke and hot metal from the wood-burning stove in the corner, very like those she had seen in hospital wards in her nursing days. There was a kettle on the center of the top, steaming gently.

Hester closed the door behind her and followed Agatha inside.

Agatha rolled her eyes. "Most, though folks reckon it'll do well in India soon. This is the best. Delicate. Know a lot, the Chinese."

In spite of herself, Hester was interested. She sat in the seat that Agatha offered her, and a few moments later accepted the cup of steaming, fragrant pale yellow tea, without milk. It had a sharp, clean fragrance she was unused to. She glanced around the walls and saw on one shelf at least thirty books in various stages of disrepair. Clearly they had been very well read indeed. On the opposite wall were glass jars with all manner of dried leaves, herbs, roots, and powders in them.

She forced her attention back to the huge woman now sitting opposite her, watching and waiting.

Hester sipped the tea again. It was quite different from any she was familiar with, but she thought she could learn to like it. "Thank you," she said aloud.

Agatha shrugged and raised her own cup.

"How did you find out about this tea?" Hester asked, sipping it again.

"Plenty o' Chinese in London," Agatha replied. "They know a lot about medicine, poor devils. Showed me some." She looked up quickly at Hester, sharp-eyed. It was a warning that her secrets were precious. She had won them hard and was not going to share them without a price.

Hester had a degree of respect for that. Her own skills had been learned on the battlefield. "I wish we'd had enough opium in the Crimea," she said quietly. "Would have helped a bit, especially when we had to amputate."

Agatha looked at her carefully, eyes narrowed. "Do that a lot, did yer?"

"Enough," Hester replied; memory brought it back to her, as if she were crouching in the mud and desolation of the battlefield, trying to block the cries out of her mind and concentrate only on the silent, ashen face in front of her, the eyes sunken in shock and pain.

Agatha nodded slowly. "Don't do to go over it," she said. "Drive yerself mad. Do yer get 'em now, people with the worst pain, torn-open guts, smashed bones an' the like?"

"Not often." Hester took the chance she had been hoping for. "Sometimes. Stones that won't pass, or torn open after a bad birth. Terrible beatings. That's why I need good opium."

Agatha hesitated as if making a difficult decision.

Hester waited. Seconds ticked by.

Agatha took a deep breath. "I can get yer the best opium," she said, her eyes fixed on Hester's. "Good price. But I can do better than that.

Eatin' it's better than nothin', not as good as smokin' it. But there's better still. Scottish man made this needle where you can stick it straight into the vein, right wherever the pain's worst. Fifteen years ago, or more. I can get you one of them needles."

"I've heard of them," Hester said with a sudden lurch of excitement. "Can you teach me how to use it? And how much to give?"

Agatha nodded. "Have to be careful, mind. You can kill someone easy, if you get it wrong. And worse than that, if you give it to them more than a few times, they get so they want it every day, can't do without it."

Hester frowned, her heart beating faster. "How do you stop that from happening?" Her voice was a little hoarse.

"You make it less, then you stop them getting it at all. They learn. Least, most do. Some don't, an' they go on taking it, one way or another for the rest o' their lives. More an' more. Makes them as sells it rich." The look of fury on her face made Hester wince.

"Is there another way to deal with pain?" Hester asked softly, knowing the answer.

"No." Agatha let the one word fall into the silence.

"Is that what Dr. Lambourn was asking about?" Hester asked. "Needles?"

"Not at first," Agatha replied. "'E were mostly on about deaths of children 'cos women gave 'em medicines they don't know what's in. He didn't get nothin' out of it one way or the other."

"You talked with him?" Hester pressed.

"Course I did. I told you, even if the government'd taken his report, it wouldn't 'ave made no difference to me nor you. An' they didn't anyway, so what do you care?" Her eyes were sharp, clever, watching Hester's face.

"But he asked about addiction to smoking opium?" Hester pressed again.

Agatha grimaced. "Not much, but I told 'im anyway. 'E listened."

"Do you think he killed himself?" Hester said bluntly.

Agatha frowned. "He didn't look to me like that kind of coward, but I s'pose yer never know. What difference does it make to you?"

Hester wondered how much truth to tell. She looked at Agatha more carefully, and decided not to lie at all. The whole question of opium in medicines was complicated by the abuse of it. Where was the dividing line between supplying a need, and profiteering? And had any of it to do with Joel Lambourn's death, or Zenia Gadney's?

"I think maybe he was murdered and it was made to look like suicide," she said aloud to Agatha. "Some of it doesn't make sense."

"Yeah? Like I said, why do you care?" Agatha repeated, looking at Hester narrowly.

"Because if he was murdered, then that makes more sense of Zenia Gadney's murder on Limehouse Pier," Hester explained.

Agatha shivered. "Since when did bloody lunatics make sense? What's the matter wi' you?"

"Mrs. Lambourn's on trial for the murder of Zenia Gadney because the doctor visited Zenia every month and paid her rent and all her other expenses," Hester replied with some heat.

"Stupid bitch," Agatha said bitterly. "What the hell good did that do 'er?"

"None at all."

"So why'd she do it then?" Agatha said, frowning, her eyes full of anger.

"Maybe she didn't. She says the doctor didn't kill himself, either."

Agatha stared at her, a new comprehension in her face. "An' you reckon as it was something to do with him asking about the opium?"

"Don't you? There's a lot of money in opium," Hester pointed out.

"Bleedin' right there is," Agatha said with scathing savagery, as if some memory had returned to her with the thought. "Fortunes made in it, an' reputations lost. Nobody wants to think o' the Opium Wars now. Lot o' secrets, most of 'em bloody an' full o' death an' money." She leaned forward a little. "You be careful," she warned. "You'd be surprised what big families got rich on that an' don't say nothing about it now."

"Did Dr. Lambourn know that?"

"Didn't say, but he weren't nobody's fool—an' neither am I. Don't go messin' around with opium sellers, lady, or you'll maybe end up somewhere cut up in an alley, or floatin' down the river, belly up. I'll get yer what yer need. An' I ain't sayin' that fer profit. Those bastards will 'ave yer for breakfast, but they won't cross me."

"Did Zenia know about all this?" Hester said quickly.

Agatha's eyes widened. "How the 'ell do I know?"

"I'd wager good money you know a great deal about anything that interests you," Hester retorted instantly.

Agatha laughed very quietly, almost under her breath.

"So I do, but madmen wot butcher women in't my concern, less they're after me. An' if they do that . . ." She lifted up her big hands and deliberately cracked her knuckles. "An' I got a big carving knife o' me own, if I 'ave to use it! Mind your own business, lady. I'll get yer opium for yer, best in the world. Fair price."

"And the needle?" Hester asked tentatively.

Agatha blinked. "An' the needle. But yer got ter be real careful with it!"

"I will." Hester stood up. She was glad the weight of her skirt hid the fact that her knees were trembling a little. She kept her voice very steady. "Thank you."

Agatha sighed and rolled her eyes, then suddenly she smiled, showing her big white teeth.

14

Oliver Rathbone was eating his breakfast when the maid interrupted him to announce that Mrs. Monk had called to see him regarding a matter she said was urgent.

Rathbone put down his knife and fork and rose to his feet. "Ask her to come in." He gestured toward his half-finished food. He had no taste for it anyway. He ate it at all simply because he knew he required the nourishment. "Thank you, I don't need any more, but please bring fresh toast and tea for Mrs. Monk," he requested.

"Yes, Sir Oliver," the maid said obediently, and left, taking the plate with her.

A moment later Hester came in, her cheeks flushed from the wind.

"I'm sorry," she apologized, her eyes taking in the table and the obvious fact that she had interrupted. "I had to catch you before you left for court."

"Sit down. More tea is coming." He gestured toward the chair where Margaret used to sit, then, as she took it, he sat also. "You must have left home very early. Has something happened? I'm afraid I have no good news to tell you."

"Bad news?" she asked quickly, anxiety shadowing her face.

He had learned not to lie to her, even to soften a blow.

"I'm beginning to think Mrs. Lambourn could be right, at least insofar as there being a government agreement not to allow Lambourn's report to be given any credibility," he answered. "I've tried to question his suicide, and the judge has cut me off every time. I think Coniston has also been briefed to head off any mention of it at all."

"But you'll not let him get away with that." It was half a question; the doubt was still there in her voice, and in her eyes.

"We're not beaten yet," he said ruefully. "In a sense their possible agreement in keeping it out of the evidence suggests that there is something to hide. It certainly isn't in order to spare anyone's feelings, as they say it is."

The maid came in with fresh tea and toast, and Rathbone thanked her for it. He poured for Hester without asking, and she took it with a smile, then reached also for toast and butter.

"Oliver, I've been doing a little asking around among people I know. I had a long talk with a prostitute near Copenhagen Place. She knew Zenia Gadney, possibly as well as anyone did."

He heard the pity in her voice and found himself knotted inside. He wished he were more convinced of Dinah Lambourn's innocence. But even if Joel Lambourn had been murdered, it did not prove that Dinah had not killed Zenia out of revenge for her betrayal during all the years before.

Except, of course, if anyone had betrayed Dinah, it was Joel himself. But he was already dead, and beyond her reach. The only things that made Rathbone question Dinah's guilt at all were the senseless timing of Zenia's death, and the fact that Pendock and Coniston both seemed so determined to block Rathbone from raising any doubt, however reasonable, about Joel's suicide.

Hester knew she did not have his attention.

"Oliver?"

He concentrated again. "Yes? I'm sorry. What did you learn that you need to tell me before I go into court again?"

She spread marmalade on her toast. "That Zenia was a very quiet woman, kept very much to herself. She used to walk often, especially by the river. She stood and gazed southward, watching the water and the sky."

"You mean toward Greenwich?" he asked curiously.

"Well, toward the south bank anyway. She had a past that she spoke of very seldom, once to Gladys, the girl I mentioned."

Rathbone felt a little chilled. "What kind of a past? Is it one that could provide another motive for killing her with such violence?"

Hester shook her head. "Not as far as I can see. She said she was married once, but apparently she drank so hard she ruined her life, and possibly she left him, or he left her."

"Who was he?" Rathbone asked quickly, feeling a lift of hope he hardly dared acknowledge. "Where can we find him? Could he have followed her to Limehouse and killed her? Perhaps he wanted to marry again, and she was standing in his way?" His mind was racing. At last there were other possibilities surfacing, which had nothing to do with Dinah Lambourn.

"Gladys guessed at it, based on something Zenia said once, when a woman was falling down drunk in the street," Hester answered. "She didn't even know if it was true, and no one has ever seen another man in Copenhagen Place, visiting her, or even looking for her. He could be dead by now, if he ever existed at all."

Her voice dropped and she looked sad, and apologetic. "She could have invented him, to make herself sound more respectable, or even more interesting. It could have been daydreaming, a bit of wishing that it had been so."

He felt the sadness inside him also, a sudden understanding of the woman's wistful dreams that he would prefer not to have understood. "Then why did you come to tell it to me so urgently before I went into court?" The sharp edge of disappointment was raw in his voice.

"I'm sorry, that was misleading." She brushed it away with a slender hand. "What I really came to tell you was that I also found a woman called Agatha Nisbet, who runs something of a makeshift hospital on the south bank of the river, near Greenland Dock. It is mainly for injured dockers, lightermen, and so on. She has a pretty steady supply of opium . . ."

"Opium?" Now he was listening, his attention quickened.

"Yes." She smiled bleakly. "I made a deal with her to buy the best quality myself, for the clinic. She spoke to Joel Lambourn several times.

He sought her out in his inquiries into opium. He wasn't out to stop the trade, just to get it properly labeled so people knew what they were taking. Agnes Nisbet said it was the deaths of children that upset him especially."

Rathbone nodded. He knew that already.

"But she warned me that a lot of people make money out of opium, ever since the Opium Wars," Hester went on. "They are quite happy, some of the worst of them, to get people addicted so they will have a permanent market." Her face was pinched with misery and anger as she said it. "A lot of very powerful families built their fortunes on opium, and they wouldn't be at all happy with the exposure Lambourn's report would inevitably have brought when it was argued in Parliament. All kinds of ghosts would've been dug up."

"You can't dig up a ghost," he said irrelevantly. "Do you think Dinah is right, at least as far as Lambourn's report is concerned?"

"Yes," she said without hesitation. "It makes sense, Oliver. We don't even know whose fortune comes from opium, and what they could lose if it's all brought out into the open, and regulated. Some companies are going to go out of business, simply because they wouldn't make the same level of profit if they are forced to measure and label."

He thought about it for a moment or two. It opened up new, alternative explanations for the death of both Joel Lambourn and Zenia Gadney—but they had no proof of anything. Great fortunes had always been made in appalling ways: through buccaneering—which was only another name for piracy—slaving, before the abolition half a century ago; and then in opium. Few wealthy families were free from one stain or another. With the fear and anger running rampant in the courtroom, and far beyond it, he did not think that "reasonable doubt" was going to save Dinah Lambourn.

"Do you know anything about the Opium Wars?" Hester interrupted his thoughts.

"Not much," he admitted. "It was all in China. Trade war of some sort, as far as I know. Our part in it has been justified by some, but it was pretty ugly. I believe we introduced opium into China and now hundreds of thousands of people are addicted to it. Not something to be proud of."

"Perhaps we should find out more, just in case it matters," she said quietly.

"Did you believe this woman, this Agatha?" he asked her. "Not her honesty, but her knowledge?"

"Yes . . . I think so. It compared in ways to my own experience in the Crimea."

"Are there any wars that aren't ugly?" He thought bitterly of all he knew and had heard of the Crimean War, its violence, futility, and loss. "This Civil War in America—God knows what those losses will be by the end—pretty good market for opium there, too. I hear the slaughter is appalling, and the injuries to those who survived. I don't suppose they even know the extent of it themselves yet. And it's not just the dead, it's the ruin of the land, and the hatred left behind."

"I think there's a good deal of hatred left behind the Opium Wars, too," Hester replied. "And money, and guilt. A lot of secrets to bury."

"Secrets don't stay buried," Rathbone said quietly. He wanted to tell her about his own secret, those photographs still sitting in his home, waiting to be stored in a bank vault where only he could disinter them.

She was staring at him. "Oliver?" she said with concern. "Do you know something about Dinah that we don't? Something bad?"

"No!" he said with a rush of relief. "It . . . it was . . . I was thinking about something else entirely."

She looked doubtful. "It?" she asked. "What are we talking about?"

"It was . . . it . . ." He breathed in and out deeply. The weight of the knowledge he carried was almost unbearable alone. "Do you know what happened to Arthur Ballinger's photographs after he was killed?"

Her face paled a little, and there was pain in her eyes.

"I have no idea. Why? Are you afraid someone has them?" She reached across the table and touched his hand gently. "There's no point in worrying. They're probably locked up somewhere where nobody will ever find them. But if they're not, there's still nothing you can do about it." Her hand was warm on his. "If somebody has them they can only blackmail the guilty, and do you really have any sympathy for men who abused children like that? I know they may have been fools more than villains to begin with, but you still can't protect them."

"I would have no sympathy if it were about money, Hester, but it isn't. It's about power," he said simply.

"Power?" There was sharper fear in her face now, and perhaps the beginning of understanding as to what he meant.

"Power to make the men in those photographs do anything, which they would, out of fear of being exposed," he elaborated.

"Do you think there are other people in those pictures who are . . . judges and politicians, or . . . ?" She saw it in his face. "You do! Did Ballinger say there were?"

"No. He did far worse than that, Hester. He left them to me." He looked at her intently, waiting for the horror in her eyes, even the revulsion.

She sat motionless and very slowly the full impact of it settled over her, like a shadow. She studied him. Perhaps she saw in him something of the burden he felt, and the bitterness of the irony. It was both Ballinger's legacy and his revenge. He might not know what it would do to Rathbone, but he must have relished the possibilities.

"I'm sorry," she said at last. "If you had destroyed them you would have told me differently, wouldn't you." It was not a question; she was letting him know that she understood.

"Yes," he confessed. "I would. I will hide them. If I die then they will be destroyed. I meant to do it at the time I saw them; then when I saw who was in them, I couldn't. Maybe I still will. The power of it is . . . so very great. Ballinger began by using them only for good, you know? He told me. It was to force people to take action against injustice or abuse, when they wouldn't do it any other way." Was he making excuses for Ballinger? Or for himself, because he had not destroyed the pictures? He looked at Hester's face and saw the confusion in her, and the comprehension. He waited for her to ask if he would use them, and she did not.

 . "Do you think Dinah is innocent?" she asked instead.

"I don't know," he said honestly. "At first I thought it was possible, then after the beginning of the trial, I seriously doubted it. Now I don't know whether she killed Zenia Gadney or not, but I'm beginning to have very serious doubts as to whether Lambourn committed suicide.

And if he was murdered, then that opens up a lot of other doubts, and questions."

There was a sound of footsteps outside the door to the hall. A moment later Ardmore came in and very courteously reminded Rathbone that it was time for him to go.

Hester smiled and rose to her feet. There was no need for further discussion, simply a quiet good-bye.

LAMBOURN'S SUICIDE WAS STILL in Rathbone's mind as the trial resumed an hour and a half later, when he met Sorley Coniston in the hall and they exchanged brief greetings.

"Morning," Coniston said with a slight smile. "Tough one for you, Rathbone. Whatever made you take it? I used to wonder if you accepted cases for notoriety sometimes, but I always decided you didn't. Haven't changed, have you?"

"Not that much," Rathbone replied drily. He did not know Coniston well, though they had been acquainted for years, but thought he might like the man if he did. He was unpredictable, and occasionally his opinions were startlingly honest. "This time I can't make up my mind myself."

"For heaven's sake!" Coniston said, shaking his head. "The only question in this one is how far you can bring in the damn opium question. Lambourn might have gone off the rails in his personal life, but he was a decent man, and honest. Don't drag his private mistakes out in front of the world. His children don't deserve that, even if you think he does."

Rathbone smiled back at him. "Cold feet?" he asked wryly.

"Going to hold them to the fire," Coniston replied. "Yours, I mean."

"Really?" Rathbone shrugged with confidence he did not feel, and they went into the courtroom.

Twenty minutes later, Coniston rose to question his first witness of the day, Dinah's sister-in-law, Amity Herne.

Rathbone watched as she walked across the open space toward the witness box. With one hand delicately lifting her skirt so she did not trip, she climbed up the steps to the top and stood facing the body of the court.

Rathbone would like to have looked across at Dinah to see her expression, but he did not want to draw the jury's attention to her, when they were all watching Amity Herne so closely. He could not imagine the pain of seeing your own family testify against you. Did they blame her for Lambourn's death? For any degree of the unhappiness that they believed had led to his suicide? He might soon know. He realized his hands were knotted in his lap beneath the table where they could not see them, his muscles aching already, at the very beginning of the morning.

Amity Herne swore to her name, and to tell the truth, all of it, and nothing but. She acknowledged that she was the sister of the accused woman's late husband, Joel Lambourn.

"I offer my condolences for the recent loss of your brother, Mrs. Herne," Coniston began. "And I apologize for being obliged to open up so publicly a subject that must be additionally painful to you in the recent tragedy that has afflicted your family."

"Thank you," she said graciously. She was an attractive woman, although not beautiful, and now appeared a little too unemotional for Rathbone's taste. Perhaps in the circumstances a certain stiffness was the only defense she had to preserve any composure at all, when all privacy was denied her. There was something in the dignity with which she stood waiting for Coniston to open up the wounds that reminded him of Margaret. He should have admired her more. How much was his own disillusion warping his views of the people around him?

Surely Coniston, standing gracefully and even a little deferentially, realized that the jury would not take kindly to anyone who was unnecessarily rough with Amity Herne. He would begin gently, set a pattern Rathbone would have no choice but to follow.

"Mrs. Herne," Coniston began, "were you aware of the nature of the work that your brother, Dr. Lambourn, was doing for the government?"

Rathbone sat up a little straighter. Surely Coniston was not going to allow that subject to be raised?

"Only in the vaguest terms," Amity replied calmly, her voice soft and very precise. "It was a medical investigation of some kind, that is all he would say."

"Confidential?" Coniston said.

"I imagine so," she agreed. She kept her gaze fixed on him, never allowing it to wander toward the gallery and not once even glancing over to the dock, where Dinah sat between her jailers.

"But I did not ask him further anyway," she continued. "I do know that it troubled him. He felt very deeply about it, and I was concerned that he was allowing himself to become too involved in it."

Rathbone rose to his feet. "My lord, Mrs. Herne has just said that she has very little idea what the work was concerned with. How, then, could she judge whether his involvement was too great?" He would like to have argued that it was also completely irrelevant to Zenia Gadney's death, but he intended to introduce the exact point later on, and this opened the door for him nicely.

Coniston smiled. "She might not have known specifically what the work was, but she can judge if it had bearing on the state of his mind. And if it bears on his state of mind, my lord, it will automatically bear on the state of mind of the accused."

"My lord!" Rathbone was still on his feet. "How can Dr. Lambourn's concern for his work have been on the accused's state of mind two months after he was dead? Is my learned friend suggesting there was some kind of communicable madness involved?"

There was a ripple of nervous laughter around the gallery. One juror sneezed and put his handkerchief up to his face, hiding his expression.

"I will permit this kind of questioning," Pendock said, clearing his throat, "on condition that you reach some relevance very soon, Mr. Coniston." He did not look at Rathbone.

"Thank you, my lord." Coniston turned again to Amity Herne. "Mrs. Herne, was Dr. Lambourn more involved with this task, whatever it was, than was usual for him?"

"Yes," she said decisively, a look of grief shadowing her face. "He became completely absorbed in it."

"What do you mean by that, Mrs. Herne? What is unusual about a doctor being absorbed in his work?" Coniston was still overly polite.

"When the government did not accept his conclusions he was distraught. At times he was almost hysterical. I . . ." She looked uncomfortable. Her hands gripped the rail in front of her and she gulped, as if to control tears. "I believe that was why he took his own life. I wish I had been more aware how serious it was. Perhaps I could have said or done something! I didn't realize that everything he valued in his life was disintegrating in front of him. Or he believed it was."

Coniston stood perfectly still in the middle of the floor, an elegant figure, even kindly. "Disintegrating, Mrs. Herne? Isn't that rather extreme? Because the government did not accept his views on . . . whatever it was?"

"That and . . ." Her voice dropped so low it was difficult to hear her. No one in the room moved. The crowd in the gallery were still, as if frozen.

Coniston waited.

"That, and his personal life," Amity finished in no more than a murmur.

Pendock leaned forward a little. "Mrs. Herne, I realize this must be appallingly difficult for you, but I must ask you to speak a little more loudly, so the jury may hear you."

"I'm sorry," she said contritely. "I find this . . . most embarrassing to mention in public. Joel was a very quiet man, very private. I am not sure how to put this delicately." She stared at Coniston; never once did her eyes stray to Rathbone. It was as if she were not aware that he was there, and would question her next. In fact, it seemed as if she was deliberately excluding the rest of the court altogether.

"His personal life?" Coniston prompted her. "He was your brother, Mrs. Herne. If he confided in you, even indirectly, you must tell the court. I am sorry to force you, but this is a murder case. One woman has lost her life, hideously, and another stands accused of her murder, and if found guilty will assuredly also lose hers. We cannot allow ourselves the luxury of being delicate at the expense of truth."

With an immense effort Amity Herne raised her head. "He implied to me that he had needs that his wife was not willing to meet, and that he visited another woman for that purpose." She said the words clearly and distinctly, like delivering knife wounds to herself. "The pressure of living up to his wife's vision of him as a perfect man was becoming more than he could bear." She bit her lip. "I wish you had not made me say that, but it is true. It should have been allowed to die with him." She could no longer stop the tears spilling down her cheeks.

"I wish it had been possible," Coniston said contritely. "This other woman that you speak of, did you know who she was? Did he mention her name, or anything about her? Such as where she lived?"

"He said her name was Zenia. He did not say where she lived, at least not to me." The implication that she might have said so to someone else was left delicately in the air.

"Zenia?" Coniston repeated. "You are certain?"

Amity stood very stiffly. "Yes. I have never heard of anyone else with the name."

"And was his wife, Dinah Lambourn, aware of this . . . arrangement?" Coniston asked.

"I was told that she learned of it," Amity replied.

"How did she learn?"

"I don't know. Joel didn't say."

"Did he say when she learned?"

"No. At least not to me."

"Thank you, Mrs. Herne. Again, I am deeply sorry that I had to raise this distressing subject, but the circumstances left me no choice." He turned to Rathbone. "Your witness, Sir Oliver."

Rathbone thanked him and rose slowly to his feet. He walked out across the floor toward the witness stand. He could feel the jury's eyes on him, cautious, ready to blame him if he was the least bit insensitive. They were naturally predisposed against him because he represented a woman accused of a bestial crime. And now, added to that, he was about to ask pointed and cruel questions, adding to this innocent woman's grief and very natural embarrassment.

"You have already suffered more than enough, Mrs. Herne," Rathbone began gently. "I shall be as brief with you as I can. I commend you for being so honest regarding your brother's . . . tastes. That cannot have been easy for you. You and your brother were close?" He already knew the answer to that from Monk's questioning of her.

She blinked. In that instant he knew she was considering a lie, and as their eyes met, she decided against it.

"Not until recently," she admitted. "My husband and I lived some distance away. Visiting was difficult. But we always kept in touch. There were just the two of us, Joel and I. Our parents have been dead a long time." There was an ache of sadness in her voice, and a loneliness in her face. She was the perfect witness for Coniston.

Rathbone changed his tactics. There was very little, if anything at all, that he could win.

"Did you at that time also come to know your sister-in-law better?"

She hesitated again.

He felt his stomach knot. Should he have asked her that? If she said yes, then she would either defend her, or be seen to betray her. If she said no, she would have to give a reason. He had made an error.

"I tried," she said guiltily, a slight flush in her cheeks. "I think if things had been different, we might have become close. But when Joel died, she was beside herself with grief, as if she blamed herself . . ." She tailed off.

In the gallery several people moved, sighed, and rustled fabric or paper.

"Did you blame her?" Rathbone asked clearly.

"No, of course not." She looked startled.

"It was not her fault that Dr. Lambourn's work was rejected?"

Coniston made as if to stand up. Rathbone turned to look at him, eyebrows raised. Coniston relaxed again.

"Mrs. Herne?" Rathbone prompted.

"How could it be?" she answered. "That isn't possible."

"Should she have . . . complied with his needs? The ones for which he went to the woman named Zenia?" he suggested.

"I . . . I . . ." At last she was stuck for words. She did not look to Coniston for help but lowered her gaze modestly.

Coniston stood up. "My lord, my learned friend's question is embarrassing and unnecessary. How could Mrs. Herne be—"

Rathbone gave a gracious little wave. "That's all right, Mrs. Herne. Your silence is answer enough. Thank you. I have no further questions."

Coniston next called Barclay Herne, and asked him to give the briefest possible account of Lambourn's being asked by the government to make a confidential report on the use and sale of certain medicines. Herne added the now-accepted fact that, to his profound regret, Lambourn had become too passionately involved in the issues and it had warped his judgment to the degree that the government had been unable to accept his work.

"How did Dr. Lambourn take your rejection of his report, Mr. Herne?" Coniston said somberly.

Herne allowed grief to fill his expression. "I'm afraid he took it very badly," he answered, his voice soft and a little husky. "He saw it as some kind of personal insult. I was worried for the balance of his mind. I profoundly regret that I did not take more care, perhaps persuade him to consult a colleague, but I really did not think it would affect him so . . . frankly, so out of proportion to reality." He looked miserable, forced publicly to expose his family's very personal tragedy.

Rathbone was surprised to feel a touch of pity for him. He turned as discreetly as he could to see if his wife had remained in the gallery, now that her own evidence was given. He saw her after a moment of searching, when a large man bent forward. Amity Herne was sitting immediately behind him, next to Sinden Bawtry. His handsome head was turned sideways, as if speaking to her.

The next moment the man in front straightened up again, and Rathbone drew his attention back to the witness stand.

"I wondered afterward if perhaps he had indulged in the use of opium far more than we guessed at the time." Herne was answering the next question. "I'm sorry to say that. I feel very guilty that I did not take his whole breakdown far more gravely than I did."

"Thank you, Mr. Herne." Again Coniston bowed to Rathbone. "Your witness, Sir Oliver."

Rathbone thanked him and took his place in the center of the floor, like a gladiator in the arena—exposed. "You mentioned opium, Mr. Herne. Were you aware that Dr. Lambourn was using it?"

"Not until after his death!" Herne said quickly.

"But you just said that you blamed yourself for not having realized that he was using it so much. How could you be expected to do that, if you were not aware that he was using it at all?"

"I meant that maybe I should have been aware," Herne corrected himself.

"Could he have used more than he was aware of himself?" Rathbone suggested.

Herne looked puzzled. "I don't know what you mean."

"Wasn't his research into the issue of opium being available in patent medicines, purchasable on any high street in the country, but without labeling to allow the person buying to know—"

Coniston jerked up to his feet. "My lord, Dr. Lambourn's work was confidential. This is not an appropriate place to debate what has not yet been proved as to its accuracy."

"Yes, your objection is noted, Mr. Coniston." Pendock turned to Rathbone. "This kind of questioning is irrelevant, Sir Oliver. You cannot connect it with the murder of Zenia Gadney. Are you suggesting that Mrs. Lambourn was somehow affected by taking opium incorrectly labeled, to the extent that she is not guilty for her acts?"

"No, my lord. But my learned friend raised the question of taking opium—"

"Yes," Pendock said quickly. "Mr. Coniston, Sir Oliver did not object to your reference, but I do. It has nothing to do with the murder of Zenia Gadney. Please restrict yourself to that subject. You are wasting the court's time and patience, and run the risk of confusing the jury. Proceed, Sir Oliver, if you have anything more to ask the witness that has bearing on the issue at trial."

Rathbone stood in the middle of the floor and stared up at Pendock in his magnificent seat. His full-bottomed white wig and scarlet robes marked him out as a man set apart, a man with superior power. He saw in Pendock's face that he was immovable on the subject. It was a strange, chill moment of understanding. Pendock was not impartial; he had his own agenda, perhaps even his orders.

"No more questions, my lord," Rathbone replied. He turned and walked back to his seat. It was at that moment, facing the gallery, that he saw Sinden Bawtry staring across the heads of the people in front of him, directly at Pendock.

At the end of the day Rathbone went to see Dinah in the prison. As her lawyer, he was allowed to speak to her alone. As soon as the cell door clanged shut, closing them into the narrow space with its echoing stone and stale smell, he began. Time was short, and precious.

"When did you first know about your husband and Zenia Gadney?" he asked. "You are fighting for your life. Don't lie to me now. Believe me, you cannot afford it."

She looked ashen pale, her eyes hollow, her whole body tense, but there was no wavering in her. He could not imagine what effort that cost her.

"I don't remember exactly. About fifteen years ago," she replied.

"And is what your sister-in-law said true? He wanted certain practices from you that you were not prepared to give?"

A quick anger flared up in her eyes. "No! Joel was . . . gentle . . . perfectly normal. He would never have said anything like that to Amity. One does not discuss such a thing, even if it were true!"

Rathbone looked at her closely. She was angry, defensive—but of Joel, or of herself? Did she deny it so fiercely because it was a lie, or because it was horribly and painfully true? He wanted to believe her.

"Then why did he go to her for all those years, and pay her?" he asked. Everything might hang on that answer.

She blinked, but she did not lower her eyes. "She was a friend. She . . . used to be respectable, married. She had an accident, and was in a lot of pain. She became addicted to opium. She . . ." Dinah drew in a deep breath, and began again. "Her husband was a friend of Joel's. When Zenia took to the streets, Joel helped her, financially. He did not tell Amity because she was living elsewhere at that time, and it was none of her concern. Anyway, she and Joel were never close, even growing up. He was seven years older than she and they had little in common. He was always studious, she was not." She shook her head briefly. "And why would he tell her such a thing? He was a doctor. He kept confidences. He told me only to explain why he went to Limehouse, and why he gave her money to live on."

He almost believed her. But there was something in the tension of her neck, the way her eyes never wavered from his, that left him fearing it was only part of the truth, and there was something vital that she had deliberately left out.

Yet Hester had told him that Zenia had said to Gladys that she had been married at one time, and her drinking had ended it. If the problem had been opium, why had she not said so? Or had Gladys simply assumed it was drink because of Zenia's pity for the woman drunk in the street?

It fitted together perfectly—almost!

"Mrs. Lambourn," Rathbone said earnestly, "you have no more time left to keep secrets, no matter how painful. You are fighting for your life, and believe me, the fact that you are a woman will not save you. If you are found guilty, three Sundays after the verdict is passed, you will walk to the gallows."

She was so white he thought she was going to faint. He felt brutal, and yet she left him no choice if he was to have any chance at all of saving her.

"For God's sake, tell me the truth!" he said desperately.

"That is the truth!" Her voice was so strangled in her throat he could barely hear it. "Joel took money to her every month, so she could survive without resorting to prostitution."

"Can you prove that? Any part of it?" he demanded.

"Of course not. How could I?"

"Did you know the money went regularly?" He was clutching at straws.

Her eyes widened a fraction. "Yes. It was paid on the twenty-first of every month. It was in the household ledger."

"Entered as what?"

"Under her initials—Z.G. He did not lie to me, Sir Oliver."

He could see that that was what she believed. But then how could she bear to believe differently? What woman in her place would?

"Unfortunately there is no proof of that which we could show the court," he said quietly. "The fact that he told you he gave her the money as an act of friendship does not prove that that was the truth. What happened to Zenia's husband? Why did he not provide for her?"

"He's dead," she said simply, an unexpected finality of grief in her face.

"What was his name?"

"I . . . I don't know."

This time he was sure she was lying; he just could not understand why.

He changed the subject. "Why did you tell the police that you were at a soirée with Mrs. Moulton when you knew she would not support that? It was not only a lie; it was one you were bound to be caught in."

She looked down at her hands. "I know."

"Did you panic?" he asked more gently.

"No," she whispered.

"What on earth did you hope to gain by speaking to Zenia?" he persisted. "What did you think she would tell you about your husband? Did you think he left papers from his report with her? Or that somehow she had helped him? Did she know something about opium that would have validated his findings?"

She faced him again. "I didn't go to Copenhagen Place. I don't know who that woman was. Clearly she tried to look like me. There's not much point in bringing the shopkeeper and other people in to testify, because they'll say what everybody expects them to—and what they will now believe is the truth. But I did not go. That I know as well as I know I'm sitting here."

She took a deep, shaky breath. "And I will never believe that Joel killed himself. He knew his report was right and he was determined to fight his detractors. You have no idea of the evil and the shame of the opium trade, Sir Oliver, or of the people who are involved in it." Her voice was trembling now. "Joel wept for what we have done in China. It is a very hard thing to acknowledge that your own country has committed atrocities. Many people cannot do that. They will go on to create more lies to cover the first." There was a curious look in her eyes, almost a challenge.

Suddenly a new truth became shatteringly clear to him, bringing the sweat out on his body and choking the breath in his throat. She had lied about being with Helena Moulton quite deliberately, knowing it would be exposed, and that Monk would have no choice but to charge her with Zenia's murder—and she would stand trial for her life. She had meant it to happen. She had asked Monk to have Rathbone to defend her because she believed he would force the truth of Joel's murder into the open, and clear his name. Perhaps his work would even be continued by someone else. That was the depth of her belief in him—and her love.

Ridiculously, he found his mouth dry and he had to swallow hard in order to speak. He looked away from her, blinking rapidly to stop the tears in his eyes.

"I'll do everything I can." It was a promise he would keep, but he had no idea if it would be enough to save her, let alone to restore Joel Lambourn's reputation. She must have seen that Pendock was against them, just as he had. And yet she had not given in.

How different she was from Margaret! How brave, reckless, and loyal. Beautiful and a little frightening. What must Joel Lambourn have been like to be worthy of such a woman?

He stood up very slowly. "I'll see you tomorrow," he said a little hoarsely. "I know somewhere I can at least try to get help." ·

Monk had received a message from Rathbone late the previous evening requesting him to be at his chambers at eight o'clock so that they would have time to speak before Rathbone was due in court. Consequently Monk was up at six. He ate breakfast with Hester, both of them saying little in a silent understanding of the growing desperation of the case. He was on the river by seven, sitting in the ferry from Princes Stairs across to Wapping, still aware of a steady ache in his shoulder from his battle in the street. Since then he and Runcorn had both been more careful.

He was not looking forward to the meeting. A brawl on one of the docks, in which a man had been killed, had kept him busy during the previous day, and in the little time he had been able to spare in the evening he had achieved nothing. He knew Hester had already told Rathbone about the nurse, Agatha Nisbet, but all that did was to confirm that Joel Lambourn had been investigating opium in patent medicines, which they already knew.

Orme was still questioning people in Limehouse, especially the area near the pier, but no one had seen anything useful. One person admitted seeing three men, considerably the worse for drink, but he was not certain if it was that evening or another. Someone else had seen two women walking to the pier at the right sort of time, and the right day, but definitely not a man.

The boat reached the steps at Wapping and he paid the ferryman and got out. The tide was low and the stones were wet. He had to be careful he did not slip. He reached the top and strode across the open stretch of the dock. The wind was rising as the tide started to flow again, coming in from the sea. It smelled of salt and fish, and now and again an unpleasant odor of effluent. Even so, it was better than the smell of the city streets, and there was a vitality in the air he had come to love. Here the sky was wide. No buildings closed in the vision and there was always light, no matter how dark the weather. Even at night the lamps' yellow glow marked the ships.

He had no time to call in at the station first. He went straight toward the high street and the first hansom cab he could catch.

He found Rathbone tense but remarkably full of energy. He welcomed Monk into the familiar quiet sitting room. There was a small fire in the grate, in spite of the fact that Rathbone would be in court most of the day.

"Come in. Sit down." Rathbone indicated one of the leather chairs. "Monk, I need your help. This has suddenly become urgent. Lambourn's sister gave evidence yesterday, which is pretty damning against Dinah, and Lambourn also. I think she's much more loyal to her husband than to her brother."

"Her husband is still alive," Monk pointed out a little cynically.

Rathbone's face tightened but he made no comment on it. "Sinden Bawtry was in court for the second time."

"Protecting the government's interest in the Pharmacy Act?" Monk asked.

"Possibly. The judge is ruling against me every time he can, even stretching it a bit. I can't help feeling he's been instructed." He continued pacing, too restless to sit himself. "Monk, I've suddenly realized what this is about. I don't know how I can have been so blind! Well, I do. But that's all irrelevant now." He paced from Monk's chair to the door, turned, and came back again.

"Dinah lied about being at the soirée precisely in order that you should arrest her, and she would beg you to have me to defend her!" He watched Monk's face intently.

Monk was incredulous. Rathbone's grief over Margaret had damaged his judgment even more than he had feared.

"Dinah Lambourn implicated herself in a particularly obscene murder simply in order to create the opportunity for you to defend her?" he said, unable to keep the disbelief out of his face. "Why, for God's sake? Couldn't she simply have contrived an introduction?"

"Not to meet me, you fool!" Rathbone said with a glimmer of bitter amusement. "To get the story of Joel's death into open court. She saw the opportunity in Zenia Gadney's murder, and took it. She is willing to risk being condemned to death in order to clear her husband's name and restore the reputation he earned for diligence and honor."

Monk's understanding came when he saw the light in Rathbone's face, the softness and the grief in his eyes. His body was stiff, and he was thinner than he had been only a few months ago, before the end of the Ballinger case. But this morning there was a vitality in him; he had a great cause to fight for.

Monk had no idea if Rathbone was right or not, but he did not want to crush the possibility.

"What is it you want me to do?" he asked, dreading the answer would be impossible to meet.

"Dinah said Lambourn supported Zenia because she was the widow of a friend of his," Rathbone answered. "Dinah knew about it almost from the beginning. The money went from the household ledgers, under the initials Z.G. on the twenty-first of every month. If we can prove that's true, then her principal motive is gone."

Monk felt his heart sink. "Oliver, that's what he told her—or else she's just thought of a very clever excuse for his behavior. It's—"

"Capable of proof!" Rathbone cut across him urgently. "Trace back where Zenia came from. Look at the records. We know her age—she must have been married within the last twenty-nine years. Find the husband." He was lit with eagerness now, his voice low and keen. "Find his connection to Joel Lambourn. Perhaps they studied together, practiced medicine together. Somewhere their paths crossed and they became such close friends that Lambourn supported his widow all his life. Even went to see her once a month, unfailingly. That's a hell of a loyalty. There'll be ways of tracing it."

Monk said nothing.

"Find it!" Rathbone repeated more sharply.

"You believe it?" Monk asked, wishing he did not have to.

Rathbone hesitated, a split second too long. "*Basically*, yes," he said with a faint smile of self-mockery. "She's lying about something, I don't know what. I do believe that she implicated herself deliberately by lying as to where she was, in order to stand trial, hoping that the whole issue of Joel's suicide would have to be examined again, and somehow we would prove that it was murder, because his work was totally valid, and somebody wants it concealed."

Monk pushed himself up onto his feet. "Then I'll reopen my investigation," he said quietly. "And I'll get Runcorn to reopen his."

Rathbone smiled, the ease relaxing his body, hope in his eyes. "Thank you."

Monk went directly to Runcorn's office. It was still a long journey eastward and back across the river in a rising wind with sleet on the edge of it. Maybe it would snow for Christmas.

He met Runcorn at the door, just as he was leaving.

Runcorn saw his face and, without speaking, he turned back and went up the stairs to his office, motioning Monk to follow him. As soon as he closed the door, Monk repeated the essence of what Rathbone had told him. Runcorn did not interrupt until he was finished.

Runcorn nodded. He did not ask if Monk believed it.

"We'd better see if anyone knows where Zenia came from," he said practically. "Trouble is, asking too many people. Better it doesn't get back to Lambourn's enemies that we're still looking."

Monk assumed for a moment that Runcorn was thinking of his own safety. Then a glance at his face, a memory of him in the firelight looking at Melisande, made him ashamed of the thought.

"Has anyone said anything to you?" he asked. He should have expected it, after the attack in the street, especially given what Rathbone had said about Sinden Bawtry being in court, and his conviction that Pendock was deliberately blocking him at every turn.

Runcorn gave a slight shrug. "Obliquely," he said, treating it lightly, although Monk heard the slight rasp in his voice. "Not only a warning, more a thank-you in advance, for acting with discretion."

Monk wondered if he should tell Runcorn that he would understand if he did not wish to pursue the matter. His career might be jeopardized. He remembered how much that had mattered to him in the past, how all the times the next step upward had been the goal.

"We'll have to be careful." Runcorn's voice cut across his thoughts. "Check Zenia, not Lambourn. It would have been easier to check Lambourn's career and see who he might have been close to and who died about fifteen years ago, but they'd spot that. Zenia's not a common name. Be a lot harder if she were Mary or Betty." He smiled lopsidedly. "Wonder if Gadney's her maiden name, or married. D'you know?"

"We'll check Gadney for deaths around fifteen years ago," Monk replied with a sudden lift of enthusiasm. It would be good to work with Runcorn again, as he knew they had at the beginning of their careers. Runcorn would remember it. He wished he could. Perhaps he would have flashes of recall, as he'd had at the beginning of his amnesia, sudden jolts when something was desperately familiar, and for an instant he could see it clearly.

"Then we'd better start now." Runcorn picked up his jacket again. "It could take awhile. How many more days does Rathbone think we have?"

"A week, maybe," Monk replied. "He'll drag it out as long as he can." Neither of them needed to say that once the verdict was in it would be all but impossible to get the case reopened. Evidence would no longer sway a jury. It would have to be an error in law, or some new fact so irrefutable that no one could deny it, before they would overturn the court's decision. Time was their enemy, along with the vested interests of money and reputation.

Obligatory civil records of births, deaths, and marriages had begun in 1838, twenty-six years ago. But to begin with there had been omissions, and there was always the possibility that an event had not taken place in the county. People made mistakes, misread a name or a number, mistook a 5 for an 8, or even a 3, and that altered everything. And, of course, people lied, especially about their age.

They left Runcorn's office in Blackheath and went back across the river. As they sat hunched up in the ferry, their faces were stung with fine pellets of ice as the sleet drove westward off the water.

At Wapping they went ashore and took a cab west again. They rode in an oddly comfortable silence. There was no need to make conversation. Each was quietly consumed in thoughts of the case, and how much might rest on it.

They were conducted into the vast, silent storerooms of the registry office, and Monk began looking for a death in the name of Gadney, although neither of them had any idea what the man's Christian name might be, or even the year of the death. He started fifteen years earlier and moved forward.

Runcorn began at that time and worked back.

They searched until both were bleary-eyed and dry-mouthed, then stopped for something to take away the taste of dust and paper in the air.

"Nothing," Runcorn said, failing to keep the disappointment out of his voice.

"We need to think again," Monk admitted, returning the last heavy book to its place on the shelf. "Let's do it in a pub with a decent lunch. I feel as if I can taste that ink."

"Maybe Gadney's her maiden name, not her husband's," Monk said a quarter of an hour later as they ate thick slices of fresh bread with crumbling Caerphilly cheese and pickles. They were both thirsty enough to get through a pint of cider and ask for a second. "They called her Mrs. Gadney, but that doesn't necessarily mean the title was accurate."

"Then his name could be anything." Runcorn wiped crumbs off his mouth. "Did anyone mention an accent? Please don't tell me she was Irish! We haven't time to start looking for anything that far away."

"No one mentioned it." Monk reached for a piece of sharp-flavored apple pie, cooked till the slices of fruit were tender but still whole. "And I think they would have. Anyway, her birth would be before they kept general records. We'd have to go to the parish for the church register. What good would it do anyway? It doesn't help to know where she was born."

"It might," Runcorn argued. "Women often get married wherever they grew up rather than where the husband lives."

He was right. Once Monk would have argued, and then pointed out that it didn't help anyway. Now he took it in its value simply as a word of encouragement to continue. He finished his cider. "You go on looking for anything with Gadney, a marriage with either bride or groom of that name. I'll start tracing Lambourn's career. See if anyone can remember who his friends were fifteen years ago. Someone might remember the name Gadney."

Runcorn frowned heavily. "They'll hear about it," he warned. "How long do you think you have before it's reported to Bawtry, or someone below him?" There was anxiety in his face. "I'll come with you. Two of us'll get there faster than one."

Monk shook his head. "Look for the marriage. If Bawtry, or anyone else, questions what I'm doing, I've got a reason. Or I can think of one."

"Like what?" Runcorn asked. His face reflected he knew the risk they were taking, and Monk was trying to protect him from it.

Monk thought for a moment. "Like I want to make sure the case against Dinah Lambourn is perfect." He smiled with a little twist of irony. "I don't mind lying to them."

"Don't get caught!" There was no answering humor in Runcorn's eyes, only concern.

"I'll meet you back here at six o'clock." Monk stood up.

"What if I find something?" Runcorn asked quickly.

"Nothing I can do about it because I don't know where I'll be," Monk answered. "Wait for me."

Runcorn did not argue but rose as well and they went out together into the blustery afternoon.

MONK SPENT SEVERAL EXHAUSTING and completely fruitless hours. As discreetly as he could he asked questions of people Lambourn had studied with, and stifled his impatience with difficulty. They were hard to track down, claiming to be too busy to spare him time. Perhaps they were embarrassed to discuss someone whose life had ended in such tragedy, but Monk could not help being crowded by the suspicion that they had been warned they would find great disfavor with their superiors if they were to be indiscreet. Doors that had been open before might inexplicably become closed to them in the future.

He found professors who had taught Lambourn, others who had graduated in medicine at the same time, one man who had changed his studies to chemistry. They remembered Lambourn but could offer nothing of use beyond the facts Monk already knew.

He could go on for many more hours without exhausting the possibilities, and each time increasing the chances of attracting more attention to his inquiries. Also he did not wish to keep Runcorn waiting. He had a dim recollection that he had done so rather often in the past.

He found Runcorn sitting at the same small table in the corner of the public house, drumming his fingers impatiently on the wood.

Monk knew he was not late, but all the same he took out his watch and glanced at it to make doubly certain. He sat down opposite Runcorn.

Runcorn was frowning, his face troubled. "You're not going to like it," he said quietly.

Monk felt his muscles tighten and his breath catch in his throat. "You found something?"

Runcorn did not stretch out the tension. "Marriage, no death."

Monk was stunned. "So the husband is still alive?"

"Not now." Runcorn took a deep breath. "Zenia Gadney was married all right—to Joel Lambourn."

"What?" Monk froze. He must have misheard. It was not a bitter or ill-conceived joke; there was not a shred of humor in Runcorn's eyes.

"It gets worse," Runcorn said grimly. "It was about five years before he appeared to have married Dinah."

"Why is that worse?" Monk did not want to hear the answer.

"I looked hard, believe me. I searched everything twice," Runcorn said miserably. "There was no divorce."

"Then . . . then the marriage to Dinah wasn't legal. Damn!" Monk buried his head in his hands. That was the last thing he wanted to hear. "Do you think Dinah found out?" he asked, raising his eyes slowly and meeting Runcorn's.

"There's no record of a marriage between Joel Lambourn and Dinah," Runcorn told him. "I should think she always knew."

"That's it," Monk said quietly. "That's the lie Rathbone sensed. He knew she wasn't telling him the complete truth. Lambourn was providing for his wife, not visiting a prostitute at all. Dinah knew that, too. She had no cause to be jealous."

Runcorn looked wretched. "But she had every cause to wish Zenia Gadney dead," he said, biting his lip.

Monk realized the truth of this the moment he spoke. "So Zenia Gadney was the legal heir to whatever he possessed. She was still his wife. Dinah is the mistress, and the children are illegitimate. What a bloody mess!"

"It is," agreed Runcorn soberly.

"Maybe Dinah went to Copenhagen Place to keep up the payments?" Monk suggested, grabbing desperately for any straw at all.

"A bit late, wasn't she?" Runcorn said drily. "Zenia'd already taken to the streets."

"Had she?" Monk questioned him. "We only assumed that because she was killed in the street, and other people hadn't seen Lambourn in the area. They assumed she was out of money because she was later than usual with a few bills, and because she had taken in bits of sewing and mending. But she'd always done that.

"Dinah was devastated by Lambourn's death," he went on. "She must have had a lot of other things on her mind more urgent than seeing that Zenia was all right. And she would not have had much money to spare, until the estate was probated—maybe no more than she needed to feed herself and her children. Her children would come first, long before Zenia."

"We need to find out how much estate there is," Runcorn said unhappily. "You'll have the right to ask that."

Monk nodded. "I'm going to ask quite a lot of things—including how much did Amity Herne actually know about her brother, and she lied on the stand saying that he told her Zenia was a prostitute he went to because Dinah refused to meet his needs."

"Maybe she knows a great deal," Runcorn said with disgust. "Like the fact that Dinah won't inherit and Zenia would, if she were still alive. But since she isn't, Amity Herne herself is the next of kin!"

Monk stared at him. "I don't even know if this makes it better or worse!" he said hoarsely.

"Depends on the estate." Runcorn stared at him, his face bleak. "Both what it really is, and what either Dinah or Amity Herne thought it was."

"Herne is already wealthy enough," Monk pointed out.

"What's wealthy enough?" Runcorn asked. "For some people there's no such thing. You don't always kill because you're desperate—sometimes you kill because you want more than you have." He stood up slowly. "I'll get you a pint. You should have something to eat. They have really good pork pies."

"Thank you," Monk said with profound gratitude. "Thank you very much."

Runcorn gave him a sudden smile—there and then gone again—before he turned to make his way over to the bar with its gleaming tankards and the well-polished handles for pumping up the ale from the barrels.

"Yes, sir," the solicitor said grimly to Monk's inquiry the following day. "A very considerable amount. Can't tell you exactly, but very wise, very prudent, Dr. Lambourn was. Always lived within his means."

"To whom did he leave his estate, Mr. Bredenstoke?" Monk asked.

Bredenstoke's face did not change in the slightest, nor did his blue eyes blink. "To his natural daughters, sir. Marianne and Adah."

"All of it?"

"Less a few small bequests, yes, sir."

"Not to his wife?"

"No, sir. She has only sufficient to care for her children."

Monk felt an unexpected glow of warmth. "Thank you."

16

I T WAS A SATURDAY morning and the court was not sitting, a fact that gave Rathbone a most welcome respite. He wrote several letters with good wishes for Christmas, now only days away, and put them in the hall for Ardmore to post.

The silence of the house did not trouble him as much as usual. He was not even conscious of the thought that it was not the peace of hopeful waiting, temporary before the return of one he loved. It was an emptiness that stretched before him endlessly, and now that disillusion had bitten so deep, in some way it stretched behind also.

Had he and Margaret ever been as happy as he had imagined? Or had he loved only who he believed she was—as it turned out, so terribly wrongly? Did she feel the same: that she had given her life and herself to a man who was so much less than she thought, and whom she had trusted blindly—and mistakenly also?

Surely neither of them had intended deception, just made assumptions? Had they seen what they wanted and expected to see? If he had really loved her, would he have acted the same way or not? He had thought so at the time, but with hindsight, and the reality of loss, he questioned it now. Did love require more generosity than he had? Did it forgive regardless?

If it had been Hester, would he have forgiven her for acting the same way? For what? Weakness because she could not face the truth about her father? The sheer inability to see the truth in the first place? Or simply that she was not what he had believed her to be, had needed her to be for his own happiness?

But Hester would not have placed anyone before what she knew was right. It would have bruised her emotions, even broken her heart, but she would have expected people to answer for their mistakes, whatever they were, whoever made them. She would not have withdrawn her love, but she would have been honest with herself and to the best she knew and believed.

He realized with only momentary surprise that if he had betrayed himself to do what Margaret wanted of him, he would have forfeited Hester's respect and a level of her friendship he would perhaps never regain. He knew also that that was a price he was not willing to pay: not at the time, and not now.

Monk's friendship he would miss also, but in a different way, and a little less.

He was still turning these thoughts over in his mind when the maid came to tell him that Monk was in the morning room. He put away the pen and closed the inkwell, then stood up and went across the hall to meet Monk.

Monk was facing the door. He looked grave and tense, and a little out of breath, as if he had hurried.

"What is it?" Rathbone asked without bothering with the usual niceties.

"You were right," Monk replied. "She was lying, by omission at the very least."

Rathbone's stomach lurched. He realized how much he had wanted Dinah to be innocent, and this was a blow he had not prepared himself to meet.

"There was nothing wrong with Lambourn," Monk went on. "No peculiar tastes at all, so far as I know. In fact, in all respects except one, he was a highly honorable man, more than he needed to be."

Rathbone forced the words out. "And the one?"

"He did not divorce his wife in order to marry Dinah. Dinah must have accepted it, because there is no record of a marriage between Lambourn and her."

"What . . . ? You mean . . . ?" Rathbone stammered, still not really understanding.

"His only marriage on record was to Zenia Gadney," Monk replied. "More accurately, Zenia Lambourn. That's why he supported her out of loyalty, and compassion. It seems that for a while she was addicted to opium, because of the pain of some old injury. If Dinah went to Copenhagen Place at all, looking for Zenia, it may well have been to continue supporting her. If she missed the first month after Joel's death, that would have been from grief, or the practical difficulty of obtaining the finances while the will was still in probate."

Rathbone's relief burst out in anger. "Then why the devil are you standing there looking like a funeral director?" he demanded. "That means she's innocent, for God's sake! She has no motive!"

"Of course she has!" Monk snapped, his face flushed, equally angry. "With Lambourn dead, she has nothing! Zenia was the widow, and the estate is apparently very considerable."

Rathbone's mind raced to make sense of it, and to salvage some kind of redeeming solution from the tangle. "Did she know that?" he asked.

"She must have known the estate was considerable," Monk replied. "And she certainly knew she wasn't married to Lambourn. Whatever she wanted for herself, or didn't, she would have needed money to provide for her children. Actually the question is, did she know what was in his will at all?"

"Do you?" Rathbone shot back.

"Yes. After a few small bequests, the bulk of his estate is left to his two daughters, Adah and Marianne."

"Damn it, Monk! Why didn't you say that?" Rathbone snapped.

"Because I don't know whether Dinah knew that or not," Monk answered him. "It depends on whether he told her. She was no party to the will, according to the lawyer. Whether he asked Lambourn what he was doing, or why he was not leaving any money to Dinah, he wouldn't tell me."

Rathbone sat down hard, the deep upholstery of the chair enveloping him. "So what are we left with? Lambourn wasn't keeping a mistress, or a whore, he was supporting his wife, and living with the woman he loved—and who is now willing to risk being hanged in order to clear his professional name, and his personal reputation."

Monk sat down in the other chair opposite him. "And the fact that Amity Herne lied through her teeth from the witness box to convince the court that her brother was an incompetent who committed suicide because of his professional failure and his personal sexual deviancy," he added. "Not to mention clearing his wife of murdering and eviscerating the woman with whom he was betraying her. Which raises the question as to what the whole blood-soaked nightmare is about! Is it really about opium, and the right to import it and sell it at immense profit without the restrictions that the proposed Pharmacy Act would enforce?"

"It's looking more and more that way, isn't it?" Rathbone concluded. "Someone with a vested interest in opium killed Lambourn in a way intended to disgrace him, and therefore his report. Then when Dinah tried to defend him, they killed Zenia Gadney in the most hideous way imaginable and blamed her, so they could silence her also. That's monstrous. Is anyone in our government really so profoundly corrupt? God, I hope not!" He remembered the courtroom, the gallery, and Sinden Bawtry sitting on the end of the row, almost concealed by the shadow of the pillar and the roof. What was he there for? To guard the Pharmacy Act, or to sabotage it?

"Then who?" Monk asked. "And there's a very serious question as to whether Dinah Lambourn is guilty and, personally, I no longer think she is. Certainly it is not beyond a serious doubt."

"I need to know a great deal more about this Pharmacy Act, who is for it and who against," Rathbone said, forcing himself to think coherently. "And what results there will be if it is passed. Who will lose? Would any sane man, however greedy, really go to these lengths to delay an act of Parliament that is bound to be passed in a year or two?"

"No," Monk admitted, shaking his head a little. "There must be more than the Pharmacy Act involved. But you haven't time to waste on this."

Rathbone stood up. "I can't afford not to have. It may not be the Pharmacy Act, or even the Opium Wars, but it's tied to them. Otherwise why destroy Lambourn and his report? Come with me." It sounded like an instruction, and that was how he meant it.

"Where are we going?" Monk rose obediently.

"To see Mr. Gladstone, the chancellor of the Exchequer," Rathbone replied. "At least I hope so. He's the coming man, a great believer in reform and the welfare of ordinary people." As he went to the door and out into the hall he was already absorbed in plans to speak to people he knew: to one man in particular for whom he had done a remarkable favor. That man could gain him entrance to Number 11 Downing Street, and Gladstone's attention, even on a Saturday morning, if he believed the matter urgent enough.

Monk, at his heels, was impressed into silence.

It was mid-afternoon by the time all the favors had been called in, and William Ewart Gladstone had made a space in his day to receive Rathbone and Monk. They were shown into the study, where the chancellor stood by the hearth. He was a solid, imposing figure with muttonchop whiskers and an oddly familiar face, as if a newspaper picture had come to life.

"Well, gentlemen?" he said, staring first at one, then the other. "This must be of remarkable importance. Please be brief. I can give you half an hour, precisely."

"Thank you, sir." Rathbone had been summarizing in several different forms what he had to say, omitting one thing and then another, trying to find not only the essence of the matter, but also that part of it that would most appeal to the crusader in Gladstone, the moral preacher that was so often at the forefront of his character.

"I am defending the widow of Joel Lambourn, who is charged with a repulsive murder, of which I believe her innocent," he began. He saw the distaste in Gladstone's face and made his decision immediately. It was something of a risk, knowing Gladstone's puritanical streak, but he was used to watching the expressions of juries and surmising whether he was winning or losing them, and what line of argument would serve him best.

"She is a woman of intense loyalty, especially to her late husband," he continued. "I have just this morning discovered from Commander Monk"—he gestured in Monk's direction—"that they were not actually married, because he was still married to the murder victim, Zenia Gadney. His visits to see her in Limehouse were not sexual liaisons, as everyone is claiming, but in order to continue in his support for her financially, and to do what he could to ensure her comfort. That was in spite of her previous terrible addiction to opium, from which he helped her to recover."

He saw the sudden pity in Gladstone's eyes, and a wave of anger. "The addiction to opium is one of the greatest curses of our age," he said quietly. "And yet the good it can do for those in agonies of pain, we cannot forfeit. God help us, we must be very careful what we do in this pharmacy bill."

"Dinah Lambourn intentionally implicated herself in Zenia Gadney's death," Rathbone went on hastily. "When the police questioned her, she did so because she wanted to stand trial in a hugely publicized murder."

"Why?" Gladstone said incredulously, his craggy face momentarily slack as he struggled to understand.

"To bring to light her husband's work on the medical facts of opium deaths," Rathbone replied, using the word husband intentionally. "Especially in children. He had given his report to the government, and they had rejected it as incompetent, and then blackened his name by accusing him of taking his own life."

"I remember the case." Gladstone shook his head. "A sin of despair, poor man."

"With respect, sir," Rathbone said as hastily as he could without rudeness, "I am beginning to believe that it was not a suicide, but actually a very clever murder." He turned toward Monk, inviting him to explain.

Monk picked up the story.

"To begin with, sir, it appeared to be suicide," he agreed. "But the police inspector in charge was in some respects overridden by government officers claiming to be acting in the best interests of Lambourn's family, as a matter of loyalty and discretion. Certain evidence in the murder of Zenia Gadney led me to Dinah Lambourn. When I was questioning her, she brought up Lambourn, and denied passionately that his death was suicide, or that his report was incompetent." Monk was speaking hastily, before he could be interrupted. Rathbone heard him deliberately slow his pace.

"She said he had been murdered, in order to discredit him," he continued. "I was obliged to investigate what she had said, as a matter of fairness, and I found several unexplained discrepancies in the story as told by the police looking into the matter. I can tell you of them all if you wish; for example, the fact that there was no knife or blade found anywhere near him, even though he slit his wrists."

Rathbone was watching Gladstone's face and he saw his interest suddenly sharpen.

"Do you believe he was murdered, sir?" he asked Monk.

"Yes, Mr. Gladstone," Monk said immediately. "I think there are people with certain interests who were willing to kill Lambourn to silence him, and then kill the unfortunate Zenia Gadney in order to blame Dinah Lambourn and thus silence her also. That way the whole report on the dangers of opium could be buried."

"What interests, exactly?" Gladstone asked.

"I don't know, sir," Monk admitted. "We haven't been able to find any copies of Dr. Lambourn's report, even though we searched both his house and Mrs. Gadney's, so we don't know what new information or conclusions he offered, or whose interests he endangered."

"A very slender case, Commander Monk," Gladstone said grimly. "What is it you wish of me?"

Monk took a deep breath. He had much to gain, and to lose.

"A summary of what the bill will contain, and anything in the way of letters or notes Dr. Lambourn may have offered ahead of his full report," he answered.

"Quite a lot," Gladstone observed drily. "Do you really believe this woman is innocent?"

"I do believe it," Monk answered, sweat breaking out on his skin at the risk he was taking. What had he done to his own career if Dinah was guilty?

Gladstone pondered for several moments. "That seems both remarkable, and very foolish. The bill will pass. It is necessary for the welfare of the people that it should. I can have a summary of it delivered to you easily enough. Anything on Lambourn's report may be more difficult, but I will do what I can."

"Thank you, sir," Rathbone said warmly, then bit his lip and looked at Gladstone. "There is probably no more than one day left of prosecution evidence; then I will have to begin the defense. I can stretch that out for three or four days at best. Once the verdict is in—and at the moment there is hardly any doubt that they will convict her—then sentence of death will be passed and that may prove all but impossible to overturn."

He glanced at Monk, then back at the chancellor. "It is not only that an innocent woman will pay with her life for her loyalty to her husband, but the Pharmacy Act may be delayed, or diluted in its efficacy. No one can measure how many people will die unnecessarily if that were to happen, perhaps most of them children."

Gladstone's face was tight and grim. He was clearly laboring under some great emotion. He did not look at them when he spoke, but into some place in the depth of his own memory.

"It is to our shame that we have many stains in our history, gentlemen, but one of the most shameful episodes in all of our nation's long life is that of the Opium Wars. There have been glorious times of courage and honor, intellectual genius and Christian humanity. The wars embody the opposite: greed, dishonor, and barbarous cruelty. Britain is addicted to tea, which at the time of those conflicts we could buy only from China. We are also very fond of porcelain, and of silk, similarly purchased largely from China. The only currency they will accept in exchange is silver bullion, of which we have very little."

Rathbone glanced across at Monk, but neither of them interrupted.

Gladstone's voice was edged with shame when he continued. "We responded with arguments and pleas, and when those failed to influence the Chinese, we began to sell them opium from India. They may have begun to use it for the relief of pain, but that swiftly changed to smoking it for pleasure. I have not the time, or desire, to spell out the progress of that abomination for you, but within a few years tens of thousands of Chinese became so addicted to it that they were incapable of work, or even of sustaining themselves or their families.

"We brought in ever more, smuggled it in, despite every effort on the part of the Chinese government to prevent the trade. Finally we poisoned a nation and reduced much of it to a state of helplessness, even death. Of course, many of us choose to deny it. It is peculiarly powerful to acknowledge that your country has behaved with dishonor. There are many who believe it is patriotism to deny it, conceal it, even to lie and blame others. Men have been murdered to cover up less, and those who did it felt justified." His voice was low and hoarse. "'My family, my country—right or wrong.' It is the ultimate betrayal of God."

Neither Monk nor Rathbone responded, not knowing how to. And the depth of Gladstone's emotion seemed to make it not only unnecessary but intrusive.

As if recalling himself to their presence he began again.

"It might have started in our own minds as a reasonable trade. Indeed there are those who argue that had we not supplied the Chinese from India, then others would have done so. The French and the Americans are involved."

"Is that true?" Rathbone asked, then wished he had kept silent. He should not have interrupted the prime minister.

Gladstone looked up at him momentarily. "Yes, but a specious argument. One man's sin does not justify another's."

"And the wars, sir?" Monk asked.

"Against the Chinese, of course," Gladstone replied. "They tried to reason with us to prevent us selling opium, with argument, trade tariffs, very little diplomacy. Even the emissaries of the queen were treated as if they were servants bringing tribute from some subject princeling." He was so affronted he found it difficult to say the words. "As the most powerful nation on earth, we did not respond well to such insult. Tempers were controlled with difficulty." He lowered his voice. "Or not at all."

Rathbone could imagine it, but he did not speak.

"There were incidents of violence," Gladstone continued, "some of them bestial beyond belief, and we are not free from blame. Although I cannot imagine that we descended to such things as I have heard tell." He shook himself very slightly. "But that is not an excuse. We have dealt with savages before, and we should not assume that because a man can create exquisite beauty or invent such blessings for mankind as paper and porcelain, even gunpowder with all its uses, that he is a civilized creature in his soul. And whatever he is, it does not excuse us from our own duty to God as Christian men." His face was dark with anger and his body shook.

Rathbone looked across at Monk and saw the pity in his face, and also a degree of confusion.

Gladstone regained his self-control and went on with his lesson. "Incident after incident escalated until the Chinese confiscated thousands of pounds of opium, an act in which they were justified. Some deny this, but it is the truth. It was a contraband substance, smuggled into China by us. The Royal Navy attacked. The Chinese ships were small, and their weapons and armor medieval. Our broadsides sank them, drowned their sailors with barely any loss to us. We attacked the land fortifications at river mouths, bombarded city walls, and the women and children sheltering within them. Our ships—such as *Nemesis*, which was steel-hulled, and a paddle-wheeler, independent of wind and tide—were beyond their power to fight. Some of them had primitive firelock guns; others merely bows and arrows, God help them. Our victory was total."

The enormity of it slowly took shape in Rathbone's mind.

"Three hundred million people," Gladstone went on quickly, as if in haste to get the entire tale out. "We made them ransom their own port of Canton for six million silver dollars. By 1842 we controlled Shanghai, and the whole mouth of the Yangtze River, and we forced on them one shameful treaty after another. We took from them the island of Hong Kong, and the ports of Canton, Amoy, Foochow, Shanghai, and Mingbo, and nine million dollars, which is nearly two million pounds in reparation for the contraband opium they had seized and destroyed."

He shook his head. "That was only part of it. There were other concessions as well. In 1844, France and the United States exacted the same concessions, but that does not excuse us. It was our war, our weapons and our greed that began it and forced it to a conclusion."

Finally he faced Rathbone and Monk. "The Second Opium War, a few years later, was no better. Again we grew rich on the ruin of another race. France, the United States, and this time Russia as well joined us in war and plunder. But we played the major part, and most certainly took the largest gain in treaties, and seizures of further ports along the coast. All the while we continued to sell opium to a wretched people, who were drowning in a sunless sea of addiction. It is an episode of appalling shame, and you will find many who would deny it."

Rathbone cleared his throat. "And the Pharmacy Act will regulate the sale and labeling of all medicines in Britain, and prevent them being sold by people who have no medical knowledge or skill?"

"It will," Gladstone agreed. He looked from one to the other of them. "Mr. Wilkie Collins, a writer of considerable skill and, more important, a great reputation, is a keen supporter of the bill, but it was Dr. Lambourn who was going to provide the professional evidence. His death was a great blow; his discredit an even greater one. But we will surmount it, I promise you. However, I would dearly like to know what it was that he discovered that would make anyone wish both to kill him and then to discredit him. Perhaps, gentlemen, we need to know.

"Sinden Bawtry told me the report was too ill-conceived to be of use and that out of respect for Lambourn's memory it was destroyed. I believed him at the time, but what you have said has caused me grave doubt. I have known Bawtry for some years, a man of skill, intellect, and great generosity to the country. Even so, he may have been deceived. There are ugly truths that Dr. Lambourn might have uncovered accidentally in his research."

Gladstone smiled with bleak goodwill but no pleasure at all. "Do what you can to save Mrs. Lambourn," he urged. "I shudder to think of our shame exposed in the courts, but it would be doubly evil to conceal it by sacrificing an innocent woman. To do so would be to defile not only our trade but our justice as well. But I warn you, it will earn you some bitter enemies, Sir Oliver. Do what you can, gentlemen. And keep me apprised. Good day to you."

"Thank you, sir," Rathbone said gratefully.

OUTSIDE, IN THE SOMBER dignity of Downing Street, Rathbone turned to Monk.

"I'm not sure if this makes it better or worse. Nothing is what I thought it was. I had assumed a clever but deeply flawed man whose distorted sexual appetites had finally ended his life in tragedy and suicide; and a wife whose grief and sense of betrayal had driven her to an obscene revenge. Instead it now seems we have a remarkable man whose only flaw was to leave his opium-addicted wife without the formality of a divorce. He lived with the woman he truly loved, without deceiving her as to her situation. Out of compassion, or sense of duty, he maintained support for his wife both financial and emotional.

"He could not be misled or bought off from writing a report on the dangers of opium use without restrictions, and was murdered for his courage. His widow, or apparent widow, loved him enough to risk her own life to redeem his reputation. His wife was not a prostitute at all, as assumed, but a woman supported by one decent man who asked nothing whatever from her. Is anything the way it appears to be?"

Monk shook his head. "I don't know."

Rathbone thought of other times in his life when suddenly nothing turned out as he had expected. The familiar had unaccountably become alien and all his confidence was swept away. Did that happen to everyone?

He kept pace with Monk, their footsteps all but silent in the quiet street.

"This close to a verdict, it may be impossible to turn things around, and that frightens me," Rathbone went on. "Someone has committed two murders. I can't believe that Lambourn's death and Zenia Gadney's are not connected. Amity Herne has lied on oath, but I don't know why. Is it enmity against her brother, or against Dinah, or to justify her husband having condemned Joel's report? Or does she have some vested interest in blocking the bill herself?"

"I don't know, either," Monk admitted. "But Gladstone is right. No one is going to like us for opening up the horror of the Opium Wars!" He stopped in the street and stared at Rathbone. "But you'll do it!"

"Oh, yes," Rathbone said. Then, the moment the words were past his lips, he wondered if he had just committed himself to ruining his career.

CHAPTER

17

Monk was deeply shaken by what Gladstone had told him. Perhaps before his amnesia he had been aware of at least some of the shame of Britain's part in the Opium Wars, but not the depth of the greed. The violence of it and the duplicity horrified him. There was arrogance in the assumption that any country had the right to smuggle such a poisonous substance to a less technically advanced people, and by weight of superior weaponry, conquer them. Then on top of all that, they had demanded reparation for what had been the results of their own savagery.

Had Britain been the victim, not the attacker, he would have burned with outrage at it. He would have condemned the invaders and thirsted for revenge.

But it was his own people who had been the barbarians, the people he had believed to be civilized, to have carried some core of honor, and a better system of beliefs, to races with a dimmer sense of what was right and with laws less just.

He sat in the glow of the firelight in his own house with the familiar pictures on the walls of the parlor, the books he had read and loved on the shelves. Scuff was asleep upstairs. Quietly he related to Hester what Mr. Gladstone had told him.

Eventually he stood up and turned on the lamps, watching her face as she listened to him. He saw the sadness in her as he described some of the details, although he did not include them all. Did she feel as ashamed as he did? She did not look as surprised as he had expected her to.

"Did you know all this?" He could not help asking her.

"No," she said quietly. "But I have seen ignorance and stupidity before. To begin with, I tried not to believe it, or to find excuses, or reasons why it was not the way it seemed. In the end I had to accept that most of it was true; some of it was even understated. People lie to conceal their mistakes, and then make even worse ones to cover the lies."

She looked at him with anxiety and a strange gentleness, as if she would have protected him from it. "Once I used to imagine that those in power were different, but most of them aren't," she went on. "No one likes to admit that their own people can be as greedy and cruel as any foreigners. We perform all kinds of contortions of the mind to make a reason why it isn't really the way it looks, but we only fool the people who want to be fooled."

"Maybe I knew, and forgot," he said, thinking back to his struggle to learn about himself, to piece together the evidence of what kind of a man he was, the good and the bad. There was so much then that it would have been more pleasant to deny. Some of it—small cruelties, unnecessary ones—he had in the end been unable to avoid, and had learned to face, and regret. But there was a kind of comfort in that— honesty could be its own healing.

As if reading his thoughts, or perhaps thinking back and tracing the same path, Hester smiled at him. It was a moment of understanding that was amazingly sweet. All pain was shared, and melted away into something calmer.

He reached out and touched her gently, and her hand closed over his.

The silence came to a natural end.

"Do you think that Joel Lambourn discovered something during his research that was to do with more than the damage opium can cause if used without knowledge?" she asked. "Something outside that altogether, and far more dangerous?"

Monk had been puzzling about that himself. "I don't see why his research would matter so much if all it contained was figures of opium misuse, deaths of children, and perhaps of addicts here and there," he answered. "It might delay the Pharmacy Act a year or so, but other people will eventually find the same evidence. And there are other medicines that should be regulated as well. Opium importers will have to deal more honestly; apothecaries will have to take more care, measure and label acceptably. Many small traders will have to stop selling it. Thousands of people will lose a few pennies a week. Would any one of them murder Lambourn for that? And also murder Zenia Gadney in such a hideous way?"

"No," she said gravely. "We have missed something. Or someone. Someone who has far more to lose than a small profit."

"Gladstone suggested there were details that might ruin some people, if they came to be known," Monk suggested, searching for an answer that made sense. "Is there some atrocity that Lambourn could have exposed that would ruin a reputation?"

Hester shook her head a little. "Why would he? He didn't need to go into details of the smuggling or the violence to prove that opium in patent medicines can kill people because they don't know what the dosage is. And isn't that all he wanted to prove?"

"Perhaps he found out something else by accident?" Monk's imagination was racing. His own ignorance appalled him. "Someone could be lying to hide . . . whatever it is . . . because they know humiliation is a bitterly painful thing to bear. Some people would rather die than be shamed—in fact, many people."

"I know," she said very quietly.

He watched her face, the sudden deep sorrow in it, and remembered too late that her father had committed suicide rather than bear the shame of the debt he owed because Joscelyn Gray had swindled him out of his money. That was the first case he had dealt with in his new life, which had begun after the amnesia. It was the case in which he and Hester had met, and he had not even thought of it in his talk of shame and suicide. He could not believe his own clumsiness.

"Hester . . ." What could he say? A tide of embarrassment burned hot up his face.

She smiled, tears in her eyes. "I wasn't thinking of him," she said gently. "He was unwise, he trusted an evil man, and I wasn't there to help. I was too busy following my own somewhat self-concerned conscience in the Crimea. National shame is different." She looked down at her lap. "Tomorrow I'll go and see Winfarthing again, and perhaps one or two other people who might know more about the Opium Wars, and the way we fought them."

"I don't think you should . . . ," Monk began. Then he saw the level resolve in her eyes, and his words faded away. She would do it, whatever he said, for her own well-being, just as she had gone to the Crimea without her parents' approval, and into the streets to create the clinic without his. It would have been very much more comfortable if she were to care more for her own well-being, or for his, certainly for her safety. But then the unhappiness would come in other ways, steadily mounting as she denied who she was and what she believed.

"At least be very careful!" he ended. "Think of Scuff!"

She hesitated, and colored a little. She drew in her breath as if to retaliate, then bit her lip. "I will," she promised.

HESTER BEGAN BY RETURNING to see Winfarthing. She was obliged to wait nearly an hour before he finished treating patients, then he gave her his entire attention. As usual, his office was littered with books and papers. A very small cat was curled up on the most thoroughly scattered heap, as if it had intentionally made them into a bed for itself. It did not stir when Hester sat down on the chair nearest to it.

Winfarthing did not appear to have noticed. He looked tired and unhappy. His thick hair was standing up on end where he had run his fingers through it.

"I don't have anything that will help," he said before she had time to ask. "I'd have told you if I had."

She recounted to him what they had learned about Dinah and about Zenia Gadney.

"Good God!" he said with amazement, his face crumpled in an expression of profound pity. "I would do anything for her that I could, but what is there? If she didn't kill the woman, then who did?" His expression filled with disgust. "I have no great love for politicians, or respect, either, but I find it very difficult to believe any one of them would cold-bloodedly murder Lambourn just to delay the Pharmacy Act. It will come sooner or later—probably sooner, whatever they do. Is there really so much money to be made in a year or two that it's worth a man's life? Not to mention a man's soul?"

"No, I don't think so," she answered. "There has to be more to it, far more."

He looked at her curiously. "What? Something that Lambourn knew and would have put in his report?"

"Don't you think so?" She was uncertain now, fumbling for answers. She did not want Dinah to be guilty, or Joel Lambourn to be an incompetent suicide. Was that what was driving her, rather than reason? She saw the thought far too clearly in Winfarthing's face, and felt the slight heat burn up her own cheeks.

"Lambourn's suicide doesn't make sense," she said defensively. "The physical evidence is wrong."

He ignored the argument. Perhaps it was irrelevant now anyway. "What are you thinking of?" he asked instead. "Something he discovered about the sale of opium? Smuggling? No one in Britain cares about the East India Company smuggling off the coast of China." He snapped his fingers in the air in a gesture of dismissal. "China could be on Mars, for all it means to most of us—except their tea, silk, and porcelain, of course. But what happens there is nothing to the man in the street. Theft? In any moral sense it's all theft: corruption, violence, and the poisoning of half a nation simply because we have the means and the desire to do it, and it's absurdly profitable."

"I don't know!" Hester said again, a little more desperately. "There has to be something we do care about. We can butcher foreigners and find a way to justify it to ourselves but we can't steal from our own, and we certainly can't betray them."

"And have we, Hester?" he said quietly. "What makes you think Lambourn discovered something like that? We all know that we introduced opium into China to pay for the luxuries we buy from them; we smuggle it into their country and it is killing them, an inch at a time.

They go through caverns of the soul, measureless to man, down to a sunless sea. Read Coleridge—or De Quincey!"

"'A sunless sea,'" she repeated. "That sounds like imprisonment, like drowning. How bad is real dependency on opium?"

He looked at her with sudden concentration, his eyes narrowed. "Why do you ask? Why now?"

"We don't smoke it like the Chinese, we eat it, take it in medicines mixed with lots of other things," she answered slowly. "It's the only cure we have for the worst pain."

"I know that, girl. What are you saying?"

"I met a woman in the docklands who runs a clinic for badly injured navvies and sailors. She showed me a syringe with a hollow needle that can put it straight into the blood, if you want to. That kills pain far more swiftly, and thoroughly. Less opium but more effect."

Winfarthing nodded slowly. "And more dependency," he growled. "Of course. Be careful, Hester. Be very careful. Opium addiction's a wicked thing. You're right, it's a sea in which a million men can drown at once, and still each one do it alone. Give it just for pain, then just to get to the next day, finally to stave off the madness. Good men use it on others to ease unbearable suffering, evil ones to create a passion from which few escape."

"Who has these needles?" she asked.

"I don't know. Do you?"

"No. I don't even know if there are many or few. I don't know if it has anything to do with Dr. Lambourn's death or not. No one seems to know what was in his report."

Winfarthing sat up, his huge body stiff, his eyes wide. "Is that what you think this is about? Not the Pharmacy Act, or the Opium Wars, but someone creating a sickness only they can treat?"

"I don't know," she said again.

"My dear, people will call you a liar, a traitor to your country for even suggesting such things," he said gently. "They will defend the perpetrators because it is not easy for us to admit that we have been deceived. No one gives up his delusion of self-worth willingly. Some prefer even to die."

"Or to kill?" she said quickly. "Silence the voice that challenges their beliefs? It's a very old thought, to punish a blasphemer, isn't it? It could be an easy justification to make."

"If somebody had been stoned I might accept that." He shook his head. "To slit a man's wrists and make him look like a suicide is not an act of righteous anger, Hester. It is cold-blooded; the sort of thing a man does to protect his own interests, not anyone else's."

She sat silently, picturing Joel Lambourn alone in the darkness on One Tree Hill.

"To do what was done to Zenia Gadney is the act of a man without even humanity," Winfarthing went on. "And to do it in order to condemn someone else is beyond even a lunatic to justify."

"I believe it was done out of self-interest to protect a fortune made, and still being made, in the opium business." She refused to give up.

"Protect it from what?" he asked

"I already told you I don't know!" She felt confused and defensive, as if a horrible truth were slipping out of her hands but leaving even uglier lies in its place. "But do you think Lambourn was a failure and a suicide?" she demanded. "Are you trying to prevent me stirring up something embarrassing—at the cost of Dinah Lambourn's life?"

A sharp unhappiness filled his face, and she knew she had hurt him.

"I'm sorry," she apologized. "That wasn't fair, and I wish I hadn't said it. I feel helpless. I know there's something terribly wrong, and I have too little time to make sense of it."

He made a small gesture with his hand, dismissing her accusation. "You haven't changed, have you? Haven't learned." He dropped his voice a little and there was a great gentleness in his face. "I'm glad. Some people should never grow old—not inside. But be careful, girl. If there really is something to this, then it is very bad indeed, and very dangerous." He leaned across to the desk and picked up a pen and a piece of paper. He scribbled a name and address and passed it to her.

"This is a man who helped Lambourn. He asked a lot of questions about opium, its use and its dangers. He works among the poor, scraping a living the best he can. He may not be easy to find. He's erratic, happy one day, wretched the next, but he's a good man. Be careful who you ask for him."

She took the paper and glanced at it. Alvar Doulting. It was a name she did not know. "Thank you," she said, putting it into her small reticule. "I'll see if I can find him."

It took her well into the next day before she at last found Alvar Doulting, working in a room next to a warehouse down by St. Saviour's Dock. He had half a dozen patients, suffering mostly deep bruises and crushed or broken bones. With only the briefest of introductions, merely a mention of the Crimea, she began to help him.

He was a young man, earnest and pale, perhaps from exhaustion and the sudden, harsh change in the weather. His lean face was both powerful and sensitive, at the moment marred by a growth of stubble and deep lines of weariness. He wore ragged clothes, several layers of them to try to keep warm, even a woolen scarf instead of a tie or cravat around his neck.

He watched her for only a moment or two before seeing that she was experienced with wounds, and that the obvious poverty and physical dirtiness of the patients were of no importance to her. She noticed only the pain, and the dangers, first of bleeding and then of gangrene, always of shock, and—at this time of year—the cold.

They worked with rags, makeshift bandages made from torn strips of fabric, splints fashioned from anything that was strong enough, cheap brandy given both as a drink to dull pain and as a way to clean wounds before stitching them with needles and gut. He had little opium, and he used it only on the worst cases.

It was more than two hours later when they were alone and there was finally time to speak.

They sat in his tiny office cluttered with books and piles of papers, which at a glance looked like notes on patients he was possibly too tired or too busy to trust to memory. She remembered doing the same. There was a small wood-burning stove in one corner and on it a kettle. He offered her tea and she took it gratefully.

"Thank you for your help," he said, handing her the steaming tin mug.

She dismissed his gratitude with a gesture so tiny he might not even have seen it. She did not waste time with preamble.

"I'm trying to save Joel Lambourn's widow from being hanged," she said bluntly. "I don't believe she killed anyone, but I don't know who did."

He was sitting on a makeshift stool. He looked up at her with hopelessness in his eyes, and a pity so deep he did not attempt to express it in words.

"You can't save her," he said simply. "You're fighting a war nobody's going to win. We ruined the Chinese, now we're ruining ourselves." He gave a bitter little laugh. "A little drink of opium to still the baby's crying, ease the stomachache, get a little sleep. A deeper draft of it to dull the agony of wounds for the soldier, the man with the crushed leg, with the kidney stones he can't pass."

His face twisted sharply. "A pipe full for the man whose life is a gray drudgery, the one who'd rather be dead than give up his escape into dreams." His voice dropped. "And in a few cases, a hollow needle and a thin glass vialful into a vein, and for a while hell becomes heaven—but just awhile—then you need some more."

He blinked. "The blood spilt and the profit made on this drug will drown you. Believe me, I know. I lost my home, my practice, and the woman I was going to marry."

She felt fear closing in as if the shadows were darker around her, and yet a surge of strength also; she had finally found someone who wasn't offering her denials.

"What did Joel Lambourn find out that was worth killing him to hide?" she asked.

"I don't know," Doulting replied. "All he told me about was the number of children who died unnecessarily, because packages were not labeled. Their mothers gave them gripe water, teething medicine, dosages against colic and diarrhea that didn't say how much or how often it should be taken. The figures are terrible, and its names are proprietary brands we all know and think we can trust."

"What else?" she pressed, sipping from her tea. It was too strong, and certainly not fresh, but it was hot. It reminded her of her army days.

"He didn't tell me," Doulting assured her. "He knew someone was trying to stop him, to make him look incompetent. He was careful. Everything was documented." His face was very pale as if misery and guilt crowded him. Every now and again he winced, as if he too had his own pain to battle. "I tried collecting information myself, and I gave him all I had. I asked questions, took notes. Some of the stories would break your heart."

"Where are your notes?"

"My office was burned, and all my papers and records were lost. Even my instruments, my scalpels and needles, all my medicines— everything was destroyed. I had to start again in a new place, begging and borrowing what I could."

Hester was cold, chilled from the inside. "Do you know who did it?"

"Names? No. Intent, I'm not sure. More than simply to stop the report that would regulate the sale of opium. It will cost to measure and label everything, and require that all medicines are sold only by people qualified to say what they are, but not that much. There are those who consider it to be limiting the freedom of poor people to buy the only relief from pain that we know, but it won't. What they're really concerned about is their own freedom to sell it to the desperate as often and as easily as possible.

"But there's no point in your asking me who 'they' are, because Lambourn didn't tell me. Said I was safer not to know it. But I'm certain he knew."

"But it's someone here in London?" Hester persisted.

Doulting nodded, his face haunted by other people's pain. "Killing Lambourn, gutting poor Zenia Gadney and seeing Dinah Lambourn hang for it would not add more weight to their souls. Perhaps there is nothing left that would."

She believed that he was telling the truth as he had heard it. The fear was written in his face, and the meager instruments and few medicines in the room testified to it. But would Lambourn have had proof of someone creating an addiction in order to feed it? And was that even a crime? A sin, of course—but a crime punishable by law? And how would Lambourn have used that proof, even if he did have it? It would not have furthered his cause of regulating sales.

Was it not a completely separate issue, to be faced at another time, if at all? Who would listen? People did not want to hear that those they trusted were capable of such brutality and greed, such utter disregard for human destruction. Would they even believe it, or would they say that if a man chose to go to hell, he had the right to do it in his own fashion? It was so much easier, and safer, to condemn the bringer of such news, destroy the words rather than the fearful, indelible acts.

"If he was collecting information on illness and death from ignorance of dosage, how would he learn of the deeper addiction caused by using the needle?" Hester asked. "He was looking at harassed mothers who'd lost children: ordinary people, who'd never been more than a few miles from their homes."

Doulting looked tired. "I don't know. I don't know where he went or who else he spoke to. He probably found it by accident from old soldiers. He didn't say."

"Old soldiers?" she said quickly.

He smiled very bitterly. "From the Crimean War, and the Opium Wars: men with injuries that will always pain them. They take opium to ease the ache of old wounds, to sleep through the nightmares of memory. For some it is to take the edge off the fevers and cramps of returning malaria and ague, and other things they don't even know the names of."

She felt stupid for not having realized. Her mind had been fixed on Lambourn's concern for infant mortality.

"You won't get it into evidence to save Dinah Lambourn," Doulting said quietly, no hope at all in his eyes. "We won't admit its evils because we sold it to an entire nation. We robbed, plundered, we murdered civilians, poisoned the men, women, and children of a nation too militarily backward to resist us, and we are barbarians: all of us, those who did it, and those who let them, and we who choose not to admit it now." He let out a quiet sigh. "If we admit it, then we have to make reparation, and we have to give back the profits. Can you see anyone doing that?"

Hester could think of no answer. "There's still time to find out who is behind this!" she said, not as a reply but as an admission.

"But who will we help if we die trying to prove it?" he asked.

"All I want at the moment is to save Dinah from being hanged," she told him.

"And you think knowing what Lambourn found out will help?" He smiled, but there was no belief of it in his eyes.

"Yes! It's possible," she insisted. "It will at least make the jury realize that there is a very great deal more to this than domestic jealousy. Tell me where I can find the soldiers Dr. Lambourn saw?" she asked. "I could look for them myself, but I haven't any time to waste."

"I'll write down for you what I know," Doulting offered. "Then I need to get back to work."

She finished her tea and set the mug down in one of the few clear spaces. "Thank you."

18

Rathbone knew that the case was slipping out of his grasp. He could not help his conviction that Dinah was innocent, yet he wondered if he felt that way because he was drawn to her loyalty to Lambourn by his own inner need to believe in the existence of such a love: deeper than her need for her own survival, deeper even than the evidence. Even Lambourn's betrayal of her with another woman and his own apparent suicide had not shaken Dinah's devotion.

He lay awake, alone in his silent bedroom, and came no closer to an answer. The sky was paling in the east, and the light came through the crack in the curtains where he had not closed them properly. It was going to be one of those bright winter days that made the coming of Christmas even more charming, more festive. Soon it would be the shortest day. People were collecting wreaths of holly and ivy and garlanding doors with ribbons. There would be carol singers in the street.

Out in the garden, the very last chrysanthemums were shaggy and drooping, some touched with frost. There was a smell of damp leaves and blue woodsmoke, all the beauty that awoke an awareness of the passing of time and the inability to hold on to even the most precious of things.

This Christmas he would be alone.

Could he even save Dinah? His professional brilliance was the one thing he had believed he could cling to: safe, beyond the ability of even Margaret to take away. Now that too seemed less certain.

If Dinah was innocent, then who was guilty?

Who on earth could he turn to as a witness?

Was it even conceivable that Lambourn's death and the murder of Zenia were not connected, just two terrible events that afflicted the same family within the space of two months? Was he looking for a pattern that was not there?

If that was true, then Dinah was innocent and Zenia Gadney was the victim of some random lunatic they might never find. Certainly he would not find even the proof of his existence in the next few days. Today was Sunday. He knew that Pendock would want to put the case to the jury before Christmas, which was at the weekend. Otherwise it would have to be carried over to the following week. The jury would hate that, and blame him for it.

He felt the weight of despair as if he were drowning, sinking as the water closed over his head and he could not draw breath. It was absurd. He was lying rigid in his own bed, staring up at the broadening light across the ceiling. His health was exactly the same as always. It was disillusion that weighed him down. He wanted Dinah to be innocent, to be sane, brave, and loyal, and to love Joel Lambourn—even though he was dead—more than she loved herself.

It was at that moment that he made up his mind to go and see Amity Herne, and somehow gain from her a stronger understanding of Lambourn, and his complicated relationships. He might learn things he did not want to, but it was too late now to balk at any truth, if it proved Dinah's guilt. There was no time left to flatter his own wishes.

Sunday luncheon was a most unseemly time to call upon anyone, especially uninvited, but circumstances left no choice. Moreover, Rathbone admitted to himself, he really did not care how inconvenienced or offended Amity and her husband might be.

He dressed with conservative elegance, as if he had just come from church, although he had not. This morning he would have found the ritual assurance of it, and the rather pompous certainty of the minister, anything but soothing. He needed to think, to plan, to face the ugliest and worst of possibilities.

At half-past twelve he was on Barclay Herne's doorstep. A few moments later, the butler somewhat reluctantly showed him into the morning room and asked him to wait while he informed his master that Sir Oliver Rathbone had called.

Actually it was Amity Herne that Rathbone wished to see, but he would take the opportunity to speak with both of them. If it could be arranged, he would like to observe their reaction to each other. He had wondered if it was possible Amity was being influenced by Barclay and by his ambition, to distance herself from Lambourn. Rathbone was perfectly willing to put every emotional pressure on her that he could in order to learn anything that would change the jury's perception of Dinah, even long enough to stretch out the trial beyond Christmas and give Monk a chance to find something more.

As the thoughts went through his head, he moved restlessly in the rather pretentious morning room. Its shelves held matching leather-bound books and there was a large, flattering painting over the fireplace of Amity, about twenty years younger, with blemishless face and shoulders.

The door opened and Barclay Herne came in, closing it behind him. He was quite casually dressed, in a loose cravat rather than a more formal tie, and a smoking jacket mismatched with his trousers. He looked puzzled and ill at ease.

"Good afternoon, Sir Oliver. Has something happened to Dinah? I hope she has not collapsed?" It was definitely a question and he searched Rathbone's face anxiously for the answer.

"No," Rathbone assured him. "As far as I know, her health is still at least moderate. But I am afraid I cannot offer much hope that it will remain so."

Herne flinched. "I don't know what to do for her," he said helplessly.

Rathbone felt uncomfortable, aware that he was embarrassing both of them, possibly to no purpose. He plunged on. "I feel that there is something vital that I don't understand. I would appreciate it very much if I am allowed to speak to you and Mrs. Herne frankly. I am aware that it is Sunday afternoon, and you may well have other plans, especially this close to Christmas. However, this is the final opportunity for me to find any cause whatever to raise reasonable doubt as to Mrs. Lambourn's guilt, or even to ask for mercy."

The last vestige of color drained from Herne's face, leaving him pasty, a fine beading of sweat on his brow. "Perhaps if you would come through to the withdrawing room . . . We have not yet eaten. You may care to join us."

· "I'm sorry to inconvenience you," Rathbone apologized, following Herne out of the door and across the handsome hallway into the withdrawing room. This was lush with burgundy velvet curtains and rich, dark wine-colored furniture with carved mahogany feet. The low, matching tables had shining surfaces, and were as immaculate as if they were never used.

Amity Herne was sitting in one of the chairs by the side of the fire, which was already burning vividly, even this early in the afternoon. Beyond the windows, the winter sun lit a small garden. All the perennial plants had been clipped back and the fresh, black earth weeded and raked.

She did not rise to her feet. "Good afternoon, Sir Oliver." She was surprised to see him, and clearly not pleased. She glanced at her husband and read his expression, then looked back at Rathbone.

Herne answered her implicit question.

"Sir Oliver would like to speak with us to see if there is anything we can tell him that might help Dinah," he explained.

Amity looked at Rathbone. Her hazel eyes were cool, guarded. She must dislike everything he had reminded her of on this quiet Sunday when perhaps she had hoped for a day's respite from the inevitable.

"I'm sorry," he apologized again. "Were it possible to choose a better time, I would." She had not invited him to sit down, but he preempted her and did anyway, choosing the chair diagonally across from her. Deliberately he made himself comfortable, indicating his intention to stay. He saw from the slight change in her expression that she understood.

"I don't know what you think I can tell you that would be of any assistance whatever," she said a little coolly. "Isn't it a trifle late now?" It was a brutal question, but honest.

"It is," he agreed. "But I have a strong feeling that there is something of importance that I don't know, and any defense may rest upon it."

"What defense can there be for killing a woman . . . like that?" Herne interrupted, walking past Rathbone to sit in the chair on the other side of the fireplace, opposite his wife. "There can be no cause on earth to justify doing that to someone. She . . . she cut her open, Sir Oliver. She did not merely fight with her and hit her too hard. That, one might understand, but not this . . . atrocity." He breathed in quickly, as if to change his choice of word, mumbling something unintelligible.

"You do not need to explain yourself, Barclay," Amity said quickly. "Zenia Gadney may have been a woman of loose morals, and an embarrassment to the family, but she did not deserve to be gutted like a fish."

Again Herne opened his mouth to protest; then again he fell silent instead.

"Of course you are perfectly right," Rathbone agreed. "There doesn't seem to be anything that would make sense of such complete barbarity. You say, and Dinah has admitted it, that she was always aware of Zenia Gadney's existence, of her relationship to Dr. Lambourn, and that he had supported her for over fifteen years. Indeed, the money came out of the housekeeping account and was noted in the household ledger, on the twenty-first day of every month. Dinah says that she admired Dr. Lambourn for caring for Mrs. Gadney in that way, and when the will was probated she intended to continue doing so."

Amity's eyes widened. "And you believe her? Sir Oliver, perhaps there is something you are unaware of. I would not mention it, even now—I find it distasteful, a discredit to my brother, and it is something I would much rather remain a family secret. But in light of what you just said, I feel it is my responsibility to tell you. Zenia Gadney, or should I say Zenia *Lambourn*, was my brother's widow, legally. She was entitled to his entire estate, not a few pounds every month, bestowed on her at the discretion of a woman who was actually no more than his mistress."

Rathbone stared at Amity. "So you do know the truth, then," he said grimly.

She met his gaze unflinchingly. She showed no sign of being embarrassed by her lie, or surprised that Rathbone knew her brother's secret. "I do. But I saw no reason to make that truth publicly known, for Dinah's sake. Can you imagine how she would look in the jury's eyes when they find out that she was nothing more than Joel's mistress, mother of two illegitimate children? It is better for the world to see poor Zenia as the other woman. But I imagine if you have discovered the fact that Joel and Zenia were married, Coniston will be able to as well."

"Amity . . . ," Herne protested.

She ignored him. "If Coniston brings the facts to light, you would have difficulty in presenting your theory to a jury in a sympathetic light, Sir Oliver. Killing for money, even to feed your children, is not justified. Most particularly with that insane degree of savagery. If I were Mr. Coniston, I would suggest to them that Joel had begun to grow tired of Dinah, and was considering asking Zenia to return to him, as his lawful wife, and that was what threw Dinah into such a frenzy of hatred."

"For God's sake, Amity!" Herne burst out. "Do you need to—"

"Please do not blaspheme, Barclay," she said quietly. "Especially on the Sabbath, and in front of our guest. I am not advocating such a course, only warning Sir Oliver what may happen in the prosecutor's summing up of the case. Surely it is better he be prepared for it?"

Rathbone felt the coldness increase inside him. He hated what she had said, and the calm, intelligent way in which she had framed it, but it was true. In Coniston's place he might do the same.

"I had not considered such a thing," he admitted aloud. "But of course you are right. While I do not believe what you suggest, neither can I offer any proof that it is untrue."

"I'm sorry. I wish we could help you," Amity said more gently. "But in the end only the truth will serve."

Barclay leaned forward, his elbows on his knees, and buried his face in his hands. Was he more deeply distressed than his wife? Or was he simply more overtly emotional? Lambourn had been Amity's brother. Perhaps there was an element in her that could not forgive Dinah for the grief she had caused him.

"Did you know Zenia well?" Rathbone asked, looking at Amity. "I mean before whatever it was that caused her addiction, and her separation from Dr. Lambourn."

A look of confusion crossed Amity's face. Clearly she had not anticipated the question. She hesitated, searching for the right answer.

"No," Herne put in for her. "We were not living in the same area then, and at that time my wife was not well enough to travel. Joel told us that Zenia was quiet, gentle, a very decent woman but somewhat ordinary."

Amity turned to Rathbone, irritation marking two tiny lines between her fine brows. "What my husband means is that she was not eccentric, and she did not draw attention to herself."

Unlike Dinah, Rathbone thought, but he did not say so. Against his will, he thought of Margaret, and then of Hester. There had been a time when he had found Margaret's quiet dignity, her grace and composure, to be beautiful, and exactly what he most wished in a woman, particularly in a wife. The passion and energy of Hester had been too exhausting, far too unpredictable. But perhaps he had been in love with Hester in a way he never was with Margaret?

Then why had he not pursued Hester, before she married Monk? Had that been out of wisdom, knowing better than to imagine she would bring him happiness? Or had he just been a coward? Had Joel Lambourn left Zenia out of boredom, captured by the color and vitality of Dinah, and her obvious love for him? And had he grown to regret that?

Would Rathbone have grown tired of Hester? Would her fire and intelligence have demanded of him more than he was willing to give, perhaps more passion than he possessed?

He did not need to think about it. Monk had loved Hester when they were married—probably long before. Rathbone knew, merely by watching Monk's face, that he loved her far more deeply now. Time, experiences—good and bad—had hollowed out a larger vessel of both of them, able to hold a more profound emotion. If he himself were worth anything at all, it would have done so of him as well.

He looked at Amity. "Did Dr. Lambourn confide his feelings to you, Mrs. Herne? I appreciate your sensitivity in protecting his privacy, especially since he is no longer able to do so himself, but I am in great need of understanding the truth."

Herne lifted his eyes to watch Amity, waiting for her answer.

Amity seemed to be struggling with herself.

"I can judge only by his actions," she said at last. "He visited Zenia more and more often, possibly more frequently than he allowed Dinah to know. Perhaps she found that out. Joel was a very quiet man. He hated emotional scenes, as I believe most men do. Some women use them as a weapon—implicitly, of course, not openly. Dinah had a tendency to dramatize. She was self-centered and demanding. Some beautiful women are very spoiled, and never learn that good looks are as much a burden as a gift. One can come to rely upon them."

"And Zenia was . . . ordinary," Rathbone put in softly.

Amity smiled. "Very. She was not plain, just—how can I say it without being cruel?—she was dull. But she was gentle and unselfish. Perhaps that is a different kind of beauty, one that improves with time, whereas superb coloring and fine features can do the opposite. Constant drama can become very wearing, after a while. One longs for an ordinariness, honesty without effort."

Herne was staring at her, his face creased in distress. However, there was nothing in his expression to indicate what it was that hurt him.

"I see." Rathbone heard his own voice sounding flat. "This would be before he became so distressed over the rejection of his report on the use of opium, and his recommendation for control of its sales?"

"We have already covered that," Herne interrupted sharply. "The report was full of anecdotes, which was totally inappropriate. Joel allowed himself to become sentimentally involved with the tragedies of the issue, which is understandable; it would be inhuman not to pity a woman who has quite accidentally killed her own child." He winced, and his emotion showed naked in his face. He drew his breath in with a gasp and continued hoarsely, "But such feelings have no place in a scientific study. I tried to explain that to him, to point out that the whole thing should be reduced to facts and figures, material details that could be measured, so we might calmly take the necessary measures to reduce the risks, without at the same time being overrestrictive and denying legitimate use of medicines. But he was . . . hysterical about it. He refused to listen." He looked across at Amity, as if for her confirmation of what he said.

She gave it immediately, turning to Rathbone. "Joel was completely unreasonable. He seemed to have lost his balance. I respected him for his compassion for those who suffer, of course—we all do—but to allow yourself to become emotionally overwrought is of no help to the cause. We both tried . . ." She looked at Herne, who nodded quickly. "But we could not persuade him to take the hearsay out of his paper and keep it strictly to the numbers. He should have provided in each case the proper details and dates of all his witnesses, and of course the places where they lived, and the records of the products used, and such doctors' or coroners' reports as were reliable."

Rathbone was surprised. What he had heard from others of Lambourn's professional conduct was very different.

"I see," he said grimly. "No court of law would accept only anecdotal evidence. I can quite see why Parliament would not, either. Do you think his health was affected by this time?" He asked this of Amity.

She weighed her answer for several moments. In the silence Rathbone could hear footsteps across the hall, and then voices.

Amity froze, upright and absolutely motionless in her seat.

Herne rose very slowly to his feet, his face stiff with apprehension. He turned to Rathbone.

"Mr. Bawtry is joining us for luncheon," he said a little breathlessly. "He said he would if he was able. I'm sorry. I appreciate that this is a family matter, but he is my superior, and I cannot refuse him."

Rathbone made a small, gracious gesture to dismiss the matter. "Of course not. And we have already discussed the more personal side of the subject. Should there be anything more that concerns the report, or Dr. Lambourn's reactions to its rejection, Mr. Bawtry will be as much involved with it as you are. I shall be as brief as I can."

He looked at Amity, expecting to see ice in her eyes, and saw instead a vitality that completely took him aback. Then she blinked and stood up, turning toward the door as the footman opened it. An instant later Sinden Bawtry came in. Clearly he had been warned of Rathbone's presence. He came forward, smiling at Amity, then held out his hand to Rathbone.

"Good afternoon, Sir Oliver. Very agreeable to see you, but I imagine you are here to gain any last-minute knowledge you can in order to get this very wretched trial over with as decently as is possible, and if we may, before Christmas."

Rathbone took his hand, which was firm and cool, his grip powerful but without any attempt to crush. He had no need to. This was not his house, but he dominated the room as naturally as if he had been the host and the other three of them friends.

"There's nothing we can do," Herne said with a rising note of desperation. "We've already explained that poor Joel was rather losing his grip, overemotional, and all that. Couldn't accept the report. Not professional."

Amity shot a glance of irritation at him but was prevented from saying anything by Bawtry's intervention.

"I think the least said about poor Joel the better," he observed, smiling at Rathbone. "It would be most unfortunate for your case to be trying to justify the murder of that woman by suggesting there was some kind of cause for it. Frankly the only hope I can see for Mrs. Lambourn is to raise some reasonable doubt that Mrs. Gadney was desperate for money and tried her somewhat unpracticed hand at prostitution."

He smiled bleakly, almost as an apology. "You could do it easily enough without soiling her name too badly. For heaven's sake don't suggest she deserved it, only that she was unlucky enough not to be able to defend herself because she was alone at the time of the attack. If she screamed, no one heard her. A woman who was accustomed to life in the streets might have been careful enough not to frequent such a place without a . . . whatever they are called . . . a pimp."

Herne looked wretched. "She was once a decent woman!" he protested.

"So was Dinah!" Amity said sharply. "For heaven's sake, Barclay, let us have it over with. There is only one way it can end. We are deluding no one by making all this pretense that it was some kind of mischance, and nothing to do with Dinah's jealousy or her desperation to make sure that she inherited Joel's money. The fairy story that he didn't take his own life but was killed by some mysterious conspiracy in Greenwich Park is absurd. No one believes it." She turned to Rathbone. "If you have any—"

Bawtry put his hand on her arm, very gently, almost in a caress.

"Mrs. Herne, it is only natural, and speaks to both your honesty and your humanity, that you wish to see an end to the torture of the mind that this trial forces upon us, but we must wait it through to the end, in silence if necessary."

He turned to Rathbone. "Sir Oliver will do the best he can for your sister-in-law, but it is a doomed effort, and he is as aware of that as we are. It is a matter of the law being seen to be done." He gave Rathbone a brief smile that reached all the way to his eyes.

Amity seemed to relax and a kind of ease washed through her face. Her eyes became bright again. "I'm sorry," she said quietly. "Of course. I don't mean to contest the inevitable. I suppose it would be unnatural not to find it distressing."

"Indeed it would," Bawtry agreed. He moved his gaze from her to her husband. "I know you were fond of him, Barclay, and therefore must find these revelations about his wife shocking. It is natural to wish to deny them, but I am sure you will find your strength in your own wife, and gratitude that you are not losing control of your skills or your professional reputation, as poor Lambourn was."

Herne made a painful and quite visible effort to compose himself, to stand up straight with his shoulders back and his eyes forward.

"Of course," he agreed. Then he turned to Rathbone. "I'm sorry we could not be of more help, Sir Oliver. I'm afraid the facts are beyond argument. Thank you for calling."

Rathbone had no choice but to depart gracefully, his mind seething with impressions, none of them even remotely helpful.

CHAPTER

———————

19

AT MID-AFTERNOON OF THE following day, Monk stood by the dockside in the wind as the ferry drew near the steps and Runcorn climbed out. He looked tired and cold, but there was no hesitation as he came forward, his eyes meeting Monk's.

Monk gave him a brief nod of acknowledgment, then turned to walk with him toward the River Police Station. They knew each other too well to need the unnecessary niceties.

Inside they went to Monk's office, and a moment later a constable brought them tea. Monk thanked him, and he and Runcorn faced each other across the desk. There had been a short note from Rathbone, delivered by messenger. Monk passed it to Runcorn to read. It brought them up to date with both the trial and Rathbone's own thoughts, and his visit to Barclay Herne.

Runcorn looked up, his face even grimmer than before.

"The more I think of it, the less certain I am that Lambourn killed himself," he said unhappily. "It looked clear at the time, and the government people were absolutely certain." He shook his head. "I believed them. All I could think of was the widow and the daughters, and trying not to make it any worse for them than it had to be. I used not to be so . . . sentimental!" He said the word with disgust.

Words of denial, even comfort, came to Monk's mind, but he knew they would sound patronizing.

"I'm not any better," Monk said wryly. "If Dinah had been plain and timid, I might not have gone to Rathbone for her, and for that matter, I'm pretty certain he wouldn't have taken the case."

Runcorn gave a quick, bleak smile. "I've been supposing Lambourn told the truth about the opium and the damage it does without proper labels. Suppose they'll have to be pretty clear, too. Lots of people don't read. They'll need figures. It will cost. But I don't see any of the people who import the stuff killing him for that."

His face took on a vulnerable, almost bruised look. "And I have to accept that what we did in China was horrible, a betrayal of all that most of us think we stand for. We think we're civilized, even Christian, for that matter. Seems like when we're out of sight of home, some of us at least are bloody savages. But is anyone going to murder Lambourn because he knew that? We all know at least part of it." He sighed. "And whoever killed that poor woman qualifies as a savage, in my mind."

Monk had been thinking many of the same things. But there was the additional element that Hester had mentioned—the desperate dependence upon opium among those captured first by pain, then by addiction. "I'd like to know in more detail what Lambourn did in his last week alive."

Runcorn saw the point instantly. "You mean what did he learn that provoked someone to kill him? Who did he speak to? How did this person know that he learned whatever it was?"

"Yes. And what the devil was it? What could be a danger to anyone here in London? What could Lambourn have discovered, and been able to prove? Proof is the point. It has to be something personal, something very precious to lose or it wouldn't provoke a murder like that."

"There was plenty of barbarity," Runcorn said, his mouth drawn down, lips tight together. "I've heard that as many as twelve million Chinese people are addicted to opium." He looked at Monk more closely. "Have you ever seen them here, in parts of Limehouse? Opium dens, I mean? Filthy houses in back alleys where people lie on beds smoking the stuff, tiers of them packed like cargo in a ship's hold. Place is so full of smoke you can hardly see the walls. Like walking through a pea-soup fog. They just lie there. Don't even know where they are, half the time. Like the living dead." He shivered in spite of himself.

"I know," Monk agreed quietly. He had seen it, too, although not often. "I could understand if some Chinamen had come over here and killed scores of us, especially the families that made their fortunes on it. But why Lambourn?"

"It doesn't make sense," Runcorn agreed. "He found out something else. But what?" He rubbed his hand across his face. There was a faint rasping sound, as if he had shaved badly, missed a bit where the stubble was gray, and in the cold morning light he had not noticed it.

"We should follow his path, as well as we can. I should have done that earlier. They told me it was all to do with the report being rejected, and I believed them."

"Nothing on the report from Gladstone yet," Monk responded. "Who did Lambourn give it to?"

"His brother-in-law, Barclay Herne," Runcorn said. "He told me he passed it on before getting it back and destroying it."

"Which may or may not be true," Monk observed.

"He'd have to say that. If he didn't, his own guilt in suppressing it would be obvious," Runcorn pointed out.

"Perhaps he edited out whatever was the problem for him." Monk was reasoning to himself as much as to Runcorn. Even as he spoke he did not really believe what he was saying.

Runcorn looked at him critically. "If it wasn't to do with the labeling of opium and the damage it could do if that wasn't correct, why would Lambourn even put it in the report? Even if Hester is right about these needles, and the addiction, it has nothing to do with the Pharmacy Act."

Monk did not reply. Runcorn was right and they both knew it.

They finished their tea and sat in silence for several moments.

Then a different idea flashed into Monk's mind, sharp and bright.

"Perhaps they destroyed the report because there was nothing wrong with it," he said urgently.

Runcorn looked totally blank.

Monk leaned forward. "There was nothing in it that damaged anyone, nothing that didn't make sense. Lambourn knew about the opium addiction and knew who was feeding it, but he didn't include it in the report because it wasn't relevant to it. It was Lambourn himself they needed to destroy, so he would never speak of it."

"Ah!" Comprehension lit Runcorn's face. "They needed to discredit him sufficiently to make a suicide believable. God in heaven, what a bloody wicked thing to do! Ruin the man's reputation so when they murder him it can be accepted as suicide?" He ran his hand over his brow, pushing back the short, thick hair. "No wonder Dinah felt so helpless. I suppose she has no idea who it was? He wouldn't have told her, for her safety, apart from anything else."

"Exactly," Monk agreed. "He found out who was involved while researching this paper, because . . ." He drew in a deep breath and let it out in a sigh. "Actually all we know for certain is that he found it out recently, too recently for him to have done anything about it before he was killed. So presumably it was during his research. And the people he gave his report to are connected to what Lambourn discovered some-how, because they suppressed his work."

"We need to know exactly what he did, where he went, who he spoke with in his last week alive," Runcorn said decisively. "Have you got any men you can spare? We haven't long, a few days at most. Can Rathbone hold out until after Christmas?"

"He'll have to!" Monk said desperately. "The trouble is that selling opium is not illegal, even with the syringe needles. Even if we find who-ever it is, the law won't touch him."

Runcorn frowned. "Depends what else he's doing," he said thought-fully. "Isn't an easy thing, distributing things people are desperate for, especially if they can't always pay." He looked across at Monk, his eyes shadowed, mouth pulled tight.

Monk nodded slowly. "We need to know a lot more about it. Above all, we need to know if we're right."

"Hester?" Runcorn asked, almost as if he dared not even make the suggestion.

Monk met his gaze without flinching. "Maybe."

He stood up and went to the door. "I'll get Orme," he answered. "We'll start immediately."

"I've got a couple I can trust," Runcorn added, also standing. "Just for the details, anyway. Check with Lambourn's household servants for times and dates. We may be able to get a ferryman who can help. Lambourn probably used the same ferries all the time. Most of us are creatures of habit."

TWO HOURS LATER, THEY had filled out several sheets of paper with what they already knew of Lambourn's last week. The information came both from Runcorn's original inquiry and from what Hester had told Monk about Lambourn's visits with Agnes Nisbet and other sellers of opium-containing medicines. It was now a matter of honing it with more accurate details of times and places, in the hope of finding the one piece that did not fit, and which had been the cause of his murder.

Monk pushed his chair back from the table and stretched. He had been concentrating so intensely he was stiff, and his back and neck ached.

"Orme, can you check the ferrymen again? They'll speak to you, even if you have to go back and forth across the water, or pay them to sit still." He smiled grimly. "Should be an easy fare, no bending the back to earn a few pence, just rest on the oars and remember." He turned to one of his other men. "Taylor, see if Lambourn spent any time in the opium dens in Limehouse. I doubt it. There's probably nothing there we don't already know about, but you've got sources. We need to be sure."

"Yes, sir. Want me to try the Isle of Dogs as well? There's a fair few dens there, too," Taylor asked.

"Yes. Good idea. If Lambourn found something he'd have gone back to make certain. Look particularly for opium dealers out of the ordinary." He looked at Runcorn questioningly. It was the moment when in the past he would have given orders. There would have been a brief struggle for authority, each guarding his own territory. This time he bit back the words and waited.

He saw the flash of recognition in Runcorn's eyes, and then the relaxing of his body. "I'm going back to Lambourn's house to question the servants," he said calmly. "The valet will know when he came and went, and, I dare say, the cook. Between them they'll have a good idea. When I spoke to them before they were very loyal to him. If they know it's to prove he was murdered, they'll help. The difficulty'll be not put-ting words into their mouths." He opened his eyes wide and looked at Monk.

Monk gave him a momentary smile, in an acknowledgment of the changed balance of power between them. "I'm going to find this Ag-atha Nisbet that Hester told me about, and speak to her again. I want to know what Lambourn said to her, and anything else she knows about him."

"Good. Where'll we meet?" Runcorn asked.

"Back here, nine o'clock tonight," Monk replied.

"My home, ten o'clock," Runcorn argued. "You can walk from here. And we'll need that long. Rathbone won't be able to string the trial much more than a couple of days after Christmas. That gives us only a few more days to find whatever it is."

Monk nodded. "That's sense. But make it my house. The kitchen. Hot tea and something to eat." He looked at Orme.

"Yes, sir," Orme replied. "Taylor, too?"

"Certainly," Monk answered. "Paradise Place, Rotherhithe."

"Yes, sir, I know." Taylor nodded, smiling as if he had been given some kind of accolade.

It took Monk more than an hour to find the makeshift clinic that Hester had described to him, but far longer than that to oblige Agatha to make time for him and sit down in her tiny office, uninterrupted, and answer his questions.

She was a huge woman, about his height but much larger boned. He could imagine very easily being intimidated by her. Only when he looked at her eyes did he see any of the compassion or intelligence Hes-ter had spoken of.

"Wot d'yer want, then?" she said bluntly. "I in't got nothin' to tell the River Police."

Whatever chance he had of her cooperation, it would die the mo-ment she suspected he was lying. He decided to be as blunt with her as he imagined she would be with him.

"I'm trying to solve the murder of a good man, before his wife is convicted and hanged for it. Or, more accurately, she's convicted of another murder the same person also committed. I believe the good man, a doctor, was killed because he discovered something very bad about someone connected with the opium trade."

Suddenly Agatha's boredom changed to interest.

"That'd be Dr. Lambourn, an' that poor creature they slit open over on Limehouse Pier. If it wasn't the doctor's wife 'oo killed 'er, then 'oo was it?" She looked at Monk with hard, bright eyes, and he noticed that her hands, bigger than his, were slowly clenching and unclenching among the scattered papers on top of the wooden table.

"Yes," he agreed. "When Dr. Lambourn was searching for information about opium he accidentally found out a few other things. One of those things was so dangerous to someone that they defamed Lambourn professionally and then killed him, trying to make it look like suicide. That way they would be certain that their own secret would stay buried."

She waited, still watching him, an unmoving mountain of a woman.

"I think he discovered this in the last week of his life," Monk went on. "So I'm following as closely as I can in his footsteps."

"Soft, like," she said with bitter humor. "You don't want ter end up in the river yerself, wi' yer throat cut, or worse."

"I see you understand perfectly. What was Lambourn looking for from you, and what did you tell him?" He wondered if he should add anything about her safety, but to offer to protect her would be insulting. She would know as well as he did that it would be impossible.

"Opium," she said thoughtfully. "Lot o' things to do with it in't so nice."

"Such as what?" he asked. "Stealing? Cutting it with bad substitutes so it's impure? There's no smuggling; it comes in perfectly legally. What's worth killing anyone for?"

"Yer can kill to corner the trade in anything!" Agatha said with disgust. "Bakers an' fishmongers do it! You try cutting inter the meat market, an' see 'ow long yer last!"

"Is that what Lambourn asked you about?" he said.

Her face tightened. "I got me own ways o' getting opium—pure. I give it for pain, not for some rich fool to escape 'is troubles. I told 'im that."

"Then why would anyone bother to murder Dr. Lambourn? Come on, Miss Nisbet!" he urged. "He was a good man, a doctor trying to get medicine labeled properly so people didn't kill themselves accidentally. They murdered him to keep him quiet, and then butchered his first wife to hang his second wife for it. Whatever it was he found out it was a damn sight worse than a petty trade war that I could hear about in common speech on the dockside."

She nodded her head slowly. "There's worse than thievin'," she agreed. "There's slow poison. There's good men gone bad an' a kind o' living death that's worse than a grave. Opium's a powerful thing, like fire. Warm yer hearth, or burn yer 'ouse down."

Monk was aware of how closely she was watching him. The slightest flicker in his face, an instant's movement of his eyes, and she would see it. For a brief second he wondered what this woman had seen and done; what life had denied her that she had chosen this path. Then his attention returned to the present, to Joel Lambourn dead in disgrace and Dinah waiting to face the hangman.

"My horrors have all been commonplace," he answered her, knowing that she would not continue until he had made some acknowledgment. "A woman raped and beaten to death, a man hacked up and left to rot, children tortured and starved. It's all happened before, and it will happen again. The best I can do is try to prevent it as often as I can. What do you know that's going to ruin anyone in London, now?"

Something inside her closed up tight and hard. "Murder," she answered quietly. "It all comes down ter murder in the end, don't it? Murder for money. Murder for silence. Murder for dreams, for peace instead o' screamin' pain, murder for a needle an' a packet o' white powder."

He said nothing. He heard footsteps on the other side of the door, fast and light, someone hurrying, and beyond that the noises of pain. No creak of bedsprings, only the rustle of straw palliasses on the floor.

"Who?" he said at last. "Who did Lambourn find out about?"

"Dunno," she answered without a second's hesitation. "Don't want ter, 'cos then I'd 'ave ter kill 'im."

Monk had no doubt that she would. He was uncertain of his own morality, because he might feel the same, but he smiled.

She smiled back at him, showing huge, white teeth. "Ye're an odd duck, aren't yer?" she said with interest. "If yer find the bastard, put an extra twist in the noose fer me, will yer? He's ruined two right good men, an' there in't enough o' them ter waste one, Gawd knows. Lambourn, and the 'ooever 'ee's got sellin' for 'im." Her voice was hoarse, as if she held back tears far too long and her throat ached from it.

"Yes," he said without hesitation. "When I get him."

"They said Lambourn slit 'is wrists?" she went on, staring at him steadily.

"Yes," he agreed.

"But 'e didn't," she pressed. Her voice was firm now, no doubt in it.

"I don't think so," Monk said quietly. He would not pretend to be certain.

"Better off than some, but it shouldn't 'ave 'appened."

"What sort of person am I looking for?" he asked. "Can you tell me anything?"

She gave a little grunt of disgust. "If I knew that, I'd get 'im meself. Someone secret, 'oo don't look like 'e'd know opium from corn flour. Someone 'oo's clean an' polite an' never seen wot 'appens to them as sticks that stuff in their veins an' takes a one-way visit to madness. But now an' again the ones like me sees their faces lookin' out between the bars at the rest of us."

Monk was silent for several moments, then he stood up.

"Thank you," he said, then turned and walked away.

He went back to Wapping, his mind teeming with what Agatha Nisbet had said. He was looking for the man who profited from selling not just opium, but the needles that made it possible to become lethally addicted to it within a matter of weeks, even days. It was nothing to do with ordinary doses anyone could buy in patent medicines, or even the Chinese habit of smoking it, bad enough in its slow destruction.

The problem was not only to find him, but even when he did, what would he do about it? To sell such damnation might be one of the vilest of sins, but it was not against the law. Unless, of course, the man was also involved in the murder of Lambourn and of Zenia Gadney.

But since it was not a crime to sell opium, and needles, even if Joel Lambourn found out, why kill him? What could he have done to harm such a man? What could he prove?

It was still a tangle too dense to penetrate.

In his office Monk reread all he had on the people concerned in the research for the Pharmacy Act, making a list of all of those who had come into contact with Joel Lambourn. He would have to compare this list with whatever Runcorn could find on Lambourn's movements in the last week of his life.

But then, of course, it did not have to be direct contact. It might have been indirect, someone who mentioned a name, a fact to someone else.

Who was the person that Agatha Nisbet believed had been corrupted into selling opium and needles for the man behind the scheme? How would they find him, and if they did, would he tell them anything of use?

The other half of the problem was not yet answered, perhaps the easier half: Who knew what Lambourn had learned so that it reached the man behind the sales, the real profiteer, the one who had killed him, and then killed Zenia Gadney? What was the line of reasoning that connected them all?

Was the damning information in Lambourn's report, or was its destruction a red herring to justify his apparent suicide? Monk knew he must look harder for it, at the very least find out exactly who had ordered its destruction, and who had carried it out.

He would ask Runcorn to put someone good on to the task of looking yet again.

The report had been handed to Barclay Herne, who had apparently told Sinden Bawtry that it was so ill prepared as to be no use for the purpose of persuading Parliament to pass the Pharmacy Act.

Who else had seen it? If no one had, then the seller of opium had to be one of those two. But would Herne have killed his brother-in-law? Both Bawtry and Herne had alibis. They had been at the Atheneum the night Lambourn died, as attested to by a dozen or more people.

The seller of opium would surely have others in his employ, including the man Agatha Nisbet said had once been good. How could Monk find him? And how soon?

Runcorn, Orme, and Taylor met at Paradise Place just before ten o'clock, all sitting around the kitchen table on the four hard-backed wooden chairs normally kept there for dining. One more chair had had to be brought along from Scuff's bedroom, Hester creeping in to collect it without waking him.

The oven warmed the room, which smelled of fresh bread, scrubbed wood, and clean linen.

Over tea and hot buttered toast Monk told them all what Agatha Nisbet had told him, emphasizing the need to find the other man she spoke of in particular. No one said anything. He looked up and saw Hester's eyes on him, watching, trying to judge from his face just what he thought.

"Did she tell you anything else about this man?" she asked him quietly. "Anything at all—age, experience, skills, what he does now?"

"No," he admitted. "I think she was protecting him on purpose. It grieved her badly that he had been so corrupted."

"Opium does that to you." Hester's face was bleak. "I don't know much about it, but I've heard a bit, seen a bit. Sometimes you have to use it for terrible wounds, and then it's too hard to give it up, particularly if the wounds never really heal."

Monk looked at her. Her shoulders were tense, pulling the fabric of her dress, the muscles of her neck tight, her mouth closed delicately so the pity showed like an unhealed wound of her own. He wondered how much more she had seen than he had, horror that she could never share.

He reached across the table and touched her fingers on the wooden surface, just for a moment, then pulled back.

"Do you know where to look?" he asked her. He hated doing it, but she would know that he had to, and resent it if he did less than his job, in order to spare her.

"I think so," she answered, looking at him and not any of the others around the table, all watching her, waiting.

"I'll go with you," Monk said immediately. "He could be dangerous."

"No." She shook her head. "We haven't time to send two people to do one job. We've only a few days. I have an idea of who it might be. When I saw him before, I didn't even think of him being addicted himself. I should have." There was anger in her voice, bitter self-criticism.

"You're not going alone," Monk responded without hesitation. "If he is the person who killed Lambourn and hacked Zenia Gadney to pieces, he'd do the same to you without a second thought about it. Either I come with you, or you don't go!"

She smiled very slightly, as though some tiny element of it amused her.

"Hester!" he said sharply.

"Think of what else there is to do," she replied. "Agatha said he was a good man once. The remnants of that will be left, if I don't offer any threat to him." She leaned forward a little, as if to command their attention. "We have to know who is using him. That's whoever killed Lambourn, and Zenia Gadney—or had them killed."

Monk clenched his teeth and breathed out slowly. "What if it's this man who killed them?" he asked, wishing he did not have to.

He saw the sudden awareness leap in her eyes.

It was actually Runcorn who said what she must have been thinking.

"That'll be why there was no bottle or vial where Lambourn was found," he said unhappily. "He didn't drink the opium, it was put into him with one of those needles. And of course whoever killed him took that away with them. He wouldn't want anyone to know of it. There can't be so many people have them."

"Still doesn't change that we have to know who killed Zenia Gadney." Orme spoke for the first time. "I've been back and forward around the Limehouse Pier. No one admits to seeing her there that evening, except with a woman. If she met a man, doctor or not, someone paid by Herne or Bawtry, then it was afterward." He looked at Runcorn, then at Monk. "I suppose you've thought that it could be that Dinah Lambourn did kill them both, nothing to do with jealousy or rage, but because someone paid her to, because of the opium?"

No one answered. The thought was impossible to rule out, but neither did anyone want to accept it.

It was Runcorn who broke the silence in the end.

"I've talked to everyone in the Lambourn house," he said. "I've got a fairly good list of where Dr. Lambourn went in his last week, but it's only what we already expected." He pulled two sheets of paper out of his pocket and laid them down in the middle of the table.

Monk glanced at them, but he could see in Runcorn's face that there was more.

"I tried to piece together his last day," Runcorn went on. "Whoever killed him planned it very carefully, very believably."

One by one around the table they nodded agreement. No one mentioned Dinah, but the very absence of her name hung between them.

"Who did he see that day?" Monk asked. He knew before Runcorn spoke that the answer would not be so easy. It was written in the confusion in Runcorn's eyes.

"Dr. Winfarthing," Runcorn replied, "in the morning. Just tradesmen in Deptford in the afternoon. He came home for an early dinner, then worked in his study before going for a short walk with Mrs. Lambourn in the evening. They both went to bed at about ten. No one saw him alive again. He was found the next morning by the man walking his dog up on One Tree Hill."

"That doesn't make sense," Hester said unhappily. "There's nothing in a day like that to make him kill himself that night. It wasn't even the day he heard about the report being rejected, was it?" She looked from Monk to Runcorn, and then back again.

"No," Runcorn replied. "They told him three days earlier. The idea was that it took him that long to steel himself to do it. Or perhaps he thought they would change their minds, or he'd find some other facts. Winfarthing said he was still determined to fight when he saw him that morning."

"We're back to Dinah Lambourn," Orme pointed out.

"No one contacted him?" Monk asked Runcorn. "No one called, left a message, a letter? Could there have been something in the post?"

"I asked the butler that," Runcorn replied. "He said Dr. Lambourn looked at the post when he came home at about five o'clock. There was nothing but the ordinary tradesmen's bills. No personal letters."

"He went to bed?" Hester asked, puzzled. "Are you sure? Could he have gone out again when Dinah went upstairs?" Her voice dropped a little.

"The butler said they both went up. He spoke to Lambourn and Lambourn answered him. But he could have read awhile, I suppose, and come down again," Runcorn replied.

Taylor looked embarrassed. "Unless he really did take his own life?" He bit his lip. "Are we certain she isn't innocent of killing him, but lying to restore some dignity to his name? Nobody wants to admit, even to themselves, that somebody they love did that. She'd want her daughters to think it was murder, wouldn't she? Women'll do most things to protect their children."

Hester looked at Taylor, then at Monk. Monk could see in her face that she believed it possible.

Runcorn was stubborn. "Either someone came to see him, or he went out to see someone," he said flatly.

"On One Tree Hill?" Monk asked. "It's close to a mile from Lower Park Street, and uphill. Who would he meet in the middle of the night?"

"Someone he trusted," Runcorn replied. "Someone he didn't want to be seen with, or who didn't want to be seen with him."

"And he didn't expect to go far," Hester added. "You said he didn't take a jacket, and it was October."

"Someone he trusted," Monk said gently. "Perhaps someone who could get close enough to him to put a needle in his vein and do whatever you have to do to get the opium in."

"That's like poor Mrs. Gadney," Orme said. "She was killed by someone she trusted, or she wouldn't have been standing out on the pier with them, alone in the dark."

"Certainly not a prospective client," Monk said with conviction. "Not out in the open like that."

"No," Orme cut in. "I asked more carefully this time. No one ever actually saw her with a man apart from Lambourn at any time. They assumed. The newspapers said she turned to prostitution, but there's no proof." He leaned forward across the table, his voice assured. "What if she was there with someone she knew, someone she didn't fear at all—just like Lambourn?"

"The same person?" Monk said what he knew they were all thinking. "Who would Zenia know that Lambourn also knew?"

"Someone respectable," Runcorn said slowly. "Someone Lambourn trusted, and someone she would never suspect of hurting her. Maybe . . ." He thought for a moment. "Maybe someone who said they were Lambourn's solicitor, or a friend."

"A doctor," Hester said very slowly. "Or a member of the family."

"Or his wife," Orme said sadly.

No one argued.

"Now we've got until the day after Boxing Day to prove it," Runcorn said, looking from one to the other of them. "If Sir Oliver can make the trial last that long."

RATHBONE LAY AWAKE A good deal of that night, his mind in turmoil. Monk had sent him regular notes to keep him aware of what he had discovered. But as yet there was no proof that could be presented in court.

Dinah's only defense was that she believed her husband had been murdered because he discovered something that would ruin the reputation of someone, someone who would commit murder rather than be exposed. And she, in turn, was willing to risk her own life on the gallows in order to force the police and the court to find the truth.

When should Rathbone tell that to the jury? If he told them too soon it would have lost its power by the time he summed up. If he waited too long it would look like a desperate, last-minute invention.

He stared up at the ceiling, eyes wide open in the total darkness, and felt as if he had lost control of the case. He must get it back. Even if he was actually working on trust that Dinah was innocent, and hope that Monk would find a thread of proof that he could unravel, he could not let Coniston know that. Above all he must not let the jury see it.

Monk's note had spoken quite clearly of an opium addiction far more profound than even that of those who smoked it, one where the substance was injected directly into the bloodstream through a vein.

Someone was deliberately introducing people to it, in a time of their weakness because of physical or emotional agony, and then when they were dependent, exploiting that desperation.

It was an evil of almost limitless proportion, but it was not technically a crime in the eyes of the law. Monk had acknowledged that himself. So why kill Lambourn? What had he discovered that he must die for?

Rathbone had to guess the answer, and guess correctly. Then he could hope to spin out the trial until Monk found the beginning of proof. Rathbone would have built up the foundations of a case, and would have to add only the final piece that tied it all together and name the man behind the murders of both Lambourn and Zenia Gadney.

Would he be able to do that? He fell asleep at last with only the outline of a plan in his mind.

WHEN THE TRIAL RESUMED in the morning, Rathbone looked across at Sorley Coniston and saw the smooth pleasure in his face. As things were now, he could hardly lose.

Rathbone must begin to take control of the pace and the temper of the evidence now. The end of the week was Christmas. As it stood, the best verdict he could hope for was reasonable doubt, and looking across the room to the twelve men in the jury box, he could not see even one doubter among them. They sat motionless, grim-faced, as if steeling themselves to answer levelly that they were prepared to condemn a woman to death for what they believed she had done.

Rathbone had no other suspect even to suggest to them, but he had to create one. In his own mind it was a nameless, faceless assassin employed by someone guilty of wanting to destroy Lambourn's credibility and see his report buried. Repeated like that, it sounded as desperate to Rathbone as it would to anyone else. He must give this person reality, ambitions, fear of loss, greed—evil.

Everyone came to order for Judge Pendock. Coniston rose to his feet and called his final witness. Rathbone had been advised who it was, as the law required, but he had no defense against what he knew the man would say. He had been hoping Coniston would not think to look for him, but considering Amity Herne's knowledge, and her loathing of Dinah Lambourn, it was to be expected.

Rathbone had managed to raise just a shadow of doubt as to whether Lambourn had taken his own life or whether, in view of the absence of a weapon or anything in which to dilute or drink the opium, there had been someone else present. No one had yet suggested the use of a syringe.

The new witness swore as to his name and occupation, and to tell the truth.

"Mr. Blakelock," Coniston began, "you are a registrar of births, deaths, and marriages?"

"Yes, sir," Blakelock answered. He was a handsome man, prematurely gray but otherwise wearing his years well.

"Did you register the marriage, eighteen years ago, of Dr. Joel Lambourn?"

"I did."

"To whom?" Coniston asked.

There was no interest in the courtroom. Only Rathbone sat stiff, his eyes on the jury.

"Zenia Gadney," Blakelock replied.

"Zenia Gadney?" Coniston repeated, his voice ringing out, high and sharp, as if the answer astonished him.

Even Pendock jolted forward, his jaw slack.

In the jury box there was a ripple of amazement. One man gasped and all but choked.

Coniston waited for the full impact to sink in, and then with a very slight smile he continued.

"And was that marriage dissolved, sir?"

"No," Blakelock answered.

Coniston shrugged and made a wide, helpless gesture with his hands. "Then who is Dinah Lambourn, the mother of his children, and with whom he has lived for the last fifteen years, until his death?"

"I presume 'his mistress' would be the most appropriate term," Blakelock replied.

"Then when Lambourn died, Zenia . . . Lambourn would be his widow, not the accused?" Coniston went on.

"Yes."

"And so heir to his estate?" Coniston added.

Rathbone rose to his feet. "My lord, that is an assumption that Mr. Blakelock is not qualified to make, and indeed it is an error. If you wish it, I can call Dr. Lambourn's solicitor, who will tell you that his estate is left to his daughters, Adah and Marianne. There was a small bequest, an annuity, to Zenia Gadney. It would amount to approximately the same amount as he gave her when he was alive."

Pendock glared at him. "You were aware of this, Sir Oliver?"

"I was aware of the provisions of the will, my lord. It seemed a fairly obvious inquiry to make," Rathbone answered.

Pendock drew in his breath to add something further, and then changed his mind. It would have been improper to ask what Dinah had confided in Rathbone, and the jury would draw their own conclusions anyway.

Coniston realized as much; he certainly had no need to win such minor skirmishes as this. "I apologize, my lord," he said with a slight smile. "It was an assumption, and as my learned friend has pointed out, in this case, unjustified. Perhaps for the defense, he will call someone to prove that the accused was aware that her children would inherit? Then her very natural fear of being left destitute by her husband's suicide would be set aside, leaving only the motive of an equally natural jealousy."

Rathbone allowed a look of incredulity to cross his face.

"Is the prosecution suggesting that the accused was jealous of the woman she so obviously supplanted in Dr. Lambourn's affections?" he asked. "Or perhaps that Zenia Gadney was so jealous, after all these years, that she attacked Dinah Lambourn? In which case the mutilation is repellent and unnecessary, but the blow that caused Mrs. Gadney's death may very well be considered self-defense!"

"This is preposterous!" Coniston said with disbelief, but no apparent ill humor. "My lord—"

Pendock held up his hand. "Enough, Mr. Coniston. I can see for myself the absurdity of it." He glared at Rathbone. "Sir Oliver, I will not have this grave and very terrible trial turned into a farce. The accused went to seek the victim where she lived. Whatever happened after she found her ended in the victim's death by violence, and then her hideous mutilation. These facts are beyond dispute. Is that the end of your case for the prosecution, Mr. Coniston?"

"Yes, my lord, it is."

"Have you any questions for Mr. Blakelock?" Pendock turned to Rathbone.

"No, thank you, my lord."

"Then we shall adjourn for luncheon. After that you may call your first witness for the defense." Pendock turned to Blakelock. "Thank you. You may leave the stand."

RATHBONE STOOD IN THE center of the floor feeling as if he were in an arena waiting for lions, naked of armor and without a sword to attack. He had never felt so vulnerable before, even in cases where he knew his client was guilty. He realized with a shock that it was not his faith in Dinah that was wounded, perhaps critically, but his belief in himself. His confidence, and some of his hope, had bled away.

Now he must lay very careful suggestions of a powerful figure bent on protecting himself. And all the time, in everything, he must believe that Dinah was innocent, no matter how far against reason that seemed to be. It must be in his mind always that Lambourn discovered something in his research that imperiled a man of power, and he was murdered to silence him. It was made to look like suicide to discredit him. Zenia Gadney was murdered to destroy Dinah and her crusade to save Lambourn's reputation, and therefore his cause.

He made himself smile, feeling as if it were ghastly on his face.

"I call Mrs. Helena Moulton."

Helena Moulton was called by the usher. A moment later, she appeared and rather hesitantly climbed the steps up to the witness stand. She was clearly nervous. Her voice shook as she swore to tell the truth.

"Mrs. Moulton," Rathbone began gently, "are you acquainted with the accused, Dinah Lambourn?"

"Yes." Mrs. Moulton avoided looking up at the dock. She stared straight ahead of her at Rathbone as if her neck were fixed in a brace.

"Were you friends?" he pursued.

"I . . . yes. Yes, we were friends." She gulped. She was very pale and her hands were locked together on the rail of the stand. The light glinted on the gems in her rings.

"Think back to your feelings during that friendship," Rathbone began. He was painfully aware that Helena Moulton was embarrassed now about owning to having been Dinah's friend, afraid the society in which she lived would then associate her with Dinah, as if testifying were somehow condoning what Dinah was accused of having done.

Rathbone did not believe her testimony would sway the case in Dinah's favor, even that it would necessarily make any difference at all, but he needed every extra hour he could to stretch out the testimony of the few witnesses he had to create the outline of someone else to suspect. Perhaps even now Monk would find something that would prove this person's existence. And curiously enough, Rathbone had almost as much faith in Runcorn as he did in Monk. There was stubbornness in the man that would cling on to the very end, especially because he was angry at having been used and misled in the first place.

Mrs. Moulton was waiting for the question, as was Pendock, who was beginning to be irritated.

"You spent time together?" Rathbone continued. "You went to afternoon parties, exhibitions of art and photographs of travel and exploration, soirées, dinner parties at times, even the theater, and of course garden parties in the summer?"

"I did with many people," she replied guardedly.

"Of course. Without lots of people, it is hardly a party, is it?" he said smoothly. "You enjoyed each other's company?"

It was a question to which she could hardly say no. That would be to suggest some ulterior motive.

"Yes, yes, I . . . did," she agreed a shade reluctantly.

"You must have spoken of many things?"

Coniston rose to his feet. "My lord, this is wasting the court's time. The prosecution concedes that Mrs. Moulton was friends with the accused."

Rathbone wanted to object, but he had no grounds on which to argue the point. If he lost, it would be only one more defeat for him in the minds of the jury.

Pendock looked at Rathbone with annoyance. "You have some point, Sir Oliver? If so, please proceed to make it. The social comings and goings of Mrs. Moulton and the accused seem totally irrelevant."

"I am trying to establish, my lord, Mrs. Moulton's standing in her ability to comment on the accused's state of mind."

"Then please consider it established and ask your question," Pendock said tartly.

"Yes, my lord." Rathbone had hoped for more time, but there was nothing with which to argue. "Mrs. Moulton was the accused anxious or worried in the week or so before Dr. Lambourn's death?"

She hesitated. She looked up for an instant, as if to meet Dinah's eyes in the dock above the courtroom gallery, then changed her mind and stared fixedly at Rathbone.

"As I recall, she was just as usual. She . . . she did mention that he was working very hard and seemed rather tired."

"And after his death?" he asked.

Her face filled with compassion, the tension vanishing as all consciousness of herself and the courtroom was swallowed up by her pity. "She was like a woman walking in her sleep," she said huskily. "I have never seen anyone more numbed with grief. I knew they were close. He was a very gentle man, a good man . . ." She gulped and composed herself again with difficulty. "I felt for her deeply, but there was nothing I could do. There was nothing anyone could do."

"Indeed not," he agreed softly. "Even the very closest of friends cannot reach out far enough to touch such a loss. Death is terrible in itself, but that a person should have taken his own life is so very much worse."

"She never believed that!" Mrs. Moulton said urgently, leaning forward over the rail as if three or four inches less between them would lend power to her words. "She always said that he had been killed to . . . to keep his work from being accepted. I am sure she believed that."

"Indeed, Mrs. Moulton, so do I," Rathbone agreed. "In fact I intend to make that clear to the jury."

A flicker of displeasure crossed Coniston's face.

Pendock was irritated but he did not interrupt.

Rathbone hurried on, gaining a lick of confidence, which was like a flame in the wind, any moment to be extinguished.

"When the police arrested her and accused her of murdering Zenia Gadney, she told them that she had been with you at the time she was said to have been seen in Copenhagen Place, searching for Mrs. Gadney. Is that correct?"

Helena Moulton looked uncomfortable. "Yes." She said it so quietly that Pendock had to ask her to repeat her answer so the jury could hear her. "Yes," she said with a sudden jolt.

Rathbone smiled at her, very slightly, in reassurance. "And was she with you at that time, Mrs. Moulton?" he asked.

"No."

Pendock leaned forward.

"No," she said more clearly. "She . . . she said that she was with me at a soirée. I don't know why on earth she said that. I couldn't support her. I was at an art exhibition, and dozens of people saw me. There wasn't a soirée anywhere near us that day."

"So it was quite impossible that she was telling the truth," Rathbone concluded.

"Yes, it was."

Coniston rose to his feet again. "My lord, my learned friend is wasting time again. We have already established that the accused was lying! That is not an issue."

"My lord." Rathbone faced Pendock. "That is not the point I am trying to make. What Mr. Coniston has apparently missed is the fact that Dinah Lambourn could never have expected to be believed in that statement."

Coniston spread his hands. It was a gesture of helplessness, inviting the court in general, and the jury in particular, to conclude that Rathbone was indeed doing no more than using up time in a desperate attempt to stave off the inevitable.

"Sir Oliver." Pendock was exasperated. "This seems to be a completely pointless exercise. If you have some conclusion to all this . . . farrago, please let the court know what it is."

Rathbone was being hurried far more than he wished, but he could see in Pendock's face that he was going to get no more latitude. Now was the moment to tell them Dinah's brave and desperate gamble.

"My lord, I am trying to show the jury that Dinah Lambourn believed that her husband had been defamed by having his report refused, and his professional ability slandered. Then when he would not accept that and go away quietly, denying what he knew to be true, he was murdered, and his death made to appear as suicide."

There was a burst of noise from the gallery. Someone shouted out abuse. Another cheered. The jury swung round in their seats, looking one way and then another.

Pendock demanded order.

Coniston appeared impatient and then disgusted.

As soon as he could be heard, Rathbone continued, raising his voice above the rustle of movement and mutter of voices. "She was willing to face trial for a murder she did not commit," he said loudly. "In order to gain a public hearing for her husband's contrived disgrace and to oblige at least someone to investigate his death again." He turned to face the astonished jury. "She is willing to risk her own life so that you, as representatives of the people of England, can hear the truth of what Joel Lambourn discovered, and judge for yourselves whether he was a good man, honest and capable, trying to serve the people of this country, or whether he was deluded, vain, and in the end suicidal."

He pointed up toward the dock. "That is how much she loved him—still loves him. She killed no one—nor does she know who did—either Joel Lambourn, or the unfortunate Zenia Gadney. And, by the grace of God, and the laws of England, I will prove that to you."

There was uproar in the gallery and this time Pendock's calls for order were useless. He cleared the court, ordering an early adjournment for the day. Then he rose to his feet and strode out, his great red gown flying out behind him like broken scarlet wings.

THE NEXT DAY, RATHBONE was prepared to call both Adah and Marianne Lambourn if necessary, simply to stretch out the time and give Monk every chance to find at least some element of truth that would raise doubt. Originally, Rathbone had hoped to learn who had killed Zenia, and be able to prove it. If he could even prove Lambourn did not commit suicide, it would make Dinah look rational, sympathetic, but so far he had been blocked in that at every step. Now there was only the suggestion of a manipulative figure behind the murder that he must give flesh to.

Perhaps he should not have been surprised. If Dinah was right then someone with power had a great deal to hide, and both Coniston and Pendock had been advised of it. There must also have been the threat that his exposure would damage someone's reputation irrevocably, and with it, perhaps, the honor of the government.

He admitted to himself he was depending on proving reasonable doubt: the possibility of there being any other answers, no matter how vague, whose existence he could prove. He just had to last today and tomorrow, then the courts were closed for Christmas, which would give them a brief reprieve, until Tuesday. But he also knew that darkening Christmas with the necessity to return immediately after would not endear him to anyone. He would not have done it had he any other choice.

In the morning he called Dinah Lambourn's servants, who had nothing to reveal of their mistress's behavior on the nights her husband and Zenia Gadney died that would implicate her in any way.

Rathbone's first witness of the afternoon was the shopkeeper who had described Dinah's visit to Copenhagen Place, and the extreme emotion she had exhibited, so much so that most of the shoppers in the street now felt as if they had seen her, and should have realized who and what she was.

But Rathbone knew that the mind can deceive the eye. He hoped that his discussion with Mr. Jenkins had shown the man how much had been suggested by circumstance, and that what he was experiencing was not in fact memory but hindsight. It was something of a risk to put him on the stand where Coniston could question him immediately afterward, but he had nothing left to lose. Please God, Monk or Runcorn had learned something of value, however fragile.

Mr. Jenkins took the stand looking very nervous to be out of the security of his own shop and the trade with which he was familiar. He gripped the rail as though he were at sea and the whole stand was tossing like the bridge of a ship. Was that the very understandable anxiety of a man in extraordinary surroundings, knowing that a woman's life might rest on what he said? Or did he plan now to go back on what he had told Rathbone, and he was afraid of Rathbone's anger—or of Coniston's anger, and the weight of the established law should he displease them?

Rathbone must set him at his ease as much as he could. He walked forward to be close enough to the witness stand not to have to raise his voice to be heard.

"Good afternoon, Mr. Jenkins," he began. "Thank you for giving us your time. We appreciate that you have a business to run and that your customers require you every day but Sunday. I will not keep you long. You have a general grocery shop in Copenhagen Place, Limehouse, is that correct?"

Jenkins cleared his throat. "Yes, sir, I do."

"Are most of your customers local people, living, say, within half a mile or so of your shop?"

"Yes, sir."

"Because people need groceries of one sort or another almost every day and naturally would not wish to carry them farther than necessary?" Rathbone asked.

Coniston shifted impatiently in his seat.

Pendock looked annoyed.

Only the jury were listening with attention, believing something pertinent and perhaps controversial was coming. Rathbone was famous, his reputation formidable. If they had not known that before the trial began, they knew it now.

"Yes, sir," Jenkins agreed. "I know 'em, like. I keep the things they need. They don't 'ave ter ask."

"So you would notice a stranger in your shop?" Rathbone smiled as he said it. "Someone who did not live locally, perhaps whose needs you did not know."

Jenkins gulped. He knew the importance of the question. "I reckon so." Already he was less sure, an equivocation in his words, not a certainty.

"Say, a well-dressed woman who was not from Limehouse, who had never bought her groceries from you, and who carried no bag or basket in which to put whatever she bought," Rathbone elaborated.

Jenkins stared at him.

Rathbone had to be as absolute as possible. There would be no going back and retracing his steps or he would sound desperate, and the jury would hear it.

"I imagine you are friendly or at least comfortable with most of your customers, Mr. Jenkins? They are decent people going about their business?"

"Yes . . . yes, course they are," Jenkins agreed.

"So a woman behaving wildly, hysterically, would be extraordinary in your shop?"

Coniston rose to his feet.

Rathbone turned to him, carefully assuming a look of amazement and questioning on his face and in the angle of his head.

Coniston gave a sigh of exasperation, as if infinitely bored, and resumed his seat. None of this would be lost on the jury. But their concentration would have been momentarily broken, the emotion lessened.

"My learned friend appears not to have perceived the importance of my question, Mr. Jenkins," Rathbone said with a smile. "Perhaps it is unclear to others as well. I am trying to show that your shop is a local service. You know all the women in the area who use your establishment to purchase their daily needs of tea, sugar, flour, vegetables, and so on. They are decent and civil people, feeling that they are among friends. A woman you have never seen before, and nobody else appears to know, and whose manner is hysterical and demanding, is highly unusual, and you would be likely to remember her, in fact be almost certain to. Is that correct?"

Jenkins now had no alternative but to agree. Perhaps Coniston, by interrupting, had unintentionally done the defense a favor? Rathbone did not dare to look at him to see. It would be obvious to the jury, and they would see gamesmanship behind it.

"I . . . I suppose I would," Jenkins conceded.

"Then would you please look up at the dock and tell me if you are certain that the woman sitting there is the same woman who came into your shop and asked to know where Zenia Gadney lived? We have already heard that it was a woman tall and dark, who looked something like her, but there are thousands of such women in London. Are you sure, beyond doubt, that it was this woman? She swears that it was not."

Jenkins peered up at Dinah, blinking a little as if he could not see clearly.

"My lord," Rathbone looked up at Pendock, "may I have the court's permission to ask the accused to rise to her feet?"

Pendock had no choice; the request was only a courtesy. He would have to explain any refusal, and he had no grounds for it.

"You may," he replied.

Rathbone turned to the dock and Dinah rose to her feet. It was an advantage. Rathbone realized it immediately. They could all see her more clearly, and every single juror was craning his neck to stare. She looked pale and grief-ravaged, and in a way more beautiful than when she had been in her own home, surrounded by familiar things. She had not yet been found guilty in the law, even if she had by the public, so she was permitted to wear her own clothes. Since she was still in mourning for her husband, it was expected she wear black, and with her dramatic features and pale, blemishless skin the loveliness of her face was startling, as was the suffering in it. She was composed, as if she had no energy left to hope, or to struggle.

Jenkins gulped again. "No." He shook his head. "I can't say as it were 'er. She . . . she looks different. I don't recall 'er face being like that."

"Thank you, Mr. Jenkins," Rathbone said, gasping with relief inside. "My learned friend may wish to question you, but as far as I am concerned, I appreciate your time, and you are free to go back to your business and your service to the community in Copenhagen Place."

"Yes, sir." Jenkins turned anxiously toward Coniston.

Coniston's hesitation was only fractional, but it was there. At least one or two of the jurors must have seen it.

"Mr. Jenkins," Coniston began gently, aware of the court's sympathy with the shopkeeper. He was a man like themselves, probably with family to support, trying to do his best in a situation he hated. He was eager to be done with it and free to carry on with his quiet, hardworking life, complete with its small pleasures, its opinions that were not weighed and measured, its very limited responsibility.

Rathbone knew all this was going through Coniston's mind, because it had gone through his own.

Coniston smiled. "Actually, Mr. Jenkins, I find I have nothing to ask you. You are an honest man in a wretched situation, placed there by chance, and none of your own doing. Your compassion, carefulness, and modesty are to be admired. Please accept my thanks also, and return to your business, which I'm sure must need you, most particularly this close to Christmas." Coniston gave a very slight bow and walked back gracefully to his seat.

Pendock's face was tense. He glanced at the clock, then at Rathbone.

"Sir Oliver?"

Rathbone rose to his feet.

"My next witness may testify at some length, my lord, and I believe Mr. Coniston is bound to wish to question some of his evidence quite closely." He too looked at the clock. He would not like to have to admit that he could not locate Runcorn at this hour, but he would if Pendock forced him into it.

"Very well, Sir Oliver," Pendock sighed. "The court is adjourned until tomorrow morning."

"Yes, my lord. Thank you."

As soon as Rathbone was in his chambers he wrote a note to Runcorn, telling him that he required him to testify when the court resumed the following morning. What small chance they had of success depended upon it. He told Runcorn he would string it out as long as possible, for which he apologized, but he had little else, except Dinah herself, unless Monk had found something more to give shape to another suspect the jury could believe in. He would at least raise the subject of the syringe, and the far deeper and more terrible addiction it led to.

As soon as he had sent the messenger with the letter folded in an envelope, and sealed with wax, he wondered if he had said too much.

He went home tired, but unable to rest.

IN THE MORNING RATHBONE took a hansom to the court, exhausted and worried. He did not even know if Runcorn would be there, and he had no excuses to offer. Not that he believed Pendock would accept any, however valid. He did not know for certain if Runcorn had even received his note. He had sent it to his home, in case he did not call in to the police station. But perhaps Runcorn had returned home late, tired, and had not even looked at any letters.

The traffic was jammed at Ludgate Circus, with shoppers, friends exchanging well wishes, celebrators beginning Christmas early, calling out cheerfully to one another.

Rathbone banged on the front of the hansom to attract the driver's attention.

"Can't you find a way around this? I have to be in court in the Old Bailey!" he demanded.

"Doin' my best, sir," the cabby answered. "It's nearly Christmas!"

Rathbone bit back the answer that rose to his lips. It was not the man's fault and being rude would only make matters worse. Why had there been no answer from Runcorn? What on earth was he going to say to the court if the man did not appear? Who else could he call at short notice? He would look totally incompetent. His face burned at the thought of it.

Perhaps he should have sent the note to the police station after all.

Then the hansom stopped again. All around there were vehicles of one sort or another, drivers shouting, laughing, demanding right-of-way.

He was too impatient to wait any longer. It was only a short walk along Ludgate Hill to the Old Bailey. The huge dome of St. Paul's rose into the winter sky ahead of him and the Central Criminal Court to his left, Newgate Prison just beyond. He lunged out of the cab, pushing a handful of coins at the driver, and began to walk rapidly, then to run along the pavement.

He raced up the steps and almost bumped into Runcorn just inside the doors. Why was he so overwhelmingly relieved? He should have trusted the man. There was no time or opportunity to speak to him now. It was his own fault for being late. Coniston was standing a few yards away, and Pendock was coming down the hallway. If he attempted to confer with Runcorn, he would look as if he were uncertain about what evidence Runcorn had to offer. That was a gift he could not offer Coniston.

Fifteen minutes later he was behind his table. His notes were in front of him, a letter from Runcorn on the top. He tore it open and read the few lines.

> Dear Sir Oliver,
>> All ready. Been looking into a few other things of interest. Don't know for certain, but I think Mrs. Monk has been looking for the doctor.
>
>> Runcorn

Again Rathbone blamed himself for lacking in trust.

"Please call your witness, Sir Oliver," Pendock ordered. His voice gravelly, a little tight, as if he also had slept little.

"I call Superintendent Runcorn of the Blackheath Police," Rathbone replied.

Runcorn came in, watched by every eye in the room as he walked past the gallery. He was an imposing figure: burly, exuding confidence. He took the oath and stood upright waiting for the questions. His hands were by his sides: no clinging to the railing for him.

Rathbone cleared his throat. "Superintendent, you are in command of the police in the Blackheath area, are you not?"

"Yes, sir," Runcorn said gravely.

"Were you called out when the body of Joel Lambourn was discovered on One Tree Hill in Greenwich Park nearly three months ago?"

"Yes, sir. Dr. Lambourn was a noted and much-admired figure in the area. Because of his importance, the investigation into his death was extended to include my force in Blackheath."

Coniston rose to his feet. "My lord, we have already heard about Dr. Lambourn's death in some detail, and the accused's reaction to it. I fail to see what Mr. Runcorn can add to what has already been said. My learned friend is desperate and wasting the court's time. If it will help, the prosecution will accede to the facts as already presented."

Rathbone would see Runcorn's testimony barred before he had even begun. He interrupted before Pendock could speak.

"Since it was presented by the prosecution, my lord, it is really meaningless to say that they accede to it."

"It is wasting the court's time to hear it again," Pendock snapped.

"If you have nothing new to add, Sir Oliver, I sympathize with your predicament, but it is not my place to indulge it. Mr. Coniston's point is well taken." He turned to Coniston. "Mr.—"

"My lord!" Rathbone raised his voice, trying hard to keep his emotion out of it. "Mr. Coniston introduced evidence regarding Dr. Lambourn's death, but for some reason best known to himself, he did not question Superintendent Runcorn, the man in charge of the inquiry into it. Had he not considered the matter relevant he would not have raised it at all. Indeed, your lordship would not have permitted him to. With respect, I put to the court that the defense has the right to question Mr. Runcorn about it, now, in light of further evidence discovered."

There was total silence in the room. No one moved.

Pendock's mouth was closed in a thin, hard line. Coniston looked at Pendock, then at Rathbone.

Runcorn stared across at the jury and smiled.

One of the jurors fidgeted.

"Keep to the point, Sir Oliver," Pendock said at last. "Whether Mr. Coniston objects or not, if you deviate from it, then I will stop you."

"Thank you, my lord," Rathbone said, keeping control of himself with an effort. Again he was sharply aware that Pendock was watching to catch him in any error at all.

Rathbone turned to Runcorn again.

"You were called to the death of Dr. Joel Lambourn when his body was found on One Tree Hill." He said this to the jury, even though it was Runcorn he addressed.

"Yes." Runcorn took it on, adding to it. "A man walking his dog had found Lambourn's body more or less propped up—"

Coniston rose to his feet. "My lord, Mr. Runcorn is suggesting that—"

"Yes, yes," Pendock agreed. He turned to the witness stand. "Mr. Runcorn, please watch your language. Do not make suggestions outside your knowledge. Simply what you saw, do you understand?"

It was patronizing in the extreme. Rathbone saw the color wash up Runcorn's face, and prayed he would control his temper.

"I was going to say 'propped up by the trunk of the tree,'" Runcorn said between clenched teeth. "Without its support he would have fallen. In fact he was leaning over anyway."

Pendock did not apologize, but Rathbone saw the irritation with himself in his face, and the jurors must have seen it, too.

Rathbone forced himself not to smile. "He was dead?" he asked.

"Yes. Cold, in fact," Runcorn agreed. "But the night had been chilly and there was something of a light wind, colder than usual for the time of year. His wrists had been cut across the inside and he appeared to have bled to death."

Pendock leaned forward. "Appeared? Are you implying that it was not the case, Mr. Runcorn?"

"No, my lord." Runcorn's face was almost expressionless. "I am trying to say no more than I was aware of myself at the time. The police surgeon confirmed that. Then the autopsy afterward added that he also had a considerable dose of opium in him, but not sufficient enough to kill him. I presumed at the time that it had been taken to dull the pain of the cuts in his wrists."

"At the time?" Rathbone said quickly. "Did you afterward learn anything for certain? Surely the police surgeon could not tell you the reason for taking the opium, only the facts?"

Runcorn stared back at Rathbone. "No, sir. I changed my own mind. I don't believe Dr. Lambourn cut his own wrists, sir. I believe the opium was to make him sleepy, slow to react, possibly even unconscious, so he would not fight back. Defensive wounds would be very difficult to explain in a supposed suicide."

Coniston was on his feet again.

Pendock glared at Runcorn. "Mr. Runcorn! I will not tolerate wild and unprovable assertions in this court. This is not the reopening of a case already closed and with a verdict returned, the fact of which I know you are perfectly aware. If you have something to offer pertinent to the murder of Zenia Gadney, then tell us. Nothing else is permissible here. Do you understand me?"

"Yes, my lord," Runcorn said boldly. There was no defensiveness in his voice or his manner. He stood head high, his gaze straight. "But since we now know that Zenia Gadney was also Joel Lambourn's wife, a fact we were not aware of at the time of his death, the manner of it, so shortly before her murder, seems to raise a number of questions. It is hard to be sure there is no connection."

"Of course there is a connection!" Pendock snapped. "It is Dinah Lambourn, the accused! Are you going to tell me that she murdered her husband also? That is hardly of service to the defense, who have called you."

Coniston almost hid his smile, but not quite.

The jury members were looking completely bemused.

"It seems likely that it was by the same person," Runcorn answered Pendock. "At least a possibility it would be irresponsible not to look into. But after questioning Marianne Lambourn, I am satisfied it could not have been Dinah Lambourn. Marianne was awake in the night, having had a nightmare. She heard her father go out. Her mother did not."

Rathbone was stunned. Was Runcorn sure of what he said? What would happen if he called Marianne to the stand? Would Coniston then tear her apart and show that she could not possibly be certain she had not fallen asleep, and simply not heard her mother leave also?

Even if that happened, it would buy him at least half a day! Had Monk found nothing further yet? Had Runcorn any ideas at all?

Coniston was staring at Rathbone, trying to read his face.

"Sir Oliver!" Pendock said slowly. "Were you aware of this? If you are presenting some—"

"No, my lord," Rathbone replied quickly, gathering his wits. "I have not had the opportunity to speak to Superintendent Runcorn since last Friday."

Pendock turned to Runcorn.

"I learned this only yesterday, my lord," Runcorn said with sudden humility. "I had occasion to reinvestigate Dr. Lambourn's death because of certain other facts that have come to light concerning his report on the sale of opium in England, and reflecting on the opium trade in general, and in particular the means of administering it through a new kind of hollow needle attached to a syringe, which sends the drug straight into the bloodstream, making it immeasurably more addictive—"

"This is the trial of Dinah Lambourn for the murder of Zenia Gadney!" Pendock overrode him loudly. "I will not have it turned into a political circus in an attempt to divert the jury from the issue at hand. Still less will I permit any attempt to argue the merits or otherwise of the sale or the uses of opium. They have no place in this courtroom." He turned to Rathbone. "Evidence, Sir Oliver, not speculation, and above all I will not tolerate malicious scandal. Do I make myself clear?"

"Absolutely, my lord," Rathbone replied with as much semblance of humility as he could manage. "This place, above all others, is one where no one should make accusations they cannot substantiate." He kept his face as devoid of expression as he could. Only because of the rise of color up Pendock's cheeks did he realize he had not entirely succeeded.

Coniston sneezed, or perhaps he choked. He apologized half under his breath.

Rathbone looked again at Runcorn.

"Please be very careful, Superintendent," he warned him. "Do these facts that you uncovered have any direct bearing on the murder of Zenia Gadney, or the fact that Dinah Lambourn has been charged with that crime?"

Runcorn considered for a moment.

Rathbone had the intense impression that he was weighing up exactly how much he could get away with.

"Superintendent?" Rathbone felt he had better speak before Coniston could rise to his feet yet again.

"Yes, sir, I believe it does," Runcorn answered. "If Dr. Lambourn and Zenia Gadney were killed by the same person, and it could not have been the accused, then it was someone else, and we must find that person. It is appearing to the police more and more likely that it was someone whom Dr. Lambourn learned about in his investigations into the use of opium—someone who was making a vast profit, first causing people to become addicted to the drug by their taking it directly into the blood for the relief of pain from broken bones and the like, and then becoming so dependent on it they couldn't live without it. Then he can charge them whatever he likes—"

Coniston was on his feet. "My lord, can Mr. Runcorn, or anyone else, offer even a shred of proof as to this supposed poison? It's a fairy tale! Speculation without any proof at all." He took a hasty breath and changed the subject. "And as to anyone swearing that Mrs. Lambourn did not leave the house again that night—we have heard nothing whatever to substantiate any of this except the word, reported secondhand, of a fourteen-year-old girl, very naturally loyal to her mother. What child of this age would be willing to believe that her mother could have cold-bloodedly slit her father's wrists and then watched him until he bled to death?"

Rathbone felt as if the ground had suddenly lurched beneath him, pitching him off balance, and he was left struggling to regain his posture.

"Sir Oliver," Pendock said with evident relief, "you are risking becoming absurd. This is all a rather desperate attempt to waste time, I don't know for what purpose. Who are you imagining will ride to your rescue? You have provided absolutely nothing to support this fantasy of conspiracy that you are asking us to believe in. Either produce it, sir, or provide us with some credible defense. If you have none, then save this fruitless distress to your client and allow her to plead guilty."

Rathbone felt the blood burn up his face. "My client has told me she is not guilty, my lord," he said, the bitterness harsh in his voice. "I cannot ask her to say that she beat to death and then eviscerated a woman, in order to save the court's time!"

"Be very careful, Sir Oliver," Pendock warned, "or I shall hold you in contempt."

"That would only delay the trial even longer, my lord," Rathbone retorted, then the instant after regretted it, and knew it was too late. He had made an irrevocable enemy of Pendock.

There was a ripple of excitement in the gallery. Even the jurors were suddenly intensely alive, their eyes moving from Rathbone to Pendock, then to Coniston, lastly to Runcorn, still waiting for further questions.

Dinah Lambourn was not the only one on trial. Perhaps in one way or another, everyone in the court was. They each had a part to play in finding justice.

Rathbone now chose his words with meticulous care. Dinah Lambourn's life might hang on his skill, and his ability to forget his own vanity or temper and think only of her, and whatever truth he could force the jury to hear.

He had no idea what else Runcorn knew. Staring at his face now, he wondered what on earth the man wanted him to ask. What could it concern that he could not raise without Pendock stopping him again? What tied Zenia Lambourn to the sale of opium and needles, except Lambourn and his research?

"Mr. Runcorn, did you have occasion to consider the possibility that Zenia Gadney might have known something of Dr. Lambourn's research into crimes involving, or following from, the sale of opium pure enough to inject into the blood, and the degeneration into madness or death that can result from it?"

Now the jurors were craning forward to listen, faces tense, fascinated and frightened.

Runcorn seized the chance. "Yes, sir. We thought it possible that Dr. Lambourn made more than one copy, at least of the most controversial parts of his report. Since it was not found in his own home, we thought he might well have left it with his first wife, Zenia Gadney. He may have believed that no one else, apart from Dinah Lambourn, knew of her existence."

Coniston stood. "Then the poor woman cannot have been murdered for it, except by Dinah Lambourn, which is our contention. All Sir Oliver has done is provide the accused with a second motive, my lord."

Pendock looked at Rathbone with a faint smile on his face.

"You appear to have shot yourself in the foot, Sir Oliver," he observed.

Runcorn drew in a sharp breath, looked at Rathbone, and then beyond him into the body of the gallery.

Rathbone understood instantly what Runcorn meant. He gave him the slightest of nods, then smiled back at Pendock.

"If Dinah Lambourn were the only one to have known the truth, that would be so, my lord. Perhaps you are unaware that both Barclay Herne and his wife, Amity Herne, Joel Lambourn's sister, both knew of his first marriage." Rathbone allowed his voice to take on a slightly sarcastic tone. "I believe they . . . forgot to mention this in their earlier testimony, though they have both confessed as much to me in the privacy of their own home."

Again the color drained from Pendock's face and he sat rigid, his hand in front of him, a closed fist on his great carved bench.

"Are you suggesting that one of them murdered this unfortunate woman, Sir Oliver?" he said very slowly. "I assume you have ascertained their whereabouts at the time in question?"

Rathbone felt as if he had been physically struck. In a matter of seconds victory had turned to defeat.

"No, my lord," he said quietly. "I was pointing out that Dinah Lambourn was not the only person aware of the fact that Joel Lambourn was married to Zenia Gadney, and visited her once a month, that we know of. It is always possible that either Barclay or Mrs. Herne may have told other people, perhaps their acquaintances from that earlier time when Dr. Lambourn was still together with Zenia Gadney, or should I say Zenia Lambourn?"

"Why on earth would either of them do such a thing?" Pendock asked incredulously. "Surely it is something no one would wish to make public? It would be most embarrassing. Your suggestion is eccentric, to put it at its kindest."

Rathbone made one last attempt.

"My lord, we are uncertain whether Dr. Lambourn's report contained references to the sale of opium and these needles, with details of the horror of the addiction such methods cause. Whether the stories are entirely true or not we do not know. But it remains likely that people's names are mentioned, either as dealers of this poison or addicts to it. Finding every copy of these papers and making certain they do not fall into the wrong hands could be regarded as a service to anyone mentioned in them—and perhaps the country in general. Opium, used properly, and under medical supervision, remains the only ease we have for mortal pain."

Pendock was silent for a long time.

The court waited. Every face in the gallery and in the jury box was turned toward the judge. Even Runcorn in the witness box turned to watch and wait.

Seconds ticked by. No one moved.

Finally Pendock reached a decision.

"Do you have any evidence of this, Mr. Runcorn?" he said quietly. "Evidence, not supposition and scandal?"

"Yes, my lord," Runcorn answered. "But it is all in bits and pieces, scattered among the accounts of tragic infant deaths that Dr. Lambourn was looking for. He came across this other evidence by accident and we think he only pieced together who was behind it in the last few days of his life."

Rathbone took a step forward.

"My lord, if we might have the rest of the day to assemble it sensibly, and make certain that no innocent person is unintentionally slandered, we might be able to present it to the court, or to your lordship in chambers, and see what the value of it may be."

Pendock sighed heavily. "Very well. The court is adjourned until Tuesday morning."

"Thank you, my lord." Rathbone inclined his head, suddenly almost sick with relief.

Runcorn came down from the stand and walked toward him.

"Sir Oliver, Mr. Monk would like to see you, as soon as possible," he said quietly. "We have more."

21

WHILE RATHBONE WAS IN court questioning Runcorn, and Monk was endeavoring to learn more about Barclay Herne and Sinden Bawtry, Hester quietly returned to see Dr. Winfarthing.

As always, Winfarthing was pleased to see her, but after he had greeted her with his usual warmth, he sat back in his chair and the heaviness of apprehension was too clear for her to miss.

"I assume you are here about that poor woman Dinah Lambourn," he said bleakly.

"Yes. We haven't long before they'll bring in a verdict," she replied. "You knew Joel Lambourn—you worked with him."

He grunted. "So what do you want of me, girl? If I had any proof he didn't kill himself, don't you think I'd have said so at the time?"

"Of course. But things are different now. What do you know about opium and syringes?"

His eyes opened very wide and he let his breath out slowly.

"Is that what you're thinking about? That he stumbled onto someone selling needles, and opium pure enough to put directly into the blood? Can kill people with that, if you don't get it exactly right. At best, you're likely to get them addicted unless you keep it to just a few days."

"I know," she agreed. "Some of the doctors in the American Civil War have used morphine to help the badly injured. Thought it wouldn't be so addictive. They were wrong. But they were doing it for the best of reasons. What if someone was doing it for money, and worse, for power?"

Winfarthing nodded very slowly. "God Almighty, girl! Are you sure? What a monstrous evil. Have you ever seen what opium addiction does to a man? Have you seen the withdrawal, if he doesn't get his supply?" His face was pinched with misery at the memory of it in his mind.

"No, I haven't."

"There's pain," he told her. "And nausea, vomiting, diarrhea, panic, depression, anxiety, sleeplessness, muscle twitching, cramps, chills, tremors, headaches, gooseflesh, lack of appetite—and other things as well, if you're really unlucky."

She felt her body clenching, as if she were threatened herself. "For how long?" she asked huskily.

"Depends," he said, watching her with his face squashed up in pity. "As little as two days—as long as two months."

She rubbed her hand over her face. "And it isn't even illegal, what this person is doing! Getting people addicted. Taking away their free will."

"Don't you think I know that?" he said wearily. "There's a big profit in it for the seller. Once you're on the opium you'll pay anything you have or do anything you're told to in order to keep on getting your supply. It's the doing anything that's the bigger problem. If you're right, and that's what Lambourn found, then you're dealing with a very wicked man."

She frowned. "But why did they kill Lambourn?" she asked. "What could he do to them?"

Winfarthing sat totally still, staring at her as if seeing her more clearly than ever before.

"What is it?" she asked.

"Did he see anyone in withdrawal?" he demanded.

"I don't know . . ." Then she saw what he was thinking. "You mean that was what was in his report? A description of addiction to opium through the syringe, and then the severity of the withdrawal process— and the request that that be dealt with in the bill? Made illegal?"

"Exactly! It has to be possible to draft a bill to allow the use of a restricted and labeled amount in medicines to be swallowed, as it is now," he agreed. "But against the law to give it or take it by needle, except when given by a doctor, and even then carefully watched. That would make our mystery man a criminal of the worst kind. Changes everything."

"Then how can we get that into court to clear Dinah Lambourn?" she said urgently. "We have only days! Will you testify?"

"Of course I will, but we'll need more than me, girl. We'll need the man your nurse Agatha spoke of. Who is he? Do you know?"

"No . . . although I have a guess. But I don't know how to make him come to court. He might . . . if . . ." She stopped, too uncertain to make it sound like a real hope.

"Do it," he insisted. "I'll come with you. God in heaven, I'll do any damn thing I can to stop this. If you'd seen a man in withdrawal, heard him scream and retch as the cramps all but tore him apart, so would you."

"To see Dinah hanged for a crime she didn't commit is enough for me," Hester answered. "But nobody believes that. We must make sense of it . . . and this will. I'll see that Oliver Rathbone calls you to testify. Now I must go and see Agatha Nisbet."

"Do you want me to come with you?" he offered anxiously.

She considered for a moment. It would be safer, more comfortable if he did, and yet she knew that it would also make Agatha far less likely to agree.

"No, thank you. But I'm grateful."

He scowled at her. "You're a fool. I should insist."

"No, you shouldn't. You know as well as I do that this must be done, and she'll refuse if you go."

Winfarthing grimaced and eased his weight back into his chair. "Be careful," he warned. "If she agrees, give me your word that you'll take her with you? Otherwise I'm coming, regardless."

"I give you my word," she promised.

He gave her a sudden, beaming smile. "I'll see you in court!"

Two hours later Hester stood in Agony Nisbet's cramped office.

"No," Agatha said flatly. "I'll not do that to him."

Hester stared at her, ignoring the fury in her eyes. "What gives you the right to make that decision for him? You said he was a good man once, and it was the opium seller with the syringe that changed him. Give him the chance to be that good man again. If he won't take it, then there's nothing we can do. Lambourn will go down as a suicide, Dinah will hang, and nobody will stop the opium sellers, or even punish the ones we catch."

Agatha did not answer.

Hester waited.

"I won't try to make 'im," Agatha said at last. "You 'aven't seen what the withdrawal's like, or you wouldn't ask. You wouldn't put anyone through it, let alone someone you cared about . . . a friend."

"Maybe not," Hester conceded, "but I wouldn't make the decision for them, either."

"It'd be the man who gives 'im the opium 'e needs," Agatha pointed out. "Without it 'e'll be in withdrawal for months—maybe on an' off forever."

"Can't you get it for him?"

"I've 'ardly got enough for the injured. You want me to give 'im yours? D'yer know 'ow much it takes ter keep an addict going?"

"No. Does it make any difference?"

"You're a hard bitch!" Agatha said between her teeth.

"I'm a nurse," Hester corrected her. "That means I'm a realist . . . like you."

Agatha snorted, was silent for a few moments, then straightened her huge shoulders. "Well, come on then! By the sound of it, you 'aven't got time ter waste!"

Hester relaxed and smiled at last, then turned for the door.

Alvar Doulting knew as soon as he saw Agatha what they had come for. He shook his head, backing into the room as if there were a form of escape in the stacks of shelves behind him.

Agatha stopped and her raw-boned hand clasped Hester so hard it bruised the flesh of her arm. She had to bite her lip not to cry out.

"You don't 'ave ter do it," Agatha said to Doulting.

"If you don't, Dinah Lambourn will hang," Hester told him. "And Joel Lambourn's report will never be seen. In particular the part about opium needles. There'll still be people addicted, whatever we do, but if it's made illegal, there'll be fewer. It's time to decide what you want to do . . . to be."

"You don't 'ave ter!" Agatha said again. Her face was pale, her voice strained. Her fingers were like a vise on Hester's arm.

Doulting looked from one to the other of them as the seconds ticked by. He seemed beaten, as if he could no longer fight. Perhaps he knew there was nothing left that he could gain, except the last shred of the man he used to be.

"Don't stop me, Agatha," he said quietly. "If I can find the courage, I'll do it."

"You'll testify that you told Joel Lambourn about the addiction that taking opium by needle causes, and he included it in his report?" Hester said it clearly. "And you'll tell them what it's like, and how it affects those it captures?"

Doulting looked at her and very slowly nodded.

She did not know whether she dared believe him. "Thank you," she whispered. "I'll tell Sir Oliver Rathbone."

He sank back against the bench, turning to Agatha.

"I'll get you enough," she promised rashly, yanking at Hester's arm. "Come on. We done enough 'ere." She looked at Doulting again. "I'll be back."

RATHBONE SAT IN MONK's kitchen, untouched tea steaming gently in front of him. There were pastries cooling on a rack, sweetmeats ready for Christmas.

"Are you certain?" Rathbone pressed, looking at Monk, then at Runcorn. "Is the evidence absolutely irrefutable?"

Hester nodded her head. "Yes. Dr. Winfarthing will come first, then

Alvar Doulting. They'll confirm that Joel Lambourn came to Winfarthing, who told him about the selling of opium and needles, and then Doulting will tell the court that Lambourn came to him, and repeat what he told him. Lambourn put it in his report. That was why he was killed. If they made it illegal to take opium that way, the sellers would lose a fortune. It was worth murdering Lambourn for, and Zenia Gadney."

"And hanging Dinah Lambourn," Runcorn added grimly.

"Then who actually killed Lambourn?" Monk asked.

"The seller of opium pure enough to inject without killing people, and the needles to do it," Hester said quietly. "Or someone he paid. Morally, it's him."

"Who? Barclay Herne?" Rathbone asked, looking from one to the other of them.

This time it was Monk who answered him. "Possibly, but from what we can tell, he hasn't the sort of money such a trade would bring. Apart from the bestiality of it, it's too dangerous to do for small reward."

"Then who? Sinden Bawtry? My God, that would be appalling," Rathbone exclaimed, the full enormity of it burgeoning to fill his imagination. "Word is that he's about to fill a very high cabinet post. If that's possible, then no wonder Joel Lambourn was desperate to expose him. He could have had the power to stop that provision from being included in the Pharmacy Act." He took a deep breath, his tea still ignored. "But Bawtry and Herne were dining at the Atheneum that night. There are witnesses. And that was miles away, on the other side of the river."

"Is Herne involved?" Rathbone asked doubtfully. "Organizing everything for Bawtry? For a suitable reward afterward?" He could not see Barclay Herne with the fire or the courage to do anything dangerous, or requiring that kind of ruthless and passionate greed, unless he was an addict, too. He remembered the confidence one day, and the pasty skin and nervousness the Sunday he had called unexpectedly. "We can't afford a mistake. If I say something I have to be right and be able to prove it—at least as probable, even if not certain," he finished.

Runcorn bit his lip. "That isn't going to be easy. The judge may not know what he's defending, but he's been told there's something. He may think it's to do with England's reputation, and nothing more personal than that, but I dare say his future's dependent on keeping it quiet."

"I'm damned sure of it," Rathbone agreed. He turned to Hester. "Are you certain this Agatha Nisbet will turn up? And what about Doulting? He could be drugged out of his senses, or dead in an alley by then."

They all looked at Hester, faces tense, bodies stiff.

"I don't know," she admitted. "We can only try."

"We haven't much to lose," Rathbone said to all of them. "As it is now, they're going to find Dinah guilty. I have no one else left to put on the stand. She's lied to me before, and I'm not sure if she knew anything at all about what Lambourn found out. I don't think her belief in him is going to be enough to change this outcome."

He looked at Hester. "Do you believe this Agatha Nisbet?"

She did not hesitate. "Yes. But it won't be so easy with Alvar Doulting. She'll bring him if he's all right, but she won't force him. You may have to string it out at least another day. I'll help her to get him as strong as we can."

"I've no one else," Rathbone told them.

"Then you must call Dinah," Hester said, her voice uncertain, a little husky. "Immediately after Christmas."

The more Rathbone heard of what Hester had learned, and the further disclosures it threatened, the more certain he was that both Coniston and Pendock knew at least of the existence of a scandal that they had been warned must be kept a secret, even at the cost of hanging a woman without exhausting the last possibility that she was innocent. Who else was addicted to the pervasive poison? Who else's fortune relied on its sale?

He looked across at Monk. It was a gamble. They were all painfully aware of it.

"I'll speak to Dinah," he said. He had not had time to talk to her since the revelation that she had never actually been Lambourn's wife. "But we've got to provide an alternative better than some shadowy form of an opium seller we also can't name."

Monk glanced at Hester, then back at Rathbone. "I know. We won't stop trying to prove who's behind it. But we need time. Can you stretch it out another day?"

Rathbone wanted to say yes, but he doubted it. If he could not, and the court could see that he was increasingly desperate, asking questions to which they all knew the answer, Coniston would object that he was wasting the court's time, and Pendock would very justifiably uphold him. Most important, the jury would know he had no defense left, or else he would have used it.

They could very reasonably try to close the case on Tuesday to keep what was left of the Christmas season clear.

Hester was frowning. She had seen the indecision in his eyes.

"Call Dr. Winfarthing on Tuesday, after Dinah," she suggested.

"Are you certain about him?" he asked.

She gave a very slight shrug. "Can you think of anything better?"

"I can't think of anything at all," he admitted. "Are you certain he won't say anything damning, even unintentionally?"

"Almost," she said.

"And this woman, Nisbet?" He realized when he heard the harshness in his voice how deeply afraid he was that in his own sense of loss and disillusion he would let Dinah Lambourn down, and she would pay with her life.

Hester smiled. "There are no certainties. We've been here before. We play the best hand we have. We've never been certain of winning. That's not the way it is."

He knew she was right; he was simply less brave than he used to be, less certain of the other things that mattered. Or maybe at the heart of it, he was less certain of himself.

RATHBONE WENT BACK ACROSS the river by ferry, perversely enjoying the hard, cold wind in his face, even the discomfort of the choppy water. There seemed to be a lot of traffic in the Pool of London today, big ships at anchor waiting to unload cargo from half the ports on earth, lighters carrying freight down from the waterways inland, up from the sea, ferryboats weaving in and out, even a River Police boat making its way over to St. Saviour's Dock. Everyone seemed to be working twice as hard, hurrying along the streets, laden with parcels, calling out good wishes, making ready for Christmas.

On the northern side he alighted and paid his fare. Then he walked quickly to the Commercial Road and caught a hansom back toward the Old Bailey, and the prison where Dinah Lambourn was housed.

Before he faced her he stopped at a quiet inn and had a large luncheon of steak and kidney pudding, with oysters and a thick suet crust, and a half bottle of really good red wine. He was too worried for the richness or the flavor of it to please him, but afterward he felt warmer and had a renewed sense of determination. A great deal of this was fueled by anger within himself that he was so nearly beaten.

He had thought hard about what to say to Dinah, and as he walked the last couple of hundred yards he made his final decision. At the prison he gave the jailer all the necessary information, identifying himself for the umpteenth time, as if they did not know him.

He was escorted along to the familiar stone cell where he waited alone until they brought Dinah to him. She looked thinner and even paler than the last time he had seen her here, as if she knew the fight was over, and she had lost. He felt the guilt of failure like a wound deep in his gut.

"Please sit down, Mrs. Lambourn," he said. Then, as she lowered herself into the chair opposite him, he sat down also. He realized, watching her awkwardness, that she was stiff with fear.

"I have just been speaking with Mr. Monk," he told her. "He and Mr. Runcorn have discovered many things about Dr. Lambourn, all of them bearing out what you yourself have told me. However, I cannot raise your hopes more than a little, because we have no proof that will stand up in court. To call those people who might be of help will be a very great risk, and I need to be certain that you understand that."

"You've found people?" There was a sudden, wild, infinitely painful leap of hope in her face, her eyes almost feverishly brilliant.

He swallowed hard. "People who may not be believed, Mrs. Lambourn. One is a doctor who is, I am told, something of a renegade. The other is a self-proclaimed nurse running an unofficial clinic for dockworkers in the Rotherhithe area. She says that Dr. Lambourn consulted her when he was gathering information about the uses and dangers of opium. So far we have nothing whatever to substantiate what she says, and she is hardly a reputable person. However, she did tell these things to Dr. Lambourn, and as a result he then sought out others, who said the same things."

Dinah was confused. "To do with opium? I don't understand."

"No, not merely to do with opium. That is the point. What she says is to do with the new invention of a hollow needle, and a syringe that can deliver pure opium directly into the blood. It is very much more effective for dealing with pain, but also it can create an addiction to opium that is terrible in its effects." He grimaced. "A brief heaven, bought at the price of a life of hell afterward."

"What does that have to do with Joel?" she asked. "Or with poor Zenia's death? All Joel was reporting on was the need to label the quantity and dosage of opium in patent medicines."

"I know," Rathbone said gently. "We think he found out about the syringe and its effects by accident, and included it in his report. If that were so, then it might well have made its way into the Pharmacy Act; then sale in that way would probably be made illegal."

"If it is as terrible as you say, then it has to be made illegal," she said slowly, understanding filling her eyes, and then horror.

He nodded. "They destroyed the report, but in case he had told anyone, such as you, for example, he had to be discredited as well."

Her eyes widened. "They killed him, so he couldn't repeat it," she said in a hoarse whisper.

"Yes."

"And poor Zenia?"

"That was probably as you said, to get rid of you, and anything you might have been told."

"Who is the doctor you spoke of?"

"Dr. Winfarthing? I don't know him. Mrs. Monk says Dr. Lambourn consulted him. I want to question him mostly to hold the court's attention until Monk can persuade Agnes Nisbet, the woman who runs the clinic, to come forward and testify. That might take a whole day. In fact I need to call someone on Tuesday morning immediately after Christmas and Boxing Day, until Winfarthing can be spoken to and fore-warned, in fairness, that the prosecution will try to discredit him on the witness stand."

"And then he might not testify?" she said shakily.

"Apart from being unfair, it might be very much against our interest to have him testify before I have had the opportunity to find out exactly what he will say, and possibly what to avoid asking him. Don't forget, Mr. Coniston will have the chance to question him after I do. I think you have seen enough of Coniston to know that he will give Winfarthing, or anybody else, a very hard time indeed. He'll try everything he knows to destroy his credibility, even his reputation, if he can."

He lowered his voice, trying to be as gentle as he could. "It is not only your life or freedom that may rest on the outcome of this case. If you are not guilty, then someone else is."

"I don't know who." She closed her eyes and the tears escaped under her lids. "Don't you think I would tell you if I did?"

"Yes, of course I do," Rathbone said softly. "All I have to do now is to make the jury see that there is such a person. But you have to decide if you want me to do this. It will be very rough. And before I can get Winfarthing on the stand, I shall have to fill Tuesday morning with something else, or the judge will declare the defense closed, and it will be too late. If I call you, you are all I have left, except your daughters. Believe me, Coniston will crucify them before he allows the truth to come out. I believe he really thinks you are guilty, and he won't spare your children."

"I'll testify," she said, cutting across everything else he might have added, although in truth there was nothing more. He had always known what she would say.

"And you understand what Coniston will try to do to you?"

"Of course. He will try to paint me as a hysterical woman trying to cling to the memory of a man who wouldn't marry me, as a woman afraid of losing his money to live on and raise my illegitimate children with." She gave a brief, forced smile, which was painful to see in its attempt at courage. "It will hardly be worse than facing the hangman in three weeks."

He drew in his breath to argue, and then decided it would only be

an insult to offer her false promises. He looked down at the scarred ta-
bletop and then up at her. "I know you didn't kill Zenia Gadney, and
that you made it look as if you might have in order to stand trial so you
could try to save Joel's reputation and honor. We might lose, but we
aren't there yet."

"Aren't we?" she whispered.

"No—no, we aren't. I will call you on Tuesday as my first witness,
and keep you there until Winfarthing turns up."

"Will he?"

"Yes." It was a rash promise.

He hoped he could keep it. He stood up. "Now I must go home and
think what to ask you, and then what to ask Winfarthing."

She looked up at him. "And Miss Nisbet?"

"Ah, that's different. I know very well what I will ask her."

Perhaps that was overstating it a little, but it was whether Agatha
Nisbet would come at all that troubled him, not what he would ask her.
He could only rely on Hester for that. Monk and Runcorn he knew
would still be working on the actual murder, and searching frantically
for the person who had walked up One Tree Hill with Lambourn, and
left him up there to bleed to death.

BOTH HESTER AND MONK had done all they could to keep the desperation of the trial away from Scuff, but he was far too observant for
them to have succeeded. Christmas morning was bright and cold, at
least to begin with, although it closed over and there was a promise of
snow later on.

Hester was up very early, long before daylight, to put the goose in
the oven, and to hang garlands of ribbons and holly up around the
house.

She and Monk had in the end decided to get Scuff a watch, the best
one they could afford, with his initials and the date engraved on the
back. As well as that there were other small things, such as little bags of
sweets, homemade fudge, and his favorite nuts. Monk had found him a
pair of really warm woolen socks and Hester had very carefully cut
down one of Monk's cravats to make it the right size for Scuff's slender

neck. And of course she had also chosen a book for him, one he would thoroughly enjoy reading.

About eight o'clock in the morning, when it was at last truly daylight, she heard the kitchen door open and Scuff put his head around nervously. Then he saw the holly and the ribbons, and his eyes widened.

"Is it Christmas?" he said a little breathlessly.

"Yes it is," she replied with a wide smile. "Merry Christmas!" She put down the spoon she had been using to stir the porridge and walked over to him. She considered asking his permission to kiss him, then decided it would give him the opportunity to refuse, even if he actually wanted her to, so she just put both arms around him and hugged him hard. She kissed his warm cheek. "Merry Christmas, Scuff!" she said again.

He froze for a moment, then shyly he kissed her back.

"Merry Christmas, Hester," he replied, then blushed scarlet at the familiarity of using her name.

She ignored it, trying not to let him see her smile. "Would you like breakfast?" she asked. "There's porridge first, but don't eat too much, because there are bacon and eggs after. And of course there's a roast goose for dinner."

He drew in a deep breath. "A real one?"

"Of course. It's a real Christmas," she told him.

He gulped. "I got a present for yer. Do yer want it now?" He was fidgeting on his seat, already halfway to standing up again.

She had not the heart to make him wait. His eyes were bright, his face flushed. "I'd love to see it now," she answered.

He slid to the floor and ran out into the hall, and she heard his feet on the stairs. Only moments later he was back again with something in his hand that was small and wrapped in a piece of cloth. Watching her face intently, he held it out to her.

She took it and unwrapped it, wondering what she would find, and already anxious. It was a small silver pendent with a single pearl in it. It hung on a fine chain. In that moment it was the most beautiful piece of jewelry she had ever seen. And she was terrified as to where he had got it.

She looked up and met his eyes.

"D'yer like it?" he asked almost under his breath.

There was a lump in her throat she had to swallow before she could speak. "Of course I do. It's perfect. How could anyone not love it?" Dare she ask where he got it? Would he think she didn't trust him?

He relaxed and his face flooded with relief. "I got it from a tosher," he said proudly. "I done errands fer 'im. 'E let me 'ave it."

Suddenly he looked embarrassed and his gaze slid away from hers. "I said it were for me ma. Is that all right?"

Now it was she who felt the warmth wash up her face. "It's . . . it's more than all right," she told him as she carefully put the chain around her neck and fastened the clasp. She saw his eyes shine with pleasure, and she couldn't resist reaching down and hugging him gently.

"In fact it couldn't be better," she added, releasing him before he could feel uncomfortable. "We have a couple of things for you, when William comes down."

"I got summink for 'im too," Scuff said, reassuring her.

"I'm sure you have," she replied. "Are you ready for porridge? We've got a very special, busy day ahead."

"How long is it Christmas?" he asked, seating himself at the table.

"All day, actually until the middle of the night," she answered. "Then it's Boxing Day, and that's a holiday, too."

"Good. I like Christmas," he said with satisfaction.

22

O N Tuesday the trial reopened with Coniston looking considerably more relaxed, as if the end of a long and weary journey were almost
reached. There was something in his face that could even have been
sympathy for Rathbone.

Pendock brought them to order very quickly.

"Have you a witness, Sir Oliver?" he asked.

"Yes, my lord," Rathbone replied. "I call the accused, known as
Dinah Lambourn."

Pendock looked slightly startled, as if he considered it a mistake,
but he made no comment.

Dinah was brought down from the dock. Carefully, her whole body
trembling, she climbed the steps to the witness stand, gripping the rails
as if she was afraid of falling. Indeed, she might have been. She looked
ashen; her face seemed to have no blood beneath the alabaster skin.

Rathbone walked out into the center of the court and looked up at
her. How long would he have to keep her here? He must speak with
Winfarthing before he put him on the stand. Any lawyer who did less
than that was a fool. He trusted Hester, but he still needed his own
preparation.

"You lived with Joel Lambourn for fifteen years as his wife?" he asked, his voice a little strained.

"Yes," she replied.

"Did you ever marry him?"

"No."

"Why not?" It seemed a brutal question, but he wanted the jury to understand her and be in no doubt whatsoever that she had always known of Zenia Gadney.

"Because he was already married to Zenia, his wife from before we met," she answered.

"And he did not put her aside in order to marry you?" He tried to put surprise into his voice without cruelty, but it was impossible. He winced at the sound of it.

"I didn't ever ask him to," she replied. "I knew Zenia had had a bad accident and the pain had caused her to become addicted first to alcohol, and then to opium. She finally recovered from the gin, but never completely from the opium. There was a time when the one thing she clung to, and which saved her from suicide, was the fact that Joel did not abandon her. I loved him, I always will. I would not ask him to do something he believed to be cruel and wrong. I wouldn't want him to be a man who wished to."

"And was it not wrong to live with you, then?" he asked but only because he knew Coniston would if he did not.

"He didn't ask me to live with him," she replied. "I chose to. And yes, I suppose society would say that was wrong. I really don't care very much."

"You don't care for right and wrong, or you don't care what society thinks of you?" Rathbone asked.

"I suppose I care," she replied with the ghost of a smile. "About society, I mean. But not enough to give up the only man I ever loved. We offended propriety, or we would have done, had they known. But we hurt no one else. Perhaps even they would not have cared a great deal. Thousands of people have mistresses or lovers. Thousands more make use of women of the street. As long as it is private, no one minds very much."

What she said was perfectly true, but he wished she had not been quite so candid—although possibly Coniston would have made the same point if she had not. Now there was very little left for him to say.

Rathbone knew he must keep the questions going all morning. Better anything than silence, and Pendock putting the case to the jury. Had Hester really persuaded Winfarthing to come? What would he do if the man refused to testify?

"Were you happy?" he asked, looking up at Dinah.

Coniston rose to his feet. "My lord, my learned friend is yet again wasting the court's time. If it will help to move the proceedings along, I shall willingly stipulate that the accused and Dr. Lambourn had an ideal life together, and until the last few weeks of his life they were as happy as any other husband and wife. There is no need whatever to call a procession of witnesses to that effect."

"I had no intention of doing so, my lord," Rathbone said indignantly.

Pendock was impatient. "Then please come to the point that you do wish to make, Sir Oliver."

Rathbone kept his temper with difficulty. He must not allow himself to be distracted by anger or pride. "Yes, my lord." He looked up at Dinah again. "Did Dr. Lambourn speak with you about his work, specifically that report he was asked to write on the sale and labeling of opium?"

"Yes, he did. It was something he cared about very deeply. He wanted to have all patent medicines clearly labeled, with numbers anyone could read, so they would know what doses were safe to take."

"Is this a highly controversial matter, so far as you know?"

Coniston stood up again. "My lord, the accused has no expertise on the subject, as my learned friend is well aware."

Pendock sighed. "Your objection is noted. Sir Oliver, please do not ask the witness questions you are perfectly aware she has no expertise from which to answer. I will not permit you to drag this trial out any further with pointless time-wasting exercises."

Rathbone bit back his anger. He turned to Dinah again.

"Did Dr. Lambourn ever tell you that he had met with any criticism or obstruction from the government, or any medical authorities while he was seeking to gather information on the subject of accidental deaths from opium?"

"No. It was the government who asked him to write the report," she replied.

"Who in the government, specifically?" he asked.

"Mr. Barclay Herne." Carefully she refrained from saying that he was her brother-in-law. She had been about to, and checked herself just in time.

"Dr. Lambourn's brother-in-law?" Rathbone clarified.

"Yes."

Pendock was growing impatient. He scowled and his large-knuckled hands fidgeted in front of him on the polished surface of the bench.

"Is Mr. Herne in charge of the project for the government?" Rathbone asked.

"I believe so," Dinah replied. "It was Barclay to whom Joel reported."

Aware of Pendock's irritation, Rathbone hurried on, resenting the pressure. "So it was Barclay Herne who told him that his report was unacceptable?" he asked.

"Yes."

"Was Dr. Lambourn very distressed by this?"

"He was angry and puzzled," she replied. "The facts were very carefully recorded and he had all the evidence. He didn't understand what Barclay considered the problem to be, but he was determined to rewrite it with some detail and notation so that it would be accepted."

"He did not feel himself rejected, or his career ruined?" Rathbone affected surprise.

"Not at all," she answered. "It was a report. The rejection distressed him, but it certainly did not drive him to despair."

"Did he mention to you having discovered anything else distressing during his research?" Rathbone asked.

Coniston stood again. "My lord, the details of Dr. Lambourn's research and what may have saddened him or not are hardly relevant. We are trying the accused for the murder of Dr. Lambourn's first wife—"

"I take your point, Mr. Coniston." Pendock turned to Rathbone.

Before he could speak, Rathbone swung around to face Coniston, as if he were unaware of the judge.

"On the contrary," Rathbone said loudly. "You claim that Dr. Lambourn took his own life in despair at something that occurred during this period of time. At first you said that it was some sexual deviancy and his consequent use of a prostitute in Limehouse, and the possibility that his wife would find this out. Now that you know the 'prostitute,' as you called her, was in fact a perfectly respectable woman who was once, and legally still was, Dr. Lambourn's wife, you have had to withdraw that!"

Coniston looked startled, even discomfited.

"Then you said that the accused killed the victim out of jealousy because she had just discovered Dr. Lambourn's visits to her," Rathbone went on. "Only as soon as you said that, you discovered that she had known of his visits for the last fifteen years; so that reasoning was clearly absurd. Now you are saying that he killed himself because an important but very detailed report he made was refused, and he had to go back and write it again. I am trying to establish whether or not that was actually so. I intend to call other professional witnesses in that field to give evidence on the subject."

"Sir Oliver!" Pendock's voice was so forceful there was a sudden, total silence in the courtroom. "We are trying the accused for the murder of Zenia Gadney Lambourn, not for the death of Joel Lambourn, which has already been ruled by the courts to be suicide. His reasons for taking his life, however tragic, are not relevant here."

"I submit, my lord, that they are acutely relevant, and I shall show the jury that that is so," Rathbone said recklessly.

"Indeed," Pendock replied skeptically. "We wait impatiently. Please proceed."

Heart pounding, Rathbone turned back to Dinah.

"I know that you find it hard to believe that Dr. Lambourn took his own life," he began, "but during the last week before his body was found, was he at any time unusually distressed, angry, at a loss to know what to do? Was he different from his normal self?"

Coniston moved in his seat, but he did not rise, although he made ready to.

Reading Rathbone's cue, Dinah replied. "Yes. He returned home from questioning people in the dockside areas, about two or three days before his death. He was most distraught by something he had learned."

"Did he tell you what that was?" Rathbone asked.

There was total silence in the room. The gallery seemed to be holding their breath. Not a juror moved so much as a hand.

"No." Dinah sighed the word, then made an effort to speak more clearly. "I asked him, but he said it was something too terrible to tell anyone until he knew who was behind it. I asked him again, but he said it was something I should not know about, for my own sake, since such suffering was involved. Once it was in my mind, I would never be able to forget it, he said. It would haunt my dreams, waking and sleeping, for the rest of my life." The tears were running down her face unchecked now. "I saw the grief in him, and I knew that he spoke the truth. I didn't ask him again. I don't know which was easier for him, my knowing, or not knowing. I never learned, because two days later he was dead."

"Could it have been the number of deaths caused by accidental overdose of opium in some new area he was researching?" he asked.

She shook her head. "I don't see how. Had there been something appalling, a large number of deaths in one place, then surely that would have been something Mr. Herne would have wished to know about, and it would not have been secret. It must have been something else."

"Yes, I see what you mean," Rathbone agreed. "Did he at any time say to you what he intended to do about this terrible thing that brought about so much suffering?"

Dinah was silent for several moments.

One of the jurors moved uncomfortably; another leaned forward as if to look at her more closely.

Coniston stared at Rathbone, then looked up at the judge.

Rathbone wanted to know if Barclay Herne was in the court or not. He had his back to the gallery and did not dare disturb his concentration to look.

"I am trying to think back on what he said," Dinah replied at last. "To think of his words, and what he might have meant. He was very disturbed by it, very distressed."

"Did he know who was involved in this abomination?" Rathbone asked. "Or anything about the nature of it?"

"Only that it concerned opium," she replied quietly. "And that he cared about it passionately."

This time Coniston did rise to his feet. "My lord! We have not in any way whatever established that there was any abomination to discover, only that something happened that Dr. Lambourn was disturbed about." He spread his hands out wide. "It could have been an accident, a misfortune of nature, anything at all. Or for that matter, it could have been nothing. We have only the accused's word that we are talking about anything more than an excuse to drag this trial out as long as possible."

"You are quite right, Mr. Coniston," Pendock agreed. "I have no more patience with your time-wasting, Sir Oliver. If you have no further evidence to bring forward, then we shall put the matter to the jury."

Rathbone was desperate. He had nothing else to ask Dinah. She had pleaded not guilty when she was charged. There was not even a denial to add.

"I have two more witnesses, my lord," he said, hearing his own voice sound hollow, even faintly ridiculous. Where the devil was Monk? Where were Hester and her Dr. Winfarthing?

Pendock turned to Coniston. "Have you any questions to ask the accused, Mr. Coniston?"

Coniston hesitated, then either in cowardice not to take any chances, or in mercy not to drag out the pointless ritual, he answered quietly.

"No, my lord, thank you."

Rathbone was beaten. "I wish to call Dr. Gustavus Winfarthing, my lord, but he is not yet in court. I apologize, and ask—"

The doors at the back of the court burst open and a huge figure strode through, jacket flying, his mane of graying hair standing on end as if he had come in from a high wind.

"Don't you dare apologize on my behalf!" he cried loudly. "I most certainly am here. Good heavens, sir, a blind man on a galloping horse could not miss me."

There was a ripple of laughter around the gallery, perhaps as much a release of tension as any amusement. Even one or two of the jurors smiled widely, then suddenly realized that perhaps it was inappropriate, and forced their faces into expressions of gravity again.

Winfarthing walked right up to the edge of the table where Rathbone sat, and then stopped.

"Are you ready for me, Sir Oliver? Or shall I wait outside again?"

"No!" Rathbone controlled his relief and his anxiety with an effort. "We are perfectly ready for you, Dr. Winfarthing. If you would take the stand, sir, you will be sworn in." He was not at all ready for him. He needed to speak to him alone, learn what he had to say and keep some grasp on the testimony, but he dared not try Pendock's patience, or he might lose even this chance.

Winfarthing obeyed, climbing with some difficulty up the narrow, curving steps to the witness box, finding it awkward to get his bulk between the railings. He swore to tell the truth, the whole truth, and nothing but the truth, then stood meekly waiting for Rathbone to begin.

Rathbone had never seen the man before. In fact he knew nothing of him except the little that Hester had told him, and the rather larger amount he deduced from the warmth with which she had spoken. Even the mention of his name had made her smile. Rathbone now had almost nothing left to lose. He set out with a bravado he was far from feeling.

"Dr. Winfarthing, were you acquainted with Joel Lambourn?"

"Of course I was," Winfarthing replied, raising his eyebrows and staring at Rathbone as if he were a peculiarly inept student in front of him for some childish prank. "Excellent man, both professionally and personally." Then, as if anticipating Coniston's objection to the fact that he had not been asked to assess Lambourn's character, he turned toward him and glared ferociously.

"Thank you," Rathbone said quickly. "Did he seek your opinions or experiences regarding the use of opium when he was doing research for his report in the three or four months before he died?"

"Of course he did," Winfarthing said with surprise in his face and his voice again, as if the question were redundant.

Already the gallery was silent. Behind him Rathbone could not hear even the rustle of movement in the seats. Please heaven, Winfarthing had something to say, more than the details, with which he could take the afternoon until Monk would find and bring Agatha Nisbet.

"Why, Dr. Winfarthing?" Rathbone prompted. "Have you some expertise in the study of infant deaths from opium overdose?"

"Tragically, yes," Winfarthing replied. "I was able to confirm a good deal of what he had found, and add my own figures to his, which incidentally were almost exactly the same."

Coniston rose to his feet. "My lord, if it will save the court's time, I am willing to agree that Dr. Lambourn's figures were honestly obtained, and may well have been accurate regarding the misuse of opium in dosing children. Whether that is a tragedy that can be overcome by better dispensing is not within our remit. But since Sir Oliver himself has implied, properly or not, that the reason for Dr. Lambourn's death had nothing to do with his report on opium labeling, I do not see how it has even the remotest relevance to the murder of Zenia Gadney, even in the unlikely, and totally unproven, event that she was privy to any part of this report. Or, for that matter, that she could have had a copy of part of it in her keeping."

"Your point is well taken, Mr. Coniston," Pendock replied. "Sir Oliver, you are wasting time again. I will not allow it. If Dr. Winfarthing has nothing to add except his opinion that Lambourn was a good doctor, then we have heard it, and it is, as Mr. Coniston has said, irrelevant. If Mr. Coniston has no questions of this witness, call your next witness, whoever it is, and let us proceed."

Winfarthing's eyes widened and his large face flushed red with anger. He swung around in the confines of the witness box with some difficulty, and glared at the judge in his scarlet robes and white, full-bottomed wig.

"Sir, I have a great deal of evidence to give," he thundered, "though I am very aware that it may not be pleasant to hear, since it concerns the most exquisitely degrading and painful ways of abusing the human body and spirit known to man. It concerns the abuse of the relief for pain, turning it into blood money in another's hands. But if we want to be counted as men of virtue, or even of honor—indeed, to be included in the bonds of humanity—then we do not have the luxury or the right to say we prefer not to distress ourselves by listening to the truth." Then he swiveled around a quarter turn, gripping the rails, and glared equally fiercely at the twelve men of the jury.

The jury gave him not only their attention but their obvious respect.

Pendock was very clearly taken aback. He avoided looking at Winfarthing, glanced at Coniston and saw nothing that helped him, and turned at last to Rathbone.

"Will you keep your witness in order, Sir Oliver," he said angrily. "I will not have chaos in my courtroom. If you have something to ask that is relevant to the murder of Zenia Gadney, and I warn you to be careful that it is so, then please get to it without further rambling or delay."

"Rambling?" Winfarthing hissed a stage whisper so loud it must have been audible at the back of the gallery.

Rathbone could feel the last shred of control slipping out of his grasp. He looked back at Winfarthing. He could see why Hester liked the man; he was totally ungovernable. That would appeal to her own anarchic nature.

"Dr. Winfarthing," he said sternly, "did you give Dr. Lambourn any information that he might have included in his report, and with which, at that point, he was unfamiliar? I am asking specifically about something that might have disturbed him sufficiently to account for his deep concern shortly before his death, but which he refused to confide in the accused, because it was too distressing?"

Winfarthing regarded him with amazement. "Of course I did!" he said loudly. "I told him that opium you swallow, even the damn stuff you smoke, is less than half your problem. The Pharmacy Act, if it sees the light of day, will be a toothless hag to deal with the problem that is now beginning—"

Pendock leaned forward, his hatchet face pale. "Sir Oliver, if you cannot keep your witness to the point, then I—"

"The needle!" Winfarthing said very loudly, his voice sharp with exasperation. He held up both huge hands, looking now straight at the jury. "A little contraption with a hollow down the middle and a point sharp enough to prick the human skin all the way to the veins. They attach the other end of it to a kind of vial or tiny bottle, with a solution of opium in it. Has to be pure, no cough mixture or stomach remedies. They push the plunger . . ." He made a dramatic gesture, closing his huge fist as if there were something inside it. "And the opium is in the blood in your veins, carried throughout your body, into your heart and lungs, into your brain! You see? Ecstasy—and then madness. The beast bites you once, and slowly, through tortures you cannot imagine—agony, vomiting, cramps, cold sweats, trembling and gooseflesh and chills— brings on nightmares no sane man has to endure. Of course you don't want to hear it."

He leaned forward over the railing as if peering into the jury's faces.

"But what you really don't want, my friends, is to live it! Or your children to live it . . . or, if you claim to be God-fearing men, any fellow human being on the face of this fair earth."

He ignored Pendock, who seemed about to speak, and Coniston now standing, ready to interrupt.

"I know! I know." Winfarthing would not be stopped. "Not relevant to the death of this wretched woman in Limehouse—Gadney, or what- ever her name was, poor creature." He leaned forward over the railing, peering at Rathbone. "But maybe it was, you see? Uncomfortable to talk about it. Makes us face the fact that we are responsible. My God, if you're man enough to allow it, for the love of heaven, be man enough to stand up and look at what it is!" His voice had risen until the volume of it, and the outrage in it, filled the room.

"We brought opium into this country. We take the money for its sale. We use it to ease our own pain when we are injured. We drink it to stop our coughs, our bellyaches, and our sleeplessness. Thank God for it—used wisely."

His voice sank to a growl. "But that does not give us the right to turn away from the misuse, the horrific knowledge of what it is like for those whose ignorance allows them to stumble into the living death of addic- tion. They're drowning in it! A great ocean of gray, endless half-life.

"And those who sell it to them, put this magic needle into their hands, peddle hell for a profit, are not breaking any laws! Then is it not our duty before God and man to change those laws so that it is?"

No one moved in the gallery. The jurors stared at him, ashen-faced.

Coniston looked wretched. He gazed at Pendock, then at the jury, then finally at Rathbone, but he did not say anything.

Rathbone cleared his throat. "Did you tell Dr. Lambourn the hor- ror of addiction through taking opium by needle, Dr. Winfarthing?"

"Goddamnit, man!" Winfarthing roared. "What the devil do you think I've been telling you?"

Pendock suddenly jumped into life, shouting, "Order!"

Winfarthing swiveled around and glowered at him. "What now?" he demanded. "My lord," he added with just a whisper of sarcasm.

"I will not have blasphemy in my court, Dr. . . . Winfarthing." He affected to forget his name and find it only with an effort. "If you repeat that offense I shall hold you in contempt."

A look of incredulity filled Winfarthing's face. Quite clearly a suitable retort came to his mind, and with an equally clear effort he restrained himself from giving it.

"I apologize to the Almighty," he said without a shred of humility. "Although I am certain He knows in what sense I call on His name." He looked again at Rathbone. "To answer your question, sir. I told Dr. Lambourn about the sale of opium fit to let into the blood, and the use to which these needles are put. Which is that a man—or woman, for that matter—may enter into their own private hell after only a few days on the poison, and be captive for ever afterward until death releases them to whatever damnation eternity offers—please God—to the seller of this nightmare and to those of us who deliberately choose not to distress ourselves with knowledge of it!"

Coniston was on his feet, his voice sharp and high above the hubbub in the room. "My lord! I must speak with you in chambers. It is of the utmost importance."

"Order!" Pendock roared. "I will have order in my court!"

Very gradually the uproar subsided. People shifted uncomfortably, angry, frightened, wanting someone to tell them that it was not true.

Pendock was furious, his face purple.

"Sir Oliver, Mr. Coniston, I will see you in my chambers immediately. The court is adjourned." He rose to his feet and strode out, his scarlet robe swirling wide, as if he were oblivious of what he brushed past or knocked into on the way.

Feeling a little sick, Rathbone followed Coniston and the court usher out of the side entrance and across the hall. As soon as the usher had knocked and received permission, they went into Pendock's chambers.

The door closed behind them. They both stood before Pendock, who barely glanced at Rathbone before looking up at Coniston.

"Well, what is it, Mr. Coniston?" he demanded. "If you are going to tell me that this man Winfarthing is outrageous, I am acutely aware of it. And if Sir Oliver cannot keep him in some kind of control then I shall hold him in contempt, and that will be the end of his evidence. So far it seems to me to be inflammatory, unproven, and irrelevant to this case."

Rathbone drew in his breath to defend Winfarthing on all counts, but before he could speak, Coniston cut across him.

"My lord, all you say is perfectly true, and I imagine that the jury can see it as the last ploy of a desperate man, as well as we can. However, there is another, more urgent and serious issue at stake here." He leaned forward just a fraction, as if he could impress the importance of it on Pendock even more. "Winfarthing was suggesting high crimes committed by certain men, without proof, or names, but leaving the implication with which to brand innocent men, simply because they have been mentioned as knowing this wretched Lambourn. There are matters of state concerned, my lord, great dangers of bringing Her Majesty's Government into disrepute, at home and abroad."

"Rubbish!" Rathbone exploded in fury and frustration. "That's a ridiculous excuse to present—"

"No, it isn't!" Coniston was speaking to him, momentarily ignoring Pendock. "I give you credit for not knowing what this man was going to say, but now that you do, you must dismiss him, with an apology to the court, and a denial of the truth of any of it—"

"I will not deny the truth of it," Rathbone cut across him. "I can't, and neither can you. And if that is what he said to Lambourn, then it is relevant, whether it is true or not. It is what Lambourn then believed."

"You don't know whether Lambourn believed it or not!" Coniston protested, his face flushed. "You have only Winfarthing's word for any of it. This seller of opium, if he exists at all, could be . . . anybody! This is totally irresponsible, and terrifies the public for no good reason at all."

"What is irresponsible is to condemn Dinah Lambourn without giving her the best possible defense," Rathbone retorted. "And hearing every argument and witness who—"

"Enough!" Pendock held up his hand. "This issue of needles is irrelevant to the murder of Zenia Gadney. She was beaten and disemboweled. Whatever Winfarthing thinks he knows, or has heard about opium selling or addiction, it has nothing to do with the obscene murder of one woman on Limehouse Pier. She was not buying or selling opium, and you have not proved that she had any connection to this mystery seller, or any other buyer, whatsoever."

"Thank you, my lord," Coniston said gratefully, his face at last ironed smooth of anxiety. He did not look at Rathbone.

Pendock's face was pinched, but he acknowledged Coniston's thanks. He turned to Rathbone. "Tomorrow you will begin closing arguments and we will put the matter to the jury. Is that understood?"

Rathbone felt crushed. "I have two more witnesses, my lord," he began.

Coniston jerked upright, almost to attention. "Witnesses to what?" he asked sharply. "More horrors of degradation in our backstreets by those who choose to addict themselves?"

"Are there more?" Rathbone snapped back at him. "Then it seems you know more of it than I do!"

"I know there's a lot of loose talk and scandalmongering," Coniston replied. "A lot of sensationalism and seeking to frighten the public and drag their attention from the murder of Zenia Gadney, poor woman. You talk about justice! What about justice for her?"

"Justice for her would be finding the truth," Rathbone said equally angrily. When he swung round to face Pendock again, for the first time he noticed the framed photograph on the table a little to his right, normally in the judge's line of sight, not his visitor's. It was of a woman and two young men, one not unlike Pendock himself. It might have been him, thirty-five years earlier. The other boy bore a resemblance also, but far less so. Brothers?

But the woman's fashionable gown was modern. And when Pendock had been twenty-two or -three, as the young man was, it would have been 1832, or thereabouts. There was no such photography as this then. They had to be Pendock's wife and sons. Rathbone was almost certain he had seen one of them, the son who did not look like Pendock, in a photograph before, in a very different setting from this elegant pose with his mother. In the other photograph he had been wearing far fewer clothes, his nakedness had been erotic, and the other person in the image had been a small, narrow-chested boy, perhaps five or six years old.

Coniston was talking. Rathbone turned to face him, waiting for him to speak again. He felt numb, as if he were at sea and the room were swaying around him. His face was hot.

Coniston was staring at him, his eyes narrowed in concern.

"Are you all right?" he demanded.

"Yes . . ." Rathbone lied. "Thank you. Yes. I'm . . . I'm quite well."

"Then you will begin your closing argument tomorrow morning," Pendock said stiffly.

"Yes . . . my lord," Rathbone answered. "I'll . . . I'll be here." It was a dismissal. He glanced one more time at the photograph in its ornate silver frame, then excused himself and walked out of the office, leaving Coniston and Pendock alone.

RATHBONE WENT HOME IN a daze. The hansom could have taken him almost anywhere and he might not have been aware of it. The driver had to call out to him when he reached his own door.

He alighted, paid the man, and went up the steps. He spoke only briefly as he went in, thanking Ardmore and asking him not to allow anyone to disturb him until he should call.

"Dinner, sir?" Ardmore asked with some concern.

Rathbone forced himself to be polite. The man more than deserved that much. "I don't think so, thank you. If I change my mind, I'll send for a couple of sandwiches, or a slice of pie, whatever Mrs. Wilton has. I'll have a glass of brandy. In an hour or two. I need to think. I doubt anyone will call, but unless it is Mr. Monk, I cannot see them."

Ardmore was in no way comforted. "Are you quite well, Sir Oliver? Are you certain there is nothing else I can do for you?"

"I am perfectly well, thank you, Ardmore. I have to make a very difficult decision about this case. I need time to consider what the right thing to do is, for a woman accused of a murder she did not commit—at least I don't believe she did—and for the woman who was very brutally killed, I think merely to serve a purpose. For a man or men who committed these crimes, and for the sake of a larger justice altogether."

"Yes, sir." Ardmore blinked. "I shall see that you are not disturbed."

Rathbone sat alone for nearly an hour, weighing up in his mind if he even wished to be certain that the young man in Ballinger's photograph was Pendock's son. If he did not use it then it did not really matter who it was.

If it was Hadley Pendock, then how would he use it? Not to get a particular verdict. There was no question in his mind that that would be irredeemably wrong. But Grover Pendock had ruled against Dinah all the way through the trial where it had mattered. Now he was attempting to end the trial before Agatha Nisbet could testify, and even if she did come on the following day, she would then not be allowed to say anything that could expose Herne, or Bawtry, or whoever it was who had brought about the murder of Joel Lambourn, Zenia Gadney, and thus also the murder of Dinah Lambourn.

That must not be allowed to happen.

There was a knock on the door.

"Come in?" he called, surprised to be glad of the interruption he had specifically asked should not occur.

Ardmore came in with a tray of sandwiches, brown bread with roast beef and some of Mrs. Wilton's best, sharp sweet pickles in a little dish. There was a wedge of fruit cake and a glass of brandy.

"In case you feel like it, sir," he said, putting it on the table at Rathbone's side. "Would you like a cup of tea as well, perhaps? Or coffee?"

"No, thank you, that's excellent. Please tell Mrs. Wilton I appreciate her care, as well as yours. You may retire now. I shan't need you again."

"Yes, sir. Thank you, sir." Ardmore withdrew and closed the door gently behind him. Rathbone heard his footsteps, a mere whisper of sound, tap across the hall floor toward the kitchen.

He picked up the first sandwich. He could use a few minutes' respite from thought, and he realized he was hungry. The sandwich was fresh, the pickles very pleasant. He ate one, then another, then a third.

Had Arthur Ballinger begun this way, feeling and thinking exactly what he was—a dirty tool to save an innocent person? What use was an advocate who was more concerned with his own moral comfort than his client's life? If Rathbone used the photograph of Hadley Pendock, if it was indeed he, then he would feel soiled afterward. Judge Pendock would hate him. He would not tell others what had been the instrument Rathbone had used, but he might tell them it was unusual, not a thing a gentleman would ever stoop even to touch, let alone injure another by wielding. He would not tell them Rathbone was able to do so only because Pendock's son had seduced and violated vulnerable, homeless children.

And if he did not use it and Dinah Lambourn was hanged, how then would he feel? What would Monk and Hester think of him? More important than that, what would he think of himself?

What would he ever fight for again? He would have abdicated his responsibility to act. Could anything excuse that?

Either way, whether he used the photographs or not, what was Rathbone making of himself? A safe, morally clean coward who acquiesced while an innocent woman walked to the gallows? A safe man who would have nightmares for the rest of his life as he lay alone in his magnificent bed, in a silent house?

Or a man whose hands were soiled by the use of what amounted to blackmail, to force a weak judge to be honest?

He finished the last sandwich and ate the cake, then drank the last drop of the brandy. Tomorrow he was going to carry out a decision that would change his life—and maybe Dinah's, and that of whoever had murdered Lambourn, and Zenia Gadney.

He stood up and went to the safe where he kept Arthur Ballinger's photographs. One day he must find a better place for them, not in this house. But for now, he was glad they were still here.

He opened the safe and took out the case. He opened that, calm now that the decision had been made. He went through the images slowly, one by one. He was disgusted, sickened by the coarseness of them, by the cruelty, the indifference to the humiliation and pain of children.

He found it. It was the same face as that in Pendock's silver-framed photograph. And on the bottom of this one, in Ballinger's hand, was written "Hadley Pendock," and the date and place in which it was taken.

Rathbone put it back again, made a note in his diary, checked that it was correct, then locked the case and put it back in the safe.

He knew what he must do tomorrow morning before the trial resumed, however hard, however painful and repellent. Shame was bitter, but it was a small thing compared with the hangman's noose.

23

In the morning, long before the court sat, Rathbone unlocked the safe again and took one of the prints that Ballinger had made of the photograph of Hadley Pendock. It was quite small, only three inches by four, a sample to show anyone what the original contained. Even so, the faces were clearly identifiable.

Rathbone put it in his pocket between two clean sheets of white notepaper, then left the house, taking a hansom to the Old Bailey. Today he needed to be early. As he rode through the gray icy morning streets he refused to let his mind even touch on what he must do, how he would say it, or how Pendock might respond. He had made up his mind, not that this was good, only that the alternative was unbearable.

He arrived at the court even before the usher, and had to wait until the man came in, startled to see Rathbone there before him.

"Are you all right, Sir Oliver?" he asked anxiously. He must know how the case was going. There was pity in his face.

"Yes, thank you, Rogers," Rathbone said bleakly. "I need to speak to his lordship before we begin today. It is of the greatest possible importance, and it may take half an hour or so. I apologize for the inconveniences I am causing you."

"No inconvenience at all, Sir Oliver," Rogers said quickly. "It's a miserable case. Maybe I shouldn't be sorry for Mrs. Lambourn, but I am."

"It speaks well for you, Rogers," Rathbone replied with the ghost of a smile. "May I wait here?"

"Yes, of course, sir. As soon as I see his lordship I'll tell him you're here, and it's urgent."

"Thank you."

It was another twenty-five minutes before Pendock came up the wide hallway and saw Rathbone. He looked grim, and clearly not at all pleased with what he feared was going to be an unpleasant interview.

"What is it?" he asked as soon as they were both inside his chambers and the door closed. "I cannot allow you any further latitude, Rathbone. You have exhausted all the leniency the court can allow. I'm sorry. You are on a loser this time. Accept it, man. Don't string this out, for all our sakes, even hers."

Rathbone sat down deliberately, as a signal that he would not be dismissed with a word. He saw the flicker of irritation on Pendock's face.

"It is not over, my lord, until all the evidence has been heard, and the jury has delivered a verdict," he replied. He drew in his breath and let it out very slowly.

"Due to circumstance," he continued, "and entirely against my wish, I have recently inherited a very remarkable collection of photographs, which I keep in a safe place, away from my home." That would soon be true.

"For God's sake, Rathbone, I don't care what you've inherited!" Pendock said with disbelief. "What on earth is the matter with you? Are you ill?"

Rathbone reached into his pocket and pulled out the sheets of paper and the photograph between them. Once he showed it to Pendock he would, like Caesar, have crossed the Rubicon, the line marking one side from the other; and he would, like Caesar, have declared war on his own people.

Pendock made a move to stand up, in effect a dismissal.

Rathbone took the top sheet off and laid the photograph bare.

Pendock glanced at it. Perhaps he did not see it clearly. His face filled with revulsion.

"God Almighty, man! That's obscene!" He raised his eyes. "What on earth makes you imagine I might want to look at such filth?"

"I would not have thought so until yesterday," Rathbone answered, his voice shaking in spite of his intense effort to control it. "Then I saw the same young man's face in that picture over there." He looked toward the silver-framed photograph on the table.

Pendock followed his gaze and his face flooded with scarlet. He seized the photograph where Rathbone had left it and held it close enough to the silver frame to compare one with another. Then the blood drained from his skin, leaving him as gray as the dead ashes in the morning fireplace. He staggered back and all but collapsed into his chair.

Rathbone felt worse than he could ever remember in his life, worse than when he had faced Ballinger in his cell, or found his murdered body so soon after; worse than when Margaret had left, even, because this was his own deliberate doing. It was open to him to have chosen differently. But what alternative could he have chosen?

Pendock lifted his head and looked at Rathbone with the same contempt with which he had regarded the small photograph when he had not known who it portrayed.

"I will not find Dinah Lambourn not guilty!" he said slowly, his voice a croak from a dry throat. "I . . . I'll pay you anything you want, but I will not mock the law!"

"Damn you!" Rathbone shouted at him, half rising to his feet. "I don't want your bloody money! And I don't want a directed verdict. I've never looked for one in my life, and I'm not now. I just want you to preside over this trial fairly. I want you to allow my witnesses to testify and the jury to hear what they have to say. Then I'll give you the original of the photograph, and all copies, and you can do what you like with them. Whether you speak to your son or not is your own choice and God help you."

He leaned across the table toward Pendock. "You were willing to give me money to keep your son from paying the price of his criminal use of children, revolting as you find it. Is it so repellent to you to give Dinah Lambourn at least the justice of a fair hearing? She's somebody's child as well; somewhere there are people who love her. And if there weren't, would that make her any less deserving?"

"It's the natural . . . the natural instinct," Pendock stammered. "This slander will damage the government, good men. We cannot change the law to alter people's freedom to take whatever ease of pain they can, for the sake of the few who abuse it."

"I love my freedom as much as the next man," Rathbone answered. "But not at the cost this is to the weaker and more vulnerable, and those who exploit them for gain. Do you love your son more than you love justice?"

Pendock sank his head into his hands. "It looks like it, doesn't it?" he whispered. "No. No, I don't. I think. But . . ." He opened his eyes slowly, his face now that of an old man. "Bring on your witnesses, Rathbone."

TWENTY MINUTES LATER RATHBONE was standing in the open space before the witness stand, which was occupied by the largest woman he could ever remember having seen. She was not immensely fat, and only just over six foot tall, but at the top of the steps as she was, she seemed to tower above them all. She was broad-shouldered like a stevedore, huge-chested, her arms heavy and muscular. Thank heaven, she was soberly dressed, even though her expression was fierce, as if defying the ritual and establishment of the law to intimidate her.

Rathbone knew what she was going to say because he had spoken to her himself. He knew her passion to ease the pain of those who had nowhere else to turn, her knowledge of opium addiction and withdrawal, and her pity for Alvar Doulting and what he had once been. Hester had warned him that Agatha might be difficult to handle. Rathbone had a powerful feeling that that would prove to be an understatement. Still, he had used the means he dreaded most to force this chance and there was no turning back.

The court was waiting, the gallery hushed, the jurors surprised that there was still something to hear. Coniston was more than surprised. He looked confused. Obviously Pendock had not attempted to explain anything to him. How could he?

Rathbone cleared his throat. He must win. The cost had already been too high.

"Miss Nisbet," he began, "it is my understanding that you run a voluntary clinic on the south bank of the river for the treatment of dockworkers and sailors who are injured or have illnesses due to the dangerous nature of their work. Is that correct?"

"Yes it is," she answered. Her voice was unexpectedly gentle for so large a woman. One would not have been surprised were it baritone, like a man's.

"Do you use opium to treat their pain?" He was asking his way gently toward the connection with Lambourn.

"Yes, course I do. There in't nothing else as'll do it. Some of them is hurtin' very bad," she answered. "Break 'alf a dozen bones an' yer'll know what pain is. Crush an arm, or a leg, an' yer'll know even better."

"I was going to say that I can imagine," Rathbone spoke gently, too, "but that would be a lie. I have no idea, for which I am profoundly grateful." He hesitated a moment to allow the jury to place themselves in the same situation, facing pain beyond their nightmares, grasping some concept of what this woman dealt with every day.

"So you use a great deal of opium. You must know where to buy it, and perhaps something about opium dealing in general?" He made it a question. "And, of course, its effects on people after the pain is healed?"

Coniston was looking puzzled, but he had not yet interrupted. Surely he would any moment now.

"Course I do," Agatha answered him.

"In this context, did Dr. Joel Lambourn come to see you within the last few weeks of his life? That would be between three and four months ago."

"Yeah. 'E were askin' questions about quality of opium, an' if I knew 'ow ter give it without overdosin' anyone," she said.

Coniston could not endure it any longer. He rose to his feet.

"My lord, is this going anywhere of relevance? Surely my learned friend is not trying to damage the work this woman is doing to relieve the agony of injured men, just because she might have no medical training? If that is, indeed, what Lambourn was trying to do, no wonder the government judged the report to be better suppressed!"

There were murmurs of agreement and approval from the gallery.

Pendock appeared undecided. He looked from Coniston to Rathbone, and then back again.

Rathbone interrupted. "No, my lord. That is the·opposite of my intention. I am only trying to establish Miss Nisbet's skill and dedication, the fact that she is familiar with the opium market, and therefore a natural person for Dr. Lambourn to consult, possibly in some depth."

"Proceed," Pendock said with relief.

Coniston sat down again, even more puzzled.

Rathbone turned back to Agatha Nisbet.

"Miss Nisbet, I don't believe it is necessary for the court to know all the details of your conversations with Dr. Lambourn regarding the purchase and availability of opium, or the ways in which you are able to know its quality. I will accept that you are an expert, and I will ask his lordship if the court will accept the evidence of your success in treating men as sufficient proof of it." He turned to Pendock. "My lord?"

"We will accept it," Pendock replied. "Please move on to your purpose in calling the witness regarding Zenia Gadney's death."

Coniston relaxed and leaned back in his seat.

"Thank you, my lord," Rathbone said graciously. He looked up at Agatha again. "What was Dr. Lambourn interested in learning from you, Miss Nisbet?"

"About opium. Specially 'oo cut it wi' wot so it weren't pure anymore," she answered. "So I told 'im about the trade as I know. 'E listened to all of it, poor devil." Her face, shadowed with some dark and complex emotion, was impossible to read. "I told 'im all I knew about it."

"About shipping opium and its entry into the Port of London?" Rathbone continued.

"That's wot 'e wanted, ter start with," she replied.

"And then?"

"My lord!" Coniston shot up from his seat and protested again.

"Sit down, Mr. Coniston," Pendock ordered. "We must allow the defense to reach a point of some relevance, which I assume will not be much longer in coming."

Coniston was taken aback. He had clearly expected Pendock to support him, but at least for the time being he was willing to wait.

Rathbone began again. "But I assume that you told him more than simply details of shipping," he said to Agatha. "That would not seem to relate in any way at all to the death of Zenia Gadney, or indeed to Dr. Lambourn's own death, apparently by suicide."

"Course not," Agatha said with heavy disgust. "I told 'im about the new way o' giving 'igh-quality opium with a needle. Acts faster and stronger for pain. Trouble is, it's a hell of a lot 'arder ter stop when yer 'ave to. Longer you take it, 'arder it gets. Weeks or more, an' some can't stop it at all. Then yer got 'em fer life. Sell their own mothers for a dose of it."

This time Coniston did not hesitate. He was on his feet and striding out into the main space of the floor before he even began to speak.

"My lord! We have already established that it is possible for the unskilled or ignorant to misuse opium, probably any other medicine, and your lordship has ruled that raking it up here in this trial, which has nothing to do with opium except in the most oblique way, is irrelevant. It is a waste of time; it will frighten the public unnecessarily, and may well be slanderous to doctors who are not here to defend themselves, their honor and their good name."

Pendock was ashen gray, and he controlled himself with a difficulty that was clearly visible to everyone.

"I think we must allow Miss Nisbet to tell us what troubled Dr. Lambourn so much, if indeed she knows," he answered. "I will warn her that no names are to be mentioned, unless she has proof of what she says. That should allay your anxieties about slander." He looked at Rathbone. "Please continue, Sir Oliver, but arrive at something relevant as soon as you can, preferably before luncheon."

"Thank you, my lord." Rathbone inclined his head graciously. Even before Coniston had returned to his seat, confused and angry, he asked Agatha Nisbet to continue.

"'E asked me a lot o' questions about addiction," she said quietly. "An 'ow yer can get over it. I told 'im that for most people, yer can't."

Now the silence in the room was intense, as if every man and woman in it were holding his or her breath, afraid to move in case the slightest rustle of fabric distorted a word.

The moment was here. Rathbone hesitated, breathed in and out slowly, then asked the question, his voice a trifle husky.

"And what was his response, Miss Nisbet?"

" 'E were gutted," she said simply. " 'E asked me if I would show 'im some proof of it, so 'e would know what 'e were talkin' about, an' so 'e could put it in 'is report for the government."

"Did he say why he wanted to put it in his report?"

"Course 'e didn't, but I ain't bleedin' stupid! 'E wanted to 'ave the government make a law so it would be a crime ter sell people that kind of opium, wi' needles to put it inter their blood. 'E wanted it so only doctors 'oo really knew what they was doin' could give it ter anyone." She looked back at him with a rage so deep, words seemed inadequate to serve it. She blinked several times. " 'E wanted ter see what it really did to anyone . . . to know everything about it."

"And did you agree to do that?" Rathbone said softly.

"Course I did," she answered witheringly, but there was pain in her voice, and Rathbone felt a sense of guilt himself for what he was about to do. But there was no choice. He was not only at the last, desperate point of his defense of Dinah Lambourn; he knew this was what Joel Lambourn had died for, and unequivocally, what was right. There was a horror waiting to destroy thousands, tens of thousands of people over time. He could not balk at causing this one person's pain.

Coniston was on his feet. "My lord, Miss Nisbet may be a very worthy woman, and I don't mean to belittle her efforts in any way, but all this is still hearsay. I assume she is not addicted to opium herself? If so, she seems to be managing with extraordinary ability to hide it. It would be flippant to suggest it is doing her good, but I do suggest she is an observer, and not a professionally skilled one at that. If we are to believe this of opium, then we must have doctors tell us so, not Miss Nisbet, for all her charitable work."

Pendock looked at Rathbone with the question in his face, the panic in his hollow eyes.

Rathbone turned to the witness stand. "Who did you take Dr. Lambourn to see, Miss Nisbet?"

"Dr. Alvar Doulting," she said hoarsely. "I've known 'im for year⸱ Known 'im when 'e were one o' the best doctors I ever seen."

"And he is not now?" Rathbone asked.

Her look was bitter and filled with grief. "Some days 'e's all right. Will be today, most likely."

"He is ill?" Rathbone asked.

Coniston stood up again. "My lord, if the witness is not coming, for reasons of ill health or whatever else"—he used the terms scathingly—"then what is the purpose of this hearsay?"

"He is coming, my lord," Rathbone stated, hoping to heaven he was correct. Hester was supposed to be bringing him, with Monk's help, if that should prove necessary.

Coniston looked around him as if searching for the missing doctor. He gave a very slight shrug. "Indeed?"

Rathbone was desperate. Neither Monk nor Hester had come into the courtroom to indicate that Doulting was safely here. If Rathbone called him and he failed to appear, Coniston would demand they begin their summing up and Pendock would not have any excuse to refuse him.

"I still have further questions for Miss Nisbet," Rathbone said, his mind racing to think how he could string this out any further. There really was little else Agatha Nisbet could say that would not be obvious even to the jury as playing for time.

"My lord"—Coniston's weariness was only slightly an exaggeration—"the court is being indulgent enough to the accused in allowing this doctor to testify at all. If the man cannot even appear, then—"

Pendock took it out of his control. "The court will adjourn for an ur, to allow everyone to compose themselves, perhaps take a glass of r." He rose stiffly, as if all his joints hurt, and walked from the

on as he was gone Coniston came over to Rathbone. His face le and for the first time Rathbone had ever seen it, his collar skew.

lk?" he asked urgently.

e what there is to say," Rathbone answered.

oved his hand as if to take Rathbone by the arm, then l and let it fall again. "Please? This is very serious. I'm lerstand the full implications."

"I'm not sure they're going to make any difference," Rathbone told him frankly.

"Well, I could do with a drink anyway," Coniston replied. "I feel like hell, and you look like it. What the devil have you done to Pendock? He looks like a corpse dug up!"

"That's none of your concern," Rathbone replied with a brief smile to rob the words of their sting, although he meant them. "If he wants to tell you, that is up to him."

They were out in the hall now and Coniston stopped abruptly, staring at Rathbone. For the first time he realized that something really had changed, and he was no longer in control.

Rathbone led the way now, going out of the courthouse and down the steps to the street. They went to the nearest decent public house and ordered brandy, in spite of the early hour.

"You're playing with fire," Coniston said very quietly after he had taken the first sip of his drink and allowed its burning warmth to slide down his throat. "Do you know what sort of restrictions Lambourn was going to advocate, and who would be made into a criminal because of it?"

"No!" Rathbone said quietly. "But I'm beginning to have a rather strong idea that you do."

Coniston looked grim. "You know better than to ask me that, Rathbone. I can't reveal anything told me in confidence."

"That rather depends on by whom," Rathbone pointed out. "And whether it conceals the truth of Lambourn's death, and consequently protects whoever murdered and then eviscerated Zenia Lambourn."

"It doesn't," Coniston's eyes widened. "You know me better than that."

"Are you sure?" Rathbone asked, meeting Coniston's gaze and holding it. "What about the effective murder of Dinah Lambourn? And that is what it will be if we deliberately allow her to be hanged for a crime she did not commit. I think you can see as well as I can that there is a great deal more to this case than domestic jealousy between two women who have known about each other for the best part of fifteen years."

Coniston was silent for several moments, sipping his brandy again. His hand around the glass was white-knuckled.

"Lambourn's death was the catalyst," he said finally. "Suddenly his money was at stake, Dinah's whole life as she knew it, and that of her children."

"Rubbish," Rathbone replied. "Her life as she knew it ended with his death because she loved him. He was murdered because of his proposal to add restrictions to the sales of opium because of what he discovered about the effects of taking it by needle. She is willing to risk being hanged in order to clear his name of suicide and professional incompetence, and perhaps even to see his work completed simply because he believed in it. Even though she didn't, and still doesn't, know what it really is."

"For God's sake, Rathbone!" Coniston exclaimed. "She's facing the hangman because the evidence says she's guilty. She lied to Monk and he caught her in it. From the evidence you've provided, if Lambourn didn't kill himself, it's even possible she killed him also. We have only her own, and her sister-in-law's, word for it that she knew about Zenia Gadney. There's a very reasonable case to say that she only learned about Zenia just before Lambourn's death, and that's the connection." He smiled with a bitter irony. "You might just have proved her guilty of both murders."

Rathbone sat staring at Coniston. He realized now how shallow his knowledge of the man was. Good family; excellent education; good career, improving all the time. Fortunate, if possibly dull marriage. Three daughters and a son. But he knew nothing of the inner man, the hopes or the dreams. What hurt him, or made him laugh? What was he afraid of, apart from poverty or failure? Was he afraid of making a mistake, convicting an innocent person? Was he ever lonely? Did he doubt the best in himself, or fear the worst? Had he ever loved someone, and been proved hideously wrong, as Rathbone had?

He had no idea.

"Do you give a damn what the truth is?" he said quietly.

Coniston leaned forward across the table, his face tense, the skin drawn suddenly tight with his own urgency. "Yes, I do! And I care like hell that we don't betray our country's laws and freedoms, the tolerance of individuals' rights to take whatever medicines they choose, how they choose. Information is one thing, and I'm all for that. But making opium illegal and the sellers of it criminals is quite another. You can't prove anything at all from this Nisbet woman's words."

"We may not be able to affect what the Pharmacy Act says, and whether opium sales are restricted, or not. That is not our decision," Rathbone argued. "But we can and must affect what happens in the Old Bailey this week. You'd better choose where you stand, Coniston, because you aren't going to be able to play the middle any longer. Are you sure, beyond reasonable doubt, that what this Nisbet woman says isn't true, and doesn't have any bearing on why Lambourn was killed?"

Coniston blinked. "What are you saying? That someone selling pure opium here in London, now, killed Lambourn, and then Zenia Gadney?"

"Are you saying that isn't a possibility?" Rathbone watched Coniston's face, and the realization hit him. He drew in his breath and let it out very slowly. His heart was pounding so violently he felt as if it must be making his body shake. "My God. You know who is behind this, don't you!" It was a statement, not a question, in fact all but an accusation.

"He did not kill either Lambourn or Zenia Gadney," Coniston said so softly, Rathbone barely heard him. "Do you really think I didn't make certain of that myself?"

"Did you? Are you saying that out of knowledge or belief?" Rathbone asked. Was it all slipping away from him again, in his grasp, and then gone, like mist from empty hands?

"Knowledge," Coniston answered. "Give me that much credit. He believes Lambourn's response to what Agatha Nisbet told him was hysterical and completely disproportionate. He wanted that part of his report excluded. He's not guilty of this. Lambourn was a fanatic and he took his own life. His wife couldn't accept that and chose this insane and terrible way of trying to force the government's hand." His glance wavered, but only for an instant.

"What?" Rathbone demanded.

"Bring in your witness." Coniston's voice was a whisper, all but caught in his throat. He sighed. "Play it out. I imagine you're going to anyway. But be warned, if you somehow manage to ruin an innocent man, I'll personally see that you pay for it with your career. I don't care how damn clever you are."

"An innocent man? What is he innocent of? Murder of Lambourn and Zenia Gadney, or of selling people a one-way ticket to hell?"

"Just stop dancing around and prove something!" Coniston answered.

"I mean to." Rathbone finished the last of his brandy. "But don't forget, reasonable doubt is enough." He put the empty glass down and rose to his feet. He walked away without looking back.

Rathbone saw no sign of either Monk or Hester in the hallways as he returned. His muscles locked tight with tension.

The court resumed with Agatha Nisbet back on the stand again. The jurors looked pale and unhappy, but not one of them averted his eyes or his attention from her.

"You have described some of the most terrible suffering any of us here has heard," Rathbone began. "Did you describe these things also to Dr. Joel Lambourn?"

"Yes, I did," she said simply. "I took 'im an' I showed 'im."

"And what was Dr. Lambourn's reaction?" he asked, looking up at Agatha again.

"'E were sick," she answered. "Looked like a man with the ague. At first 'e were just revolted, like anyone would be, then as we saw more, 'e got gray in the face an' I were afraid 'e were going to 'ave a seizure or an 'eart attack. I even fetched 'im brandy."

"And that revived him?"

"Not a lot. 'E looked like a man as 'ad seen death in front of 'im. Reckon as perhaps 'e 'ad, save it weren't more'n a few days before 'e were found with 'is wrists cut, poor sod." Her language was coarse, but the pity in her face, even the grief, was too powerful to belittle or ignore.

Rathbone deliberately took a risk, but time was pressing hard on him. "Did he seem to you suicidal?"

"The doctor?" she said incredulously. "Don't be a fool! 'E were 'ell-bent on stoppin' it, whatever it cost. Never reckoned as it'd cost 'im 'is life. Not ter even think of 'is wife too."

"Are you referring to Zenia Gadney?"

"Never 'eard of 'er, till now. I meant Dinah. An' if yer think she killed 'im yer dafter than them as is in Bedlam chained ter the walls an' 'owlin' at the moon."

Rathbone controlled the slightly hysterical laughter that welled up inside him.

"I do not think so, Miss Nisbet. Nor do I think she killed Miss Gadney. I think Dinah Lambourn guessed some of this. Then when Zenia Gadney was murdered, she allowed herself to be accused, even adding to her appearance of guilt by telling a lie she knew would very quickly be found out."

He hesitated only a moment. "She did this, risking her own life, so this court could discover and expose the truth. That is a truly remarkable love, a loyalty beyond death. I thank you, Miss Nisbet, for your courage in coming here to tell us of horrors I am sure you would far rather not relive. Please wait there in case Mr. Coniston has anything to ask you."

He returned to his seat, wondering what Coniston would do, and if Pendock would support him if he objected.

Coniston rose slowly. He walked out into the center of the floor with even more grace than usual. Rathbone did not know him well enough to be certain if that was a mark of excess of confidence, or a time-wasting maneuver because he lacked confidence.

As soon as Coniston spoke, he knew it was the latter. All his original certainty had evaporated, but it was a good mask, nonetheless. The jury would not read him.

"Miss Nisbet," he began courteously, "you have seen some shocking and very dreadful things. I respect you since they so clearly move your compassion, and your will to help and minister to the sick." He moved two or three steps to the left and then turned. "In all this horror, did you see the face of any man responsible for the sale of opium, and the needles to administer it into the blood? Are you certain you would even recognize him if you saw him again, unconnected to his trade?"

Rathbone saw the look of confusion in Agatha's face. He rose to his feet.

"My lord, Miss Nisbet has not stated that she would remember him, or indeed that she ever knew his name. All she said was that Dr. Lambourn had a powerful and extremely distressed reaction to her story and behaved as if he knew who it was."

"You are quite correct, Sir Oliver," Pendock agreed. He turned to Coniston. "Perhaps it would be simpler, Mr. Coniston, if you were merely to ask the witness if she believes she would recognize the man again, were she to see him, here or elsewhere."

Coniston's jaw clenched, but he obeyed.

Agatha answered simply. "I never saw 'im, far as I know. But—" She stopped abruptly.

"But . . . ?" Coniston asked quickly.

"But that in't no use," she answered, clearly lying.

Coniston drew breath to ask a further question, then changed his mind. "Thank you, Miss Nisbet," he said, turning and walking back toward his table. "Oh! Just one more thing, did Dr. Lambourn tell you that he knew who this man was, or that he was acquainted with him, that he would challenge him, ruin him, see him in prison? Anything like that?"

It was a gamble, and even the jury seemed to be aware of it. The silence was intense.

Rathbone rose again. "My lord, perhaps one question at a time might be clearer, both for Miss Nisbet and for the jury?"

"Indeed," Pendock agreed. "Mr. Coniston, if you please?"

Coniston's face colored deeply, and his jaw was clenched so tight the muscles in it bulged.

"My lord." There was the slightest edge of sarcasm in his acquiescence. "Miss Nisbet, did Dr. Lambourn say that he knew this man you say sells opium for profit?"

"No, sir, but 'e went white like 'e were going ter faint," she replied.

"Could that be the very natural horror of a decent man told of abominable human crime and suffering?"

"Course it could," she said tartly.

"Did he say that he had either the wish or the power to ruin this man? For example, send him to prison?" Coniston continued.

"I went ter get 'im brandy. 'E didn't say much at all, 'ceptin' ter thank me."

"I see. Did he at any time tell you that he was going to face this man, accuse him, or otherwise bring him to answer for his terrible trade? Did he tell you this man's name?"

"No."

"Thank you, Miss Nisbet. That is all I have to ask you."

Rathbone was on his feet yet again. "May I re-direct, my lord?"

"Of course," Pendock told him.

Rathbone looked up at Agatha. "Miss Nisbet, did you form the opinion that Dr. Lambourn was deeply horrified by what you told him?"

"Course 'e was," she said witheringly.

"Because of the suffering, the crime of it?"

"I think it were 'cos 'e 'ad an idea 'oo it were," she said slowly and distinctly. "But 'e never told me."

There was an immediate ripple of amazement and horror through the room. Rathbone turned to look at the gallery, and at that moment saw the door open and Hester come in. Their eyes met and she gave a very slight nod. Relief washed through Rathbone like a wave of heat. He turned to the judge, the smile still on his lips.

"I would like to call Dr. Alvar Doulting to the stand, my lord."

Pendock glanced at the clock on the far wall.

"Very well. You may proceed."

Alvar Doulting came up the aisle between the seats in the gallery and across the open floor. He climbed the steps of the witness stand with difficulty. When he reached the top and faced Rathbone, suddenly all that Agatha Nisbet had said of a living hell became real to Rathbone's eyes. Doulting looked like a man who lived in a nightmare. His skin was gray and sheened with sweat. In spite of the fact that he clung to the rail, he was trembling violently. A muscle in his face twitched and he was so gaunt the bones of his skull seemed to stretch his skin.

Rathbone felt a searing guilt that he had compelled the man to come here.

Doulting swore to his name and his professional qualifications, which were impressive. He had clearly once been a great doctor in the making. The man who stood in front of them now was the more horrifying because of it.

Based upon what Agatha Nisbet had told him, Rathbone began his questioning, urged on by the feeling that Doulting might not stay well long enough to say much. If the diarrhea, vomiting, and cramps that Winfarthing described in the withdrawal symptoms of addiction were to strike him, he would be unable to continue, no matter how critical his evidence was to the case. And yet still Rathbone felt brutal doing it.

"Thank you, Dr. Doulting," he said with profound sincerity. "I appreciate your coming. Since you are clearly unwell, I shall be as brief as I can. Did you speak with Dr. Joel Lambourn, shortly before his death in early October?"

"Yes, I did." Doulting's voice was steady, in spite of his physical distress.

"Did he ask you about the sale and use of opium, in the course of his investigation into the possible Pharmacy Act prepared by Parliament?"

"Yes."

"What did you tell him, if anything, beyond the dangers of people overusing it because of the fact that it was inadequately labeled?"

Doulting gripped the railing more tightly and took a deep breath.

"I told him about the relief opium gave to agonizing pain when it was administered directly into the bloodstream using the recent invention of a hollow needle attached to a syringe. I also told him how much more deeply addictive it is, acting within a matter of days to make someone so dependent upon it that it is almost beyond a person's ability to stop using it. It takes over their lives. The hell of being without it is almost as bad as the pain it relieved."

Rathbone was compelled to ask the next question, even though he hated doing so. He felt the clenching of his own body as he imagined not only the man's pain but his humiliation.

"And how do you know this, Dr. Doulting?"

"Because I am addicted to it myself," Doulting answered. "I was given it with the best intentions, after I had my pelvis crushed in an accident. My pain then was almost unbearable. The opium was given to me for some time, until the bones healed. Now that the pain is almost forgotten, I wish I had never seen opium, never heard of it. I dread the hell of withdrawal and can bear to survive only for the comfort the next dose of opium will bring."

"Where do you obtain it?" Rathbone asked.

"From a man who sells it to me, in a form pure enough to inject into my body."

"Is it expensive?"

"Yes."

"How do you afford it?"

"I have lost everything I had, my house, my family, my practice. Now I must do his bidding to sell it to others who have also become its slaves. I think perhaps I would rather be dead." There was no melodrama in his voice, no self-pity. "It would certainly be better for others, and perhaps it would be better for me also."

Rathbone wished he could reply with any comfort at all, even if only to acknowledge his dignity, but this was not the place.

"Do you know the name of this man, Dr. Doulting?" he asked.

"No. I would tell you if I did."

"Would you? What would happen to your supply then?"

"It would be stopped, as I imagine it will be now that I have testified here. I really don't think I care anymore."

Rathbone lowered his gaze. "There is nothing I can say to touch your pain. The best I can do is thank you for coming here and testifying to this court—at such price to yourself. Please wait there in case Mr. Coniston has anything to ask you."

Coniston stood up slowly. "Dr. Doulting, do you expect us to take this fearful account solely on your word? By your own admission, you are the servant of this man and will do anything for your dosage of opium."

Doulting looked at him with weary contempt. "If you doubt me, go into the back alleys and gutters where the lost and the dying are. You'll find others who'll tell you the same thing. For God's sake, man, look at me! Before the opium I was as respectable as you, and as comfortable. I had rank and position, a home, a profession. I had health. I slept at night in my own bed and woke looking forward to the day. Now all I want is redemption—and death."

There was a wave of pity from the court in sighs and murmurs so palpable that Coniston found himself unable to continue. He looked up at Doulting, then across at Rathbone. Someone in the gallery called out to him to sit down.

"Order!" Pendock said loudly. "I will have order. Thank you, Mr. Coniston. Is that all?"

"Yes, my lord, thank you."

Pendock looked at Rathbone. "Court is adjourned for today."

LATE THAT AFTERNOON AND into the evening, Rathbone, Monk, Hester, and Runcorn sat around the kitchen table eating, drinking tea, and planning the last day of the trial. Sleet battered against the windows and the oven made the room an island of warmth.

"Might have enough evidence for a verdict based on reasonable doubt," Rathbone said unhappily, "which I suppose is better than I hoped for a day or two ago. But I want to prove her innocent. Her life will still be ruined without more than this."

"And she will not have cleared Lambourn's name," Monk pointed out.

Hester was staring at the plates arranged on the dresser, but clearly her vision was beyond them, far into a space only she could see.

"Do you believe Lambourn knew who it was?" she asked, shaking her head a little and looking at Rathbone. "He must have, mustn't he? Or at the very least, whoever it is thought he knew. That has to be why he was killed. If he had handed in a revised report and the government had seen it, especially Mr. Gladstone, who is something of a moral crusader, selling opium might well be made illegal."

"It would make sense," Runcorn agreed. "If he was killed by someone he knew, that would explain why he went out to meet them alone in the evening. Maybe he even walked up One Tree Hill with them."

"If he went up the hill alone with them, at night, knowing who they were and what they did, then he was an idiot!" Monk said savagely. He ran his hands through his hair. "Sorry," he apologized. "There's something here we're missing. It does look as if he could well have gone up the hill with someone he knew. There were no marks of hoofprints or tire tracks on the path or the grass, and no one could have carried him up there single-handed. Even two would have found it difficult. It doesn't make sense."

Rathbone nodded. "We always assumed he walked willingly, but alone." He turned to Runcorn. "Were there any footprints other than his?"

"Those of the man who found him, and by the time I got there, other police, and the police surgeon," Runcorn replied. "There could have been anyone else's and I wouldn't have seen. And to be honest, at that time I assumed it was suicide, too. I didn't think of alternatives. I should have." He looked wretched, filled with guilt for an irresponsible oversight.

Rathbone glanced at Monk and saw the pity in his face. This was something that would have been unimaginable only a year or two ago.

"Actually we know it wasn't either Herne or Bawtry in person, because there are people who'll swear they were elsewhere, lots of people," Hester said. "So if it was one of them who was selling the opium, then he had somebody else actually kill Lambourn. But they can't account for their time when Zenia Gadney was killed. They wouldn't think to, because as far as anyone else knew, there was no connection."

"They paid someone to kill Lambourn?" Rathbone asked. "Zenia? Is that possible? And then killed her so she couldn't betray them, or blackmail them?"

"Why wait two months?" Monk asked.

"Perhaps she didn't try blackmail until then?" Rathbone suggested.

"Or perhaps it isn't either Herne or Bawtry anyway?" Runcorn put in. "Where do we go if it's someone else altogether?"

Monk sighed. "Let's look at who it has to be." He ticked off the points on his fingers, one by one. "Someone Lambourn knew, and who had the power to have his report rejected, and his name blackened for incompetence." He went to the second finger. "Someone who had access to raw opium of pure quality in order to sell it." He touched the third. "Someone who knew of Lambourn's connection with Zenia Gadney, and was in a position to make it look as if Dinah had killed her."

"One more," Hester added.

"What?"

"Someone who knew a woman who could pose as Dinah in the shop in Copenhagen Place. She could have worn a wig to imitate Dinah's hair, but it had to be a woman," she answered.

"Unless it really was Dinah?" Monk looked from one to the other of them to see what they thought.

Suddenly an idea came to Rathbone's mind. He looked up quickly.

"I . . . I think I know." The words seemed absurd, not courageous but idiotic and desperate. "I want to have Bawtry in court tomorrow, and Herne and his wife. I think I know how I might trick them on the stand."

"Think?" Monk said softly.

"Yes . . . I think. Do you have a better idea?"

Monk pushed his hands through his hair again. "No." He looked at Runcorn.

"We'll do whatever you want," Runcorn promised. "God help us."

"Thank you," Rathbone answered almost under his breath, wondering if he could be right, and if he could possibly pull it off.

Rathbone slept badly. There was too much racing through his mind, too many possibilities for success, and for failure. His plans were made, but everything rested in the balance of his one last, great gamble. In his mind he turned over everything he could say, every disaster he might avert, or rescue if it came down to it.

He drifted off into fitful sleep, still troubled. If he lost, Dinah would be hanged. Either way, in using the photograph to dictate Pendock's behavior, to force him into decisions he would not have otherwise made, what had Rathbone done to himself?

Would Pendock ever forgive him? Rathbone knew that if he were certain of the decision he had made in his own mind, that should not matter. But how could one ever be certain when it came to using such methods?

Was he sure Dinah was innocent? Was he seeing her as a woman who would risk anything and everything to save her dead husband's name because that was what he wanted to see, needed to believe someone would do? And did it ease any of the pain he felt from the bitter end of his own marriage?

He woke late, with a jolt of panic; what if he did not get to the Old Bailey in time? The day was jarringly cold; the sky was dark and the easterly wind carried a sleety edge of worse to come. The pavements were icy, and keeping balance was hard as he strode along.

Runcorn, his first witness, was already waiting for him in the hallway as he went toward his chambers to put on his wig and gown. He had never imagined he would find Runcorn's figure reassuring, but it was acutely so today. The man had a solidity to him, a certainty of the things he believed in.

"All present and correct, Sir Oliver," Runcorn said quietly.

For a moment Rathbone was puzzled. It seemed an oddly inclusive expression to use referring to himself.

"Mr. and Mrs. Herne, Bawtry, and the police surgeon, sir," Runcorn explained. "And Mrs. Monk says she'll do the best to fetch Dr. Doulting again, just as you said. Could be that the poor man's too ill."

Rathbone drew a deep breath and let it out in a sigh of overwhelming relief. "Thank you."

"And there's a Mr. Wilkie Collins here as well," Runcorn went on. "Something to do with the Pharmacy Act. Says he's supporting it, and to send you the message that he'll remember Joel Lambourn. I gather he's a writer of some sort."

Rathbone smiled. "Indeed he is. Please give him my compliments, Mr. Runcorn. If I survive this, I'll take him to the best dinner in town."

Runcorn smiled back. "Yes, sir."

Half an hour later Runcorn was on the witness stand and Rathbone was looking across at him. The gallery was silent, the twelve jurors sitting motionless. A few of them appeared not to have slept much either.

Upon his high chair Pendock seemed like an old man. Rathbone wanted to avoid looking at him at all, but to do so would be both foolish and impossibly rude. He was acutely aware that if he had not spoken, Pendock might have died without ever knowing of his son's aberration. The knowledge of it now was a dark burden to carry, whatever the nature of this one trial.

At the next table Coniston was tense, looking one way and then another. Even the jury must see that he had lost the certainty he had shown as recently as yesterday morning.

Rathbone cleared his throat, coughed, then coughed again.

"Mr. Runcorn, in the light of further evidence and certain facts that seem to be unclear, I must take you back to your earlier testimony regarding the death of Joel Lambourn."

Coniston half rose, but Pendock was there before him.

"I realize you object, Mr. Coniston, but nothing has been said yet. I shall stop Sir Oliver if he wanders from the point. I imagine the prosecution is as keen as the rest of the court to learn the truth of this. If indeed Dr. Lambourn was murdered, then in the interests of justice we must know that." He smiled in a ghastly gesture, looking like a man drowning. "If the accused is guilty of that also, I assume you wish to know it?"

Coniston sat back down again, looking at Rathbone with an expression of complete confusion. "Yes, my lord," he said grudgingly.

Rathbone waited a second or two, then asked his first question of Runcorn.

"You were called to take over the investigation of Dr. Lambourn's death as soon as the local police realized who he was, is that correct?"

"Yes, sir," Runcorn replied simply. This was the last stand, and there was no time or need to elaborate beyond what was absolutely necessary.

"You examined the body, and the surrounding scene?" Rathbone asked.

"Yes, sir."

"Could you tell if Dr. Lambourn had walked to the place where you found him, or been carried there in some way?"

"I can tell you that there were no marks on the ground of any kind of transport, sir," Runcorn said firmly. "Nothing with wheels anywhere near, no hoofprints of any horse, just the foot marks of several men, and those of a dog, matching the one belonging to the gentleman who found the body."

"Do you conclude from that absence of these indications that Dr. Lambourn walked?"

"Yes, sir. He was at least an average height and weight of man. It would have been impossible for one man to have carried him all the way from the path. It was some distance—hundred yards or so—and steep."

"Two men?" Rathbone asked.

Coniston rolled his eyes with exasperation, but he did not interrupt.

"No, sir, I don't think so," Runcorn answered. "Two men carrying a body would have left some kind of mark on the grass, and even on the path. It's very awkward, carrying a dead weight. Have to go sideways some of the time, or even backward. Slips out of your grip. Anyone who's tried it would know."

"But what footprints were there around the body?" Rathbone persisted.

"Clearly?" Runcorn raised his eyebrows. "Impossible to say, sir. Too many people been there. The gentleman who found him, the policemen, the surgeon. They all went up to him, naturally, at first probably to see if they could help. Pretty well mucked up everything. No harm meant, of course. Couldn't know it would ever matter."

"Just so," Rathbone agreed. "So he could have walked there himself, either alone, or with someone else?"

"Yes, sir."

"Did you ever find the knife with which he had cut his wrists?"

Runcorn shook his head. "No, sir. Looked very hard, even at some distance, to see if he could have thrown it. Don't know how far a man can throw a knife when he's just cut his wrists. Come to that, don't know why he would want to."

"Nor do I," Rathbone agreed. "Did you find anything in which he could have taken the opium? I'm thinking of a bottle for water, or a vial that contained any solution in which opium could have been dissolved."

"No, sir. Looked for that, too."

"Or a syringe with a needle?" Rathbone asked.

"No, sir, nothing."

"Nevertheless, at first you concluded that his death was suicide?"

"At first, yes, sir," Runcorn agreed. "But the more I thought about it, the unhappier I got. Still, there was nothing I could do until Mr. Monk came along about a second death, which was very definitely a murder, and asked me to look into Dr. Lambourn's death a little harder."

"But you had been told to leave the matter as it was, had you not?" Rathbone pressed.

"Yes, sir. I did it in my own time, but I'm aware I'd been ordered to leave it," Runcorn admitted. "But I began to think he was murdered. I can't leave that to rest without knowing for sure."

Coniston stood up abruptly.

"Yes, yes," Pendock said quickly. "Mr. Runcorn, please do not give us any conclusions you may have come to unless you have proof that they are correct."

"Sorry, my lord," Runcorn said contritely. He did not argue, although Rathbone could see from his face that his silence was not easy.

"Mr. Runcorn, did you see any marks of struggle on the ground, or on Dr. Lambourn's person?" Rathbone asked. "Were his clothes torn or in disarray, for example? Were his shoes scuffed, his hair tangled or his skin bruised?"

"No, sir. He looked fairly peaceful."

"As a man might who had committed suicide?"

"Yes, sir."

"Or been brought there, dosed with opium he took to be something else?" Rathbone suggested. "Given to him by someone he trusted, causing him to be insensible when that person carefully slit his wrists and left him there to bleed to death, alone in the night?"

Runcorn's face showed his imagination of the tragedy. "Yes, sir," he said quietly, his voice a little husky. "Exactly like that."

Coniston looked up at Pendock, but this time kept his silence with grim resignation.

"Thank you, Mr. Runcorn," Rathbone said courteously. "Please wait until Mr. Coniston has asked you whatever he wishes to."

Coniston stood up and walked toward the witness stand. "Mr. Runcorn, did you see anything whatsoever to prove that Dr. Lambourn was in the company of anyone when he went up One Tree Hill in the middle of the night?"

"It isn't so much what I saw as what I didn't see," Runcorn replied. "No knife to cut his wrists, nothing with which to take opium."

"And from that you deduce that it was someone he knew, and trusted, this mystery companion?" Coniston pursued.

"Yes, sir. Seems to make sense. Why would you go up a hill in the dark with someone you didn't trust? And there were no signs of a fight. Anyone fights for their life, when it comes down to it."

"Indeed." Coniston nodded. "Then it could even have been a woman, for example the accused, his . . . mistress, with whom he lived as if she were his wife, and pretended to the world that she was, who was with him?"

There was a gasp in the gallery at Coniston's blunt statement. Several jurors actually looked up at the dock, where Dinah sat white-faced.

"Could've been," Runcorn agreed quietly. "But then, it could've been the lady who really was his wife."

One of the jurors blasphemed—and immediately clapped his hand over his mouth and blushed scarlet.

Pendock glanced at him but said nothing.

"Thank you, Mr. Runcorn. I think we have heard enough of your remarkable suppositions." Coniston returned to his seat.

"Anything further, Sir Oliver?" Pendock inquired.

"No, thank you, my lord," Rathbone answered. "I would like to call Dr. Wembley, the surgeon who examined Dr. Lambourn's body."

Wembley was called, sworn in, and faced Rathbone.

"I shall be very brief, Dr. Wembley," Rathbone began, still standing out in the center of the open space, every eye upon him. "Were there any marks on the body of Joel Lambourn when you examined him on One Tree Hill, or later in your postmortem?"

"Other than the cuts on his wrists, you mean?" Wembley asked. "No, none at all. He seemed to be a healthy man in his fifties, well nourished and perfectly normal."

"Could you say whether or not he had been involved in any kind of physical struggle immediately prior to his death?" Rathbone asked.

"He had not."

"Were there any bruises, ligature marks, abrasions, anything at all on his body or his clothes to suggest he had been carried manually?" Rathbone pursued. "Or that he had been tied up, perhaps by the ankles, arms, or any other part of his body? Or bumped around? The rubbing of fabric, perhaps, twisting as if something had been used to make carrying easier?"

Wembley looked incredulous. "Nothing whatsoever. I can't think what gives you that idea."

"I do not have that idea, Doctor," Rathbone assured him. "I simply want to exclude it. I believe Dr. Lambourn walked up One Tree Hill in the company of someone he trusted completely. It never occurred to him that they might do him any harm whatsoever." He smiled bleakly. "Thank you, Dr. Wembley. That is all I have to ask you."

This time Coniston did not take the trouble to cross-examine. His face showed his belief in the total futility of the entire exercise.

Monk arrived at the Old Bailey considerably later than Rathbone, after the trial had resumed. He had been out since before dawn questioning people near the Limehouse Pier and along Narrow Street leading to it, asking the new questions that they had planned yesterday evening. He had the answers, even though he had come perilously close to putting them in the witnesses' mouths. But he believed them, and time was desperate.

He was walking up the long hall when he recognized ahead of him the figures of Barclay and Amity Herne. They were standing fairly close to each other, but there was no ease in either of them. Barclay was facing a doorway to one side of the hall, as if expecting someone to emerge out of it. There was anxiety in every line and angle of his body, and the side of his face that Monk could see was sharp with fear.

Amity was facing him, half facing Monk, but she was oblivious to everyone else aside from her husband. She was speaking to him urgently and—to judge by her expression—with both anger and contempt.

Monk stopped, pretending to search his pockets for something, and watched them discreetly.

Amity appeared to repeat something she had said and took Herne by the arm. He shook her off as though her touch soiled his clothes. Then, with a single word of dismissal, he walked briskly away, disappearing around the first corner.

Amity stood still. Her back was to Monk now, so he could not read her expression, but the rigidity of her body, the stiff, high shoulders, were expressive enough.

He was about to move forward himself when the door Herne had been watching opened and Sinden Bawtry came out. Immediately, as if by the simple drawing of a curtain, Amity Herne changed completely. She turned toward him and Monk could see most of her face. It was lit with joy, her eyes soft and bright, a slight smile parting her lips.

Could she be so good an actress? Surely this was an unguarded moment no one was meant to see, perhaps least of all her husband?

Bawtry came toward her, smiling. Was there more warmth in it than courtesy required, or was Monk imagining it because of the sudden fire in *her*? Bawtry touched her, just one hand on her arm, but the gesture was clearly gentle. His hand lingered. Her smile became even softer.

Then they remembered themselves and the moment vanished. He spoke. She answered, and formality was restored again.

Monk stepped forward from the place where he had stopped and walked briskly on toward the court where he knew he would soon be called.

RATHBONE WAS RELIEVED WHEN Monk climbed the steps to the witness stand and was sworn in again. Rathbone knew that Coniston's patience and Pendock's strength were both wearing out. He must hold the jury's attention. They must begin to believe him soon and see a totally different pattern emerging. All he had asked of Pendock, all he could or would ask, was a fair hearing.

"Mr. Monk," he began, his voice hard and clear, "I know you have already testified to finding the body of Zenia Gadney, horribly mutilated, but I must ask again details I did not ask before, because new explanations have become highly possible. Mrs. Gadney's body was found early in the morning, as was Dr. Lambourn's. Can you tell us again exactly where that was?"

"On Limehouse Pier."

"On the pier itself?"

"Yes."

"Is that a place where a prostitute might conduct her business?"

"No. It would be very easily seen from the river. Any boat going by, unless a certain distance from the shore, would observe you."

"Yet the body was not found until you came by at roughly sunrise?"

"Because it was lying down and motionless." Monk's face tightened. "She could easily have been mistaken for a heap of rags, or an old tarpaulin, the way she had been left there."

Rathbone felt a slight sickness clench in his stomach. "And your attention was drawn by a woman screaming?"

"Yes."

"Briefly, what did you then, Mr. Monk?"

"Mr. Orme and I took the boat in to the woman who had attracted our attention. She was screaming because she had discovered the dead and grossly mutilated body of a woman who proved to be Zenia Gadney, a resident of Copenhagen Place, nearly half a mile away."

"Mrs. Gadney, she had been murdered?" Rathbone asked.

"Yes."

"In the course of your investigations did you learn why she was out at night, alone, in such a place as Limehouse Pier?"

"Apparently she liked to walk in that area, in daylight." Monk hesitated a moment. Was he as aware of the gamble they were taking as Rathbone was?

"And was she alone then?" Rathbone prompted. He could not afford to slip now.

"She was seen with another woman at about sunset," Monk answered quietly.

"Another woman?" Rathbone repeated it, his voice raised to make sure no one failed to hear.

"Yes. I have several witnesses who say it was a woman. They did not know who it was, nor were they able to give any detailed description, except that she was a few inches taller than Mrs. Gadney," Monk answered him.

"Did they appear to know each other?" Rathbone asked. "According to your witnesses."

"That was their impression," Monk conceded. He looked tense, worried. Rathbone wondered how hard he had had to push for the testimony, but he was convinced it was the truth.

"So Mrs. Gadney was also out around dusk, with a person she appeared to trust, and was found murdered by morning?" he said aloud. "Is that correct?"

"Yes."

"Would it surprise you to know that Dr. Lambourn also went out alone, just after dark, and seems to have met someone he trusted, possibly a woman, and gone up One Tree Hill where he was dosed with opium and his wrists cut? He also was found alone, the following morning."

"It would have surprised me at the time," Monk replied. "It does not surprise me now."

"Had you seen this pattern initially, might you have investigated differently?"

Coniston stood up. "That is a hypothetical question, my lord, and the answer is meaningless."

"I agree. Mr. Monk, you will not answer that question," Pendock directed.

Rathbone smiled. The comment was for the jury, not for Monk to answer, and they all knew it, especially Pendock.

"Thank you," Rathbone said to Monk. "I have no more to ask you."

"I have nothing, my lord," Coniston said. "We have heard it all before."

Rathbone asked for a brief adjournment and was granted it.

He met Monk out in the hall.

"Thank you," Rathbone said quickly.

"Are you sure you know what you're doing?" Monk asked anxiously, falling in step with him as they made their way toward Rathbone's chambers.

"No, I'm not sure," Rathbone answered. "I told you that yesterday evening." They reached the door and went in, closing it after them. "I've got Bawtry coming in a moment. Are you ready?"

"Before he comes," Monk said quickly, "I saw him in the hall just before I came into court." Briefly he described the quarrel between Amity and Herne, and then the total change he had seen in her manner toward Bawtry.

"Interesting," Rathbone said thoughtfully. "Very interesting. Perhaps I shall have to amend some of my ideas. Thank you."

Before Monk could reply there was a knock on the door and the court usher told Rathbone that Mr. Sinden Bawtry was here to see him.

Rathbone glanced at Monk, then at the usher. "Ask Mr. Bawtry to come in, please. Then see that we are not interrupted."

Bawtry came in looking only slightly concerned. He shook hands with both of them, then accepted the seat Rathbone offered.

"What can I do for you, Sir Oliver?" he asked.

Rathbone had been awake half the night thinking of exactly this moment. He had everything to win, or to lose, resting on what he said in the next few minutes.

"Your advice, Mr. Bawtry," he said as calmly as he could. "I'm sure you would like this case ended as soon as possible, as we all would—but with justice completely served."

"Of course," Bawtry agreed. "What can I advise you regarding? I knew Lambourn, of course, but not his wife." He made a slight grimace. "I'm sorry, perhaps that is technically incorrect. I mean Dinah Lambourn, whom I took to be his wife. Zenia Gadney I had never even heard of until her tragic death. What is it you wish to know from me?"

"So much I had surmised," Rathbone replied with the ghost of a smile. He must judge this perfectly. Bawtry was a brilliant man, a star very much in the ascendant, even considered a possible future prime minister by some. He had the background, as well as what appeared to be a blemishless record, and he was fast gaining a formidable political reputation. No doubt within the next few years he would make a fortunate marriage. He had no need to seek money, so he could afford to marry a woman who would be a grace to his social ambitions, and of personal pleasure to him, with wit and charm, perhaps beauty. Rathbone would be a fool to underestimate him. Facing the clever, unflinching eyes he was acutely aware of that.

"Then how can I help you?" Bawtry prompted him.

"Did you see this report of Lambourn's personally, sir?" Rathbone asked, keeping his voice light, stopping the trembling of it with an effort. "Or did you perhaps take Herne's word that it was unacceptable?"

Bawtry looked slightly taken aback, as if this were something he had not even considered. "Actually I saw very little of it," he replied. "He showed me a few pages, and they did seem a bit . . . haphazard, conclusions drawn without sufficient evidence. He told me the rest was even worse. Since the man was his brother-in-law, he quite naturally wished to protect him from being publicly made a fool of. He wanted to destroy the report without having any more of its weaknesses being known. I could understand that, and frankly I admired it in him. Whether it was for his wife's sake, or for Lambourn's was irrelevant to me."

"But you never saw the rest of it?" Rathbone pressed.

"No. No, I didn't." Bawtry stared at him. "What are you suggesting? You wouldn't be asking me this now unless you believed that it had some relevance to this trial." The ghost of a smile crossed his face. "Herne didn't kill Lambourn, if that's what you're thinking. He was unquestionably at the dinner in the Atheneum. Aside from personally seeing him there, I could name at least twenty members who were there also and will swear to it."

Rathbone smiled sadly. "I know that, Mr. Bawtry. Mr. Monk already made absolutely certain of it."

Bawtry glanced at Monk, then back at Rathbone. "Then I don't understand what it is you are asking me. I did not read more than a few pages of Lambourn's report. Incidentally, I believe he was factually right. The use of opium has to be labeled, and its sale in patent medicines restricted to people who have some medical or pharmaceutical knowledge at the least. It was never his conclusions that were in doubt, only the quality of his research, and the way he presented it. He allowed his own anger and pity to destroy his objectivity. To use it in argument for a bill could only have allowed the opponents of it—and they are many and powerful—to have fuel against us."

"We don't think the labeling of patent medicines was the issue for which Dr. Lambourn was murdered." Rathbone cleared his throat. He realized with surprise that his hands—which he was keeping carefully at his sides, out of sight—were clenched so hard that they ached.

Bawtry frowned. "Then what was? And if not that report, then why are you so interested in Herne?"

"If we can be certain that it was not the report on patent medicines for which Lambourn died," Rathbone replied, and was forced to clear his throat again before he could go on, "that proves that the explanation about the report being a failure and destroying Lambourn was an excuse, a reason to misdirect the investigation. We believe that during the course of his research Lambourn learned something else, something he could not let go of, concerning the sale of pure opium for use in syringes and needles that inject it directly into the blood. The addiction to opium given this way is agonizing and lethal. It was for attempting to have that particular practice made illegal that he was murdered, and Zenia Gadney also."

Bawtry was pale-faced, his eyes wide. "That's dreadful! Appalling!" He moved a little in his chair, a slight leaning forward as if he could no longer relax. "Are you suggesting that Herne had something to do with it? How? And for God's sake . . ." He trailed off, his eyes filled with dawning horror.

"What is it?" Rathbone demanded urgently.

Bawtry licked his lips, hesitating. He looked profoundly unhappy.

"What is it?" Rathbone repeated, his voice sharpening.

Bawtry looked up and met his eyes. "I've noticed rather erratic behavior in Herne," he said quietly. "One day he's full of energy and ideas, the next time I see him he looks nervous, can't concentrate, skin clammy. Is it . . . is it possible . . . ?" He did not finish the question, but it was not necessary. The idea was already fully understood between them.

Rathbone met his gaze and held it. "You think he may be addicted to opium himself, and either he is the one who is selling it, or else he is the tool of the man who is?"

Bawtry looked wretched. "I hate even to think it of a man I know, but I suppose anyone can fall victim to such a drug, commonly used as it is. Is it possible?" His face already showed that he knew it was.

"That he paid someone to kill Lambourn?" Rathbone asked. "Someone who could do it quietly, easily, making it look like suicide, and who would never be suspected? Yes, of course it is."

Bawtry was now as tense as Rathbone. Rathbone was suddenly overwhelmingly grateful that Monk was in the room. He had wanted him here as a witness to the conversation, but now he also needed him here for his physical safety.

"Paid someone?" Bawtry affected confusion, but not total disbelief. "Who? Have you discovered something totally new that might attest to this? I have only just arrived in court."

"A woman," Rathbone said. "The obvious person who makes complete sense would be Zenia Gadney."

"Gadney?" Now Bawtry was completely incredulous. "From all accounts I've heard, she was a slight, very ordinary middle-aged woman, unremarkable in every way. Indeed, she appears totally a victim, a pawn in the game." He frowned. "Are you saying she was actually greedy, desperate, and passionate enough to have murdered her husband, the man who had supported her financially, and with some kindness, over the last fifteen years? You must have compelling evidence! It's frankly preposterous."

"There is evidence." Rathbone again chose his words delicately. "It is not compelling, but the more I weigh it, the more it seems to make sense. Consider the possibility that Herne needed desperately to silence Lambourn, indeed, to discredit him so that no whispers of what he found would ever be believed, in case he spoke of it to others. He dare not kill Lambourn himself. Lambourn may even have been aware of the danger and would have taken care not to be alone with Herne. And of course Herne had to have a way of protecting himself from suspicion."

"I see," Bawtry said cautiously.

"So he promises to pay Zenia Gadney what would be a moderate sum to him, but a fortune to her, in exchange for this favor."

"But . . . murder? Of her *husband*?" Bawtry was still far from convinced.

"A gentle murder," Rathbone explained. "She asks Lambourn to meet her alone, when Dinah will not know. There are many ways she could justify such a request. She takes a knife, or a blade of some sort, possibly an open razor. And of course she also takes a strong opium solution, possibly mixed in something palatable, to disguise it. Or it is conceivable Herne gave her a syringe with a solution in it."

Bawtry nodded, as if he were beginning to believe.

"She arranges a suitable place to meet, possibly in the park," Rathbone continued. "They walk together up One Tree Hill. On the top the view over the river is worth seeing. She offers him a drink. They have climbed a bit, and he is glad of it. Quite soon he is drowsy and they sit down. He passes out. She then slits his wrists and leaves him to bleed to death. She takes the knife or razor with her, because possibly it can be traced to her. Similarly she takes the container in which she brought the opium. It may well have been quite large. She will have pretended to drink from it herself, in case he found it odd that she didn't, when she too had walked up the hill."

Bawtry gave a slight shiver. "You paint a terrible picture, Sir Oliver. However, it is believable. But surely you cannot possibly find any way whatsoever to suggest that she then killed herself? Whatever her remorse afterward, to have inflicted those mutilations upon herself would surely have been impossible? And in that case, how do you explain her death?"

"Of course," Rathbone agreed. "Anyway, the surgeon is of the opinion that the mutilation happened after she was already dead, thank God. No, I think she may have tried to blackmail Herne for more money, and he realized that he had to kill her, not only for financial reasons, but because if he did not, he would never be safe from her. Possibly he always intended to finish her off."

Bawtry's lips were tight, but he nodded his head very slightly. "It is hideous, but I admit I can see how it might be true. What is it that you wish from me?"

"Do you know anything at all that would disprove the outline I have just given?" Rathbone asked. "Anything about Lambourn, or more probably, about Barclay Herne?"

Bawtry sat silently for some time, concentrating intently. Finally he looked up at Monk, then at Rathbone.

"No, Sir Oliver, I know of nothing. I don't know whether your theory is true or not, but there is nothing within my knowledge that makes it impossible. You have created more than reasonable doubt as to Dinah Lambourn's guilt. I think both judge and jury will be obliged to grant as much."

Rathbone felt the ease come through him at last.

"Thank you, Mr. Bawtry. I am most grateful for your time, sir."

Bawtry inclined his head in acknowledgment, then rose to his feet and left the room.

Monk looked across at Rathbone. "Ready for the next step?" he said softly.

Rathbone took a deep breath. "Yes."

WHEN THE COURT RESUMED in the early afternoon, Rathbone called his final witness, Amity Herne. She took the stand with dignity and remarkable composure. She was wearing a very elegant dark dress, which was not quite black, the color of wine in shadow. It became her, a dramatic contrast with her fair hair and skin. She gave her name, as before, and was reminded that she was still under oath.

Rathbone apologized for recalling her. Coniston objected and Pendock overruled him, directing Rathbone to proceed.

"Thank you, my lord." He turned to Amity. "Mrs. Herne, you testified earlier that you and your brother, Joel Lambourn, did not know each other well in your early adulthood, because you lived some distance apart. Is that correct?"

"Yes, I'm afraid so," she said calmly.

"But in the last ten years or so you both lived in London, and therefore were able to visit far more frequently?"

"Yes. Perhaps once a month or so," she agreed.

"And of course you were aware of his marriage to Zenia Gadney?"

"Yes. But I have been forced to be discreet about it, for reasons that must be obvious to you."

"Of course. But you knew, and you were aware that Dinah Lambourn also knew?" he asked, forcing himself to be polite, even gentle.

"Yes. I have said as much."

"And your brother, he knew where Zenia lived once they were no longer . . . together?"

"Yes." She looked puzzled and a trifle irritated.

Rathbone smiled. "Had he ever mentioned the address to you?"

She hesitated. "Not . . . not specifically, that I recall."

"Generally? For example, that it was in the Limehouse area?"

"I . . ." She gave a slight shrug. "I am not certain."

"I ask because it appears that Dinah knew Zenia's whereabouts closely enough to ask for her in Copenhagen Place. She did not wander around searching half London for her; she went almost immediately to the right street."

"Then Joel must have mentioned it," Amity replied. "You appear to have answered your own question, sir."

"It appears that he made no secret of Zenia's whereabouts," Rathbone agreed. "Are you certain you were not aware? Or your husband, perhaps? Might your brother have confided in your husband, possibly in case something should happen to him, and he would need someone he could rely on to take care of Zenia if he were not able to?"

Amity drew in her breath sharply, as if some terrible thought had suddenly come into her mind. She gazed at Rathbone in horror.

"He . . . he might've." She licked her lips to moisten them. Her hands tightened on the railing in front of her.

The tension in the courtroom crackled like the air before a thunderstorm. Every single one of the jurors was staring at Amity.

"But he was dining at the Atheneum on the night your brother was killed," Rathbone went on.

"Yes. Yes, any number of gentlemen will testify to that," she agreed, her voice a little husky.

"Just so. And on the night Zenia Gadney was killed?" he asked.

"I . . ." She bit her lip. Now she was trembling, but her eyes did not waver from his even for an instant. "I have no idea. He was not at home, that's all I can say."

Now there was rustle and movement everywhere. In the gallery people coughed and shifted position, each straining to move left or right so their view of the witness was uninterrupted. The jurors fidgeted.

Coniston was staring at Rathbone as if he had suddenly changed shape in front of his eyes.

"You don't know where he was, Mrs. Herne?" Rathbone repeated.

"No . . ." Her voice wavered. She put her hand up to her mouth. She gulped, staring almost helplessly at Rathbone.

"Mrs. Herne—"

"No!" Her voice rose and she was shaking her head violently. "No.

You cannot make me tell you any more. He is my husband." She swiveled around in the witness box and pleaded with Pendock. "My lord, surely he cannot force me to speak against my husband, can he?"

It was the desperate cry of a wife in defense of the man to whom she had given her life and her loyalty, and it utterly condemned him.

Rathbone looked at the jurors. They were frozen in horror and sudden, appalling understanding. There was no doubt left anymore, only shock.

Then he swung round to the gallery and saw Barclay Herne, ashen-faced, eyes like black sockets in his head, trying to speak. But no words came.

On either side of him people moved away, grasping at coats and shawls, pulling them closer in case even a touch should contaminate them.

Pendock demanded order, his voice cracking a little.

Herne was on his feet, staring wildly as if seeking some rescue. "Bawtry!" he shouted desperately. "For God's sake!"

Behind him, facing the judge and witness stand, Bawtry also rose to his feet, shaking his head as if in awful realization.

"I can't help you," he said in perfectly normal tones, but the sudden silence from the gallery made his voice audible.

Everyone was now staring at these two men, but no one could have missed seeing the doors swing open. Hester Monk came in, the gaunt figure of Alvar Doulting a step behind her.

Sinden Bawtry turned toward them as the sound of their entry caught his attention.

Doulting stared at Bawtry. Hester seemed to be half supporting him as he lifted one arm awkwardly to point at Bawtry.

"That's him!" he said, gasping for breath. His body was shaking so badly he looked in danger of collapse. "That is the man who sold the opium and syringes to me, and to God knows how many others. I've watched too many of them die. Buried some of them in paupers' graves. I'll find one myself soon."

The crowd erupted as pent-up terror and fury at last found release, people rising to their feet, crying out.

"Order!" Pendock shouted, also rising to his feet, his face scarlet.

But no one took any notice of him. The ushers tried to push their way through the crowds to help Bawtry, or at the very least to make sure he was not trampled.

Amity Herne, still in the witness stand, could do nothing. Her anguish was naked in her face. She cried out Bawtry's name in a howl of despair, but it was hardly audible above the din, and no one listened to her or cared.

Coniston looked like a lost child, searching this way and that for something familiar to hold on to.

Pendock was still shouting for order. Gradually the noise subsided. Ushers had helped Bawtry out and stood guarding the doors. Hester eased Doulting into a seat at the back where people made ample room for him, sitting apart, as if his private hell were contagious.

At last Pendock had restored some kind of sanity and was able to continue.

"Sir Oliver!" Pendock said savagely. "Was that outburst contrived by you? Did you arrange for that . . . that appalling scene to take place?"

"No, my lord. I had no idea that Dr. Doulting would know by sight the man who has dug his grave, so to speak." That was something less than the truth. At the time he had arranged it with Hester, he had expected Doulting to reveal Barclay Herne as both the seller and an addict.

Pendock started to speak again, and then changed his mind.

"Have you anything further to ask of Mrs. Herne?" he said instead.

"Yes, my lord, if you please," Rathbone said humbly.

"Proceed." Pendock barely lifted his hand, but the gesture was unmistakable.

"Thank you, my lord." Rathbone turned to Amity, who was now looking as if she had heard the news of her own death. Her eyes were unfocused, her entire body sagging.

It was all up to him now. He must make it plain to the jury. Reasonable doubt was no longer the verdict he sought; it was a clear and ringing "not guilty." What happened to Bawtry was up to a different jurisdiction, and would perhaps only happen on the stage of public opinion. Dinah Lambourn's life, and Joel Lambourn's reputation, were Rathbone's responsibility. And maybe he would also achieve some measure of justice for Zenia Gadney.

"Mrs. Herne," he began. The silence in court was absolute. "Mrs. Herne, you have heard the evidence making it seem highly likely that your brother, Joel Lambourn, was murdered by a woman he trusted, who arranged to meet with him on the night of his death? Together they walked up into Greenwich Park, he totally unsuspecting of any violence. On One Tree Hill they stopped. It is possible she somehow managed to inject him with a needle, but more likely she offered him a drink that was extremely heavily laced with opium. He became dizzy, then unconscious within a very short space of time. She then slit his wrists with a blade she had brought with her, leaving him to bleed to death alone in the dark."

Amity swayed in the witness box, gripping the rail to stop herself from falling.

"It was suggested that this woman he trusted was his first wife, in law his only wife, known as Zenia Gadney," Rathbone went on. "And that she did it because she was paid to by your husband."

"I know," Amity whispered.

Coniston half rose, then sat back again, his face pale, eyes wide in fascination.

"Why would your husband do such a thing?" Rathbone asked.

Amity did not answer.

"To protect his superior, Sinden Bawtry?" Rathbone answered for her. "And of course his own supply of opium. He is addicted, isn't he?"

She did not speak, but nodded her head slightly.

"Just so," Rathbone agreed. "I can well believe that Bawtry asked this of him. Your husband is a weak and ambitious man, but he is not a murderer, either of your brother, or of Zenia Gadney."

Again there were cries from the gallery and Pendock restored order only with difficulty.

"It was a woman who killed Dr. Lambourn," Rathbone continued as soon as the noise had subsided. "But it was not poor Zenia. It was you, Mrs. Herne, because Bawtry asked your husband to do it, and he had not the nerve. But you had. In fact you would have the nerve to do anything at all for your lover, Sinden Bawtry!"

Again the noise, the screams, catcalls, and gasps drowned him out.

"Order!" Pendock shouted. "One more outburst and I shall clear the court!"

This time silence returned within seconds.

"Thank you, my lord," Rathbone said politely. He turned to Amity again. "But Dinah would not let people believe Joel had killed himself. She would not let it rest, and you could not allow that. If she persisted, and cleared his name, then the opium bill would have to include making the sale of it in injectable form illegal—a crime, punishable very seriously. The prime minister would never ignore what Joel Lambourn had told him of the evil that opium in such a form caused. Your husband, addicted as he was, would sink into despair, and perhaps death. I don't know whether that mattered to you—perhaps not. It might even have been convenient. But Sinden Bawtry would be finished by such a bill. The wealth he so lavishly spends on his career, and his philanthropy, would dry up. If he continued to sell the opium, then he would become a criminal before the law, ending his days in prison. And you would've done anything to prevent that."

He stopped to draw breath.

"I don't know whether Dinah guessed at any of this." He plunged on. "I think not. She believed in her husband, believed that he would not have killed himself. And she knew that she had not killed Zenia. I think it was you, Mrs. Herne, who posed as Dinah in the shops in Copenhagen Place, already knowing perfectly well where Zenia lived, but creating a scene in order to be remembered. You knew Zenia, as she knew you. She trusted you, and quite willingly met you on the evening of her death, just as Joel had met you on the evening of his."

The court was motionless; no one interrupted him now, even by sigh or gasp.

"You walked with her to the river," he went on. "Perhaps you even stood together on the pier and watched the light fade over the water, as she loved to do. Then you struck her so hard she collapsed. Perhaps she was dead even as she fell to the ground.

"Then in the darkness you cut her open, possibly with the same blade as you had used to slit your brother's wrists. You tore out her entrails and laid them across her and onto the ground, to make as hideous a crime as you could, knowing that the newspapers would write head-lines about it.

"Public opinion would never allow the police to leave such a mur-der unsolved. They would eventually find the clues you had laid leading to Dinah, and she would at last be silenced. No one would believe her protests of innocence. She was half mad with grief; and you had reason and sanity, and an unblemished reputation on your side. Who was she? The mistress of a bigamist with a wife he still kept on the side, or so it appeared."

He looked up at her now with both awe and disgust.

"You very nearly got away with it. Joel would be dead and dishon-ored. Zenia had served her purpose and would be remembered only as the victim of a terrible crime of revenge. Dinah would be hanged as one of the most gruesome female murderers of our time. And you would be free to continue your love affair with a rich, famous, and very hand-some man, possibly even marry him when your husband's addiction ended his life. And Sinden Bawtry would forever owe you his freedom from dishonor and disgrace."

He took a deep breath. "Except, of course, that he does not love you. He used you, just as you used Zenia Gadney, and God knows who else. Surely in time he would also kill you. You have a hold on him that he cannot afford to leave at loose ends, and he will grow tired of your adoration when it is no longer useful to him. It becomes boring to be adored. We do not value that which is given to us for nothing."

She tried to speak, but no words came to her lips.

"No defense?" Rathbone said quickly. "No more lies? I could pity you, but I cannot afford to. You had no pity for anyone else." He looked up at Pendock. "Thank you, my lord. I have no more witnesses. The defense rests."

Coniston said nothing, like a man robbed of speech.

The jury retired and came back within minutes.

"Not guilty," the foreman said with perfect confidence. He even looked up at Dinah in the dock and smiled, a gentle look of both pity and relief, and something that could have been admiration.

Rathbone asked permission to speak to Pendock in chambers, pri-vately, and he walked out of the court before anyone else could catch his attention. He did not even look at Hester, Monk, or Runcorn, all waiting.

He found Pendock alone in his chambers, white-faced.

"What now?" the judge asked, his voice hoarse and shaking in spite of his attempt to remain calm.

"I have something that should belong to you," Rathbone answered. "I don't wish to carry it around, but if you come to my house at some time of your convenience, you may do with it, and all copies of it, whatever you please. I would suggest acid for the original, and a fire for the copies, which are merely paper. I . . . I regret having used them to obtain justice."

"I regret that you had to," Pendock replied. "You did not create the truth; you merely used it. I shall be retiring from the bench. I imagine after this victory, you may well be offered it. For reasons that must be obvious, I shall not mention our arrangement. You may believe me, or not, but I truly thought I was serving my country in attempting to prevent you from frightening the general public from using the only medicine easily available to them. I thought Lambourn was a foolish man wishing to curtail the freedom of ordinary people seeking some respite from the worst of their afflictions, perhaps even a man attempting to keep the sale of opium in the hands of a very few, of whom I was told he might be one. God forgive me."

"I know," Rathbone answered softly. "It was very believable. Our record of the use and abuse of opium, the smuggling and the crime already attached to it, are damnable. Alvar Doulting is only one of its victims, Joel Lambourn another, Zenia Gadney a third. We must become far wiser in the treatment of pain, of every sort. This is a warning we ignore at our peril."

"You will make a good judge," Pendock said, biting his lip, his face pale and tight with regret.

"Maybe," Rathbone answered. "I imagine it is a great deal more difficult than it looks from the floor of the courtroom, where your loyalties are defined for you."

"Indeed," Pendock answered. "I have found nothing harder in life than to be certain of my loyalties. I am sure in my head; it is my heart that ruins it all."

Rathbone thought of Margaret. "It always does. It would be easier not to love," he agreed.

"And become the walking dead? Is that what you want?" Pendock asked.

"No." Rathbone had no hesitation. "No, it isn't. Good luck, sir." He went out without looking backward, leaving Pendock to his thoughts.

Outside in the hall he almost bumped into Monk.

Monk looked at him with intense concern.

Rathbone wanted to affect indifference, but the warmth in Monk's eyes made it impossible. He stood still, waiting for Monk to speak first.

"You used them, didn't you?" Monk asked. "Ballinger's photographs."

Rathbone thought of lying, but discarded the idea. "Yes. This was too big, too monstrous to think only of my own peace of mind." He searched Monk's face now, afraid of what he would see.

Monk smiled. "So would I . . . I think," he said quietly. "The burden is heavy either way."

ABOUT THE AUTHOR

ANNE PERRY is the bestselling author of two acclaimed series set in Victorian England: the William Monk novels, including *A Sunless Sea* and *Acceptable Loss*, and the Charlotte and Thomas Pitt novels, including *Dorchester Terrace* and *Treason at Lisson Grove*. She is also the author of a series of five World War I novels, nine Christmas novels, most recently *A Christmas Homecoming*, and a historical novel, *The Sheen on the Silk*, set in the Ottoman Empire. She lives in Scotland.

www.AnnePerry.net

ABOUT THE TYPE

This book was set in Goudy Old Style, a typeface designed by Frederic William Goudy (1865–1947). Goudy began his career as a bookkeeper, but devoted the rest of his life in pursuit of "recognized quality" in a printing type.

Goudy Old Style was produced in 1914 and was an instant bestseller for the foundry. It has generous curves and smooth, even color. It is regarded as one of Goudy's finest achievements.

0550256655